How to Marry a Duke

England's *most eligible bachelor has finally met his match.*

VICKY DREILING

GRIFFIN

EARLY PRAISE FOR
HOW TO MARRY A DUKE

"Vicky Dreiling delivers a tale chock full of warmth, wit, and tenderness. She's sure to please readers everywhere!"
—**SAMANTHA JAMES,**
New York Times bestselling author

"A terrific romp of a read! . . .
Vicky is a bright new voice in romance."
—**SARAH MacLEAN,**
New York Times bestselling author

"Sexy, fresh, and witty . . . A delicious read! Better than chocolate! Vicky Dreiling is an author to watch!"
—**SOPHIE JORDAN,**
New York Times bestselling author

AND DON'T MISS

How to Seduce a Scoundrel

. . . ilable in mass market
in July 2011

. . . ase turn to the back
. . . his book for a preview.

> **"I am a matchmaker and am fully aware of the benefits of marriage, but they do not apply to me."**

Tristan cupped her cheek and turned her to face him. "You think not?"

"I-I know so."

"You do not sound certain," he murmured, caressing her silky skin.

"Wh-what are you doing?"

"I am trying to convince you of what you are missing."

A ragged breath escaped her.

He lowered his head and breathed near her ear. "Would you miss naughty whispers?"

"You are unseemly."

"Not convinced, I see." He turned his head until her breath whispered over his lips. "Would you miss tender kisses?"

She pushed his chest. "You are a tease."

He looked longingly at her mouth.

Then he did a reckless thing. He leaned forward and captured her lips...

"In her lively debut novel, Vicky Dreiling has penned a fresh, engaging take on Regency matchmaking that brims with clever wit and repartee. I found myself smiling and laughing out loud on numerous occasions. Here's hoping for more of this promising new author's historical romances!"

—Nicole Jordan, *New York Times* bestselling author

How to Marry a Duke

VICKY DREILING

FOREVER

NEW YORK   BOSTON

This book is a work of fiction. Names, characters, places, and incidents are the product of the author's imagination or are used fictitiously. Any resemblance to actual events, locales, or persons, living or dead, is coincidental.

Copyright © 2011 by Vicky Dreiling
Excerpt from *How to Seduce a Scoundrel* copyright © 2011 by Vicky Dreiling
All rights reserved. Except as permitted under the U.S. Copyright Act of 1976, no part of this publication may be reproduced, distributed, or transmitted in any form or by any means, or stored in a database or retrieval system, without the prior written permission of the publisher.

Book design by Giorgetta Bell McRee

Forever
Hachette Book Group
237 Park Avenue
New York, NY 10017
Visit our website at www.HachetteBookGroup.com.

Forever is an imprint of Grand Central Publishing. The Forever name and logo is a trademark of Hachette Book Group, Inc.

Printed in the United States of America

First Printing: January 2011

10 9 8 7 6 5 4 3 2 1

To my beautiful daughter Amber Rose, who stayed up all night to read the entire book. I love you, bunny-girl. P.S. Yes, we can have Rob and Henry audition for the hypothetical movie.

Acknowledgments

Every book is a journey, but a first book is special. With hand to heart, I wish to thank all the special people who took this journey with me in one form or another.

My deepest gratitude to my extremely talented editor, Michele Bidelspach. Michele, I am awed by the transformation your insights helped me to achieve with this book. xoxoxo

Heartfelt thanks to my fabulous agent, Lucienne Diver. We were fated to meet by accident—twice. I feel like the luckiest author in the world to have landed you as my agent.

Muchas gracias (and many margaritas) to Kristi Gold, who never stopped believing in me. *Merci beaucoup* to Karen Burns and Ellen Watkins for laughing so hard at the sheep scene; that day I dared to hope I just might sell the book.

Thanks to all the wonderful friends who supported me on this journey: Sharie, Tera, Gerry, Jan, Pat K and Pat R,

Laurie, Jo Anne, Kimber, Kerry, MJ, Sandy, Michele L, and Vicky. To my friends at WHRWA, the Beau Monde, 100 Words a Day, the River Rats, and GIAMX4. For an unforgettable moment, my thanks to my DARA friends, who cheered my first sale in the Executive Conference Room at the RWA Conference in D.C.

Most of all, my love and thanks to my supportive family: Mom, Daniel, Regina, and Jonathan.

How to
Marry a
Duke

Chapter One

The belles of the Beau Monde had resorted to clumsiness in an effort to snag a ducal husband.

Tristan James Gatewick, the Duke of Shelbourne, entered Lord and Lady Broughton's ballroom and grimaced. A quartet of giggling chits stood near the open doors, dangling their handkerchiefs as if poised to drop them. Determined to avoid playing fetch again, he strode off along the perimeter of the room.

With a long-suffering sigh, he conceded he'd contributed to this national disgrace. Ever since the scandal sheets had declared him the most eligible bachelor in England, he'd rescued twenty-nine lace handkerchiefs, five kid gloves, and twelve ivory fans.

If only he could have convinced himself to choose a bride based upon the inelegance of her fumbling, he might have wedded and bedded the most inept candidate by now. Alas, he could not abide the thought of spending a lifetime with Her Gracelessness.

He surveyed the crowd looking for the hostess of this grand squeeze, a useless endeavor. The crème de la crème swarmed the place like bees. The din of voices competed with the lively tune of a country dance, making his ears ring. He'd rather eat dirt than subject himself to the dubious delights of the marriage mart, but with his thirty-first birthday approaching, he could no longer pretend he was invincible. The dukedom had been at risk far too long.

Someone tapped a fan on his shoulder. He paused to find Genevieve and Veronica, two of his former mistresses. Seeing them together, he realized how alike the striking widows looked. Both were tall, dark-haired, and curvaceous. He canvassed the cobwebs in his brain and realized all of his past lovers had similar attributes. Well, those he could recollect.

Tristan bowed and lifted each of their hands for the requisite air kiss. "Ladies, it is a great pleasure to see you again."

"Were your ears burning?" Veronica said in an exaggerated boudoir voice. "You are the subject du jour."

"I am delighted," he lied. He'd grown increasingly frustrated with the notoriety the papers had whipped up. How the devil he'd ever find a bride in this circuslike atmosphere evaded him. But find one he must.

Genevieve tittered. "We were comparing you to all of our other gentlemen admirers."

He'd bedded more than his fare share of mistresses, but this situation was certainly unique among his experiences. "What did you conclude?"

Genevieve leaned closer and squeezed his arm. "We agreed you were the naughtiest of all our lovers."

He regarded her with a wicked grin. "Praise indeed."

Veronica glanced at him from beneath her lashes. "How does it feel to be England's most sought-after bachelor?"

High-pitched giggling rang out from behind him. He rolled his eyes. Not again.

Genevieve's shoulders shook with laughter. "Watch out, Shelbourne. A bevy of little misses are stalking you."

He grimaced. "Rescue me?"

The two women laughed, blew him a kiss, and drifted away, leaving him to the predators. When he turned round, the four silly chits he'd seen earlier halted and stared at him, agog. Given their youthful faces and puritanical white gowns, he surmised not one of them was a day over seventeen. He needed a wife, but he'd no intention of robbing the proverbial cradle.

When they continued to gape at him as if he were a Greek statue come to life, he took a step closer. "Boo."

Their shrieks rang in his ears as he walked off into the crowd. Ignoring the avid stares directed at him, Tristan squeezed past numerous hot, perspiring bodies, and not the kind one hoped to find naked and willing in bed. With more than a little regret, he banished thoughts of Naked and Willing in order to concentrate on Virtuous and Virginal. First he must locate Lord and Lady Broughton. Perhaps his hostess would introduce him to a sensible young lady of good breeding. Perhaps pigs would fly, too.

He might have avoided all this nonsense if his dear mama had cooperated. When he'd informed her of his bridal requirements a month ago, she'd swatted him with her fan and told him he had rocks in his head.

A loud bang nearly sent him ducking for cover. Feminine gasps erupted all around him. Alarmed, he sought the source of the disturbance and realized it was only the slamming of the card room door. The gentleman responsible for this discourteous act was none other than his oldest friend, Marc Darcett, Earl of Hawkfield.

Tristan hailed Hawk with a wave and walked in that direction. Intent upon reaching his friend, Tristan failed to notice the impending danger until something crunched beneath his shoe. A quick glance to the floor confirmed his worst fear—the thirteenth incident of a dropped fan. Damn and blast, he'd crushed it.

He lifted his gaze, expecting a devious mama and her blushing daughter. Instead, a petite young woman with honey-blond hair stood staring at his shoe. She said something that sounded suspiciously like *ashes to ashes, dust to dust*. With all the voices ringing in his ears, he assumed he'd misheard.

Though he was tempted to walk past her, he couldn't ignore the fan he'd broken. "I beg your pardon," he said, bending to retrieve the mangled ivory sticks.

"You are not to blame. Someone jostled my arm."

Her excuse was the worst he'd heard yet. He didn't even bother to hide his cynicism as his gaze traveled up her white gown. Blue ribbons trimmed her bodice, drawing his attention to her generous décolletage. He continued his perusal to her heart-shaped face. She watched him with twitching lips. Pillow-plump lips. He inhaled on a constricted breath. Lord, with that mouth she could make a fortune as a courtesan.

Her long-lashed eyes twinkled. "Sir, if you will return the remains, I will see to its burial."

Her witty remark stunned him. Belatedly, he realized he was grinning up at her. She probably thought he'd fallen for her ruse. Exasperated with himself, he grasped the broken sticks, rose, and placed the ruined fan in her small gloved hands.

He met her amused gaze again, noting she did not simper or blush. She was no miss fresh out of the schoolroom. "I apologize for the damage. Allow me to make reparations," he said.

"It is quite beyond repair," she said.

"I insist upon compensating you for—"

"My pain and suffering?" She laughed. "I assure you the fan's death is a relief to me. Look, you can see it is exceedingly ugly."

They'd not had a proper introduction, and yet, she'd invited him to come closer. He decided to oblige her and find out if her intentions extended beyond droll quips. While she chattered about a dim shop light and putrid green paint, he stole another glance at her mouth, picturing those lips damp and kiss-swollen. Slow heat eddied in his veins.

She continued speaking in an unreserved manner as if they were old friends rather than strangers. "Even my maids refused to take the fan," she said. "So I decided to carry the pitiful thing at least once."

A footman carrying a tray of champagne paused before them. She lifted up on her toes like a ballerina to place the ruined fan upon it. Pint-sized she might be, but her flimsy skirts outlined a deliciously rounded bottom. He liked voluptuous women, and his practiced eye told him this one had the body of a goddess.

His blood stirred. He wanted her.

A warning clanged in his head. She was probably

married, and he never dallied with other men's wives. Then again, maybe she wasn't. He found himself hoping she was a willing and lonely widow, but he meant to do more than hope.

"Poor little fan. May you rest in peace." She pirouetted and gave him a dazzling smile. "There now, I'm done mourning."

She was exceptionally clever, but without the brittle artifice common among the ton. He caught her gaze, willing her with his eyes. "Now that the funeral is over, perhaps you would allow me to escort you to the refreshment table." And thence to a more private location.

"You are too kind, but I must return to my friends."

Triumph surged inside him. She'd said friends, but made no mention of a husband. "Will you allow me the *pleasure* of your company a little longer? I mean to persuade you to accept my offer."

"I have dozens of other fans," she said. "Your apology is more than sufficient."

She intended to play hard to get. Since he'd come of age, women had always pursued him. At the prospect of a chase, excitement raced through his blood. But he must proceed with caution. If he'd misjudged her, she would take offense. A smile tugged at his mouth. He knew exactly which card to play.

He reached inside his coat and produced his engraved card. "Take it. In the event you change your mind, send round a note." If she refused, he'd have his answer. But if she accepted, he'd have her name. And soon her.

When she started to reach for the card, he held his breath. *Take it, little charmer. I'll ride you to the stars all night.*

She hesitated and then peered at his card. Her doll-like

eyes grew round as carriage wheels. She curtseyed, mumbled something he couldn't hear, and disappeared into the crowd.

Her sudden departure caught him off guard. He took two steps, searching for her, but the crowd had swallowed her. Obviously she'd not known his identity beforehand. But why had she fled?

"There you are."

At the sound of Hawk's voice, Tristan turned.

"I tried to save you," Hawk said, "but that dragon Lady Durmont waylaid me. So who was the latest clumsy belle to accost you?"

"I've no idea," Tristan said. "I take it you do not know her."

"I never saw her face." Hawk frowned. "What the devil were you doing engaging a strange lady in conversation?"

"I stepped on her fan."

Hawk made a sound of disgust. "Follow me."

As he walked with his friend, Tristan frowned, wondering how he could have misread her signals. Then again, the women who pursued him made no secret of their illicit intentions with their risqué innuendos. The mysterious lady had surprised and intrigued him, but she'd not taken the bait, so he dismissed her from his mind.

Hawk led him over to a wall niche displaying a winged statue of Fortuna, goddess of fortune and fate. "Old boy, you've got to be more careful," Hawk said. "These chits are desperate. One of them might trick you into a compromising situation."

Tristan huffed. "A cautionary tale in reverse. Lady Rake seduces unsuspecting bachelor."

"There are plenty of schemers on the marriage mart who would throw away their virtue to marry a duke."

"Ridiculous." He'd never fall for such tricks.

"Forget this bridal business for now," Hawk said. "You needn't rush to the altar."

"I've left the dukedom unsecured for thirteen years." With good reason, he silently amended.

Hawk released a loud sigh. "You're determined to wed."

"Determined, yes. Whether I'll succeed is debatable."

"As usual, you're making matters much too complicated. You're in luck. I have a brilliant plan."

"This ought to prove entertaining," he said.

"It's simple," Hawk said. "Choose the most beautiful belle in the ballroom, get an introduction, and ask her to dance. Then call on her tomorrow and propose. In less than twenty-four hours, you'll be an engaged man."

"You call that a brilliant plan?"

Hawk folded his arms over his chest. "What's wrong with it?"

He huffed. "Most of the beauties I've met are vain, silly, and clumsy."

"You want an ugly wife?"

Tristan scowled. "That's not what I meant."

"What the devil do you want?"

"A sensible, respectable, and graceful woman." He wanted more, but he wasn't about to confess his fantasies.

"If it's a boring and plain bride you're wanting, you need look no further than the wall," Hawk said, indicating a group of pitiful-looking gels sitting with the dowagers.

Tristan had started to turn away when he saw the amusing lady he'd spoken to earlier. His heartbeat drummed in his ears. She led two gangly young cubs over to the forlorn girls. The chandelier's soft candlelight illuminated her curly golden hair.

Within minutes, both cubs were escorting wallflowers toward the dance floor. The lady responsible for this turn of events clasped her small gloved hands. As she watched the couples, her plump lips curved into a dreamy smile, and her eyes softened. Transfixed, Tristan forgot to breathe. He'd last seen that expression on a woman after a vigorous bout between the sheets.

Then Lord Broughton and his new bride approached her. All signs of the temptress disappeared as the lady faced the couple. "That's her," Tristan said.

Hawk squinted. "Who?"

"The lady I spoke to earlier. She is standing with Broughton and his wife."

"Lord help us. It's Miss Mansfield."

Miss Mansfield? She was a virtuous, unmarried lady? The devil. He'd almost made her an indecent proposition.

Hawk laughed. "You've never heard about her?"

"You're obviously itching to tell me," he grumbled.

"She makes matches for every ugly duckling in London," Hawk said, wagging his brows.

Tristan scoffed. "You're funning me."

"I'm not jesting. She's not called Miss Mantrap for nothing," Hawk said. "The woman is a menace to bachelors. Good old Broughton is a prime example."

Good old Broughton gazed down at his pretty blond bride. The man looked as if he were suffering from unbridled lust, a term women euphemistically called love.

Hawk regarded Tristan with suspicion. "Why are you so interested in her?"

"Mere curiosity," he said with a shrug.

Hawk smirked. "Cut line. You thought she was available for dalliance."

He'd never admit it. No doubt she was as poor as a church mouse, without noble family connections. She probably found matchmaking preferable to taking a position as a lady's maid or governess. Most likely, she'd only received an invitation to the ball because she'd made Broughton's match.

He wished she'd not refused his offer to pay for the fan. But he understood her pride all too well, and though he thought her chosen career odd, he couldn't deny she'd made a successful match for Broughton.

Tristan's skin tingled. No, he would not stoop to hiring her to find him a bride. He could practically picture the news in the scandal rags. *The Desperate Duke has hired a matchmaker*.

He was not desperate. He was a bloody duke. With a mere crook of his finger, he could have any woman he wanted. The problem was he didn't want just any woman. He'd formulated requirements for his ideal bride.

All he needed was to find someone who met them.

He thought about spending week after week trolling for a wife in ballrooms. He thought about fetching fans, handkerchiefs, and parasols. He thought about his need for an heir. His chances of finding his perfect duchess seemed remote at best.

Tristan glanced at Miss Mansfield again and reconsidered. She needed money. He needed a bride. For the right price, Miss Mansfield would keep her involvement a secret from all but the chosen girl and her grateful family.

He frowned, realizing he was basing his decision on

one example—Broughton. Hiring Miss Mansfield meant taking a risk, but if her efforts proved unsatisfactory, he could dismiss her. Truthfully, a larger risk loomed. Marriage was for life, and as matters now stood, he was in serious danger of tying himself forever to an unsuitable wife. Or no wife at all, at this rate.

Tristan sized up the situation and realized he had two choices: continue his haphazard search or hire Miss Mansfield. After weeks of pure hell shopping at the marriage mart, the matchmaker won hands-down.

Of course, he had no intention of enlightening his friend. "I'm off to pay my respects to Broughton and his wife."

Hawk snorted. "This marriage business has addled your brain."

"I fail to understand what you find so amusing."

"Miss Mansfield is a happily-ever-after spinster." Hawk clapped him on the shoulder. "Congratulations, old boy. You've just chosen the only woman in the kingdom who won't wed you."

Tessa Mansfield wanted to kick herself.

Heaven above, she'd practically flirted with that rake, the Duke of Shelbourne. She'd never seen him before tonight, but she'd heard about his reputation. The gentleman rake, they called him. Everyone said he didn't gamble to excess. They said he never seduced innocents. Every other female, however, was apparently fair game.

She prided herself on her ability to spot a rake at twenty paces. This particular rake had fooled her with his agreeable manner. But she knew rakes used their charm to disarm their intended victims. She recalled the duke's slow smile and could not deny she'd let his handsome face turn her head.

Tessa cringed as she recalled the way she'd chattered like a monkey. He must have thought she'd dropped her fan on purpose like all those silly girls she'd read about in the scandal sheets. Oh, how lowering.

She took a deep breath, reminding herself she was unlikely to encounter him again. Thank goodness.

"I am glad to see you, Tessa. I've missed you so."

Tessa returned her attention to Anne, her former companion and dearest friend in the world. "I missed you as well."

Anne's eyes misted. "I never imagined I would make such a happy marriage. You made all my dreams come true."

For nearly a year, Tessa had promoted the match between Anne Mortland and Lord Broughton. More than once, Tessa had feared all would come to naught, but true love and a dusting of luck had culminated in this fairy tale marriage.

Tessa glanced at Lord Broughton. "You both look well, my lord."

Broughton gazed at his bride with adoration. "I am the happiest of men."

Tessa's heart contracted with a yearning for something she could never have.

Anne clasped her arm. "Tessa, look quickly. You do not want to miss seeing Jane dance."

Tessa lifted up on her toes to see past the crowd. She caught a glimpse of her new companion, Jane Powell, but the fast approach of two fashionable and handsome gentlemen diverted her attention. As they neared, her heart thudded. She recognized the taller man with tousled black hair. It was the Duke of Shelbourne.

She turned round, hoping he'd not seen her. To her mortification, Shelbourne and the other gentleman approached Lord Broughton.

"Shelbourne, Hawk, this is an unexpected pleasure," Broughton said, rubbing his hands.

Tessa gazed up at the chandelier, wishing she could melt like the wax oozing from the candles. When she'd run away, he'd probably thought she wanted him to chase her. Belatedly, she realized her behavior only made her look guilty and a little foolish. She planted a serene smile on her face as Lord Broughton introduced her to the duke and Lord Hawkfield. Then she curtseyed and rose to find Shelbourne gazing at her. In the light of the chandelier, she could see his eyes were marine blue and fringed by thick black lashes.

"Miss Mansfield and my wife are friends," Lord Broughton said. "She is the one responsible for our happy union."

Lord Hawkfield raised his brows in an exaggerated fashion. "I say, a matchmaker? If only I had known of your skills when my sisters were single, Miss Mansfield. You might have saved me the trouble of finding them husbands."

His mocking tone vexed her. She'd encountered plenty of his kind before, always quick to ridicule her avocation. "I had no idea I had a competitor. Or do you only make matches for relatives?"

Before Lord Hawkfield could reply, the duke cut in. "His self-proclaimed talent is highly overrated."

She arched her brows. "Should I be relieved?"

"He never stood a chance against you."

His distinctive baritone voice sent an exquisite shiver along her arms. She mentally shook herself. *He's a rake, he's a rake, he's a rake.*

The music ended. Lord Hawkfield excused himself and disappeared into the crowd. The duke glanced at her, and then he closed the distance between them.

She looked at him warily. Could he not see she wished him to leave her in peace?

"I apologize for detaining you so long earlier," he said. "Without a proper introduction, I fear you might have taken offense."

He'd apologized in a gentlemanly manner, even though she was equally at fault, perhaps more so, since she'd done most of the talking. "No apology is necessary. The circumstances were unusual."

He inclined his head. Though he did not smile, there was a natural curve to his full lips. His was not the pretty face of a dandy, however. Oh, no, not at all. His thick brows, angular cheekbones, and square jaw were all male. Little wonder women reportedly swooned at his perfection. No, not quite perfect, she thought, detecting a faint shadow along his jaw and above his full upper lip. His valet probably had to shave him twice a day. Her skin prickled at this evidence of the duke's masculinity.

"There is something I wish to ask you." His voice rumbled, a sound as rich and irresistible as a cup of chocolate.

Her heart thumped at the low, seductive notes in his voice. She'd thought herself unsusceptible to such tricks, but evidently her traitorous body was not.

"May I call upon you tomorrow afternoon?" he asked.

"Your Grace, if this concerns my fan, I beg you to forget the matter." There, that should settle his concern once and for all.

"It is not about the fan," he said. "I have appointments early in the afternoon. May I call at four o'clock?"

She regarded him with suspicion. "Why not tell me now?"

"I prefer to discuss it in private, if you are amenable."

In private? Did he mean to make her a dishonorable proposal? Then her common sense prevailed. A handsome rake like him would have no interest in a plump spinster.

His mouth curved in the merest of smiles. "You hesitate. I can hardly blame you after I discomposed you earlier."

She lifted her chin. "I was not discomposed." What a bouncer. She'd fled as if the engraving on his card read His Grace, the Duke of Devilbourne.

"I will of course abide by your decision." Then he gazed into her eyes with such intensity, she stilled like a rabbit in the woods. He drew her in, mesmerizing her with his arresting blue eyes. She felt the pull of his will like a swift current. And everything inside her said *yes*. "Very well," she said breathlessly.

"Thank you. Until tomorrow." He sketched a formal bow and walked away.

She let out her pent-up breath. Good God, he'd seduced her into agreeing.

Anne approached, using her fan to shield her voice. "What were you and the duke discussing?"

Tessa thought it best not to reveal his intended visit until she knew his purpose. "Nothing of consequence." But he wanted something from her. She suppressed a shiver.

"He spoke to you at length," Anne said. "You must tell me what he said."

"You make too much of the matter." Why had she let him turn her head?

"He looked at you like a starving wolf. Stay away from him," Anne said. "He is well-respected for his politics, but even Geoffrey admitted the duke has a notorious reputation with women. He probably has one hundred notches in his bedpost."

Tessa scoffed. "I'm sure he has no interest in carving one for an aging spinster like me."

"You are only six and twenty," Anne said. "Why must you always demean your charms?"

She ignored her friend's question. "Do not worry. I am in no danger of falling for a rake's wiles." Even if he'd persuaded her to let him call tomorrow, and she'd accepted against her better judgment.

Anne drew closer. "He has a reputation as a legendary lover. Women throw themselves in his path. I heard he can persuade a woman to do his bidding with his eyes."

Tessa gulped, knowing it was true.

Anne surveyed the crowd and grabbed Tessa's arm. "Look, there he is now by the hearth. Do you see that woman with him? That is Lady Endicott, a formerly respectable widow—until she met Shelbourne."

Tessa glanced in that direction. A tall, raven-haired beauty with jade feathers in her bandeau slid her finger along Shelbourne's lapel. Then the widow leaned against him and whispered in his ear. He turned his head and flicked her earbob.

Tessa gasped. Stars above. She'd invited that shameless rake to her drawing room.

His teeth flashed in a roguish grin. Then he winked at the lady and strode off.

"How could he engage in such brazen flirtation when his sister is present?" Anne said, her voice outraged.

Tessa swerved her gaze to Anne. "His sister?"

"Lady Julianne," Anne said. "She is dancing with Lord Holbrook."

The dark-haired young woman laughed as she skipped past her partner. Her complexion glowed with the radiance of youth, and her gold-netted gown set off her slender figure to perfection. A sliver of envy lodged in Tessa's throat. Long ago, she'd missed her own opportunity to have a season. Most of the time, she refused to dwell on the past, but once in a while, regret shadowed her heart.

Anne regarded Tessa. "Lady Julianne is purported to have declined more than a dozen marriage proposals since her come-out three years ago."

"She sounds very particular."

"Perhaps it is her brother who is particular," Anne said. "Some say the duke believes no man is good enough for his sister."

Tessa stilled. Did he mean to ask her to make a match for his sister tomorrow? No, surely he would rely on his mother's advice. Why then had he insisted on calling?

Chapter Two

$\mathscr{A}$t half past three o'clock, Tessa set aside her book, walked over to the window, and peered out the wavy glass. Shadows from her town house crept halfway to the wrought-iron gates. A curricle with enormous yellow wheels rumbled past, splashing puddles from an earlier shower.

What did Shelbourne want? The question played like a refrain in her head. She'd tossed and turned for hours last night, trying to guess, but she'd not thought of a single reasonable explanation.

Gravesend shuffled inside, wearing a solemn expression on his heavily lined face. Tessa smiled at her faithful butler. "You are looking dapper today," she said.

He tugged on his lapels. "Everything is in readiness for the duke's visit."

"Thank you, Gravesend," she said. "That is a relief to me." She watched her elderly butler exit with a smile on her face. He'd served her late uncle for many years and refused to retire with a pension, because he felt an obligation to her.

"Oh, I've made a shambles," Jane Powell said.

Tessa padded over to the round table where her new companion sat ripping out stitches. "Troubles?"

Jane set aside her needlework and brushed back an auburn curl. "I confess I'm all aflutter. In all my wildest dreams, I never thought to meet a real duke."

"You need do nothing more than stitch quietly."

"I promise not to utter a sound," Jane said, her expression anxious.

"I'm sure you will do fine." Tessa sat next to her. "Before the duke arrives, there is one issue I must address. Whatever transpires today must never leave this room."

"Oh, yes, of course. My lips are sealed," she said, tracing her finger over her mouth.

The rap of the knocker downstairs startled Tessa. A glance at the clock showed it was a quarter of four. Was the duke early? She walked over to the settee and perched upon the cushion, not allowing her spine to touch the mahogany back carved in the shape of shields.

When footsteps sounded on the stairs, her stomach flopped like a hooked fish. She told herself she had nothing to worry about. It was only the unknown making her nerves jangle.

Gravesend entered, puffed out his chest, and announced the duke.

Tessa smiled at Gravesend, rose, and curtseyed as Shelbourne strode inside.

When he bowed, his movements were quick and efficient. "Miss Mansfield, thank you for receiving me."

She introduced her companion and then indicated one of the armchairs across from her. "Will you be seated?"

Her chest constricted as he crossed over to the chair. In the light of day, his imposing height and powerful physique dominated her drawing room. Every sculpted and commanding inch of the man bespoke an ancestry of warriors. She could easily picture him, broadsword in hand, storming castle walls.

After they were seated, Tessa looked inquiringly at him. "May I offer you tea?"

"No, thank you."

She gazed at him expectantly. He tapped his fingers on the arm of the chair as he surveyed the drawing room. She imagined it from his perspective. No doubt he found the pale green walls with plasterwork of gold swags and ribbons entirely too feminine for his taste.

He returned his gaze to her. "Is your family from home?"

A tiny pin pricked her heart. "I have no living family."

"My deepest sympathy for your misfortune," he said.

"I consider myself quite fortunate. I have wonderful friends, and Miss Powell is a perfect companion."

He considered her for a moment. "You have taken charge of your life in spite of a difficult situation. An admirable quality."

His unexpected praise surprised her. She knew the ton looked upon her independence with suspicion.

After an uncomfortable silence, Tessa realized she would have to start the conversation. "Lady Broughton pointed out your sister to me last night. She is a lovely young woman."

"I thank you on her behalf." He glanced at Jane and then returned his attention to Tessa. "Miss Mansfield, I wish to discuss a matter with you in private. With your permission, of course."

Tessa hesitated. Meeting a gentleman alone wasn't strictly proper, unless a couple rode in an open carriage. Clearly he had no intention of speaking in front of her companion. Practicality must prevail—or she would go mad with curiosity.

"Jane," Tessa said, facing her companion. "The light is growing too dim here for needlework. You may return to your bedchamber to finish."

Wide-eyed, Jane quit the drawing room, leaving behind her sewing basket. Tessa suppressed a smile at Jane's forgetfulness.

When the door shut, Shelbourne squared his shoulders. "I must apologize for asking you to meet me alone. In doing so, I am putting your reputation at risk. I would not have asked if I did not believe it necessary."

"I take responsibility for all my decisions, Your Grace. Since the matter is a sensitive one, it is in both our best interests to ensure the conversation remains private."

"Thank you," he said.

She respected him for acknowledging the risk to her reputation, but he'd yet to state his purpose. "You have kept me in suspense. How may I help you?"

"I wish to hire you."

She stiffened. He'd insisted on speaking to her privately. Did he mean to hire her as a—a mistress?

He regarded her curiously. "Last night, I understood you offer matchmaking services."

Her shoulders slumped with relief. "My matchmaking is not a business."

"Nevertheless, I will compensate you for your efforts,"

he said. "Name a fair price, and I'll see you're paid half upon agreement, and the remainder upon a successful conclusion."

"I have no need of remuneration." Thanks to her late uncle, she had inherited a considerable fortune.

His dark brows drew together. "Surely you expect something in return."

She shook her head. "My matchmaking endeavors are entirely altruistic."

"Very well," he said. "I am prepared to provide you with the necessary information to aid in your search."

So he meant to ask her to make a match for his sister after all. "While I am flattered, I fear your mother would object if I were to make a match for Lady Julianne."

He frowned. "You misunderstand. I am not seeking your services for my sister."

Oh, dear, she'd made a mistake. How many times had Uncle George warned her never to make assumptions? "Your Grace, who is the lucky bride-to-be?"

The corners of his mouth lifted just a little. "If I knew that, I wouldn't need your assistance."

She gaped at him. "You want me to find *you* a bride?"

"Yes."

She couldn't countenance any man seeking her services, let alone a duke. "You are the most sought-after bachelor in England. Why do you need my help?"

"Finding a suitable bride on the marriage mart is a chancy business. Since I never leave matters to chance, I decided to consult an expert."

Tessa figured he'd grown weary of dodging fans, hand-kerchiefs, and parasols. "There is a certain amount of luck involved in all matrimonial matters. I simply facilitate opportunities for those who have few choices." She smiled. "You have the opposite problem."

"The number doesn't signify," he said. "What matters is making the right choice. And that is the crux of my problem."

"I do not understand."

"Do you read the papers, Miss Mansfield?"

"I am aware of your situation. Is it causing difficulties for you?"

"With such fame, I dare not ask a lady to dance for fear the scandal sheets will print my engagement the next day."

"Oh, dear, that is a problem," she said. "If it is not too impertinent, may I ask if there is a particular reason you've chosen to marry now?"

He tapped his fingers again. "I have recently set my affairs in order."

She narrowed her eyes. "What affairs?"

His fingers stilled. "I beg your pardon?"

"If I am to agree to this match, I must first assure myself that you are a man of good character." She already knew he was a rake, but she intended to make him squirm.

He regarded her from beneath his black lashes. "Do you often allow men of bad character into your drawing room, Miss Mansfield?" he drawled.

"Oh, did you not see them lined up at my door? It is truly amazing how many knaves, rogues, and rakes seek to make respectable marriages."

When he smiled, his eyes crinkled at the corners. "Are you always this satirical?"

He'd neatly diverted her, but she'd not forgotten. "About your affairs?"

His smile faded. "I inherited a number of debts more than a decade ago, but the estate is now solvent." He paused. "Some might find my decision to postpone marriage foolhardy under the circumstances."

She filled in the blanks. He'd refused to marry in order to replenish the ducal coffers. A rake he might be, but he wasn't a fortune hunter. "I find your decision honorable." If only all gentlemen were so honorable, her life might have turned out differently.

"I took a risk, one that left the dukedom unsecured for a number of years." His tone and his expression held a challenge. "I have no heir, Miss Mansfield."

She could not help but admire him. His decision must have been a difficult one, and yet he'd taken the rocky path rather than the smooth one. "You made the right choice."

His eyes registered surprise, but he quickly hid it. "Have I answered to your satisfaction?"

"Well, I am curious why you have not sought your mother's advice."

A cynical expression crossed his face. "She refused to help."

Tessa's lips parted.

"My mother and I do not agree on the subject of my bride." He paused and added, "She has rather decided opinions."

Tessa nodded. She'd met more than a few strong-willed mothers and knew the havoc they could wreak. Obviously the duchess had tried to impose her will on her son. Tessa believed ladies and gentlemen should choose with their hearts. "I always listen to those who seek my aid and try to meet their needs."

"Your professionalism is precisely what I am seeking."

Thus far, he'd reassured her, but she could not forget he

was a rake. "If I am to make this match, you must agree to one condition." Even as she spoke, she knew he would balk.

"What is the condition?" he asked.

She lifted her chin. "In order for there to be marital accord, you must agree to honor your wedding vows."

Mischief lurked in his blue eyes. "If I recall correctly, there are several parts to the vows. Is there one in particular that concerns you?"

Warmth crept into her cheeks. "You must agree to forsake all others."

He leaned forward, looked over his right shoulder and then his left. "Where are they?"

She frowned. "Who?"

"The ones I'm supposed to forsake." He gave her a roguish grin. "I assume you require proof."

"You mock me, but your reputation precedes you."

"Is that why you ran away last night?" he said, his voice rumbling with sensual overtones.

Her face flamed. "I did not run. I hurried back to my friends."

His knowing smile incited her temper. "Unlike you, I take the matter very seriously," she said, "and I have it on the best of authority that you are an infamous rake."

"I'm thirty years old, a bachelor, not a monk," he said.

"I saw you flirting with Lady Endicott last night," she bit out. "Do you deny seducing a respectable lady?"

"While I owe you no explanation, I will deny your unfounded accusation," he said in a deceptively mild yet dangerous tone. "I've never seduced anyone. All of my paramours consented freely. All were worldly widows. I make no apologies for my past liaisons."

Oh, he was unrepentant, every bit as bad as Anne had said. "Your past is an indicator of your future conduct. I can only conclude you see nothing wrong with taking a mistress after your marriage, and I do not condone infidelity."

"Neither do I," he said in a solemn voice.

Her lips parted. She could hardly believe her ears.

"You've made an assumption when you do not know me," he said. "I expect marital fidelity from my wife, and I will remain faithful to her in return."

She regarded him with suspicion. A man of his lusty appetites would yield to temptation. "How am I to know you will keep your word?"

His eyes glinted with a devilish expression. "Perhaps a record of my attendance at church would satisfy you. Or maybe a character witness? My friend Hawk is a disreputable fellow, but I'm sure he'd vouch for me."

She sniffed. "I ought to make you do it."

"Upon my honor, then."

Well, she could not express her doubts without besmirching his honor. Gentlemen were touchy about such things.

His blue eyes twinkled. "Did I pass the test?"

"So far," she said. Once again, he'd tried to charm her. She'd best watch out.

"You would make a formidable barrister," he said.

"No, but I believe I have developed some talent at matchmaking."

"Apparently Broughton agrees, and I respect his opinion."

No one had ever spoken of her career with such esteem. Excitement coursed through her veins. Finding a bride for the Duke of Shelbourne would be the ultimate feather in her matchmaking cap. Why, she would have no trouble at all making a match for him. He was handsome, honorable, and agreeable. And he'd promised to be true to his wife. What woman would not fall in love with him?

The potential benefits crashed in her head like the waves at Brighton. If she successfully married off the duke, other gentlemen might seek her services. Then she could match them with all the unfortunate young ladies who tearfully sought her help. At long last, she would earn the respect she deserved for her career. She imagined the whispers of the ton as she strolled through a ballroom. *There she is, the Duke of Shelbourne's matchmaker.*

"Do you require a contract?" he asked.

She blinked. "No, that is unnecessary."

"Ah, so you operate on the basis of a gentleman's agreement?"

"Um, I suppose one could call it that." Instinct told her something was awry. She weighed her vague misgivings against the advantages to marry matchmaking career. How could she possibly turn down the opportunity to make the match of the decade? The century!

Elated at the prospect, she rose and beamed at the duke. "Yes, I will be happy to assist you."

He unfolded from his chair, crossed the room, and held out his palm. "Will you shake hands to seal our agreement?"

"Very well." When their palms met, a giddy sensation, like champagne bubbles, raced to her head. His hand, so much larger than her own, engulfed hers, making her feel strangely possessed. The warmth of his long fingers contrasted with the cool metal of a ring. As if she were dreaming, she slowly lifted her gaze past his imposing chest and tipped her head back, only to find herself drowning in his vivid blue eyes.

The thick fan of his black lashes lowered just a little, and the sultry expression in his eyes ensnared her. The subtle scent of sandalwood invaded her senses, making her dizzy with forbidden longing.

When he released her hand, she exhaled, though tension still vibrated all along her limbs. What was the matter with her? She decided it was only the excitement of knowing she would make one of the most prestigious matches in society.

When he reached inside his coat, she glimpsed a heraldic shield on his gold band. Then he pulled out a folded piece of parchment from his coat and offered it to her. "Here is a description of the bride I am seeking."

A twinge of unease skittered down the back of her neck as she unfolded the paper and read the page.

My bride should be at least twenty-one years of age, never married, and of noble birth. The candidate must have training in planning social entertainments and managing servants. Her conversation should be of an intelligent nature, extending beyond balls and bonnets. Sound judgment based on rationality rather than emotion is a requirement. Other desired traits include gracefulness, dutifulness, modesty, and decorum. Above all, she must be virtuous and have an unassailable reputation.

A great clanging, like the bells at St. Paul's, echoed in her ears. He'd written the description as if it were an advertisement for a servant.

"There is one important quality I neglected to include." He paused a moment as if assessing her. "I should be able to detect a hint of . . . passion in the lady's nature."

Her jaw dropped.

He looked amused. "Have I shocked you?"

She tapped his paper. "You said you want a respectable bride."

"I do, but I plan to remain faithful and want a wife who will abandon her inhibitions," he said.

She huffed. "No, you want the impossible—a virtuous courtesan."

"I want an angel in the ballroom and a temptress in... private."

Heat scorched her face. "You cannot taste the wine and decide it is not to your liking. There is no way for you to know such a thing."

His gaze dipped to her mouth. With agonizing slowness, he lifted his lashes. "I'll know," he said.

His low, velvety voice stirred heat low in her belly. Fearing she would melt in a puddle at his feet, she returned to the settee, set his paper aside, and applied her fan.

When he settled in his chair, she glanced at him. At the knowing look in his eyes, she snapped her fan closed. "You've forgotten the most important ingredient to a happy marriage."

"Oh, and what is that?" he asked.

She lifted her chin. "Love."

His eyes filled with cynicism. "I think people often mistake love for something baser."

Lust. The unspoken word hovered in the air. A lady should blush at his scandalous meaning, but if she did, he would only enjoy his triumph over her. And she took greater offense at his cavalier disregard of the heart. "I believe love is what sets us apart from the animal kingdom," she said.

"I think reason and rationality set us apart from the beasts," he said.

"I'm afraid there has been a misunderstanding," she said. "I only make love matches."

"Miss Mansfield, in the matter of tender words or gestures, I've nothing to recommend me. But I take my responsibilities seriously. All who depend on me know safety and security. I cannot promise to marry for love, but I will promise to treat my wife with respect and dignity."

Tessa hesitated. There were plenty of single ladies of little fortune and no marriage prospects who would leap at his offer in order to secure their uncertain futures. Yet everything inside her rebelled at promoting a cold marriage of convenience. She had spoken at length with many of these desperate girls, and in every instance, all had admitted a yearning to marry for love.

She recalled her uncle's words spoken that day eight years ago that had changed her life forever. *I would never allow you to spend a lifetime of misery with a man who does not love you.*

As an ignorant girl, she'd not realized her uncle's beliefs were so different from those of society. Since then, she'd heard of far too many young women forced into arranged marriages. Most parents of the ton cared only about noble titles and wealth. Those parents wielded a great deal of power over their daughters and sons.

Tessa shivered. She could not make a match where there was not even a prayer of love developing.

She drew in her breath, prepared to refuse him. His jaw hardened, an indication he knew. No doubt he was accustomed to everyone complying with his wishes, but she would not sacrifice her principles, not even for a duke.

And yet, if she refused him, he *would* make a loveless marriage. But if she helped him, she might succeed in convincing him to marry for love.

She recalled something her uncle George had told her on his deathbed. *Things happen for a reason.*

Pins pricked the backs of her hands. That was the moment she knew it was her destiny to open the duke's heart to love. "Very well, Your Grace. I will assist you."

He looked taken aback, but he recovered quickly. "Excellent. Shall we agree on one week?"

She blinked. "For what?"

"For you to introduce me to my future bride," he said with a shrug.

Did he plan to propose on the spot? She cleared her throat. "Usually there is a courtship involved."

His chest shook with unsuppressed laughter. "Ah, yes, of course. A brief courtship will allow me to verify the candidate is suitable."

"You delight in teasing me," she said.

"All teasing aside, I expect you to commence immediately. I've already wasted a month and have no wish to delay further. Once I make a decision, I will act quickly."

Apparently the man didn't have a romantic bone in his body. Once again, doubts plagued her, but if she did not help the duke, he probably would find someone willing to do his bidding. Someone who would not care whether he made a happy marriage or not.

Of course she must dissuade him from choosing a wife based on his ridiculous description, but she would address that issue when he was ready to listen. "There may be more than one young lady who meets with your approval." Given his finicky requirements, she suspected he would object to one candidate after another.

"Do you have more than one lady in mind?" he asked.

"Yes, but I wish to give the matter careful study first."

He looked skeptical.

She rushed in before he could object. "Would you be willing to consider more than one? I would hate to rule out a young lady you might find agreeable."

"I suppose so, although I think it highly unlikely you will find more than one. Still, it speaks well of you to be prepared."

She smiled. If all went well, her career would soar as a result of this match.

"I have one other requirement—of you," he said. "I prefer we keep our arrangement a secret."

She averted her gaze, so he would not see her disappointment. He didn't want anyone to know because he didn't really respect her career.

"I want to keep our dealings quiet. I'm weary of all the notoriety," he said. "The papers have made a jest of my honorable intentions."

"I understand," she said, "but I cannot promise secrecy when everyone is watching you."

He let out a gusty sigh. "No matter what I do I cannot avoid drawing attention."

"I can make one promise to you," she said, meeting his gaze. "I will never reveal our conversations to another soul."

"Thank you. Do you have any questions before I leave?"

"Not at this time." When she rose, he came to his feet and bowed. Then he regarded her with a perplexed expression. "If it is not too impertinent, perhaps you might satisfy my curiosity. Why did you become a matchmaker? Obviously, it is not for money."

She shrugged. "It just happened. One evening at a ball, I saw the poor ignored girls sitting miserably by the wall, and I decided to help them." She did not tell him that her own shattered dreams had led her to make love matches for the girls whose prospects were grim.

The clock chimed five times. "I must leave," he said. "Is one week sufficient for you?"

She hid her crossed fingers behind her skirt. "Yes, I believe so."

Chapter Three

Tristan felt like a foreigner in a feminine country.

The babble of voices and laughter died the minute he stepped inside Miss Mansfield's spacious drawing room. In the silence, the clink of teacups and saucers boomed like cannon. He stood there, dazed, gazing at a crowd of young chits and matrons. They perched upon chairs set in a wide semicircle. He recognized a number of his mother's fellow she-dragons. They stared at him as if he were the last morsel of food on earth.

Clearly Miss Mansfield had made a mistake in her invitation.

The rustle of fabric drew his gaze to her. She wore an elegant yellow gown that billowed round her voluptuous figure as she came forward and curtseyed. When she rose, her serene smile was the portrait of feminine poise.

He respected her for maintaining her composure. "My apologies, Miss Mansfield," he said. "Obviously there has been a mistake."

"No apology is necessary, Your Grace. We've been expecting you."

What the devil? Shock reverberated throughout his body. The little witch had tricked him.

"Come now, Miss Mansfield," Lady Verstan called out. "You've kept us in suspense long enough. What can you mean, inviting Shelbourne and our daughters to call?"

"Have no fear, Lady Verstan," Miss Mansfield said. "I intend to enlighten everyone." She glanced at him. "Will you follow me, Your Grace?"

The temptation to walk out the door gripped him, but doing so would only create a scene. "Allow me to escort you," he said, offering his arm. Her lips twitched, but she complied. The light touch of her hand on his sleeve stirred an odd, tight feeling in his chest. Probably a digestive disorder.

She slid her hand away when they reached the hearth. "Could I have your attention, please?" The buzz of voices quieted. After a moment's silence, she spoke. "I know you are all curious. It is no coincidence that I invited England's most eligible bachelor and twenty-four single young ladies."

That pronouncement brought about a flurry of whispers. Tristan kept his stony gaze on Miss Mansfield. What mischief was she brewing?

"Before I explain," Miss Mansfield continued, "it is important to consider a little background. This may surprise many of you, but rank and power can sometimes be a burden."

Lady Durmont snorted.

Miss Mansfield's lips thinned, but she recovered her poise. "Imagine if you will," she said, "what it is like to be a man of Shelbourne's consequence. Everyone around you sees only the prestige of your title. Such an exalted position has many advantages, but the disadvantage is that no one sees you for who you really are."

He arched his brows, wondering how long she'd practiced her pretty little speech.

Miss Mansfield walked a few paces with her hands behind her back, gazing at the rich carpet as if pondering some great philosophical question. Suddenly, she halted, scanning the rapt faces before her. "What must it be like to find a wife in such circumstances? Any eligible single girl would naturally feel constrained in the duke's presence. She would feel awed and would confine her conversation to topics deemed suitable by society."

No, she would simper, giggle, and drop her fan.

Miss Mansfield's eyes glowed with fervor. "How, then, can the duke possibly find the duchess of his dreams?"

Several young ladies sighed. Damn and blast, they'd actually fallen for her sentimental drivel.

After a lengthy pause, Miss Mansfield eyed him. "When the duke sought my help a week ago, he was quite clear about the qualities he sought in a duchess. After due consideration, I made a list of single ladies who might qualify, but I encountered a problem."

He narrowed his eyes. "And what problem was that?"

"No one met all of the requirements." After a stunned silence, she continued. "So I made a decision. Twenty-four of you received invitations because you most closely fit the duke's vision of a bride. However, it is not for me to judge who is best suited. I am leaving that decision to His Grace. He will choose during a special courtship involving all the young ladies."

Tristan ground his teeth. He'd trusted her, and she'd dared to manipulate him. If she thought he'd stand for her tricks, she was sorely mistaken. He opened his mouth to put a stop to her nonsense, but before he could utter a word, Lady Verstan snapped her fan closed. "Miss Mansfield, are you suggesting that the duke court twenty-four ladies?"

"Only for the first week," she said.

His jaw worked. She would pay for her deception.

"Preposterous," Lady Durmont said.

Several other dragons murmured their agreement. No doubt they would all refuse to allow their daughters to participate in this sham of a courtship. When they did, he would dismiss Miss Mansfield, and that would ruin her career.

A pretty, blue-eyed blonde raised her hand. "Miss Mansfield? I hope it is not too impertinent of me to ask, but you said the duke would court all of us for only the first week. After that, will the courtship be limited to one of us?"

"A good question, Lady Georgette, and the answer is no," Miss Mansfield said. "The actual courtship period will last several weeks. Each week some of you will be eliminated, based on the duke's choices. Those chosen will receive an invitation to return the following week." She paused and then said, "Of course, no one is obligated to participate, which brings me to my next point. Those of you who do not want the duke to court your daughters, please raise your hands."

None of the dragons lifted a finger.

"Your Grace," she said in a deceitfully sweet voice. "Do you have an objection?"

"How could I possibly object?" Thanks to Lucifer's handmaiden, he couldn't refuse without insulting forty-eight ladies.

Apparently she missed the sarcasm in his voice because she clasped her hands like a gleeful child. "Well, then it is all settled."

It most certainly was not settled. There had to be some way out of this fiasco. He could imagine all too well the notoriety the bizarre "courtship" would engender. Damn it all. He didn't want to subject his mother and sister to a barrage of gossip, but it was too late now. By tomorrow, the entire kingdom would know.

Once again, matters had spiraled out of his control. After weeks of finding himself the unwilling subject of the scandal sheets, he could bear no more. Yet he couldn't conduct even a traditional courtship without the inevitable scrutiny of the ton.

He would find a means of eliminating all but one of the young ladies. But if he courted one lady, the damned papers would print his impending engagement long before he'd made up his mind. Whether the lady in question suited or not, he might find himself obliged to offer because of her family's expectations and those of society. However, if he courted several at once, he could avoid that trap. Of course he'd no intention of courting twenty-four of them.

Miss Mansfield leaned closer to him. "I have several plans for the courtship," she murmured.

He'd have to be daft to trust her now. An idea occurred to him, one that would eliminate most of them. He leveled a stern look at Miss Mansfield. "I have a proposal for the first session."

Her smile froze. "Oh, how lovely."

"In fact, we can begin today, if the ladies can spare another half hour or so."

"What did you have in mind?" she asked.

"A test."

Her brows furrowed. "What sort of test?"

Tristan took a menacing step toward her. "A duchess test."

He insisted on supervising the test.

Tessa sat beside the duke near the wall in her dining room. The twenty-four young women labored over their compositions at the mahogany table. The scratch, scratch, scratch of quills filled the room. With a sigh, she vowed to exercise patience with Shelbourne.

What in the world had possessed him to propose this test? Surely he wouldn't choose a bride based on a paper? Especially one titled "Why I Would Make the Perfect Duchess." Poor man, he had no notion how to court a woman. It was fortunate he'd come to her for help.

She glanced at him, only to find him watching her through narrowed eyes. Tessa lifted her chin and pretended to ignore him. From the moment he'd entered her drawing room, she'd sensed his disapproval. He'd not believed her when she said no one met all of his qualifications. But she would not let him intimidate her. Eventually he would realize she'd done him a favor.

The duke consulted his watch and announced, "Fifteen minutes remaining."

Tessa hoped Jane was faring well entertaining the matrons in the drawing room. Her companion's eyes had widened in terror at the prospect of being left alone with the most fearsome ladies of the ton. To prevent disaster, Tessa had taken drastic measures. She'd brought out the sherry decanter and told Jane to top up the glasses at every opportunity. A little happy tonic might tame the dragons.

A feminine gasp followed by several muffled giggles drew Tessa's attention back to the bridal candidates. Miss Amy Hardwick, the plainest young woman in the room, picked up the quill she'd evidently dropped. Ink spots spattered her page. All the other young ladies stared at her with obvious disdain.

Tessa rushed over to Miss Hardwick. "Do not fret. Here is another sheet of paper."

Miss Hardwick rubbed at the ugly ink stain on her finger. A frizzy red lock fell over her forehead.

"Do not worry about the stain," Tessa whispered. "Just copy what you've already written."

Miss Hardwick flushed. She hunched her shoulders and picked up her quill, her movements hesitant. Tessa backed away, fearing to add to Miss Hardwick's embarrassment. With all her heart, Tessa wished she could provide encouragement to the young woman, who had not taken well with the ton. After four seasons, she had not received a single marriage proposal.

A girlish voice startled Tessa. "Your Grace," Lady Georgette said, "how much time do we have left?"

He consulted his watch. "Nine minutes."

The other girls gasped and started writing. Lady Georgette smiled at the duke, revealing her twin dimples. Then she dropped her paper on the floor. "Oh, dear."

He started out of his chair, but Tessa shook her head at him. Then she walked over to Georgette, picked up the paper, and placed it on the table. The little flirt ignored her and waved her fingers at the duke. Tessa moved to block Georgette's view of her prey and pointed at the quill.

"I'm done." Georgette offered the paper to Tessa.

Tessa folded her arms. "Leave it on the table."

She returned to her chair and leaned toward the duke. "Have a care," she whispered. "You're distracting the girls."

"I am not," he said.

"Lower your voice," she whispered.

He made an exasperated sound.

She shielded her face with her hand. "You mustn't encourage flirtation. The girls need to concentrate."

A slow, wicked smile spread across his face. He bent his head and whispered, "Lady Georgette finished."

His breath stirred the curl by Tessa's ear, making her shiver. The lingering scent of sandalwood tickled her senses. When he sat back in his chair, he gave her a roguish grin. Her cheeks grew hot at his knowing expression. Oh, why had she reacted so foolishly to his practiced wiles?

The duke consulted his watch again and spoke in a low voice. "After everyone leaves, and that includes Miss Powell, you and I will have a private discussion."

"Yes, of course. We need to evaluate the papers," she said in an undertone. She ought to tell the duke his test would not work, but undoubtedly he would defend his decision. He would discover soon enough he couldn't choose a bride on the basis of hastily scrawled compositions.

After everyone else departed, Tristan walked to the hearth in Miss Mansfield's drawing room and pivoted to face her. "Now you will explain why you tricked me."

The compositions she clutched fluttered to the carpet, scattering round her feet. "Oh," she said, her voice squeaking.

Why did women drop things all the time? Was it something he did? Irritated, Tristan walked over to her and knelt on one knee to gather the papers. When he handed them to her, an odd sensation gripped him. The devil. He must look like a besotted swain about to propose.

That thought brought him to his feet. He straightened his sleeves and regarded her coldly. "Well?"

"It wasn't a trick," she said. "You agreed to consider more than one."

"You failed to mention there would be twenty-four," he gritted out.

"I explained my reasons earlier," she said. "Your requirements proved considerably more difficult than I anticipated."

He didn't believe her. "You should have notified me you were having difficulties."

"I decided to find a creative solution."

He scoffed. "Naturally it never occurred to you to consult me."

"I admit this courtship is somewhat irregular, but truthfully, I have handed you the opportunity of a lifetime." Grasping the papers to her chest, she ticked off her points on her slender fingers. "First, you will have sole access to twenty-four of the most eligible ladies in society. Second, you will be able to eliminate any you do not think suit. Third, every bachelor in the Beau Monde will envy you."

"Admit it. You meant to manipulate me," he said.

"I know you are vexed, but you agreed to court all the girls."

"I could not refuse after their mothers approved. You purposely arranged matters so I had no choice."

"Actually, I have given you twenty-four choices."

His head ached from listening to her ludicrous excuses. "Enough. We will judge the papers now."

Her brows furrowed. "You cannot mean to choose a wife based on a paper."

"It is my courtship, and I will do as I see fit." He would make her wait before telling her the real reason behind the test.

An hour later, Tristan realized he'd miscalculated.

He sat at the opposite end of the settee from Miss Mansfield. The compositions lay in a neat stack between them. He'd read all the papers, with the exception of the four illegible ones. The other papers all sounded alike. A litany of their accomplishments swam in his brain. Singing, dancing, painting. Lord, did they really think he cared about such nonsense?

He'd hoped to eliminate all but two or three, but he did not have enough information yet. Clearly, he would have to devise a better plan. The news would delight his mischief-maker, but he would make it clear he was in charge. He would relegate her role to chaperone.

Tristan stole a look at her. As she read the last paper, she moistened her strawberry-plump lips. Her generous mouth made him think of lush, heated kisses. She sighed, drawing his attention to her full breasts. He imagined stripping the flimsy bodice from her and gazing at her taut nipples. His body stirred, warming like the first swallow of an excellent brandy.

She set the paper on top of the stack. "You must admit

the compositions demonstrate some of the qualities you requested in a wife."

Determined to rein in his lusty thoughts, he shifted his gaze to the papers. "I failed to detect a single example."

"Oh, but you are wrong." She riffled through the papers and pointed at one smeared with ink blots. "Miss Hardwick stressed her training in managing household accounts. That indicates dutifulness, in my opinion."

Miss Hardwick must be the bashful redhead who had dropped her pen.

"All the other ladies are quite accomplished as well." Miss Mansfield regarded him with a guileless expression. Her long-lashed round eyes and full cheeks gave her an innocent appearance. Yet those ripe lips ruined the effect.

Her mouth curved into a serene smile. "Since the girls did so well, we shall have to invite them all back next week."

"Not so fast. There are four I couldn't read." He thumbed through the papers until he located them. "I cannot abide an illiterate wife."

When the mischief-maker huffed, he decided to get a little revenge, and he knew exactly how to unnerve her. "Eliminate these girls." When she reached for the papers, he let his fingers brush her soft hand.

She inhaled sharply.

He fixed an innocent schoolboy expression on his face. "Is something the matter?"

She turned her gaze away as she set the papers aside. "I think you should reconsider. Their nervousness prevented them from doing their best."

He bit back a smug grin. "The point of the exercise was for me to observe how they react in demanding situations."

She whipped her stunned gaze back to him. "You misled them."

"It was a test of their confidence. Only one of them passed."

"If you are speaking of Lady Georgette Danforth, you mistake conceit for confidence," she said in an indignant tone.

Interesting. Miss Mansfield had made no secret of her dislike for the girl during the test. "You have a long-standing acquaintance with her?"

"I know her type. She is a determined flirt."

"I imagine they all are, with the exception of that unfortunate red-haired girl."

She lifted her chin. "Miss Hardwick wrote the best paper despite her mishap. I think that shows fortitude."

Evidently she meant to champion the wallflower of the bunch. The poor girl would not suit at all, but he couldn't deny Miss Hardwick had recovered well. "I will give her one more chance." And then he would eliminate her.

Miss Mansfield's wide smile transformed her from merely alluring to breathtaking. She regarded him with shining eyes, making him feel as if he'd just saved a damsel in distress.

Bloody hell. Doubtless she'd perfected that worshipful look to add to her bag of she-devil tricks. He would not let her distract him again. "Send invitations to all but the four I mentioned previously. And make it clear they may not court other gentlemen."

"They would not risk their reputations or their chances with you," she said.

"I always make my expectations known from the

beginning," he said. "If they don't like the conditions, they may withdraw."

She grumbled under her breath.

He cupped his ear. "Sorry, I didn't hear that."

She sniffed. "For the next event, I propose an informal gathering at my town house."

"No, that will only lead to inane conversation," he said. "I will send round a plan shortly."

"Are you never spontaneous?" she asked.

"No, and I don't like surprises."

Her green eyes glimmered. "But some of the most wonderful things in life are unexpected."

"You're a hopeless optimist," he said.

"Only a pessimist could utter such a ludicrous oxymoron."

"I am a rationalist. In my experience, a logical approach prevents disorder and misunderstandings. I never allow emotions to interfere with my judgment, something you must make clear to the bridal candidates."

"No one is completely devoid of feelings," she said.

"Allow me to clarify. If any of these girls have starry-eyed visions of romance, they'd best drop out of the competition."

"Competition?" Her voice pitched up an octave. "Do you think of yourself as a prize?"

He fought back a smile. "No, but I imagine they do."

She made an exasperated sound.

Her poor opinion tickled him enough to rile her further. "Miss Mansfield, most people treat me with deference." In truth, he despised the sycophants who fawned over him.

She sniffed. "I am sorry to be the bearer of bad tidings, but beneath the ducal trappings, you are only a man."

"You wound me."

Her lips twitched. "I doubt it."

He found himself smiling at her wit. The afternoon shadows made him aware of the late hour. He couldn't remember ever spending this much time with a woman, outside of bed, without becoming restless and bored. That thought spurred him to his feet.

She rose as well. A subtle, tealike fragrance, roses, curled through his senses. The soft sound of her breathing drew his attention to her slightly parted lips. His heart beat a little faster.

She curtseyed. "Good day, Your Grace."

Her voice jolted his befuddled brain. He muttered something polite, bowed, and strode out, wondering where the devil he'd lost his mind.

The next evening, Tristan nursed a brandy while waiting impatiently for Hawk at White's. The liquor did nothing to quell his gloomy mood. His mother had confronted him about his courtship this morning. Apparently her fellow she-dragons had wasted no time in their rush to spread the news.

Masculine voices grew louder as the premises swelled with London's elite gentlemen. The aroma of sizzling beefsteak drifted from the upstairs dining room. Tristan retrieved his watch and frowned at the time. Then he turned his attention outside. Rain tapped on the window. Outside, a yellow pool of light from the gas lamp pierced the mist. A carriage rumbled along the cobbled street and jangled to a halt. When Hawk emerged, a gust of wind blew back his black greatcoat. He looked like an enormous raven as he dashed to the door.

A few minutes later, Hawk sprawled in the vacant chair across from Tristan. "Sorry I'm late." In the candlelight,

Hawk's bleary eyes, disheveled hair, and tangled cravat made a frightening picture.

"Good Lord," Tristan said. "Were you attacked by thieves?"

"No, a ballerina." A solicitous waiter brought Hawk his usual brandy. After the waiter left, Hawk eyed Tristan. "My ballerina has a friend, if you're interested."

"Don't tempt me."

"Are you too fastidious to consider a dancer?"

"No."

Hawk lifted his brows. "Are you ill? I heard about this doctor who specializes in—"

"I don't have the bloody pox," Tristan grumbled. There was no way to conduct a discreet liaison now. If he took a mistress, everyone would know, including those girls' fathers. Tristan fingered his tight cravat, imagining their furious reactions.

Damnation, he needed a woman to slake his lust. And he needed one badly. Last night, he'd awoken from a dream about *her* ripe mouth. Clearly he was a hair's breadth from losing what remained of his sanity.

Thanks to the mischief-maker, he could look forward to even more infamy. The thought seared his brain. He took a swig of brandy. The liquor burned his throat, but he refused to cough.

"What the devil ails you?" Hawk asked.

"Nothing." Tristan set the glass down with a decided thunk.

Hawk's eyes narrowed. "I heard about the courtship. Have you lost your wits?"

Probably. "I retained Miss Mansfield to find a bride who suits me."

Hawk snorted. "You wouldn't dream of allowing anyone to choose your horse, but you'd let a stranger pick your bride?"

"It's not as if I can ride her before I buy her," Tristan muttered.

Hawk gave him a dubious look. "Old boy, you're my friend, and I have to ask. What is Miss Mansfield expecting in return for this service?"

"Nothing. She says she doesn't need the money."

"I heard she inherited Wentworth's fortune."

Tristan leaned forward. "As in the late earl?"

"One and the same. She was his only living kin."

"She told me she has no family," Tristan said.

"She's as independent as any man and purported to be one of the richest women in England." Hawk shook his head. "I don't like this matchmaking business. She's in it for something other than money. What does she stand to gain by helping you?"

He'd no idea, but he'd never admit it to Hawk. "What does it matter? All I care about is finding a wife."

"Be careful," Hawk said. "Don't let her trap you into something you'll regret."

Tristan scoffed. If she made one more misstep, he'd dismiss her and expose her as a fraud. She'd never hold her head up in society again.

"There's a lot of speculation about her," Hawk said. "She has a reputation for being far too clever for her own good."

"You think I can't handle a clever woman?" he gritted out.

Hawk grinned. "Since you put it that way, I suppose Miss Mansfield has met her match."

Chapter Four

$\mathcal{I}$n moments, Tessa must face the grand dragon of the ton.

Her heart pounded as she followed the footman up the curving staircase. After receiving the terse summons from the Duchess of Shelbourne this morning, Tessa had surmised the sensational reports in the scandal sheets had prompted this meeting.

Of course it was unfair of the duchess to blame her. After all, the duchess had refused to help her son find a wife. But fairness did not signify. The curt tone of that missive left no doubt in Tessa's mind that the duchess meant to rip her to shreds.

Upon reaching the landing, Tessa drew in an unsteady breath. She could not afford to let fear overwhelm her. Above all else, she must remain poised, regardless of what the duchess said.

After the footman opened the drawing room doors, Tessa lifted her chin and walked inside. A sea of red greeted her. The crimson sofa and chairs, cherry damask wall coverings, and red draperies threatened to overwhelm her.

This must be the duchess's favored room for drawing blood.

Tessa turned her attention to the dark-haired woman glaring at her from one of the sofas. The duchess wore a mauve striped gown with a high ruff collar. Only a few silver threads marred her fashionably short curls. She looked much too young to have a grown son.

Tessa curtseyed. "Your Grace."

The duchess lifted a quizzing glass hanging from a ribbon and inspected Tessa with a curled lip. "So you are the infamous matchmaker my friends told me about."

She inclined her head, but said nothing. Her uncle had taught her never to feel compelled to fill a silence.

When it became apparent the duchess would not invite her to be seated, Tessa decided to thwart the woman's intimidation tactics. She perched upon the sofa directly across from the duchess and forced herself to smile.

The duchess released her quizzing glass. "I did not give you leave to be seated."

Tessa met her gaze. "I assumed you did not wish to keep me standing."

"I most certainly did. This interview will end shortly after you resign as my son's matchmaker."

Tessa clasped her trembling hands hard. "I beg your pardon, but I made the agreement with your son," she said in as neutral a tone as she could manage. "Any decision to discontinue must involve him."

"Impudent gel," she said.

"You flatter me," Tessa said. "It has been many years since anyone has referred to me in such youthful terms."

"I meant no compliment to you. Your reputation as a spinster precedes you."

With considerable effort, she ignored the insult and kept a serene smile on her face. "I can hardly keep my single state a secret."

The duchess gave her a freezing look. "How dare you address me in such an insolent manner? If you had even a modicum of sense, you would tremble in fear of what I can do to you."

Tessa swallowed hard, knowing the duchess had the influence to ruin her. Then her gaze lit on the newspaper on the sofa next to the duke's mother. With sudden insight, Tessa realized the courtship had humiliated the duchess. "I meant no insult to you," she murmured.

"Miss Mansfield," she said. "Your services are no longer required."

Tristan's brain seared like a hot coal upon reaching the drawing room door and hearing his mother's words. He'd warned his mother not to interfere. Clearly she'd defied him and gone behind his back. Determined to keep his anger in check, Tristan strode inside to find his mother glowering at Miss Mansfield.

Miss Mansfield stood, curtseyed, and lifted her chin. Despite her bravado, crimson flags marred her cheeks. Obviously, his mother had given her quite a tongue-lashing.

He bowed. "Miss Mansfield, this is a pleasant surprise."

The duchess remained seated. Her lips curved in a sardonic smile. "Miss Mansfield has delighted us with her presence."

He knew without a doubt his mother had summoned her.

Miss Mansfield kept her gaze on him. "Your Grace, I must take my leave now."

"I understand." It would be distasteful to subject her to his family squabbles.

The duchess sniffed. "Tristan, you will release her from this ridiculous matchmaking scheme. I am the rightful person to find you a bride."

"Is my memory failing? As I recall, you refused."

The duchess picked up a newspaper beside her. "Word has spread to the scandal sheets." Her voice shook with anger.

He shrugged. "That is nothing new. I've been a daily gossip item for weeks."

She slapped the paper on the sofa.

Miss Mansfield's uncertain gaze flitted from his mother to him.

The devil. His mother meant to have her way, even if it resulted in a scene. He turned his attention to Miss Mansfield. "I will call on you tomorrow to discuss our business."

"Business?" the duchess said in an outraged tone. "How can you refer to marriage in such cold terms?"

"Marriage is my duty," he said.

"This is a matter of the heart. When your father and I—"

Tristan held up his hand. "Enough."

His mother jerked her face away. Why she continued to mourn a man who had never deserved her mystified him. She'd conveniently forgotten her late husband's many transgressions and often spoke lovingly of him. Tristan's refusal to agree with her assertions remained a source of friction between them, but he would not aid and abet his mother's illusions.

Surprisingly, Miss Mansfield gave his mother a sympathetic look. "Your Grace," she said softly. "I am sorry for any embarrassment I may have inadvertently caused you. It was not intentional."

"An apology will not suffice. If you are truly sorry, you will resign," his mother said.

"Mama, it is not your decision," he said.

The duchess's countenance darkened as she stood. "You will regret this, Miss Mansfield." Then she whipped past Tristan, jerking the door closed behind her.

He walked over to the red velvet sofa his mother had vacated. "Please be seated," he said to Miss Mansfield.

He sat across from her and drummed his fingers on the rolled arm of the sofa. "I apologize for my mother. You should not have had to witness that."

Miss Mansfield smoothed her skirts and said nothing.

He considered her through narrowed eyes. "You are not thinking of quitting, are you?"

"No, but something must be done."

"I assume she forced you to come here. In the future, do not respond to her overtures without consulting me first."

She met his gaze. "I will do my best to abide by your wishes. There may be times, however, when it is not possible. In such cases, I will use my best judgment."

"Fair enough," he said.

"Let me assure you I did not reveal our previous discussions to your mother. As I promised earlier, I will maintain the strictest confidence about our dealings."

"My mother will not interfere again."

"We cannot exclude her," Miss Mansfield said. "Doing so will only humiliate her further."

He scowled. "I will not allow her involvement. After the way she insulted you, I'm surprised you would suggest it."

"She struck out because she felt mortified. Imagine her embarrassment when she learned from her friends that you'd retained me and then read the news in the paper."

"My mother's objections do not signify. She will have no part in this courtship."

An earnest expression filled Miss Mansfield's eyes. "I understand you are angry. However, if your mother doesn't feel she has a role, she will never accept your bride."

"She'll feel the brunt of my wrath if she doesn't. And she knows it."

"Your Grace, there is one more point you should consider. You need to choose a bride who can stand up to your mother. The best way to find out who is capable of that is to observe how the girls deal with her."

Tristan drummed his fingers again. Involving his mother would make no difference. None of those young women would dare naysay a duchess.

"Your mother's role will be restricted to occasional observation," Miss Mansfield continued. "We can listen to her opinions, but that doesn't mean we must take her advice."

He'd never met a more persistent woman in his life. Tired of her arguments, he decided to placate her. "I'll reconsider the matter after I narrow down the field of candidates." Since he intended to choose someone in a fortnight at the latest, the subject did not merit further debate.

"Very well," Miss Mansfield said. "Now, I have an idea for the courtship. I believe you should pay calls on each of the candidates in order to discover more about their characters. Of course I will accompany you."

"I have more important things to do than dally in twenty drawing rooms next week."

She widened her eyes. "Are you planning to conduct an absentee courtship?"

"I'm objecting to your ridiculous plan."

"Have you ever courted a lady?" she asked.

He figured mistresses didn't count. Besides, they chased him. "A man doesn't court a lady unless he has serious intentions."

She sighed. "Nevertheless, it is clear to me you need lessons."

Where the devil had she gotten that infernal notion?

"Your Grace, I must be honest. Ladies expect gentlemen to display some tenderness. Thus far, you've demonstrated a sad lack of the finer feelings. I know this embarrasses you."

"Dash it all. I am not embarrassed."

She gave him a pitying look. "You needn't pretend with me. I'll instruct you in the ways to please and attract a lady."

Tristan bit back laughter at her ludicrous insult and decided to have a bit of fun at her expense. "What a generous offer, Miss Mansfield." He considered her with a lazy grin. "Shall we begin now?"

"Tomorrow is soon enough," she said, her eyes narrowing with suspicion.

Her agitation tickled him. "But we've so little time," he said. "I'm anxious to benefit from your vast experience."

She leaped up. "I will not tolerate your teasing."

He rose as well. "Come here, Miss Mansfield."

She hesitated.

"You're not afraid, are you?" He deliberately lowered his voice to a sensual rumble, expecting her to rebuke him.

She sniffed. "How ridiculous."

Unable to resist, he beckoned her with his fingers, knowing she would refuse. To his surprise, she marched over to him like a general on a battlefield. He held out his hand, certain she would slap it. Silly little spinster, she took it without question. A current like the charged atmosphere before a storm sizzled his palm. Her gasp let him know she'd felt it, too.

Their gazes locked. She moistened her plump lips and knocked the breath out of him. His brain fogged. In one fluid movement, he tugged her up to his chest.

Her feminine gasp emboldened him. The urge to claim her luscious mouth gripped him. Pulling her closer, he lowered his head. When his cock stirred, a warning clanged in his addled brain. At the last second, he turned his head and whispered in her ear. "How am I doing so far?"

He might not know how to court a lady, but he'd certainly honed his seduction technique.

Shock reverberated through Tessa. Unable to move, she focused on the soft rise and fall of his breath near her ear. Heat emanated from the solid wall of his chest, blanketing her senses. A clean scent clung to him, like sunshine and soap. And something far more primal. Something undeniably male.

Propriety demanded she reprimand him for taking such liberties, but she couldn't form the words. She should be outraged, but his big, muscular body enthralled her. The slight brush of her breasts against his coat made her sensitive flesh ache.

He turned his head slightly, and his breath whispered across her cheek. Involuntarily, she followed the sound, until their lips were inches apart. Wicked anticipation thrummed through her blood.

As if bitten by a viper, he dropped her hand and stepped back, leaving her unbalanced. A fleeting, disturbed look flitted through his blue eyes. Then he clasped his hands behind his back and walked to the window.

Shock cascaded over her. She'd fallen for his rakish ruse. And *he* had walked away.

Tessa cringed. She'd not even tried to stop him. He'd probably concluded she'd encouraged him. And why would he not? Recalling the events, she realized how provocative her words must have sounded. *I'll instruct you in the ways to please and attract a woman.*

Dear God, she'd melted in his arms with nary a thought to the consequences. If he'd not had the sense to step back, she would have let him kiss her.

"We need to resolve next week's business," he said.

His voice startled her. For a moment, she could not speak, but she must recover quickly. Taking an unsteady breath, she forced herself to reply. "You have an idea for the courtship?"

He turned to face her, his expression stoic. "I agree it's important I get to know the candidates, but paying individual calls is out of the question."

Thank goodness he'd said nothing about what had

transpired between them. Then why did his sudden aloofness prick her like a hundred needle jabs? She thrust aside her strange feelings, determined to regain her poise. "Did you have something in mind?"

"Yes. Gather all of the candidates in your drawing room. I will interview those who interest me."

"But it will be difficult to converse in such a large group."

A stern expression entered his eyes. "My goal is to eliminate at least half the candidates, possibly more, next week."

She gaped at him. "How can you make such a decision before you have even spoken to them?"

"I can. And I will."

Her temper flared. "Very well. I'll inform the candidates to prepare for a very long afternoon."

"Two hours," he said. "No more."

"In two hours, you won't be able to spend even ten minutes with each candidate."

He raised his brows.

"I need more time," she said, growing exasperated.

He crossed his arms over his chest. "Two hours. Next Tuesday. Your town house. And do not invite my mother."

"It cannot be done," she said.

"It can, and it will."

She pressed her nails into her palms. Let it be just as he requested. He'd see how ludicrous his demands were.

Lady Anne Broughton sat beside Tessa on the settee. "I have news, but first, what is this I hear about your making a match for the Duke of Shelbourne? Everyone is talking about it."

"Anne, you know I never discuss the particulars of my matchmaking efforts." Tessa poured tea, secretly pleased word had spread. Already her matchmaking career was benefiting from helping the duke.

"Is it true he is courting twenty-four ladies?"

She ignored Anne's question. "Cream?"

"Yes, please." Anne sighed. "You think to evade me, but you cannot."

Tessa added a dollop of cream to both cups. She'd never intended to invite so many ladies, but somehow two had turned into five, and five into ten, and she could not leave off Lady Elizabeth Rossdale or Miss Caroline Fielding. Before she'd known it, she'd invited twenty-four of the most elite belles in society.

Anne took her cup and bit her lip.

Tessa frowned. "Is something wrong?"

"Were you discussing matchmaking with Shelbourne at my ball?"

Tessa sipped her tea and said nothing.

"Why did you not tell me?" Anne said in a hurt tone.

Tessa focused on her cup. Because he'd lured her with his gaze, and she'd not wanted Anne to know she'd fallen so easily for his wiles.

"You cannot even look me in the eyes," Anne said. "It is not like you."

"Anne, please."

"I asked you what you were discussing that night. You said nothing of consequence, but you knew," Anne said. "Why did you keep this from me?"

She met her friend's troubled gaze. "I will admit this much. All I knew that night was that he wished to call on me."

Anne drew in her breath. "Tessa, you have not developed tender feelings for him, have you?"

"I'm his matchmaker. Give me credit for discretion and sense." Such as taking a rake's hand and falling into his arms with nary a peep of protest.

Anne set her cup aside. "Dearest, I worry because of his reputation. I saw him gazing at you in an improper manner."

"You worry for nothing." But she would have let him kiss her if he'd not stopped. She decided her brain had gone on holiday.

"Tessa, we share everything," Anne said. "You have never lied to me before."

Her cup rattled as she set it on the saucer. "It was an omission, not a lie." Out of necessity, she'd learned to prevaricate and reveal only part of the truth when necessary. She'd lied to Anne by omission for years because she'd had no choice.

"You are the sister I never had," Anne said. "I cannot help being concerned about you."

"There is nothing to worry about. He is only interested in my matchmaking services." But she could not forget he'd almost kissed her, and she'd wanted him to do it. Had yearned for something that could destroy her reputation and her career.

"Tessa, I am worried. You knew his reputation and still you agreed to make him a match. Did you think of the young ladies? He is a *rake*."

"I am satisfied his intentions are true and honorable," she said. "And you must accept that this is all I can say about the matter. I swore confidentiality to him, and I will not break my promise."

"I'm sure their mothers know his reputation. They don't care about anything except his ducal title," Anne said.

Tessa suspected the girls felt the same way. She could only hope under her guidance they would see beyond his title. No, she must do more than hope. She must encourage Shelbourne and the girls to become better acquainted.

"I need not worry about you," Anne said. "Jane will be there to supervise and the girls will be present as well. So you are safe from him."

Until yesterday, she would have agreed. She set her cup aside, vowing she would not fall for his teasing ever again. He was a skilled flirt with years of experience. She dared not let her guard down again.

Tessa turned to her friend. "Enough about Shelbourne. I wish to hear your news."

"It is not news really, but I have hope for the first time in two years. Geoffrey is inquiring into my brother's disappearance at the battle of Toulouse."

Cold chills broke out on Tessa's arms, despite the heat from the fire. She searched for something to say, but there was so much she could not say. All she could do was offer her sympathy. "I know how difficult it has been for you these past two years."

Anne glanced down at her clasped hands. "Geoffrey realized I cannot reconcile my brother's loss. All I have is a report stating he went missing in action. If I knew for certain what happened to Richard, perhaps I could rest easier."

Tessa's stomach lurched involuntarily. The guilt, buried deep inside, clawed its way to the surface. She'd tried to put those events behind her, but they would follow her all the days of her life.

Anne's eyes misted as she gazed at Tessa. "If not for

you, I never would have found the strength to go on. Your support meant the world to me."

Anne's father had died shortly after they had received the news about her brother. Tessa had wanted to help her indigent and grieving friend. Yet she could not deny guilt had played some part in her decision. She'd thought that offering her friend a home would lessen the burden of remorse. A thousand times, she'd asked herself if Anne deserved the truth, but a confession would destroy their friendship forever.

"I'm so sorry," Tessa said with a heavy heart. No amount of apologies would ever change the past.

"Forgive me," Anne said, dabbing at her eyes with a handkerchief.

"You have nothing to apologize for." Tessa's words echoed in her brain as if she'd spoken in an empty room.

Anne folded her handkerchief. "It was so generous of your uncle to provide my brother's commission. Poor Papa felt so guilty. He was a wonderful vicar, but he had no talent for finances."

Thank heavens Anne knew nothing about the real circumstances behind that commission.

Anne glanced at the clock on the mantel. "I must go now. Geoffrey is expecting me."

Tessa's legs felt deadened as she accompanied Anne to the door. Once there, Anne halted. "There's one more thing, Tessa. I discussed it with Geoffrey, and he suggested I speak to you."

Tessa stiffened involuntarily. What had Anne told her husband?

"I worry that in helping me you sacrificed your own chance for marriage."

Her face grew hot, imagining Anne discussing her spinster state with Lord Broughton. "I sacrifice nothing, thanks to my uncle's generosity."

"You deserve to make a happy marriage. Think of what you are missing. A husband and children."

"In all the time you've known me, have you seen a single gentleman call for me?" she asked.

"You put my needs above your own. And I think in the process, you sent out signals that you were unavailable."

Oh, yes, she'd sent those signals out, but Anne had nothing to do with it.

"Promise me you'll consider what I'm about to say," Anne said.

"So serious," she said, a little too glibly.

"It's not too late for you to marry, Tessa. It's not."

Tessa said nothing because there was nothing she could say. In truth, it was eight years too late.

Chapter Five

Tristan's eyes watered at the overwhelming scents of roses, violets, and the devil only knew what other flowery perfumes.

Over the rim of his teacup, he surveyed the twenty misses who sat preening like plumed and ruffled peacocks in Miss Mansfield's drawing room. Their giggles and whispers made him feel ancient. Of course the age difference was customary. Women were expected to marry young.

"More tea?" Miss Mansfield asked. She was seated beside him near the hearth.

"No, thank you." Tristan set his cup aside and observed Miss Mansfield while she refilled her cup. He'd never paid much attention to women's fashions before and probably wouldn't have noticed her gown if not for the gauzelike fabric trimming her bodice. The filmy material drew his gaze to the shadowy hollow between her ivory breasts. They seemed to strain against the confines of her bodice. Heat simmered in his groin as he imagined their soft weight in his palms.

"Your Grace? Is something the matter?"

He jerked his gaze to her eyes. The heat in parts down south leaped to his face. The devil. She'd caught him ogling her. This cursed celibacy was starting to interfere with his mental faculties. "Sorry," he mumbled. "I was thinking."

She frowned. "Your face is flushed. Are you feverish?"

"Only a little warm. From the fire." The one in his groin. He'd best change the subject. "We should begin."

"Very well." Then she clapped her hands. "Ladies, your attention, please," she called out.

The feminine chatter died.

After a moment of silence, Miss Mansfield said, "Thank you all for coming today and congratulations on being selected to continue in the competition."

The lively blonde, Lady Georgette, wrinkled her slim nose. "Competition?" she said. "Is this a contest?"

Several of the young ladies giggled.

"Make no mistake," Miss Mansfield said. "You are all competing for the duke's hand. His Grace has agreed to take an entire two hours out of his busy schedule to interview you."

She'd made him sound like a pompous ass. He scowled to get her attention, but she rose and walked over to a closed door near the hearth. "The interviews," she said, opening the door, "will be conducted in the yellow drawing room under my supervision."

A brunette with slanting green eyes raised her hand.

"Do you have a question, Lady Elizabeth?" Miss Mansfield asked.

"No, an observation," Lady Elizabeth said. "By my

calculation, there is no possible way to conduct individual interviews with all twenty of us in two hours."

Tristan nodded. Lady Elizabeth's astute assessment ratcheted her up a notch in his estimation. He meant to explain that he would select a handful of candidates to interview after a general thirty-minute conversation, but Miss Mansfield intervened.

"I have devised a plan to stay within the time frame," she said. "At five minutes per interview, we will finish twenty minutes ahead of schedule." She favored him with a sugary smile. "Think of it as speedy courting."

The young ladies giggled.

He started to argue, but an idea occurred to him that could well save him from having to interview all twenty. He allowed his gaze to travel over the candidates. Their smiles disappeared and several fidgeted. "Each of you should keep in mind that I am unable to give you the consideration you deserve. That is why I plan to eliminate at least half of you today."

The drawing room rang with horrified gasps.

Their stricken faces bothered him, but he had to remain firm. "I know that sounds harsh, but keep in mind that sooner or later nineteen of you will be eliminated."

They looked stunned, as if the possibility had never occurred to them. He figured their parents were pressuring them to participate. Regardless, he must ensure they understood the odds were stacked against them.

"The season is well under way, and all twenty of you are ineligible to court other gentlemen. If you stay much beyond today, you are likely giving up the chance to marry this season. That is why I am giving you a choice. You can withdraw now, so that you may court other gentlemen.

Or you can choose to stay. If you decide to leave, I will understand."

At first none of them moved. Then the plain, red-haired girl stood, revealing a crumpled pink gown that hung sacklike on her spare frame.

Tristan stood. Poor girl, he thought, watching her awkward attempts to retrieve her reticule while keeping her eyes downcast. Honestly, what had Miss Mansfield been thinking to include this painfully shy young woman in the courtship?

Miss Mansfield rushed forward. "Miss Hardwick, how wonderful of you to volunteer for the first interview."

Tristan narrowed his eyes. Didn't Miss Mansfield understand she'd only drawn unwanted attention to the girl? Why prolong Miss Hardwick's misery when she obviously did not wish to participate?

Miss Mansfield scanned the room and called out to her companion. "Jane, please have the candidates form a queue. We'll need to be quick."

Miss Powell hurried forward, but she wasn't fast enough.

The bridal candidates leaped out of their chairs and made a mad dash for the adjoining drawing room door. As they jostled one another, a chorus of complaints arose.

"I was here first."

"Stop pushing."

"She stepped on my toes."

Tristan gaped at them. So much for genteel deportment.

Miss Mansfield had to clap her hands three times to get their attention. "Ladies, remember your manners. Have you forgotten His Grace is watching you?"

That question only set them off blaming one another.

"She pinched me."

"It's her fault."

"She called me a cow."

Miss Mansfield clapped her hands again. "Enough! The next person who utters a single word will automatically be dismissed from the competition."

A tall brunette with stormy eyes objected. "This is unfair, making everyone fight for a position."

"Thank you for your time today, Lady Beatrice," Miss Mansfield said. "A footman will show you out."

Lady Beatrice shot a venomous glare at Miss Mansfield and then quit the room with her head held high.

The other candidates looked frightened as Miss Mansfield walked the length of the queue, inspecting them. They ought to be ashamed of their childish behavior, but Miss Mansfield had stood up to them. She was entirely too soft-hearted where Miss Hardwick was concerned, but she had an iron backbone. Nevertheless, he meant to call her on the carpet for manipulating him again.

"Jane," she said to her companion. "Cut up strips of paper and number them from one to nineteen. The girls will draw the order of their interviews."

Tristan stepped forward. "Miss Mansfield, may I have a private word with you?"

She nodded and led him into the adjoining room while Miss Powell conducted the drawing.

He shut the door. "I thought we had an understanding. No more tricks. Instead, you chose to mock me with another one of your nonsensical ideas."

"I did my best to ensure all the girls have an equal chance," she said.

He narrowed his eyes. "You embarrassed Miss Hardwick when she tried to leave."

"Promise me one thing," she said, her voice low and urging.

"What?" His gruff tone startled her, but he had to resist her. And he found it difficult when she stood so near, her lush lips parted and her eyes pleading.

"Please don't eliminate Amy Hardwick yet," she said.

He took a step closer, looming over her. "You should have allowed her to withdraw."

Miss Mansfield's eyes filled with misery. "She hasn't taken well with the ton. Others mock her. You saw the other girls looking at her with disgust during the test. Her self-esteem is so battered she probably thought you directed your speech solely to her."

He wondered if her concern for Miss Hardwick was based on her own spinster state. But Miss Mansfield was no wallflower. "You did her no favor. She is too bashful to ever fit into my world."

"Please do not eliminate her yet. She will benefit from the courtship. Others will regard her with respect when they realize you have taken notice of her."

"Ridiculous," he muttered.

"All I ask is that you keep her one more week. Then when you release her, she will be free to court other gentlemen. If you keep her an extra week, others will conclude she has special qualities."

"I will judge her based on her responses to the interview, the same as the others." When she started to protest, he held up his hand. "To treat her any differently would be tantamount to pity and a dishonor to her."

An hour later, Tessa cringed as she escorted yet another weeping young lady out of the yellow drawing room. The duke had extended eight invitations so far. Now there were four remaining candidates to interview and only two invitations. Worse, there was no guarantee he would extend both of them.

She took a deep breath and called out, "Next."

Lady Georgette glided inside the yellow drawing room with a poised smile on her face. Her confidence irked Tessa. No doubt the duke would give an invitation to the pretty blonde. Men were slaves around beautiful women.

After they had taken seats, the duke asked the same question he'd posed to all the other candidates. "Lady Georgette, if we wed, what is it you expect from marriage?"

Tessa held her breath, certain Georgette would say she wanted to do her duty and give him an heir. He had eliminated the candidates who had responded in that fashion.

Georgette twirled the curl by her ear. "Well, I hardly know you, so it's difficult to answer. We may not suit at all."

What conceit, Tessa thought.

The duke looked amused. "Let's try it another way. What do you expect from marriage in general?"

"I am very close to my family," she said. "We have many traditions. When I marry, I hope to see my parents and brothers often."

"You will be creating a new family and learning your husband's traditions," he said.

"I know there will be changes, but I hope to blend both families as often as possible," she said.

"Anything else?"

She twirled her curl again. "What do you want from marriage?"

He handed her an invitation. "Perhaps you will find out."

Ugly jealousy clawed at Tessa. She averted her gaze, ashamed by her petty reaction. Why did she care that he was attracted to the blond beauty?

She pushed it all out of her mind. For now, Tessa had more important concerns than Georgette. The next two candidates made the fatal mistake of swearing they only wanted to give the duke an heir. Both fled the yellow drawing room empty-handed and in tears.

Amy Hardwick had drawn the last number. As she shuffled inside, Tessa sent Shelbourne a pleading look. His expression remained stoic, alarming her. After Tessa sat, she couldn't take her eyes off the last invitation. He'd said there was no assurance he would extend all ten. Tessa bit her lip. Just once, couldn't the girl least likely win?

Amy clutched her trembling hands and gazed at her lap.

"Miss Hardwick?" Shelbourne said.

When she didn't respond, he waited. Several anxious seconds ticked off. Finally, Amy peeped up at him.

"That's better," he said, his voice gentle. "Now, I will ask you the same question I've posed to everyone else. And I want you to be honest."

His kind tone gave Tessa hope. Perhaps he would relent and keep Amy in the competition for another round.

After he asked the question, Amy lowered her gaze once more. "I have no expectations," she mumbled.

He drummed his fingers on the arm of his chair. "Miss Hardwick, do you have an objection to me?"

She lifted her gaze. "Oh, no, Your Grace."

"Earlier you tried to leave. Can you tell me why?"

Her lashes lowered again. "I no longer wished to be in the courtship."

"Then why did you participate in the first place?"

"Mama insisted," she whispered. "I know I do not belong with all the other pretty girls."

Blinding pain, like a giant fist, slammed into Tessa's heart. Oh, dear God, she'd only wanted to help. Instead, she'd inadvertently wounded Amy.

The duke shifted in his chair. "Miss Hardwick, you give yourself too little credit. Character is more important than beauty."

"Mama says beauty is in the eye of the beholder." Her slender fingers curled into her palms. "It is not true."

"I know one thing to be true," he said. "If you do not believe yourself worthy, no one else will."

She jerked her chin up.

"Because I find your honesty refreshing, I would like to extend an invitation to you," he said. "There is one stipulation, however."

Tessa held her breath, unable to believe her ears. He was giving Amy a chance.

"You must answer the question. What do you want from marriage?"

"Oh." Amy swallowed. "I—I'm not exactly sure."

"Surely you've daydreamed about marriage," Tessa said. She could feel Shelbourne looking at her, but she kept her attention on Amy. "What do you see?"

"Mama says I must not reveal my bluestocking tendencies." Amy clutched her trembling hands. "But I always dreamed of being a great political hostess," she said in a rush. "As a means of helping my husband's career."

Tessa exchanged a stunned look with Shelbourne. She

could not envision shy Amy holding court with cynical politicians.

"I know it is foolish of me." Amy blushed. "My brain freezes when I am in a group."

"People are drawn to those who express interest in their opinions," Shelbourne said. "You need only ask a few questions. Believe me, they will think favorably of you."

She regarded him with something akin to worship. "Thank you for the advice. I will always remember your kindness."

He held out the invitation. "Will you accept this?"

Amy nodded, and for the first time that day, she smiled. Tessa blinked back the hot moisture pooling in her eyes. Oh, she'd not known he could be so wonderful. As she rose to escort Amy to the door, she glanced back at him and silently mouthed, "Thank you."

He scowled. Silly duke. He thought himself unaffected by tender emotions, but now she knew the truth.

After Amy left, Tessa returned to the yellow drawing room to find him standing and tugging at his sleeves. "May I ask why you eliminated the girls who said they only wanted to give you an heir? I thought you wanted a dutiful wife."

His eyes gleamed with a wicked expression. "I fear the answer might shock you."

"How silly. I'm not a naïve girl." She took a step closer to him. "I insist you tell me."

"Very well." He closed the distance between them. The subtle scents of sandalwood, starch, and male curled through her senses. She was aware of his powerful chest, the slight bristle shadowing his jaw, and the sound of his breathing. Every inch of her skin tingled in response to him. Everything inside her wanted him to touch her.

Then his voice startled her. "I'd rather my wife not think about duty on our wedding night," he said.

His words took a moment to register. When they did, she gasped. "You are outrageous."

He treated her to a lopsided smile. "You insisted."

Although her cheeks burned, she refused to let him best her. "Perhaps I'll tell them to think of England."

He leaned down and his breath whispered across her cheek, like a caress. "Patriotism isn't one of my requirements."

The next afternoon, Tessa brushed the feathers of her quill against her cheek as she tried without success to reply to a letter from her solicitor. She dipped the quill in the inkwell, but she blotted the paper. Frustrated, she capped the inkwell and crumpled the ruined page. She could not concentrate because her thoughts kept returning to Shelbourne.

All last night, she'd thought about his response when she'd asked him why he eliminated the girls who only wanted to do their duty. He'd flustered her by drawing too near, so near the scent of him had mesmerized her and sent a flood of heat flowing through her veins. Then he'd fobbed her off with a risqué jest.

He'd subjected her to his wicked teasing before. The rake knew exactly what he was doing. And a very secret part of her liked it.

The door sighed open, startling her. Tessa rose as Gravesend announced Shelbourne. Her pulse quickened as she drank in the sight of him. He wore a blue coat that magnified his expressive eyes. Something sweet unfurled in her chest as he sat across from her. Yesterday, he'd revealed himself to be a fair and kind man when he'd treated Amy Hardwick with special gentleness.

"Thank you for receiving me." His gaze slanted over to Jane, who sat at the round table, concentrating on her needlework.

"It is a pleasure to see you again," Tessa said. Now that there were only ten candidates left, she must accelerate her efforts to open his heart. She had to encourage the tenderness he'd revealed, not an easy task with any man, much less Shelbourne.

Jane set her needlework aside. "I will ring for a tea tray."

Pleased with her companion's initiative, Tessa nodded. Then she smiled at the duke. "I assume you wish to discuss the next round of the courtship."

"Yes. I have an idea."

Tessa stilled. Oh, heavens, what if he proposed another one of his ridiculous tests? If he did, she would have to think of some way to deter him, but she'd no intention of doing so in Jane's presence. Tessa had explained to her companion that the duke felt less inhibited without an audience, so they had arranged a private signal. Tessa glanced at Jane and nodded once.

Jane rose again, curtseyed, and slipped outside the drawing room. Shelbourne watched her with a puzzled expression.

"I ask Jane to be present only at the beginning to preserve the proprieties," Tessa said.

Shelbourne blew out his breath. "Once again, I am putting your reputation at risk."

"The risk is minimal. I've also spoken to my butler. He is a faithful retainer and served my uncle before me. Gravesend understands our meetings are confidential."

Shelbourne frowned. "But what of your other servants?"

"They are loyal." At his skeptical look, she added, "I pay them twice the standard wages and hire more than strictly necessary, so they are not overburdened." She smiled. "I treat them with respect, and in return they are devoted to me. So you need not worry on my account."

"Thank you," he said.

"You have an idea for the next round of the courtship?" she said.

He nodded. "I spoke to Hawk, and he suggested a tour of the gardens at Ashdown House. Richmond is close enough for a day trip."

"What a wonderful suggestion. I definitely approve." She'd heard the famous Capability Browne had designed the gardens. "Will Lord Hawkfield's mother join us?"

"No. All his family is in Bath visiting his ailing grandmother. Except his younger brother, who is taking his grand tour."

"How fortunate for the young man the war is over," Tessa said.

"Hawk was thankful the war ended before William reached his majority."

Tessa folded her hands in her lap. "Did you consider serving your country?"

"For me, there was no choice. I couldn't abandon my family or my responsibilities to the estate."

"What about Lord Hawkfield?"

"Oh, he was primed to go after Old Boney, but his

mother begged him not to leave." The duke looked troubled. "I discouraged him as well. To be honest, my reasons were selfish. I could not bear the possibility of my friend being maimed or killed."

Guilt seized her, thinking of Anne's brother. But he'd made his choice.

"I've often questioned my interference," Shelbourne said.

"If you had not counseled him, perhaps he would have gone to war. Had he suffered injury or death, you would forever regret not speaking your mind. Ultimately, the decision was his to make."

His intent blue gaze snared her. "How wise you are."

If only she could turn back the clock and apply that hard-earned wisdom. But dwelling on the past would change nothing. "Since Lord Hawkfield's mother will not be in residence, we should invite your mother."

"No, she'll interfere."

"You agreed to include your mother once you had eliminated several candidates," Tessa said.

"Not now."

She sighed. "I need another lady to help chaperone. The girls' families will feel more assured of the propriety of the event if your mother is present."

He tapped his thumb on the chair. "I concede your point. But this is not an invitation for my mother to participate every week."

Tessa smiled. "Now, perhaps we should think about some activities in addition to touring the gardens. I will select four candidates to make plans. Of course, I will assist them."

"Allow them to do all the planning," he said. "I wish to see if they have the proper training required of a duchess."

When the tea tray arrived, she poured. "Cream?" she asked.

"No, thank you."

She handed him a cup. Then she sliced a generous portion of cake with currants and walked over to him. When she handed him the plate, their fingers brushed. Her breath hitched at the warmth of his skin. As she returned to her seat, she told herself to stop acting like a schoolgirl. Then, unable to help herself, she stole a look at him.

He bit into the confection with an expression of decadent pleasure. Then he met her gaze. His lashes lowered in a seductive look as he slowly licked a stray crumb from his mouth.

She caught her breath, imagining his tongue on her lips. When he gave her a sultry smile, her face heated. Determined to recover her poise, she focused on drinking her tea. A few minutes later, he polished off his cake and looked at her hopefully.

She set her cup aside. "Another?"

"Yes, please," he said.

After she brought him another slice of cake, he grinned. "When I was a boy, I used to sneak into the kitchen and beg for sweets."

"And I'm sure you were indulged." She returned to the settee and picked up her dish of tea.

"Until I got sick from eating too much," he said.

"What happened?" She smiled, expecting a humorous story.

"My father sacked the cook for overfeeding me."

"Rather harsh of him." Oh, dear, she should not have let that slip.

Shelbourne shrugged. "He was in his cups."

Tessa contemplated her tea, fearing her shock showed on her face. "Did he ban you from the kitchen?"

"No, but I didn't want to be responsible for anyone else losing their position, so I stayed away." He bit into the cake.

She winced. He'd been a mere boy.

"You needn't look so stricken," he said. "It happened a long time ago."

Tessa remembered what he'd told her the day he'd requested her matchmaking services. *All who depend on me know safety and security.* Had there been none under his father's rule? "How old were you when your father died?"

"Seventeen." He took another bite.

"I was seventeen when I took over the housekeeping for my uncle after my aunt's death," she said, setting her empty cup aside.

"So we have something in common," he said. "I'm sure you were a great comfort to your uncle."

Guilt spurted in her chest. She brushed her skirts, hoping he'd not noticed her discomposure.

"I'm sorry," Shelbourne said. "Obviously, you still grieve for him."

She met his gaze. "My uncle was a wonderful man." As she often did when uncomfortable, she turned the topic away from herself. "How did you manage your university studies under the circumstances?"

Something—was it regret?—flickered in his eyes. "I had private tutors."

He'd had no choice. She wondered what else he'd sacrificed for duty. "It must have been difficult."

Shelbourne set his plate aside. "After my father's death,

I discovered we were on the brink of financial ruin. The total encumbrances of the estates were staggering compared to the annual income."

She shivered. All her life, she'd taken her family's wealth for granted, until her uncle had died and left her his fortune. Without it, she would have suffered in ways she did not like to contemplate. "I would not know where to begin in such a situation."

"At first I was overwhelmed by the extent of the debt I'd inherited, but I preferred being in control."

"However did you overcome your financial difficulties?"

"I liquidated property not subject to entail. Then I made investments in shipping expeditions. I had to make ruthless decisions," he said. "I could not afford sentimentality. So I sold whatever I could and put off repairs to the estate in Oxfordshire. I had two criteria for every decision I made. It had to be either absolutely necessary or contribute funds."

"What else could you have done?" she said.

"Oh, there is an easier path for gentlemen with pockets to let."

Marry a woman of fortune. Her eyes widened.

"I could not stomach the idea of marrying for money," he said.

"Most gentlemen in your situation would not blink an eye."

"Society considers wedding for money an acceptable option, but I had my reasons."

She wanted to know more, but he didn't volunteer the information.

"I've bored you sufficiently with my history," he said.

The cynical amusement in his blue eyes was a mask.

He'd shared a painful part of his past, and yet, he'd related it in an offhand manner. She wanted to tell him how much she admired him, but a sixth sense told her he would mock her in self-defense. Instead, she planted an impish smile on her face. "I think you have more than a few commendable traits."

He chuckled. "I shall try not to disappoint you too much."

Disappoint her? On the contrary, he'd demonstrated his unwavering commitment to family and duty. Shelbourne had already made so many sacrifices. He deserved the ultimate happiness in marriage. What he needed was a wife who would appreciate his unselfish commitment to duty. Most of all, he deserved a wife who loved him enough to open his heart.

He watched her intently. "I can practically see the cogs and wheels churning in your brain. What are you thinking?"

She must tread carefully. Playing on his droll sense of humor might keep him from balking. "Oh, I was thinking you are entirely too tender-hearted. You really must not wear your heart on your sleeve."

A warm laugh escaped him. "I see what you're about. You're trying to tease me before you lecture me."

"No lectures," she said. "Only a few suggestions."

His eyes glinted with cynicism again.

"Never mind," she said. "You need not make any special efforts. After all, the girls are courting you."

He looked affronted. "I beg your pardon?"

"You are in an enviable position compared to most gentlemen seeking a wife. You needn't exert yourself at all. All you need do is sit back and let the girls woo you."

"I fully intend to control this courtship."

"Oh," she said, biting back the urge to smile. "Do you have something particular in mind?"

He scowled. "You're the expert on these matters."

She'd hooked him. Now all she need do was reel him in. "Well, I have a few ideas."

"Such as?"

"A lady is always flattered when a gentleman asks how he might please her."

His blue eyes lit with a devilish expression. "I shall be sure to ask my bride how I might best please her."

Heat flooded her face again. Although she was embarrassed, she must not allow him to distract her. "I am referring to special gestures that show you care."

"You mean poetry and posies. I will not pretend to be romantic."

"Actually it will be far more effective if you focus on something special to the individual ladies."

"You'll have to be more specific," he said.

"Suppose you were competing with another man for a girl's affections. The other gentleman brings flowers and sends poems. What would you do to top him?"

"Shoot him."

She laughed. "As I said before, ladies expect tenderness. For a woman, these special gestures are proof of affection."

"So you're saying it isn't enough that I promise constancy, a stable home life, and respect," he said, a note of defensiveness in his voice.

"Make no mistake. Those qualities speak highly of your honorable character. But think what it would mean to you if your wife gave you some token of her regard, something she knew would make you feel special."

"I've no need of tokens. What will please me is if my wife seamlessly carries out her duties."

She must remain patient with him. "Women expect gifts, Your Grace."

"You mean jewels."

"A gift that is specially chosen is more valuable to a woman than the most expensive jewel."

"How am I to know what trinkets make a woman feel special?"

"Observation," she said.

"Men are not good at guessing what is in a woman's thoughts. We don't think alike at all."

"That isn't true of all men," she said.

He regarded her with suspicion. "You have evidence of this?"

She glanced down at her clasped hands. "After my parents died, I found a box of notes among my mother's treasures. There were literally hundreds of them. Every morning, my father left a note on my mother's pillow." She paused, remembering how those words had brought tears to her eyes. Other than her mother's jewels, those notes were all she had left of her parents.

Shelbourne looked puzzled. "Notes?"

She had never told anyone about them before. Even now the memory brought an ache to her heart. Though her parents had died ten years ago, she still missed them. "My father wrote the same thing every day. *You are my one and only, for all eternity.*"

He frowned. "Your father couldn't think of anything else to write?"

"You are being purposely obtuse." Did he not see how much those notes meant to her?

"I am a rational man," he said. "Facts and action hold meaning for me. I am not a mind reader."

He really did not understand the significance. "The reason my father wrote the same note every morning," she said gently, "was to let my mother know his love for her never wavered."

"Now I understand why you are such a romantic." He grinned. "I suppose the notes were less costly than jewels."

She shook her finger. "You tease me."

"Yes, but there is a reason. Your efforts to reform me are misguided. It's wrong to marry someone in hopes of changing the other person. People are who they are. The woman I choose to marry needs to accept me as I am. I will extend the same courtesy to my wife."

"Provided she meets all of your requirements," she muttered.

"Would you prefer I marry someone under false pretenses?"

"No, of course not." She would rather he marry for love, but he wasn't ready to hear her opinion. Although his resistance troubled her, she'd known from the beginning this would not be easy. No matter what, she must persevere.

His happiness was at stake.

Chapter Six

The dark clouds portended disaster.

Tessa noted the disgusted expression on the duchess's face at the sight of the rustic barge. The wind whipped the battered and faded canopy. As for the crude wooden benches, Tessa prayed they were free of splinters. The duchess would not appreciate being poked in her aristocratic derriere.

Thunder rumbled in the distance. All ten girls squealed and then giggled. Tessa held on to her bonnet as the wind buffeted her. "We had better board if we are to reach Ashdown House in a timely manner."

Miss Henrietta Bancroft pinched her nose as she approached the water stairs. "It stinks of fish."

The duchess sent her a scathing look. "What were you expecting, miss? Perfume?"

Tessa winced. Until this morning, she had not known of their travel arrangements. Henrietta, Lady Elizabeth, Amy Hardwick, and Lady Georgette had decided to surprise her after hearing they were to make all the arrangements for the outing. The four had arrived at Tessa's town house this morning, bursting with enthusiasm over their plans for a boat ride and a picnic. Unfortunately, none of them had taken the weather into account. When Tessa had questioned them about the menu, Henrietta had laughed and said they had relegated the task to Lord Hawkfield's chef. Amy alone had looked chagrined. Doubtless, the other three had ignored her concerns and spent all their time inventing games, giving no thought whatsoever to practicalities. Now Tessa understood why the duke didn't like surprises.

The duchess glared at the ominous sky. "Unless I miss my guess, we shall be soaked through before this journey ends."

Tessa rather hoped it would rain. The duchess might suffer an apoplexy if she learned they were to sit on blankets and cushions while dining al fresco.

The duchess took Tessa's arm. "You will sit with me. We have much to discuss."

As they picked their way down the water stairs, Tessa figured she had much to withhold.

Once aboard, the duchess steered her to a bench at the rear. The girls, including the duke's sister, Lady Julianne, crowded together on the forward benches. The covering did little to shield them. The wind whipped their skirts and tore at their bonnet ribbons.

As the barge bobbed into the open waters of the Thames, the duchess spoke in a stern tone. "What could you have been thinking to travel on the river? Did it never occur to you the weather might turn foul?"

Tessa's loyalty to the duke prevented her from telling

the duchess that she'd had no hand in the plans. "I apologize for the miserable conditions."

"It's too late now," the duchess said. "You would not need to make apologies if you considered the consequences before acting."

Tessa bristled at the rebuke, but held her tongue.

The duchess narrowed her eyes. "I still cannot figure out how you managed to persuade my son to participate in this ridiculous courtship. I want an explanation, and do not try to dissemble. You'll not fool me, gel."

Tessa smoothed her skirts. "I'm sorry, but I am not at liberty to discuss the particulars."

"A pretty way of saying you refuse. You had best curb your impetuous tendencies. I'll not stand for any more of your outrageous schemes."

Tessa wondered if the duchess meant to scold her during the entire journey.

"This is the consequence of too much independence," the duchess continued. "What could your uncle have been thinking? You would be much better off with a husband than a fortune."

Tessa inhaled sharply at the insinuation that her beloved uncle George had failed to care for her properly. "My uncle took me in when my parents died. He was as generous and loving as a father. I loved and respected him very much." Tessa braced herself for another lecture, but the duchess said nothing for several anxious seconds.

Finally, she spoke. "Your loyalty to your uncle does you credit. I knew Wentworth long ago. He was a fine gentleman." She paused. "I can only conclude you have a talent for bamboozlement. How else could you have tricked my son and those girls' mothers into agreeing to this foolhardy courtship?"

"It was not trickery, and no one was obligated."

The duchess shook her head. "My friends said you made it seem as if their daughters would have no chance with my son if they didn't agree."

Tessa again smoothed her skirts to hide her guilt. She might have made a tiny insinuation to that effect.

"You are much too clever for your own good, young lady, but heed me well. You do not want to make an enemy of me."

She glanced at the duchess. "I would much rather make an ally of you."

"You may start by telling me what prompted this courtship nonsense."

"I beg your pardon, but I promised confidentiality to your son."

"How convenient," the duchess said. "I don't like it at all. And I've yet to figure out what you're hoping to gain from this matchmaking scheme."

Tessa met her gaze. "You may not believe me, but I truly want your son's happiness." She thought it best not to mention her own ambitions.

"Do I look as if I just fell off the vegetable cart?"

The duchess started to speak again, but a commotion diverted her attention. The guttural sound of retching mingled with the roar of the wind. Tessa's eyes widened as a blond young woman seated on a bench bent over. Good heavens, Georgette was ill. "I have to help her," Tessa said, starting to rise.

"She must have motion sickness," the duchess said. "Stay. I will assist her." She carefully made her way toward Georgette. In the meantime, Amy removed Georgette's bonnet, and Julianne held her heaving back.

Within minutes, the duchess had summoned one of the rowers to bring a pail. Amy held back Georgette's hair as the young woman emptied her stomach.

"How revolting!"

Tessa's gaze whipped toward the owner of that voice. Lady Elizabeth waved her hand in front of her face, while the others laughed. Stupid, heartless girls.

The duchess glared at the laughing girls. All of them withered under her disapproving regard.

Afterward, the duchess returned and sat beside Tessa. For a while, they shared a companionable silence. The girls giggled and whispered to one another, all except Amy, who sat apart with Georgette.

Tessa watched a group of girls gather round Julianne. "Your daughter is quite vivacious."

"She has always been so," the duchess said. "She attracts friends wherever she goes. And men flock to her."

"But none have captured her heart?"

"Not yet." The duchess's shrewd eyes bored into Tessa's. "Enough about my daughter. Has my son shown any partiality to one of the girls?"

Tessa's lips twitched. "I hope he will have an opportunity to further his acquaintance with the remaining candidates today."

The duchess sighed. "I wish he would marry for love, but I fear he will choose with his head."

Tessa recalled the duchess telling her son marriage should be a matter of the heart and wondered anew why Shelbourne did not believe in love.

"In my day, all marriages were arranged, but I wed for

love," the duchess said. "I shall never forget the first time I saw him."

Clearly she wished to speak about her late husband. Curious, Tessa glanced at her. "How did you meet?"

"He asked me to dance at my come-out ball." A dreamy expression filled her eyes. "I feared I would swoon before we ever reached the dance floor. He was the most eligible bachelor that year. Three weeks later, he proposed."

Tessa managed a wan smile. The whirlwind courtship must have turned her head. As a naïve young woman, she would not have known her husband's true character.

"It was the happiest time of my life," she said.

The duchess could not have remained happy in the face of her husband's drunkenness and wild spending habits. Perhaps she had turned a blind eye to her husband's faults.

Lightning rent the sky, followed by rolling thunder. Not long afterward, the heavens opened up. Sheeting rain whipped inside the canopy. The girls screamed.

While the storm raged, Tessa and the duchess tried to calm the girls. Like children, they cried over their wet gowns and ruined bonnets. "Hush," the duchess shouted.

When a few continued to wail, she threatened to make them swim to Ashdown House.

Torrential rain continued to pound Ashdown House, preventing them from traveling home. Tessa closed the door to the bedchamber where Georgette rested. Amy Hardwick had insisted on staying with her. Tessa had taken Amy aside and urged her to join everyone else at dinner. Amy, bless her, had not wanted to leave the teary-eyed Georgette alone after the other girls had mocked her. Tessa could not fault Amy for her generosity, but she feared the minute Georgette recovered, she would drop Amy like a hot coal.

With a sigh, Tessa clutched the shawl over her borrowed gown and walked down the corridor. When they had arrived dripping wet, she'd seen the duke's worried expression, but they'd not had a chance to speak. Tessa and the duchess had led the girls upstairs immediately to change out of their sodden clothing. Fortunately, no one, save Georgette, had suffered any ill effects.

Tessa paused outside the bedchamber shared by Elizabeth and Henrietta. She lifted her fist to knock, but stopped at the sound of Elizabeth's vicious words.

"Did you see that hideous gown they found for her? If I were that plump, I would starve myself." She tittered.

Tessa's cheeks burned. The other girls had donned gowns that had once belonged to Lord Hawkfield's sisters, but none had fit Tessa. Instead, the maid had produced one of Lady Hawkfield's matronly gray gowns, a gown that had required considerable hemming.

"Perhaps she is trying to entice the duke." Henrietta's unmistakable nasal laughter grated on Tessa's nerves.

Humiliated, Tessa continued down the corridor to the next chamber. If she had known those two were so horrid, she never would have invited them to participate in the courtship. As she knocked on the next door, Tessa resolved to warn the duke about them.

After dinner, Tessa sat with everyone else in a sumptuous drawing room. She clutched a voluminous shawl over the ill-fitting gown. In comparison to the bridal candidates, she looked every inch the dowdy spinster.

Lilting laughter drew her gaze to the hearth. Several girls sat in a circle round the duke, looking elegant and slender in fashionable gowns. Elizabeth and her friend Henrietta sat on either side of the duke, teasing him relentlessly. Worse, he was laughing. To all appearances, he was enjoying their attention.

The duchess brought Tessa a cup of tea and sat next to her on the sofa.

"Thank you," Tessa said.

The duchess gazed at her son. "Well, the gels have recovered from this afternoon's fiasco. All except poor Lady Georgette."

"I checked on her earlier," Tessa said. "She was able to take a bit of broth. And Miss Hardwick is staying with her."

The duchess sipped her tea. "Lady Georgette is undoubtedly embarrassed. I will reassure her there is no shame in seasickness. It cannot be helped." She paused and considered Tessa with an enigmatic expression. "Georgette is undoubtedly the loveliest of all the girls. Do you not agree?"

"She is accounted a great beauty." Tessa drank her tea to hide her irritation. Obviously the duchess favored Georgette for her pretty face.

The duchess regarded her with a sardonic smile. "I asked for your opinion, not a general consensus."

Tessa placed her cup on the saucer. "I cannot deny beauty is a basis for initial attraction, but nature ensures it fades over time. In order for a marriage to succeed, there must be shared values and . . . affection."

"Affection." The duchess lifted her brows. "And what of love, Miss Mansfield?"

"I believe love is the foundation for the happiest of marriages."

"Ah, so you believe love conquers all?"

Tessa set her cup aside. "I think the notion far too simplistic for the complexities of a marital relationship."

"But you've never married, so what do you base your opinions upon?"

Tessa lifted her chin. "My own parents affirmed their love daily, but still they had disagreements. I believe their love for each other motivated them to work out their differences."

"An astute observation," the duchess murmured.

When the duchess said nothing further, Tessa's attention wandered to a small group of young ladies, including Julianne, who stood chatting with Lord Hawkfield. Julianne's longing gaze followed his every move. She touched his sleeve and an arrested expression crossed his face. Oh, dear, was Hawkfield the reason Julianne had turned down so many proposals?

Lord Hawkfield looked round the room. Then he caught Tessa's gaze and detached himself. "Do you play the pianoforte, Miss Mansfield?" he said after approaching.

"Yes, but perhaps we should allow the girls to display their talents."

He grinned. "Come, I will turn the pages for you."

"Yes, do play," the duchess said. "We need some diversion."

Tessa set her teacup aside. "I will start," she said, rising. "Afterward, I will encourage the girls to take a turn."

Heads turned their way as Hawkfield escorted her to the pianoforte. She shuffled through the music. Finally, she decided to play Pachelbel's Canon. Determined to focus on the haunting melody, she did not realize all conversation had ceased until she played the last note. She glanced up and met Shelbourne's gaze. In his eyes, she saw approval.

"Excellent," the duchess said, breaking the silence.

Everyone applauded. The duke rose and walked over to her. "You are more than accomplished."

"You flatter me too much," she whispered, aware of everyone staring.

"It is not flattery," he said. "You held everyone in this room spellbound."

She gazed into his appreciative blue eyes, wishing she could tell him how much his compliment meant to her. A dowdy spinster she might be, but tonight, *he* had praised her.

"Miss Mansfield has certainly set a high standard," the duchess called out. "Let us see if one of the other gels can match her talent."

Lady Elizabeth rose as if she were a princess and smiled benevolently at the other girls. "Now whom should I choose to sing while I play?"

Sally Shepherd giggled and pointed at herself.

Elizabeth overlooked her and regarded each of the girls with a superior air. "Henrietta," she said at last. "You shall be my pet tonight. Come turn the pages and sing for us."

Henrietta popped up and hurried after Elizabeth, reminding Tessa of the King Charles spaniel who had dogged her late aunt's every footstep.

Shelbourne offered his arm to Tessa. As they walked away, he spoke in a low voice. "Will you join me at the window seat? I wish to speak to you."

Tessa cast a surreptitious glance at the duchess. "It might be remarked upon," she whispered.

"Then meet me in the library a half hour after everyone else retires," he said. "I know it's a risk, but the matter is important."

"I will try." She wondered what he wished to discuss. Doubtless he wanted to hear her report on the bridal candidates before making his decision about who to eliminate. Tessa planned to tell him she found Elizabeth and Henrietta to be two of the most disagreeable young ladies she'd ever met.

"If you meet with anyone along the way, leave immediately," he said. "Above all, do not take any chances."

She nodded.

The first notes of Elizabeth's amateurish performance brought a smile to Tessa's lips. Then the screeching voice of a soprano made her wince. Shelbourne stopped and turned to stare. So did everyone else.

Seeing the delighted sparkle in Henrietta's eyes, Tessa realized the girl probably thought they were admiring her. The attention appeared to inspire her even further. She increased her volume by several decibels, all but screaming out the high notes.

Hawk appeared at Tessa's side. "Is she deaf?"

"We may be after this performance," the duke muttered.

The duchess and Julianne joined them. "That chit's voice is awful," the duchess said.

"Brother," Julianne said. "If you marry her, I swear I'll sew her lips shut."

At long last, the song ended. During the smattering of applause, Tessa knew she had to prevent a repeat performance from Henrietta. She rushed over to encourage two other girls to demonstrate their musical talents.

Afterward, she sought out Elizabeth, determined to

interrogate the girl. "Will you take a turn with me?" she asked.

"I would be honored." Elizabeth spoke with a bit too much enthusiasm.

"Are you enjoying your evening?" Tessa asked as they minced around the perimeter of the drawing room.

"Enormously," Elizabeth said. "The duke is witty and handsome. I declare, my heart fluttered the entire time he spoke to me." She glanced at Tessa. "I am so glad you included me in the courtship."

Tessa wished she'd known the girl's hateful character beforehand. "Is it not difficult competing with so many girls?"

"Not at all. All the girls are so sweet. We are all the best of friends now."

Tessa lifted her brows. "You are friends with all of them?"

"Of course I like some girls above the others, but even if I disliked someone, I would never speak of it."

Tessa decided to make her squirm. "You look particularly lovely in that shade of green. And the gown is a perfect fit."

"I do wish the maids had found a better one for you. You are such a dear," Elizabeth said, her voice dripping with insincere sympathy.

Tessa wondered what the lying witch would say if she told her what she'd overheard, but she had a better plan and led Elizabeth over to an alcove featuring a statue of Diana. "It was particularly kind of you to ask Henrietta to sing this evening."

"Her voice is not the best, but she does enjoy singing," Elizabeth said.

"So you asked her to sing out of kindness?"

"I beg your pardon?"

"You know Henrietta cannot carry a tune," Tessa said. "Yet you encouraged her to sing in front of everyone."

She pouted. "Oh, I understand why you would think it cruel of me. You have not attended any of the musicals in my circle, so you would not know everyone indulges Henrietta. It would be unkind to tell her the truth when she is so proud of her accomplishment."

Elizabeth's patronizing words irritated Tessa. "Perhaps I have misjudged you. Then again, I was surprised by your behavior when Georgette grew ill on the barge."

"Oh, that." She laughed nervously. "I felt a bit sick myself when she became violently ill. I did not know the others would laugh."

Tessa thought Elizabeth's excuse for ridiculing Georgette sorry indeed.

Elizabeth sighed. "I confess I was not sympathetic to her plight. Nor were the other girls, but if you knew the way she treats us, you would understand."

"I've yet to see her belittle anyone," Tessa said.

"Do not let her fool you. In front of the duke and his mother, Georgette pretends to be sweet, but she will not condescend to speak to any of us." Elizabeth's mouth thinned. "She thinks she's above all of us. No one likes her."

"So you admit you spoke to the other girls about her," Tessa said.

"The other girls came to me and professed their dislike of Georgette," Elizabeth said. "I could not encourage them to pursue a closer acquaintance with her."

Tessa regarded her with an icy stare. "I understand now how you gained your popularity."

Elizabeth withdrew her arm. "I beg your pardon?"

"The ploy worked well for you. You shredded one girl's character, knowing the others would agree because they fear becoming your next victim."

"I cannot believe you would think me capable of such a scheme." Elizabeth averted her face and wiped her fingers under her dry eyes.

Tessa huffed. "Your tactics may have worked on your *friends*, but I am far more worldly than they are and recognize cruelty when I see it. You would do well to remember the duke relies on my opinion."

When Elizabeth faced her again, her green cat's eyes held a cold, flat expression. "You have no proof."

Tessa walked away, digging her nails into her palms. She did have proof, but she would not give Elizabeth the satisfaction of admitting she'd overheard her insults. Soon, however, a new realization brought a triumphant smile to her lips. Shelbourne had spent a great deal of time with Elizabeth this evening. He was a shrewd man and must have noticed her malicious tendencies. Perhaps he meant to discuss eliminating her when Tessa met him in the library. She couldn't wait to see the shock on Elizabeth's face when he cut her from the competition.

When Shelbourne shut the library door, the draft doused Tessa's candle. The only light in the room came from a single flickering taper upon the mantel.

He took her candle. "I trust you met with no one," he said in an undertone.

The rumble of his low voice sounded seductive in the dimly lit room. She wet her dry lips. "I waited until everyone else retired."

Thunder boomed, startling a squeak out of her.

"Shhh," he murmured. "Take my arm."

As she wrapped her hand round his sleeve, her breath caught at the feel of his hard muscles beneath the woolen cloth. She was much too aware of the warmth emanating from his body. Her heart thudded, but she told herself it was only because of the gloomy room and the storm outside.

He led her to a small sofa. Then he walked to the hearth and used the taper to light her candle. When he returned, he set the candle on a nearby side table. "I didn't light the fire to avoid attracting the attention of a curious servant," he said quietly.

She shook off her silly misgivings until he sat beside her. Only a foot of cushion separated their bodies. She breathed in the faint scent of sandalwood, a fragrance that clouded her head.

He shifted his long legs, turning toward her. Then he rested his arm along the back of the sofa, his hand only a few inches from her shoulder. His casual pose and the flickering candlelight lent a forbidden intimacy to this secret meeting. She wondered if she'd made a mistake in coming here, but they needed to talk about the girls.

"I worried when all of you were late today," he murmured.

"I saw your concern when we arrived," she whispered.

"I told you not to interfere with the girls' plans. It never occurred to me they would take a barge here."

She knew he blamed himself. "If there had been any danger, your mother and I would have made alternative plans."

The flickering candlelight cast shadows over his face.

"The girls' families entrusted me with the welfare of their daughters. If harm had come to any of you, I would bear the responsibility. As it is, they cannot return home tonight."

She leaned forward. "We arrived safe, and that is all that matters."

"Lady Georgette is ill. If she develops a fever, I will never forgive myself."

Tessa had to reassure him. "It is merely motion sickness, and I suspect a bit of wounded pride."

Outside, driving rain pelted the windows. He looked in that direction and then turned his attention back to her. "Every day I must make decisions, some that affect hundreds of lives. It is not a duty I take lightly."

"I know something about responsibility," she said. "More than once, I've made mistakes managing servants. No one is perfect. All any of us can do is make the best decisions we can and learn from our mistakes."

Tristan took the edge of her silk shawl between his fingers. He swirled the cloth round and round as if he took sensual enjoyment in the silky feeling. Her skin heated as she imagined his fingers sliding over her flesh.

"My mother confronted me about the barge after you left the drawing room," he said, his voice rumbling. "You took all the blame."

"I made a promise to you, and I will not break it."

"You are loyal," he whispered.

"To those I believe in." *Je crois en toi.*

He let go of the shawl. "I thought you had more than a few doubts about me."

"And you had none about me?"

He chuckled. "Touché."

In the dark library, the deep notes of his voice made her think of a couple whispering in bed. Desire pooled low in her belly. Once again, she questioned the wisdom of meeting him. She was alone in the dark with an unrepentant rake. But such a simplistic description did not do justice to this complex man. In a few short weeks, she'd learned much about him. He was stubborn sometimes, but had proven himself fair in his dealings with the girls. He liked to shock her with risqué innuendo, but he'd worried about risking her reputation. He resisted all of her romantic suggestions, but he'd spoken of her career respectfully.

These paradoxical qualities should have made him an enigma to her, and yet, she somehow instinctively understood him. Perhaps it was a result of the growing familiarity that had sprung up so quickly between them. They'd spent a great deal of time alone, unfettered by the social strictures that ordinarily governed meetings between a man and a woman. She felt as if they had created their own little world and forged new rules of engagement.

"I saw you speaking to Lady Elizabeth earlier," he said, interrupting her thoughts. "What were you discussing?"

She wanted to hear his opinion first. "What did *you* think of Elizabeth and her friend Henrietta?"

"They were amusing."

"You found them agreeable?"

"You'd better keep your voice down," he murmured. "Elizabeth and Henrietta talked to me. The other girls said very little."

"They monopolized you." The knowledge that he liked them made her bitter. She'd been certain he would see through those two cruel girls.

"The others had plenty of opportunity," he said, "but

you obviously disapprove of Elizabeth and Henrietta. Why?"

"Did you not think it strange when Elizabeth asked Henrietta to sing?"

He shrugged. "Why do you ask?"

"Elizabeth knew Henrietta cannot sing. Yet she asked her to do so."

"Are you suggesting Elizabeth meant to embarrass her?"

"It is a possibility."

"I doubt it. They are friends."

Tessa huffed. How could he miss what seemed so obvious to her? Did he not realize that Elizabeth had manipulated her own friend? "I must caution you about those two girls. I have reason to believe them capable of mischief."

"Is there something you're not telling me?" he asked.

"The particulars are not important."

He leaned closer to her. "If they have done something wrong, it is important."

"I overheard them gossiping. They were unkind."

"What exactly did they say?"

She had backed herself into a corner, but she had too much pride to tell him they had mocked her. "I prefer not to reveal specific details, but their comments were cruel."

"Speaking of Miss Hardwick—"

"I did not say they were speaking of Miss Hardwick."

"You didn't have to." When Tessa started to protest, he held up his hand. "Where was Amy Hardwick tonight?"

"She chose to stay and look after Lady Georgette."

"A pity Lady Georgette is still unwell," he said. "I would have liked to further our acquaintance."

Tessa inhaled. "And what of Amy?"

"It is time to let her go," he said. "Her actions tonight proved she would prefer not to participate."

"You are punishing her because she cared enough to help Georgette. That's unfair." How could he eliminate sweet Amy and keep Georgette, who had done nothing to deserve his favor?

"I know you feel sorry for Amy, but she could have joined us for part of the evening," he said. "My guess is she was relieved to find an excuse to stay away. She's been reluctant from the beginning."

"If Lady Georgette had chosen to stay behind, you wouldn't even consider cutting her from the competition," she hissed.

"What are you insinuating?"

"You're eliminating Amy because she lacks Georgette's beauty."

"If beauty was all that mattered to me, I could have picked the belle of the season and been done with it. And you will recall, I never mentioned beauty as a requirement."

She lifted her brows. "So beauty doesn't matter to you?"

"A trick question," he said. "If I say no, you won't believe me. If I say yes, you will call me on the carpet for being shallow."

"Then be honest. Which is it?"

He stood and walked a few paces away, his back to her.

"Tell me," she said, rising.

He whirled around. "Don't."

She took a step toward him, ignoring his warning. "Tell me."

"Leave it be," he said as if gritting his teeth.

Tessa stood her ground. "I am not leaving this room until you do."

"I want to be physically attracted to my wife." He made an exasperated sound. "There, you forced me to say it."

She averted her gaze to the cold ashes in the grate. "So you proved my point. You are rejecting Amy because she isn't pretty."

The rapid thud of his footsteps jolted her. She gasped when he took her by the shoulders. "You do not understand," he said.

"Then explain."

He towered over her. The feeble light from the candles illuminated his harsh expression. "I *want* to *want* my wife."

Tessa swallowed hard.

"Do you understand?" he said.

She couldn't breathe, much less answer him.

"I *want* to *want* her so much I can't stop thinking about her."

She remembered his words. *I want an angel in the ballroom, and a temptress in private.*

His lashes lowered, thick and dark as the night. "I want to be on fire for her."

She was melting under the force of his heat.

He closed the scant distance between them. His face was but a dangerous shadow. She was aware of the drumming rain and his harsh breathing. As he drew her closer, a dim warning flashed in her brain, but his male scent lured her into a forbidden, reckless place.

Her eyes drifted closed seconds before his lips claimed hers. She braced her hands on his chest. Beneath the silk waistcoat, his heart pounded. At her touch, he grew bolder, painting her mouth with broad strokes.

Stop him now. This was wrong. So very, very wrong. Though her brain told her to walk away, a lonely place deep inside cried out for more.

Her knees wobbled. Needing support, she reached for his shoulders. Her shawl slipped to the floor. He wrapped her tighter in his arms, the heat of his body scorching her. Unable to resist, she caressed the tendrils of cropped hair brushing his collar. Damn the consequences, she thought. She'd already fallen and wanted to memorize the feel of his silky hair, his sensuous lips, and his strong arms. Because his kiss would be her last.

He parted his lips, kissing her open-mouthed, again and again, until she obeyed his command. A moan escaped her at the sweep of his tongue. He tasted of brandy and sin.

He pulled her up to her toes, arching her spine. His hands slid down to her bottom, urging her closer, closer. He flexed his hips and her belly met with unmistakable male hardness. His tongue thrust inside her mouth, retreated, and thrust again. Over and over. The wild rhythm unleashed a burning flood inside her. She strained against him, wanting, yearning to be closer, and he rocked against her.

Just a little longer, she promised herself. A little longer to feel desirable. A little longer to feel passion. A little longer to hold the world at bay.

His lips left hers, and she nearly cried out in protest, but he kissed a path to her neck. When he found the pulse point, he nipped her with his teeth. She stilled beneath his possession, a primitive acquiescence. He touched her with his tongue, and she could no longer think. All she could do was beg for more. Unable to help herself, she pressed her breasts against him, a silent plea.

As his hand swept round her hip and up the curve of her waist, she held her breath in anticipation. He cupped her breast, his long fingers splaying and teasing. His thumb circled her nipple through the cloth, and she gasped. He covered her mouth, his tongue caressing as his hand delved inside her bodice. When he touched her naked flesh, she gave herself up to the exquisite pleasure.

She was lost to everything but her need for his touch. He teased her nipple, making her ache. A wild craving built deep inside where she'd grown slick with need. She squeezed her thighs together, desperate to fill the void. Against her belly, the rigid, long length of him strained against her. She wanted to touch him *there*. Most of all, she wanted to sink to the floor and take him down with her.

He broke the kiss and jerked his head up. Outside the library, the clip of footsteps echoed on the marble floor and stopped outside the door. In a daze, Tessa stood there, her mind slow to interpret the impending threat. He grasped her shawl from the carpet, wrapped it round her shoulders, and stepped away.

Fear clawed at her belly. Her breath came in short gasps. *Go away, go away, go away.*

The door handle turned.

Chapter Seven

$\mathscr{T}$ristan's heart pounded as the library door opened. Fear of discovery made his mouth dry. Unfortunately, the lust coursing through his veins was slow to dissipate. His skintight trousers felt ready to burst. He gritted his teeth, thankful the dark interior hid his predicament.

Relief filled him at the sight of Hawk. The flickering light of Hawk's candle illuminated his stunned expression. "I beg your pardon," he said.

"We were discussing the courtship," Tristan said, his gaze flitting to Miss Mansfield. In the dim light, he couldn't make out her expression.

"I'll not interrupt," Hawk said, starting to close the door.

"Stay," Miss Mansfield said. "I was on the verge of leaving." She plucked her candle off the table and headed for the door.

Tristan wanted to stop her. They needed to discuss what had transpired between them, but he could say nothing with Hawk present. And God knew he had no idea what he would say.

After the door clicked shut, Tristan walked over to the hearth and gripped the cold marble mantel. *Idiot.* What had possessed him? He'd never touched a virtuous lady before.

Damn his sorry hide.

Hearing the clink of glasses, Tristan glanced at the sideboard. Hawk poured two brandies and brought one to him.

Tristan gulped the brandy. The fiery liquor made his eyes water. "The devil, what have I done?"

Hawk sauntered over to a chair and stretched out his legs. "Don't feel obligated to confess on my account."

"I lost my head," he muttered.

"Have no fear," Hawk drawled. "It's still attached to your neck."

"I never meant this to happen," Tristan said.

"Do I have to hear this?"

"Damn it all. I'm in trouble."

Hawk waved his hand. "No, you're lucky it was only me who burst in on you. Sorry about that, old boy."

How far would he have gone if Hawk hadn't arrived? "I kissed her," he gritted out.

"Oh, bloody hell, is that all? She'll survive a chaste peck."

Tristan jerked his head up. "Chaste peck? I had my damned tongue down her throat."

"So it was a naughty kiss. It could have been worse."

"It was." He'd had his hands all over her.

"Did she try to stop you?"

"She was probably overwhelmed by feelings she didn't understand," he said.

"Maybe she enjoyed it."

"That doesn't signify." Tristan set his glass on the mantel and started pacing. She must think him the worst sort of libertine. If she resigned, a public scandal would ensue. There was no quiet way for her to bow out with ten girls still remaining in the courtship.

"Sit down," Hawk said. "You're wearing a hole in the blasted carpet."

He retrieved his brandy and slumped on the sofa.

"Hear me out, old boy," Hawk said. "I've never known you to take risks. Until you met her."

Tristan huffed. "That's rich. You're suggesting she's a bad influence on me. You do see the irony, I hope."

"I don't know if it's good or bad. I only know she has influenced you," Hawk said. "And I still don't understand what she hopes to gain."

"Matchmaking is her career. She takes pride in it."

Hawk sipped his brandy. "It's an odd career for a woman who refuses to wed."

"Her career is not the issue," Tristan said. "I crossed a line, and now I've got to deal with the repercussions."

"No one knows but me and the two of you. So officially, she's not compromised. Miss Mansfield strikes me as a worldly woman, and frankly, she didn't protest."

He recalled her shock at his refusal to apologize for his liaisons that first day he'd called on her. "If you're insinuating she wanted me to kiss her, you're wrong. She's got high-minded notions of morality."

"If that's the case, she's likely feeling guilty," Hawk said. "After all, she's your matchmaker and owes allegiance to you and those girls you're courting. She probably thinks she's to blame."

Tristan met his friend's eyes. "The blame is mine."

"Apologize," Hawk said. "Say you were both caught up in the moment. It was a difficult day. What happened was an aberration, a momentary lapse in judgment."

"Right." Tristan tossed back the remainder of his brandy.

"It's not irreparable," Hawk said.

"And if she thinks it is? What then? She might resign."

Hawk gave him an enigmatic look. "Do you want to continue with the courtship?"

"I have to find a bride," Tristan said. "At least this way, I have a better chance of knowing the sort of woman I'm marrying."

"Are you making any progress?"

"I've eliminated fourteen," Tristan said, a little too defensively.

"Are any of them serious contenders?"

"It's too early to tell yet," Tristan said.

"I see," Hawk said, his tone dubious.

Tristan chose not to challenge Hawk. "It's probably a moot point now. Miss Mansfield is a stickler when it comes to making matches. She'll likely quit tomorrow."

"She won't," Hawk said. "Remember, she has as much to lose as you do, maybe more. All of society knows about this courtship. She won't risk causing a scandal."

"I hope you're right," Tristan said.

By early afternoon the next day, the rain had stopped and the roads had dried enough to send the girls home. Tristan paced the drawing room, waiting for all of them to assemble. Before they left, he would let them know his decision.

The last of the girls entered, but still Miss Mansfield had not arrived. A trickle of sweat beaded down his neck. What if she didn't show?

Then let her hang, he thought. She'd interrogated him about his past liaisons, but when put to the test, she'd failed. If she quit, she'd suffer the brunt of the scandal.

The devil take him. She would never have met him in secret if he'd not told her it was important. He'd treated her badly.

The silence in the room unnerved him. The candidates sat rigidly on their chairs, their expressions anxious. They were nervous, too. He cleared his throat. "Lady Georgette, you are recovered?"

She blushed. "Yes, thank you."

"Excellent," he said.

Miss Hardwick reached over and patted Georgette's hand. Obviously Amy truly cared about Georgette's welfare. Guilt burned his chest as he recalled what he'd said last night.

The rustle of skirts brought his attention to the door. Miss Mansfield entered. Her severe expression jolted him. He swallowed hard, not knowing if she meant to resign in front of the girls. Remembering Hawk's words, he could only hope an instinct for self-preservation would overcome her matchmaking principles.

"Your Grace," she said quietly. "Do you wish to meet individually with the candidates?"

Relief filled him. "That will not be necessary," he said.

She gave him a questioning look.

"Trust me," he whispered.

She averted her gaze, but not before he noted the disturbed look in her eyes. The devil. How could he have sullied her last night?

He had to brazen this out and hoped his decision would appease her until he could apologize in private. With a deep breath, he faced the bridal candidates. "Ladies," he said, "I know this is difficult for you, so I won't keep you waiting. After much deliberation, I have decided not to eliminate anyone today."

Shrieks erupted. The girls hugged one another and chattered.

From the corner of his eye, he saw Miss Mansfield whip her face toward him. He resisted the urge to return her gaze, knowing he must keep his focus on the excited girls.

"Ladies, could I have your attention again?" When they quieted, he continued. "You may wonder about my reasons. Due to the inclement weather, you were all subjected to distress. I enjoyed your company, but it was a trying day. And not everyone was able to join us last night."

He paused, gathering his thoughts. "I wish to acknowledge Miss Hardwick. She is to be commended for staying behind last evening to look after Lady Georgette. It would not be fair to eliminate either of them, but it would not be fair to eliminate anyone who attended the gathering either. In the next few days, all of you will receive invitations. For now, carriages are waiting downstairs to return you to your families."

They all rushed up to him. He noted Lady Georgette had taken a reluctant Miss Hardwick in hand and drawn her to the group. The girls spoke all at once, but his attention wandered over to Miss Mansfield, who had walked over to the window. He felt as tightly strung as a violin, thinking of their impending discussion. Had his actions today been enough to prove to her he wasn't a complete cad?

Soon a footman arrived to escort the girls downstairs. Miss Mansfield wished them all a safe journey, relieving his fear she would follow them downstairs and prevent him from apologizing.

When the last of the girls left, he shut the door and faced her. "Will you sit with me?" he asked.

She joined him on the sofa, gazing at her clasped hands.

He cleared his throat. "I will not offer you excuses for last night. My behavior was inexcusable."

"I did not stop you," she whispered.

Hawk had been right. She blamed herself. "Look at me," he said.

She shook her head.

"It was my fault," he said. "I shocked you. I shocked myself. Nothing can change what I did, but you must believe I have never done anything like this before."

"I believe you," she whispered.

"You are a virtuous lady and deserve better treatment."

She drew in a shuddering breath.

"An apology is insufficient," he said, "but I promise never to dishonor you again."

"I accused you of being unfair to Miss Hardwick," she said. "I was too forceful, even though you warned me."

"You are not to blame." Deep down, he knew it was desire, not anger, that had precipitated that kiss. He'd been stealing glances at her luscious body since the first day he'd met her. Perhaps it was his celibacy that had broken his control. Or more likely sheer lust for a high-spirited woman with curves that would tempt the devil. Regardless of the cause, he had lost all control.

"We were not ourselves last night," he said, "but I

know better than to take advantage of a maiden's innocence. If you continue to blame yourself, it will only add
to my shame."

Her throat worked. "Does Lord Hawkfield know?"

Tristan hesitated a beat too long.

"Oh, God," she said, covering her face.

"You are not to blame."

"How could I do this to the girls?"

"They will never know."

She lowered her hands and gazed at him, her face crimson. "I will."

"We made a mistake, but we are adults," he said. "We will
go forward. If you can find it in your heart to forgive me."

"There is nothing to forgive. You are one of the most
honorable men I've ever met."

He inhaled. "I don't deserve that."

"Yes, you do. You kept Amy in the competition, even
though you are not attracted to her."

"I kept her because she alone cared enough to stay with
Georgette. Her selfless act showed her kindness and maturity. You opened my eyes to her special qualities."

Her eyes shimmered with unshed tears.

He squeezed her hands. "Can we be friends?"

"You do me too much honor, Your Grace."

"Will you call me Tristan? As a friend?" The minute the words flew from his mouth, he held his breath.
Would she think it a sly attempt to seduce her into another
indiscretion?

She searched his eyes, as if trying to reach through to
his very soul. "Tristan, it is," she said. "As my friend, you
may call me Tessa. In private."

He exhaled. "You have a beautiful name."

When she blushed, he released her hands. "May I call upon you tomorrow to discuss the next round of the courtship?"

She nodded. "I must go."

He walked her to the door and breathed a sigh of relief. He was damned lucky she'd forgiven him. A weaker woman might have made a scene. Tessa, however, was stronger than any woman he'd ever met.

As she descended the stairs, she trailed her graceful fingers along the banister. Her white muslin gown whispered round her generous curves. His gaze riveted on her swaying hips. Heat sparked in his veins. He fisted his hands, determined to master his unruly desire for her.

He must not, could not, ever allow lust to overrule his head again. The risk was too high.

She wasn't alone.

The next day, Tristan entered Tessa's drawing room to find her deep in conversation with Lord and Lady Broughton. At first, he was irritated with Tessa for entertaining friends when he'd made an appointment. Then he thought it selfish of him. She'd always made time for him. He should not begrudge her friends when she gave so much and asked nothing in return.

When he saw Lady Broughton dabbing a handkerchief at her eyes, he realized he'd arrived at an inopportune time. "My apologies," he said. "I will come back another day."

Tessa turned to him. "Please join us." Her voice sounded strained.

Judging from Lady Broughton's tear-stained cheeks, something untoward had happened. Even Miss Powell looked distressed.

Broughton strode over and shook his hand. "Good to see you, Shelbourne."

"I fear I've interrupted," he said.

"Not at all. I was sharing some news with Miss Mansfield about my wife's brother, Mortland. He disappeared at the battle of Toulouse, and I'm investigating."

Tristan frowned. Two years had elapsed since that fateful battle in France. "He was an officer?"

"A lieutenant," Broughton said. "I recently corresponded with his superior officer. He recalled seeing him before the attempt to cross the Garonne River."

Tristan schooled his features. According to reports, the bridge had fallen due to flooding. If Lady Broughton's brother had survived the crossing, he would have faced fierce odds during the battle.

"I have a few other leads," Broughton continued. "I sent a few letters and hope to locate some of Mortland's fellow officers. Perhaps one of them saw him on the battlefield."

The chances of anyone recalling what had happened to Lady Broughton's brother at this late date were slim. Tristan turned to Broughton's wife. "I am deeply sorry, ma'am."

"Thank you for your condolences," she said.

Tristan regarded Broughton. "May I be of assistance in your search?"

"Thank you, but there's not much else to be done." Broughton's guarded expression spoke volumes. He didn't want his wife to know he thought the search a futile effort.

"Will you take a seat, Your Grace?" Tessa asked.

"Thank you," he said.

The conversation drifted to the typical dull observations

about the weather. Then Lady Broughton set her cup aside, opened her reticule, and drew out a letter. "I've been reading all of my brother's letters again and brought this one for you, Tessa. Richard mentioned you. I thought you might wish to read it."

Tessa hissed in a breath, drawing everyone's attention to her. All the color drained from her face. "I could not take your letter."

"You can return it later," Lady Broughton said.

Tessa regarded the letter as if it were a snake. With obvious reluctance, she took it.

"It was one of his early letters," Lady Broughton said. "He seemed anxious about you. Perhaps you can make out why he was so concerned."

An arrested expression crossed Tessa's face. "I'm sure he was only making a polite inquiry." She set the letter on the settee. Then she gripped her hands in her lap. A shadow seemed to pass over her features.

Tristan stilled. Why did that letter trouble her so much?

"I am surprised my brother did not inquire after your uncle," Lady Broughton continued.

Broughton looked at Tristan. "Wentworth purchased Mortland's commission."

Tristan gave Tessa a sympathetic look, realizing she probably felt guilty because her uncle had purchased the commission. Her guilt was misplaced, of course. He decided to speak to her about it when they were alone.

"Well," Tessa said. "I believe we're all ready for more tea." As she poured, Miss Powell handed round the cups.

Twenty minutes later, Broughton turned to his wife. "My dear, we must be off now."

After their departure, Miss Powell quit the drawing room as well. Tessa plucked the letter off the settee, walked over to the desk, and deposited it in a drawer. Then she glanced at him. "May I bring you a brandy?"

"Yes, thank you," he said.

When she brought him the drink, their fingers brushed. Alarm flitted through her eyes. Then she snatched her hand back as if scalded.

Her reaction made him feel like a devil. As she took her seat and stared at her clenched hands, he wondered if he should apologize again for that kiss at Ashdown House. But doing so would likely embarrass her. He decided to concentrate on the matchmaking business. "I've been thinking about the next round of the courtship."

"So have I," she said. "I think it's time to observe the candidates out in society." She gave him a tremulous smile.

"I thought of calling on them here." He sipped his brandy. "I prefer not to expose the courtship to the prying eyes of the ton."

"You need to see how the girls comport themselves in a public setting. We could attend the opera. That way you can control who is allowed in your box." She paused and then added, "We should invite your mother and sister. They can converse with the girls. All of society, well, those at the opera, will see that your family supports the courtship."

He groaned. "You're determined to surround me with an army of females."

"You may invite Lord Hawkfield."

"He despises the opera. So do I."

"All the more reason to focus your attention on the bridal candidates."

He took a long drink of brandy. "There are still ten candidates. It might be best to have one more private session first."

She considered his words for a long moment. "You can arrange to speak privately with a chosen few. During that time, your mother, sister, and even Lord Hawkfield can talk to the other candidates. I think it would be helpful to have their opinions."

He narrowed his eyes. "My opinion is the only one that counts."

"You will make the final choice about who will remain and who will go," she said. "However, the girls may reveal a different side of their characters to your family and to Lord Hawkfield."

"I suppose so," he said grudgingly. Damnation, he should have refused. So why had he not? Because he felt guilty for kissing her.

"Try to look on the bright side," she said. "You might actually enjoy it."

"I doubt it," he grumbled.

That earned him a laugh.

"Tessa, I hesitate to interfere in your personal affairs, but I could not help but notice your uneasiness over that letter."

Her expression grew wary.

"I suspect you feel guilty because your uncle purchased the lieutenant's commission."

She stared at her clasped hands. "Anne still grieves for her brother."

"She deserves your sympathy, but you must absolve yourself and your uncle of guilt. It was generous of him to provide the commission. No one is to blame for what happened."

"Thank you for caring."

"How long ago did your uncle die?"

"Four years have passed," she said.

How had she withstood being all alone in the world? "I take it your uncle provided you with a comfortable inheritance."

"I inherited Hollincourt, my uncle's property."

Stunned, he stared at her. "But what of the entailment?"

"I do not profess to understand all the legal complexities, but I know the settlement ended with my uncle. Since there was no heir, he did not renew it. So he was free to leave the property to whomever he chose. The title of course is extinct."

He swallowed hard. Her late uncle's failure to produce an heir was Tristan's worst fear. For three hundred years, the earls and dukes of Shelbourne had reigned. His father had nearly beggared the estates, but Tristan had let pride get in the way of doing his duty because he couldn't stomach marrying for money. He'd been a fool to wait this long to secure the title.

Tessa knit her brows. "You look troubled."

"Your uncle's predicament is a grim reminder of my own situation." In his case, the remaining property was entailed upon his future heir. He'd made provisions for his mother and sister, but nothing to equal the security Wentworth had provided for his niece.

"I am here to help you remedy that situation," Tessa said quietly.

Tristan set his brandy aside. "I heard you were an heiress, but the details aren't common knowledge. I'm surprised, given the unusual circumstances."

"Until last year, I did not venture to London. Plenty of people question me, but I do not discuss the matter. I'm considered odd enough for my independence."

"I fear I'm being impertinent, but I have wondered why you never married," he said.

She smoothed her skirt. "Circumstances were not in my favor."

"What do you mean?"

"After my aunt died, my uncle's health deteriorated. I took care of him."

"How long was he ill?"

"It came on gradually. The first two years, he suffered from melancholy, but the last three, his heart weakened."

Her words stunned him. She had nursed her uncle for five years. He'd never met a more selfless woman in all his life. "Few young women would give up so much for an ailing relative."

"He was all the family I had left," she said, her voice quavering a little. "My parents died in a carriage accident when I was sixteen."

An odd pang, swift and sharp, stung his hardened heart. She'd lost all her family in a few short years.

"I am lucky compared to most women in my situation," she said. "Poverty would have made my life much harder."

Her uncle must have worried about leaving her alone, but that only made him wonder. "I'm surprised your uncle didn't make arrangements for you to marry."

She hesitated, turning her gaze to the fire. "I had to postpone my presentation at court when my aunt died. The year after, Uncle George could not bring himself to go to London because he still grieved for my aunt. He made arrangements with his friend's wife to sponsor me." She paused. "I chose not to go."

"You could not bear to leave your grieving uncle."

She said nothing.

"You still miss him," he said.

She sighed. "Every day, but when I feel sorry for myself, I remember how lucky I am to have Anne."

"You've known her for a long time, haven't you?"

"Since I went to live with my uncle. Her father died shortly after they received the news about her brother. She had nothing at all, so I invited her to share my home."

"A generous offer," he said.

"No, she was a great comfort to me. Anne insisted on a paid position as my companion. I agreed for the sake of her pride, but she is my dearest friend, as close as a sister."

"I suppose you came to London to find her a husband."

She returned her attention to him. "No, I came to London because I wanted to experience it for myself. It was so much more than I ever imagined. I love the museums, the theater, and the balls. And the shopping best of all."

"Then it is a lucky thing your uncle left you his fortune." They exchanged smiles. "I find it ironic you chose to make matches when you have eluded marriage."

"I am firmly displayed on the spinster shelf," she said.

"You cannot be more than four and twenty." In truth, her full cheeks and button nose made her look even younger.

She flushed. "You have just earned a lifetime place as my friend."

He chuckled. "You can tell me the truth."

"Six and twenty," she muttered.

"You are far too young to dismiss marriage," he said, frowning.

"Now you sound like Anne." She rolled her eyes and said in a mimicking tone, "It's not too late for you, Tessa."

He suspected the spinster label had wounded her. The ton's cruelty angered him. By God, she deserved far better. "I think you would make a wonderful wife to some lucky man."

Tristan would say something so wonderful, today of all days.

Tessa kept the smile plastered on her face until he left, and then she sank onto the settee. She clutched her freezing hands in her lap. Her head ached from the effort of keeping her composure. When Anne had handed her that letter, she had not wanted to touch it.

She glanced at the desk. Dread filled her. She did not want to dredge up the past, but she had no choice. She must honor her promise to Anne.

Procrastinating would only make her more anxious. She would read the letter now and have done with it. Resolute, she marched over to the desk and opened the drawer. Her hands trembled as she unfolded the letter. The pages were creased from age. She spread it out on the desk and noted the date. It had been written only a few weeks after Richard Mortland had left home and before he'd been stationed on the Continent. He had told his sister not to worry because he would grow accustomed to hardship. Clearly he'd not cared that his words would cause Anne anguish.

At the end, Tessa saw her name. As Anne had said, he'd

claimed to be worried about her. *When last I saw Miss Mansfield, she seemed melancholy and wan. Pray, write and tell me how she fares.*

With jerky movements, she folded the letter and shoved it back inside the desk drawer. Tomorrow she would return it to Anne. There was nothing she could tell her friend. Nothing.

She had known that before reading the letter.

Today the past had invaded the present. She had locked the door on the proverbial skeletons in her closet, but the letter had served as a window. She had allowed Tristan to peek inside. Ordinarily she avoided all questions about her past, but he had been so kind. He had surmised that she felt guilty because her uncle provided the commission. Because he cared, she had revealed the essential details of her past, but only the essentials.

His words haunted her. *You could not bear to leave your grieving uncle.*

She had said nothing. Uncle George had taught her not to feel compelled to fill the silence. He'd neglected to tell her she would never be able to silence her regrets. She would pay for her mistakes all the days of her life. But she'd been spared the worst.

Her secrets were safe.

Chapter Eight

The next day, Tessa's hands grew clammy as she entered Anne's drawing room, which was decorated in the latest Chinese style. She planned to dispense quickly with the subject of Richard's letter. Putting it off would only increase her nervousness.

"Have you read Richard's letter?" Anne asked as they sat upon the sofa.

Guilt seized Tessa at the hopeful expression in her friend's eyes. With trembling fingers, she retrieved the letter from her reticule and handed it over. She took a deep breath before uttering the words she'd prepared. "I cannot say what your brother meant in his expression of concern for me." She'd lied by omission out of necessity. "I am sorry."

"Geoffrey warned me not to hope too much." Anne carefully added the creased letter to a bundle of missives tied with blue ribbon. "Perhaps Richard was concerned because your uncle had not recovered from his melancholy." Anne set the packet of letters aside. "Richard was grateful to your uncle, so I am surprised he did not inquire after Lord Wentworth's health."

Tessa wasn't surprised.

"Where are my manners?" Anne said. "I haven't even offered you tea yet."

Tessa accepted a cup and took the opportunity to change the subject. "I have an idea. Next week, the duke will court the girls at the opera. You must convince your husband to attend and visit Shelbourne's box at intermission."

"What a splendid idea. Are you certain the duke will not mind?"

"I'm sure he will welcome you both."

Anne sipped her tea, regarding Tessa over the rim of the cup. "Geoffrey and I were both surprised he called upon you yesterday."

Tessa shrugged. "He'd made an appointment to discuss the courtship."

Anne looked troubled. "I hesitate to say anything, but Geoffrey convinced me it would be better if you learned about the gossip from a friend."

Tessa stilled. "What gossip?"

"Lady Elizabeth is spreading a tale that you are trying to slander her."

Tessa inhaled. "Oh, that conniving witch. You would not believe how she is manipulating the other girls."

"I'm sure she is," Anne said, "but use caution when speaking to the girls. Their mothers can ruin your reputation."

Anne's wisdom made her realize she'd acted heedlessly. "You are right," she said. "I confronted her at Ashdown House. In hindsight, I should have spoken to Tris—to the duke, privately." Tessa winced at her mistake. It was too much to hope her friend had not noticed her faux pas.

Anne stared at her. "What did you almost say?"

"I made a silly mistake."

"You almost called him something other than duke," Anne said. "What was it?"

She'd certainly stepped into a pile of manure. "His Christian name is Tristan."

"I am surprised you even know it," Anne said.

"I heard his mother call him Tristan." She'd uttered another lie of omission. Anne's disturbed expression indicated she did not believe that explanation.

"Why would you even think of referring to him in such an intimate fashion? I never even considered using Geoffrey's Christian name until we were engaged."

She decided to tell Anne the truth. After all, Anne was her friend. Surely she would understand. "I know it's not strictly permissible, but Shelbourne and I are friends. We agreed to a more familiar address in private."

"So he does not call you Tessa in front of the girls?"

"No, of course not."

"But what does he call you in front of Jane?"

"He uses the proper address when she is there. Honestly, there is no cause for concern."

"But Jane would always be present when he calls." Anne set her cup aside, and then her eyes widened as if she had suddenly realized the significance of Tessa's silence. "You have spent time alone with him?"

Tessa unfurled her fan and applied it to her warm cheeks. "I'm no green girl fresh out of the schoolroom."

"You are not an elderly woman at your last prayers, either," Anne said.

"What difference does it make? No one knows."

Anne's countenance grew stern. "Jane knows you are alone with him, and I wager the servants know as well."

Tessa closed her fan. "I'm not completely ignoring the proprieties. Jane is present until the tea tray arrives. And my servants are loyal."

"You are risking your reputation. It is not like you."

Tessa moistened her dry lips. "He is more comfortable speaking to me in private. It's a business arrangement, so there is no cause for alarm."

"I have always respected you for keeping your match-making efforts confidential, but you have never had a gentleman client before." Anne looked shaken. "I am very concerned. He is a rake."

"You are making entirely too much of the matter."

"He insists on being alone with you, and he calls you by your Christian name. I cannot even imagine how he seduced you into that indiscretion."

Her cheeks flamed. "Seduced me? Indiscretion? These are gross exaggerations." Indeed, he'd not had to coax her even a little before she'd fallen witlessly into his arms at Ashdown House.

"I did not mean to cast aspersions on *your* character."

"You must not think ill of Shelbourne," Tessa said. "He is an honorable gentleman."

"I know his reputation, and so do you. I saw the way he watched you yesterday."

She'd been so worried about Richard's letter, she'd not noticed. "You are imagining things."

Anne shook her head. "Geoffrey remarked upon it as well. The duke was definitely watching you while you were pouring tea."

"He was probably hoping I'd serve cake. He is fond of sweets."

"I think he is fond of more than cake."

"Anne, your suspicions are fanciful in the extreme." But he had kissed and touched her. Was it possible he had grown attracted to her? No, she mustn't even think it. He had apologized and taken all the blame for their indiscretion, but deep down, she knew she had encouraged him. God help her, she had relived his touch and the feel of his lips every night since then. No matter how many times she'd told herself to stop, she'd invariably failed. But where was the harm? No one would ever know about her secret fantasies.

"Tessa, you're not in love with him, are you?"

The question startled her. Once again, her face burned. "How could you even ask such a question? I'm his matchmaker."

Anne touched her hand. "I know you would never betray the bridal candidates, but I worry you will lose your heart to him."

"Nonsense," she said. She had not lost her heart to him. She had *not*. But she had betrayed the bridal candidates when she'd kissed him. She'd stolen one romantic moment for herself and nearly compromised herself and Tristan. If anyone but Lord Hawkfield had come into the library, she would have brought disgrace upon Tristan, his family, and herself.

Never again, she swore. From this moment forward she would focus all her efforts on encouraging him to choose a bride with his heart. Her heart was in no danger. None at all.

Hawk lifted his glass. "A toast to your courtship."

Tristan glowered at his friend over the rim of his brandy

glass, certain Hawk would rib him endlessly when he heard about the opera. They sat at their usual spot at the club. Outside the bow window, the yellow pool of light from the gas lamps looked eerie in the misty night. Male voices rumbled, but in a nearby room, silence reigned as fools sat at the green baize tables risking their fortunes— fools like his late father.

He shoved aside the useless thoughts about his sire. "Miss Mansfield insisted I invite you to the opera next week. I'll tell her you have a previous engagement."

Hawk's brown eyes lit with merriment. "The opera? Oh, Lord, she's insisting you court the chits there, isn't she?"

"I told her you hate the opera." Damnation, he'd agreed because of his guilt. Now he'd committed himself to taking the courtship out in public.

"Why am I invited?" Hawk asked.

Tristan traced the rim of his glass. "It's just another one of her ridiculous notions. Trust me, you don't want to attend."

"And let you down? Never."

"Your ballerina will be missing you."

"I tired of her hysterics a week ago," he said. "But now that you mention it, I am in need of a new mistress. I might as well take a turn round the pit while I'm at the opera."

"You will not troll for whores in front of my mother and sister."

Hawk laughed. "Right-ho. I'll be as angelic as a choirboy. But what am I to do? Help your dear mama chaperone?"

"You're supposed to converse with the chits and report back to me. But you're not attending."

"I promise not to flirt with them."

"I'll give Miss Mansfield your regrets."

"But I wouldn't miss it for the world."

Masculine laughter erupted from the center of the room, drawing their attention. Several gentlemen took turns clapping Viscount Hunter on the back.

"What do you suppose that's all about?" Hawk asked.

Tristan shrugged and sipped his brandy. They shared a companionable silence until Lord Westerly approached a few minutes later.

"Well, Shelbourne, what do you make of this turn of events?" Westerly asked.

Tristan gave Westerly a bored look and swirled his brandy. He detested the man, finding him a pest and a notorious gossip.

Westerly grasped his lapels and rocked back on his heels. "With nine other gels to court, I don't suppose you'd miss one."

The fine hairs on the back of his neck stiffened. What the devil? One of the girls had quit the courtship?

"I confess, I never thought Hunter would come up to scratch," Westerly continued with obvious relish. "He's evaded Miss Fielding for years. Quite the rake, you know. Everyone knows she's mad for him."

The news startled Tristan. Caroline Fielding had been courting Hunter behind his back? Westerly's words echoed in Tristan's brain. *Everyone knows she's mad for him.*

Shock rippled down his spine. Did Tessa know? Surely not. Damn it all to hell, it was her responsibility to ensure the girls adhered to the rules. On that first day, he'd given Tessa his bridal requirements, and he'd expected her to investigate the girls. If she'd done so, she would have known what everyone else knew. Caroline Fielding had held a torch for Hunter—for years.

Tessa had failed him.

Loud masculine guffaws erupted from Hunter's table. Fury burned him like a live coal. She'd let him be made a fool of at his club. Damn her!

"I say, did you not know of Hunter's betrothal to Miss Caroline Fielding?" Westerly smirked. "She is one of your bridal candidates, is she not?"

"Piss off," Hawk growled.

Tristan stared at Hunter. When the man returned his gaze, Tristan lifted his brandy glass, indicating no hard feelings. He'd be damned if he would let Hunter think he'd won a contest over the chit.

Hunter held his glass aloft and inclined his head.

Tristan exchanged a speaking look with Hawk. They both rose.

"I say, do you mean to call out Hunter?" Westerly's eyes gleamed.

Tristan stared him down. "What I mean to do is bloody your nose if you don't stand aside."

Westerly held up his hands and backed up, nearly tripping over his feet. "No harm intended, Shelbourne."

Ignoring Westerly, Tristan forced himself to stroll as he took his leave, but he could feel the stares. By tomorrow morning, the bloody scandal sheets would print the news and make sport of him again. He gritted his teeth as he and Hawk collected their greatcoats, gloves, and hats.

After his father's death, Tristan had sworn no one would ever humiliate him or his family again. Tessa would pay dearly for this. He'd see to it she never made another match again.

Once they stepped outside, Hawk adjusted his hat at a jaunty angle. "I'm trying to remember which one is Miss Fielding. Is she a blonde or a brunette?"

Tristan's jaw worked. "Yes."

Hawk snorted. "You don't remember."

"Remember what?" he gritted out.

"Never mind. What are you planning to do?"

"Have a few choice words with Miss Mansfield."

"About Hunter and Miss Fielding?"

"Miss Mansfield has some explaining to do." He'd give her a tongue-lashing she'd never forget.

"Be fair," Hawk said. "She may not know."

"It's her business to know about the bridal candidates." She'd live to regret crossing him. He'd see to it everyone in society cut her.

"It's late," Hawk said. "You should wait until tomorrow before speaking to her. Let your temper cool."

"No."

"She may not be at home. Sleep on this and call on her first thing tomorrow."

"If she's not home, I'll find her." He'd scour the entire city if necessary.

"You'd better let me come with you," Hawk said as Tristan's carriage arrived.

"No."

"I'll chaperone," Hawk said.

"I don't need your help."

In the misty yellow gaslight, Hawk's teeth gleamed. "She might."

When Tessa heard a masculine voice, she rushed to the landing. Gravesend followed Tristan, who strode into the great hall. "It's after midnight," her faithful butler said. "My mistress is not receiving."

"Gravesend, I'll make an exception," she said.

Tristan looked up. The cold look in his blue eyes startled her. He knew.

Her butler shuffled off, mumbling under his breath.

The clip of Tristan's boots on the marble floor echoed in the silent house. He strode up the steps, never taking his icy gaze off her. When he reached the landing, he came so close to her, she instinctively started to take a step back but stopped. Though he towered over her, she lifted her chin. "Will you join me in the drawing room?"

He gave her a curt nod and opened the door.

"May I offer you a brandy?" she said, heading toward the sideboard.

The door clicked shut. "You may offer me an explanation."

The brusque tone of his voice made her turn. He stood near the door, looking every inch the haughty duke. A very tall, very angry duke.

"Shall we be seated?" she said, as if nothing were untoward.

He strode up to her so fast she gasped. "How long have you known about Miss Fielding's engagement to Viscount Hunter?"

She bristled at his accusing tone. "Since Mrs. Fielding and her daughter called on me at three o'clock this afternoon. I sent three missives to your town house, but you never answered. Where were you?"

"I owe you no explanations."

"I tried my best to inform you. It's not my fault you were from home."

His eyes narrowed. "What I want to know is why you invited Miss Fielding to participate when she was courting another man?"

"I questioned her about Hunter before inviting her to the courtship."

"You knew?" he said in an outraged voice. "You invited her even though you knew about her feelings for Hunter?"

"She told me she'd given up on him last year. Hunter dragged his feet too long. Evidently your interest in Miss Fielding spurred him. He must have realized he stood to lose her."

"I'm happy to have been of service." Tristan strode over to the fireplace and leaned his hands on the mantel.

"When they called today, I reminded Miss Fielding and her mother that the girls were not allowed to court other men," Tessa said. "They claimed Hunter showed up unexpectedly yesterday and made her an offer of marriage."

Tristan huffed. "And you believed them?"

"Of course I found their explanation suspect, but she accepted Hunter, so it is of no importance now."

"No importance?" he said, gripping the marble mantelpiece.

An exasperated sigh escaped her. "Why are you so vexed?"

He glanced over his shoulder, his blue eyes freezing her. "Imagine my shock when Hunter announced his betrothal at my club tonight."

She winced, realizing he'd taken a blow to his pride. "I'm sorry you found out that way."

"Sorry? That's all you have to say?" He raked her with a scathing look. "I trusted you. If you had done your duty, it never would have happened."

"I did the best I could. And if you will calm down, you will realize it is better to learn now that she still holds feelings for Hunter."

"What if I had found out too late? What if I had married her only to find out she secretly yearned for Hunter?"

"If she had married you, she would have had to relinquish all feelings for him."

"And if she didn't?"

She inhaled. "What are you suggesting?"

"When I gave you the bridal requirements, I specified my future wife should have an unblemished reputation."

"I would not have invited the girls if they did not have excellent reputations," she said.

"Do you even know if any of them are courting other men?"

"I'm sure we would have heard."

His eyes narrowed. "The same way we heard about Miss Fielding?"

"How was I supposed to know Hunter would renew his addresses to her?" she said, her voice rising.

"You needn't concern yourself. I intend to discover everything I can about the others. Something you should have done in the first place."

"I relied on reports of their characters, as anyone would do."

"You did not even try. Did it ever occur to you that their families may have covered up indiscretions?"

She scoffed. "God forbid you should find out one of them allowed a man to kiss her."

He stiffened. "Touché."

Her stomach clenched. She'd not meant to refer to their forbidden kiss.

He executed a stiff bow. "Good-bye, Miss Mansfield."

She gasped. As he strode away, she hurried after him. "Tristan, wait, please."

He reached the door. Then he leaned against it.

She walked up behind him. "Tristan, I'm so sorry. I—"

"No apologies."

"But I knew your pride—"

"Say no more."

"Please listen. When Caroline told me she no longer cared for Hunter, I believed her to be sincere," she said. "To be honest, I thought you would shrug it off. After all, you told the girls they could withdraw at any time."

"You don't understand." He pushed away from the door and regarded her with a bleak expression. "I will not marry a woman who is apt to betray me. The scandal would hurt my mother and sister."

Evidently Caroline's defection had touched off some wound deep inside him. "Tristan, did someone betray you?"

A long moment passed before he responded. "Not me."

She searched his eyes, the question unspoken.

"My father was unfaithful to my mother."

"It must have hurt her very much," she whispered. And him as well.

"She forgave him," he said. "She always did."

Her heart ached for his mother. "She loved him."

"It is her favorite illusion."

Oh, dear God. Tristan had only been seventeen when his father died. He must have been young when he'd learned about his father's indiscretions. She could only guess at his confusion over his mother's feelings and his disillusion over his parents' unhappy marriage.

No wonder he didn't believe in love.

He cleared his throat. "You should have told me about Miss Fielding at the very start. From now on, you will report everything you learn about the girls, even if it is only a rumor. Is there anything else you haven't told me?" he asked.

She had no choice but to prevaricate. "I've nothing to report about the other girls."

"You must be honest with me. If I make a mistake, I'll have to live with it for the rest of my life. And I will not risk marrying a woman who might bring disgrace upon me and my family."

She lowered her gaze, unable to look him in the eyes.

He bade her good night and strode out.

Her stomach churned as she shut the door. Tristan demanded honesty and an unblemished reputation. He had every right to both.

She had neither.

Tristan walked into her foyer. The elderly butler's weathered face puffed up like a toad as he handed over Tristan's greatcoat, gloves, and hat.

When Tristan donned his hat, the butler had the audacity to scowl at him.

Tristan gave him his best ducal glare.

"No man mistreats my mistress," Gravesend said in his gravelly voice.

The old man's words pummeled his gut. Hell, he'd burst into her home after midnight and taken out his humiliation on her. The devil. He'd mistreated her.

Tristan glanced out into the great hall, knowing he should go upstairs. And, damn it, apologize.

"Don't even think of going to her. You've bothered the little missy long enough."

Little missy? Tristan eyed the old man, remembering she'd told him the butler was her long-time favored servant. Well, hell.

The butler opened the door. Tristan gave him a curt nod and strode out, holding on to his hat as the chilly wind buffeted him. Turmoil roiled inside him. He'd let his anger overrule him tonight, and then he'd confessed about his father's infidelity.

What had possessed him? He'd buried his father thirteen years ago without a backward glance. For reasons he could not understand, Tessa had managed to penetrate his cool reserve. From now on, he would keep their discussions solely focused on the courtship. And he'd damn well better stop imagining her naked in his bed.

His driver jumped down and opened the door as Tristan approached. The light rain doused one of the two oil lamps at the gate. He'd almost reached the carriage when he noticed a hackney cab stationed half a block away. The square was empty otherwise. Suddenly, the hackney lurched into motion. Tristan watched as it circled the square and rolled away into the night.

The back of his neck prickled. London was a dangerous place, full of thieves and cutthroats. A woman alone was an easy target for ruffians.

"Hold a moment," Tristan said to his driver. Then he strode back up the walk and banged the knocker.

Gravesend opened the door and lifted his candle. "What now?" he said in a surly voice.

Tristan held his temper with an effort. "There was a

suspicious hackney down the street. You should keep extra vigil to ensure your mistress's safety."

Gravesend's weathered eyes filled with alarm. "Thank you, Your Grace. I'll set footmen to keep watch."

Tristan nodded and returned to his carriage, feeling a bit foolish. A thief wouldn't travel by hackney and risk the driver's remembering his face. Probably it was only a dandy, too drunk to recall where he lived. He almost convinced himself there was no cause for concern, but he worried about her all the same.

Chapter Nine

The roar of voices filled the King's Theatre in Haymarket.

Tessa's nerves jittered as she and Jane entered the duke's box. It was the largest one in the theater. Across the wide expanse of the horseshoe-shaped auditorium, the crème de la crème filled five tiers of ornately carved boxes. Their heads swerved in Tessa's direction. The tall feathers in the ladies' coiffures bobbed as they leaned toward one another, whispering and pointing with their fans.

Her mouth dried like dead winter leaves. She told herself not to allow their stares to bother her. After all, she'd known the duke's courtship would garner attention from every corner. But knowing in the abstract was quite different from the reality. She felt exposed, quite like one of those horrifying dreams where she found herself naked in a crowd.

Behind her, Jane gasped. "I had no idea the theatre was so enormous. Look how the light sparkles like stars."

Jewels winked from the reflection of the chandeliers suspended from brackets along each tier of boxes. The lack of glass shades, however, resulted in a profusion of wax dripping down into the pit.

"I will take my place in the chair at the back of the box," Jane said.

Tessa nodded absently as she scanned the interior. Tristan stood close to the balcony, surrounded by all the bridal candidates. The duchess sat chatting with Julianne and Hawk.

"There is Miss Mansfield."

Startled by Tristan's voice, Tessa met his gaze. His long, muscular legs showed to advantage as he strode toward her, a bright smile on his handsome face. He wore a black coat with gilt buttons. His white silk waistcoat made a dramatic contrast.

When he halted before her, she smiled. "You look every inch the most eligible and handsome bachelor in England."

His appreciative gaze swept over her blue satin dress, the netting and blond lace a frilly departure from the simpler styles she usually favored. "And you, my lady, are positively the most ravishing matchmaker I've ever known."

"Quite probably the only one you know."

He laughed.

Her heart thudded as she drank in his smile. Then reality intruded. Her only role in his life was to ensure he chose a wife for love. After what she'd learned about his parents' troubled marriage, she was even more determined to see that he found a bride capable of breaching the fortress he'd erected round his heart.

She glanced at the bridal candidates, noting that the duchess, Julianne, and Hawk now stood with the circle of girls. "Shall we join the others?" she asked.

When he offered his arm, she set her gloved hand on his sleeve. Awareness of his warm body engulfed her. The faint scent of his masculine cologne aroused forbidden yearnings in her. He glanced down at her with a boyish, lopsided grin, making his escort seem suddenly intimate. Her heart fluttered.

When they reached the young ladies, Elizabeth glared at her. Tessa withdrew from Tristan's escort and smiled, determined to rise above Elizabeth's cattiness. Elizabeth ignored her and took the opportunity to commandeer Tristan's arm. Unable to bear the sight, Tessa turned away.

Her gaze settled on Amy Hardwick. The shy girl looked elegant tonight in a jade gown that draped her slim, tall figure. She'd cut her hair, taming the frizzy red locks into soft curls.

Tessa walked over to Amy, who stood between Georgette and Julianne. "You look stunning in that gown," she said, careful to keep her voice low.

Julianne locked arms with Amy. "Isn't she lovely?" She exchanged a conspiratorial wink with Georgette.

Amy blushed. "Georgette and Julianne are responsible for my new look."

"I approve."

Lord Hawkfield sauntered over and fisted his hand on his hip. "I declare I've never seen so many pretty girls. And not a one has even the slightest interest in me."

Tessa lifted her brows. "I shall be happy to find you a bride, my lord."

Hawkfield held up his hands as if warding her off. "Have mercy on this confirmed bachelor."

Tessa laughed. Then she surveyed the group and noted that Tristan had extricated himself from Elizabeth. Satisfied, Tessa strolled about, mingling with the other girls.

A few minutes later, the duchess approached. "Miss Mansfield, I believe the performance is imminent, but my scamp of a son has managed to disappear. Will you find him while I direct the girls to their seats?"

"Yes, of course." She walked to the back of the box, where a footman stood, guarding the entrance. Tessa frowned. Perhaps Tristan had dashed out to the facilities. With a sigh, she applied her fan and turned to watch the duchess herd the girls. Her lips twitched at the duchess's obvious exasperation when the bridal candidates kept exchanging seats.

The duchess looked back at Tessa and lifted her quizzing glass to her eye. Tessa shrugged. The duchess lowered the glass and made a shooing motion with her hand. With a groan, Tessa walked out into the corridor and halted.

Tristan stood a few feet away with his back to her. A tall, dark-haired woman leaned against him and whispered in his ear. It was the widow, Lady Endicott, the woman Tessa had seen him with at Anne's ball.

Wave after wave of shock crashed over her.

When Lady Endicott saw Tessa, a smug smile played on her lips. Tessa itched to slap the hussy.

Lady Endicott stepped back, blew him a kiss, and sauntered off, swaying her hips. Tristan turned, met Tessa's gaze, and winced.

She whirled around.

"Wait," he called out.

She stood still, clenching and unclenching her shaking hands. He was having a liaison with that woman.

He strode up behind her and turned her to face him. "It's not what you think."

She snapped her fan shut. "How dare you sneak out with that hussy when you are supposed to be courting the girls?"

"I saw her talking to the footman and took her outside before someone saw her," he said in an undertone.

"You should have instructed the footman to turn her away, but you wanted to flirt with her."

A couple walked past, eyeing the two of them with open curiosity. When they were out of earshot, Tessa returned her livid gaze to him. "You're still involved with her, aren't you?"

"No," he said under his breath. "I ended it the night I met you."

"Don't lie to me. I saw her touching you. You didn't even try to stop her."

He leaned down. "Did you expect me to push her away?"

"A simple no would have sufficed." She inhaled. "How could you? What if your mother had stepped out here? What if the girls had seen you?"

"Even if I wanted her, I wouldn't dare act upon the feeling. I've told you more than once I'll not subject my family to scandal," he said. "And I certainly wouldn't risk it for a woman I know is trouble."

"You just did." She glared at him. "Your mother already marked your absence. We'd better return before she becomes suspicious."

He took her arm, led her inside, and stopped. His jaw worked as if he were battling some inner demon. "It won't happen again," he muttered.

A sliver of doubt lodged in her heart. Women chased him and freely offered themselves. Despite his vow to remain faithful to his wife, she feared he would yield to temptation in a moment of weakness.

The same way she'd yielded to him at Ashdown House. A swift burning sensation flared in her chest. She was a hypocrite.

He drew closer to her. "She means nothing to me." He hung his head. "But, my friend, you do."

"You're trying to sweet-talk me so I'll forgive you."

He glanced at her from beneath his lashes. "I didn't know I had it in me. Must be your influence," he said.

She swatted his arm with her fan. "Your rakish tricks won't work on me."

"I made a mistake. Will you forgive me?" he said.

She'd made plenty of mistakes in her life. God knew she'd give anything for a second chance. He'd admitted he was wrong. She'd come this far with him and decided to relent just this once. "Don't do it again."

He crossed his finger over his heart. "I won't."

Even though she knew he meant to charm her, her lips twitched. The rogue.

Several of the girls turned to look at them. Tessa forced herself to concentrate on the courtship. "Which one of the lucky girls will you interview first?"

He didn't hesitate. "Lady Georgette."

Hot jealousy raged like wildfire inside her. She struggled with the ugly emotion as his words came back to haunt her. *I want to want my wife.* He'd kissed and touched her, making her feel desired and wanted. The memory she'd secretly cherished crumbled like dry toast as she conjured up a vivid image of him kissing Georgette. She wanted to press her hands against her temples and push the picture out of her brain.

He glanced down at her. Fearing he would see her jealousy, she averted her gaze. "Shall I fetch her?" Her voice cracked a bit.

"No." An awkward pause followed. "I'll go."

Tessa watched as he made his way to Georgette and led her to the two chairs set apart in the front of the box. He bent his head, listening to something she said. With his jet hair and her sunshine-yellow curls, they made a striking couple.

A thousand knives stabbed Tessa's heart. Everything inside her cried out possessively, *he is mine*.

She wrenched her gaze away, fearing someone might see. That was the moment she saw the other girls watching the couple. Their tormented expressions mirrored the wretched emotions roiling inside her.

The realization brought on a wave of humiliation. She was reacting as if she were one of his bridal candidates. No, she was acting like a pathetic spinster, but that was nothing new. Whenever she attended to her correspondences these days, she found herself staring at nothing as she remembered something he'd said. Whenever she read the papers, she looked for news of him. Whenever the knocker rapped, she caught her breath, wondering if it was him.

She knew he drummed his fingers when he was impatient. She knew he stretched out his long legs when he was relaxed. She knew he liked cake and did not take cream in his tea. And every time he called, her heart leaped with giddy excitement. As if she were a young, eligible belle and he was her beau. Oh, God, had he noticed?

She could not bear the thought and prayed he didn't know. For weeks now, she'd deluded herself in the worst possible way. She'd seen no harm in befriending him. She'd thought her nightly fantasies harmless. She'd not known how much it would hurt to watch him court the most beautiful young lady in the Beau Monde.

Tonight was only a taste of what she could expect in the coming weeks. He was not her beau. He was only her friend, and even that was forbidden. She'd known it when he'd asked her to agree to a more familiar address. And she'd said yes, even though she'd fallen under his seductive spell at Ashdown House and allowed him indecent liberties.

Tessa glanced at his profile and thought about all the times he'd teased her. She'd enjoyed bantering with him. With dawning insight, she realized she'd encouraged his flirtation because she liked being the center of his attention.

Oh, dear God, what must he think of her? The answer sent another wave of humiliation through her: a lonely spinster starved for a man's attention.

The swish of skirts alerted her. Two young women walked toward her. Both Charlotte Longham and Catherine Cresswell had determined looks on their faces, looks that spelled trouble. Tessa regarded them warily.

"Miss Mansfield," Catherine said. "May we speak frankly?"

"Is something the matter?" she asked, her voice too sharp.

The two exchanged surprised glances.

With considerable effort, Tessa donned a disinterested mask. She must not let her anguish show.

"You tell her," Charlotte said.

Catherine fidgeted.

"What is it?" Tessa asked, growing impatient.

"We thought you should know Georgette is taking unfair advantage," Catherine said in a rush.

Tessa lifted her brows. Although she wasn't fond of Georgette, she must never show it. "Ladies, unless you have solid proof of wrongdoing on her part, I advise you not to tread down this path."

Charlotte's expression turned indignant. "Oh, we have proof. All the girls are talking about the way she has befriended Lady Julianne."

"Indeed," Catherine said. "Elizabeth saw her eating ices at Gunther's with the duke's sister last week."

"And Henrietta saw them shopping together," Charlotte added.

"Georgette is pretending to be Lady Julianne's friend so she can influence his sister to put in a good word for her," Catherine said in a childish, whining tone. "It's unfair."

"I see," Tessa said, measuring her words. "And Elizabeth and Henrietta took the two of you into their confidence?"

"We discussed it when we all met at Elizabeth's house yesterday," Charlotte said.

"Except for Amy Hardwick," Catherine said. "Everyone knows Georgette is pretending to be Amy's friend, so the duke will think she is kind."

Obviously Elizabeth and Henrietta had stepped up

their manipulative campaign to ensure the other girls ostracized Georgette. "I wonder why Elizabeth and Henrietta did not confide in me."

Catherine and Charlotte exchanged nervous glances.

"Did they ask you to speak to me?" Tessa said.

Charlotte shook her head. "No, but they thought someone should. When no one volunteered, Catherine and I decided to inform you."

Tessa was tempted to ask the two empty-headed girls if they had questioned why neither Elizabeth nor Henrietta had volunteered to tattle, but she held her tongue. The stage curtain rose, and a hush fell over the crowd, signaling the beginning of the performance. "Is there anything else?"

Neither of the girls spoke.

"In that case, please return to your seats."

Charlotte lifted her nose in the air. "I think we did the right thing by reporting to you, Miss Mansfield."

"You assume too much," she said, her eyes narrowing. "There is no stipulation against befriending Lady Julianne. More important, you did not actually witness the events. It is hearsay as far as I'm concerned."

Charlotte's chest heaved. "Well, Elizabeth and Henrietta saw her with their own eyes."

"They made sure all of you knew about it," Tessa said. "Yet they did not report to me. But if you believe they have your best interests at heart, who am I to naysay?"

Both Charlotte and Catherine stared at her with stunned expressions.

As Tessa escorted them to their seats, she couldn't help but wonder if Georgette *was* taking advantage of Julianne to improve her own chances with Tristan.

• • •

At intermission, Tessa stood with all the girls, only half listening to the conversation swirling around her. Her traitorous thoughts kept returning to Tristan's lengthy interview with Georgette. The entire time, she'd kept glancing over at the two of them, despising herself. The worst part was that he'd not singled out any of the other candidates.

She glanced at him. He stood near the balcony, speaking to Hawk. When he met her gaze, Tessa looked away, fearing her tumultuous emotions showed on her face.

A few moments later, Tristan approached. The girls crowded round him, all except Georgette and Amy. They stood apart, whispering with Julianne. Georgette glanced over her shoulder at Tristan. A sweet smile spread across her pretty face, emphasizing her twin dimples. Tristan returned her smile. Then Georgette's curly lashes lowered. She returned her attention to Amy and Julianne, a perfectly correct, perfectly ladylike response.

A fist slammed into Tessa's heart. She had no right to be jealous. If she were truly his friend, she would be happy for him. But she wasn't. Because even though she could never have him, she didn't want the prettiest girl to have him either.

She stared at Georgette, wondering if the blond beauty had befriended Julianne as a means of gaining advantage in the competition. Was she a calculating witch? Or had she formed an honest friendship with Tristan's sister? Tessa could not trust her judgment because she could not be objective.

Soon all the girls' parents invaded the box. Tristan shook hands with their fathers. The mothers crowded around the duchess. The excited chatter flowed. Tessa made an effort to greet the girls' mothers, but they paid scant attention to her. She wandered through the crowd, smiling and trying not to look as insignificant as she felt, but the effort seemed fruitless. Why bother when no one even noticed?

She started toward the back of the box, intending to speak to Jane, but halted when she saw her companion conversing with Mr. Hodges, the young man she'd danced with at Anne's ball. Not wishing to disturb the couple, Tessa walked to the balcony, staring sightlessly at the milling people in the pit below.

After seeing Tristan with Georgette, she suspected he would choose her. Probably soon. After tonight, it would all be over except for the formalities. The thought made her heart ache.

Did he hold tender feelings for Georgette? Did Georgette love him? Or was it to be a dynastic marriage? Tessa sighed. She'd hoped to open his heart to love and further her matchmaking career. Foolishly, she'd thought her role as his matchmaker would garner her respect from the ton. Tonight, they'd ignored her as if she were little better than a servant. Nothing she did would ever change their opinion of her.

Was she doomed to fail him and herself?

Tessa squared her shoulders, determined not to give up on him. As for society, they could go hang for all she cared. But she did care because her career meant a great deal to her. She'd helped many young women make happy marriages and changed their lives forever. Given them what she could never have.

"What are you doing standing here all alone?"

Tristan's deep voice startled her. "Oh, you surprised me," she said, pressing a hand to her fast-beating heart.

He stepped beside her. "What were you contemplating?"

She shrugged. "I wondered about your interview with Georgette." There, she'd sounded perfectly disinterested.

"She is vivacious, as I expected."

Tessa wet her dry lips. "You found her agreeable?"

"I liked her well enough."

An understated response if she'd ever heard one. Tessa glanced at him. "She must be elated. You spent the entire first half with her."

"I didn't realize so much time had passed until the curtain came down."

Tessa's heart plummeted like a brick to her stomach. He had been so taken with Georgette that he'd forgotten all about the other girls.

"There they are," the duchess called out in a hearty tone.

They both turned at the sound of his mother's voice. The duchess approached with Anne in tow.

Tessa drew closer to Tristan. "I invited Lord and Lady Broughton to call at intermission," she said in an undertone. "I hope you do not mind."

"Of course not," he said. "But where is Broughton?"

Anne quivered with excitement as she rushed up. "Oh," she said pressing a hand to her heart.

"Anne, what is it?" Tessa asked, frowning.

"Geoffrey said I must ask permission first. Your Grace, may I bring a guest? He is waiting with my husband in the corridor."

"Your friend is welcome," Tristan said.

Stunned by her friend's presumption, Tessa gave Anne a speaking look. "Who is he?"

"I mean to surprise you." Anne bobbed a curtsey, whirled round, and hurried away.

The duchess lifted her quizzing glass and inspected Tessa. "You do not look eager to meet this gentleman."

"I'm stunned, to be honest." Tessa turned her attention to Tristan. "I must apologize for her."

He shook his head. "I don't mind meeting a friend of Broughton's."

Tessa wondered why Broughton would send Anne to ask permission, but didn't voice the words.

Tristan craned his head and lifted his hand in greeting. "Ah, there is Broughton and his wife now. I don't see the other fellow."

Tessa looked about, but could not see over the tall people blocking her view.

"Come, let us meet them," the duchess said.

As they pressed through the crowd, Tessa tried to think of a reasonable explanation for Anne's odd behavior and failed.

The duchess regarded her with a crafty expression. "Perhaps your friend means to make a match for you."

Heat rushed to her face, knowing Tristan must have heard his mother. "She would never embarrass me in front of everyone." But she realized Anne's intentions would not matter. The duchess had made the assumption and others would, too. Tessa cringed as she imagined others taking note of the introduction. Oh, why had she not taken Anne aside and demanded an explanation? Everything had happened so quickly, she'd not had a chance.

Many stared as they passed. Tessa lifted her chin, determined not to show her discomfort. They had almost reached the back of the box when she saw Lord Broughton.

Next to him, Anne stood speaking to a short, muscular gentleman with curly blond hair. He stood with his face in profile. A prickling sensation stung the backs of Tessa's hands. There was something familiar about him.

The curly-headed man turned and gazed directly into Tessa's eyes. Icy shock cascaded over her. *Oh, no. Oh, no, no, no.*

Tessa halted. All the blood drained from her head.

"Miss Mansfield, are you unwell?" the duchess asked.

Her voice seemed far, far away.

Anne rushed forward and took Tessa's hands. "Is it not a miracle?" she said, her voice breaking. "My brother came home."

The crowd stirred, the low voices buzzing in Tessa's ears.

Anne released her and stepped aside. Lieutenant Richard Mortland limped forward and paused less than a foot away from Tessa. A moon-shaped scar curved from his eyebrow to his cheek. Fine lines crinkled at the corners of his puppylike brown eyes. His smile held a slightly sad quality. "Hello, Tessa."

Gasps reverberated round the box.

It took a moment for her deadened brain to comprehend the reason for the uproar. *Good God, he had called her by her Christian name.*

"I beg your pardon, Miss Mansfield." Richard glanced down and scuffed the toe of his shoe on the floor. "I did not mean, that is to say, I meant no offense. Please forgive my dreadful error."

Anne placed her hand on Richard's shoulder. "Of course Tessa will forgive you." She looked round. "We all knew one another when Miss Mansfield came to live with her uncle. My father was the vicar, so we called upon Lord Wentworth often."

Tessa released her pent-up breath. Anne's explanation had covered up Richard's mistake, though Tessa suspected he'd done it on purpose. But why would he? And where had he been for two years? It was as if he'd risen from the dead.

Richard's eyes lit with interest when Lord Broughton introduced Tristan and the duchess.

Everyone in the crowd squeezed closer. Lord Broughton cleared his throat and addressed them. He explained that his wife's brother had been reported missing in action at Toulouse and had been presumed dead. During the battle, he had been wounded and left behind. While the battle raged, a peasant French family discovered him. "He hovered near death, nursed by the kind family for two years," Broughton said.

Richard kissed his sister's cheek, a gesture that sent waves of feminine sighs through the crowd. Several ladies dabbed handkerchiefs at their eyes.

"I hope you will all forgive the disturbance tonight," Lord Broughton said. "My wife and I ask you to share our joy in Lieutenant Mortland's return."

A round of applause followed. Richard inclined his head, obviously basking in the admiration.

Tessa glanced at the crowd. The explanation about the French family sounded suspicious to her. Was she the only one who questioned the validity of the tale? Of course he would invent such a fantastic story. But really, how could he explain a total lack of communication for two years?

Thank heavens Uncle George wasn't here to witness this travesty. In truth, she was glad all the attention centered on

Richard. Years ago, he'd dreamed of rubbing shoulders with the ton. Now that he'd won their esteem, he would likely ignore her and focus on more impressive acquaintances.

With so many eyes upon her, she must regain her composure. "Anne, I am so happy for you."

"I knew you would be overjoyed," Anne said.

She tried to smile, but she could not.

Richard cupped his hand and whispered to Anne. She turned to Tessa. "Richard has something he wishes to ask you."

Pins pricked her hands again. She heard feminine sighs. No doubt the ladies all thought him handsome and heroic, his limp proof of his duty to his country. In all fairness, he had served his country. Clearly he had been injured. Guilt seized her for a moment, but sanity returned as she recalled the choice he'd made long ago.

The buzz of voices dwindled as they waited to hear his words. Richard dipped his chin in a boyish manner. She knew better than to fall for that trick. He'd used it to coax her eight years ago, but she was no longer a naïve eighteen-year-old girl.

"I hoped you would take a turn with me in the foyer," he said.

"You are kind, *Lieutenant Mortland*, but I would not take you from your sister after your recent reunion." She'd allowed her voice to carry, deliberately emphasizing the proper address, a counterpoint to his earlier indiscretion.

Anne shook her head. "You mustn't worry on my account. How could I deny such a simple pleasure to my brother and my dearest friend?"

Panic seized her. She could not go anywhere alone with Richard. "I am obliged to assist the duke this evening."

Anne's brows furrowed. "Surely you can spare a few moments."

"My duty is to His Grace."

Her words caused a ripple of whispers among the crowd. She knew her refusal was creating a scene, but she refused to let Richard trap her.

The duchess intervened. "Gel, no one will think less of you for taking a turn with the lieutenant." She regarded her son. "Tristan?"

Tessa poured all her entreaty into her eyes. *Tristan, can you not see how much I wish to avoid this man?*

"Miss Mansfield is free to do as she pleases," he said.

Everyone stared. She wished the floor would crack open and swallow her. Richard held out his arm. "Will you take a turn with me?"

She saw Anne's bewildered expression and knew she had no choice but to comply. Revulsion shot through her as she took his arm. The brief, triumphant look in his eyes sparked resentment inside her. He had planned to ask her in public, so she could not refuse. Furious with him for coercing her, she gave him a haughty look worthy of a queen.

As they departed, Tessa noted the censorious stares directed at her and knew she'd erred badly. No doubt they thought her behavior ill-bred. To them, Richard was a war hero, returned to the bosom of his family. He had deceived them with his charm and self-effacing manner, the same way he had deceived her eight years ago.

Chapter Ten

When Richard led her into the crowded corridor, Tessa placed a serene smile on her face because others were watching. No matter what happened, she must keep her composure. She could not afford to make another mistake.

She could endure a short walk with the man she loathed.

They descended the stairs. "You must forgive my earlier indiscretion," he said. "I was so overwhelmed when I saw you that I completely forgot the proprieties."

Too bad he'd not been dumbstruck. Did he actually think she would believe him? Well, why wouldn't he? Eight years ago, she'd fallen for every honeyed word that dripped from his lips.

As they minced about the foyer, Tessa surveyed the crowd. Many had taken notice of her appearance with a stranger. She could well imagine their mocking thoughts. *The spinster matchmaker has found herself a man.*

After everything that had happened, why would he ask

her to take a turn with him? Years ago, she'd learned the hard way he'd only wanted her fortune. Tessa doubted anything had changed.

He let out a loud sigh. "Must you treat me in this cold manner? I hoped to renew our friendship."

Satan would ice skate in Hades before that happened. "Is that the reason you insisted upon walking with me?"

"I wished to speak to you privately because there are things I cannot say in Anne's presence."

"The words are better left unsaid."

"Will you not allow me to apologize?"

"You have done so. Twice."

"I meant for the terrible way we parted all those years ago."

"Very well. I accept." She inclined her head. "Now we may return."

He regarded her with a mournful expression. "I cannot allow this to pass so easily."

"You're not planning to beat your breast and weep copious tears, I hope."

"Still the little vixen, aren't you?" he said in an exaggerated, seductive tone.

She held her tongue, hoping her silence would speak for itself.

His gaze lowered to her mouth. "You've no idea how often I thought of you."

She might have fallen for such a trick eight years ago, but she wouldn't now. "As much as you thought of your sister?"

"I missed you both."

"Ah, I begin to comprehend. You pined so much you couldn't bear to write Anne for two whole years."

"My severe wounds prevented me. My recuperation took many months." He sighed. "My recollection of that time is vague."

How convenient. "The French family could not write for you?"

"They were illiterate peasants."

"Naturally they could find no one in all of France to send correspondence to your family."

"It is quite impossible for a lady to understand. The confusion and difficulties of life in a war-torn country are overwhelming. Even Wellington did not know Napoleon had abdicated when he commanded the battle at Toulouse."

"I confess I am befuddled. Did the war not end nearly a year ago?"

He led her to the perimeter of the foyer. "You do not believe me. Even my limp is not proof enough for you."

"I am sorry for your suffering, but you made your choice."

"It was no choice." His puppy eyes filled with feigned pain. "Your uncle would have told you differently, but he gave me no option."

Richard had no idea she'd heard every word he'd spoken to her uncle.

He stopped before a painting depicting Venus and Mars in a lover's embrace. "I still have feelings for you," he whispered.

She inhaled sharply and tried to jerk her hand away, but he clamped his fingers over her own. For the space of a heartbeat, fear squeezed her lungs, but she would never let him see he'd discomposed her. She straightened her spine and regarded him with all the hauteur she could muster. "The air in this crowd is stifling. Please return me to the box now."

"No, let me say these words," he said. "I've kept them bottled inside for eight years. I was willing to risk everything for you because I lo—"

"Hush." She almost left him on the spot, but she couldn't return to the box alone without stirring up more gossip. Others had already marked her animosity toward Richard. She didn't dare give them more ammunition.

He closed his eyes momentarily as if he were in pain. "Forgive me. I was overcome with emotion. This is neither the time nor the place."

"Now that you are recovered, let us return to the box. I have duties."

"Not until you allow me to reassure you."

He obviously thought she was still the same stupid girl who had believed everything he said. "I neither want nor need reassurance from the likes of you," she said in a warning tone.

"I was not to the manor born," he said, "but I am a gentleman. What transpired all those years ago will never pass my lips."

But once it had.

"You doubt me," he said. "I am not the selfish being you suppose me, but I'm no fool either. I would never risk the condemnation of my family and all of society."

She had multiple reasons to distrust him, but whether she trusted him or not mattered little. In truth, she had no choice but to depend upon his discretion.

"After I left home, I worried about you," he said, "but I could not write, not without risking your uncle's wrath."

"I do not wish to hear another word." He had never

cared about her. She had overheard him say as much to her uncle.

His brandy-soaked breath soughed over her cheek. "I wrote a few lines to Anne before I left for the Continent. All I could do was inquire after your health. Anything else might have caused suspicion."

Her stomach roiled. He'd referred to the letter Anne had given her only a week ago. She gazed at the painting without really seeing it.

"Can we not be friends?" he asked.

He had extended the olive branch, so she would take it for Anne's sake, with conditions. "Out of respect for your sister, we will maintain a polite acquaintance."

"I suppose I must accept, though I hope in time we can be friends again."

All she would ever offer him was a truce, and that only because of Anne. Though she would never let down her guard, he had allayed her worst fears. He would not reveal their secrets because he had as much to lose as she did.

Tristan gripped the balcony rail, his back to his guests. He could not walk about, making small talk. Hot anger swirled through his veins. He still wanted to plant his fist in Mortland's face.

How dare that upstart, that nobody, call her Tessa? The insolent cad had staked a claim on her in front of everyone. She'd only stood there, staring at him as if she'd seen a ghost. What else could she have done? While Lady Broughton had made excuses about youthful acquaintances, Tristan did not believe it was a slip of the tongue.

The lout had played the crowd like a card sharp. Tristan recognized the type. His father had manipulated his mother with lies and half truths. Tristan had learned at an early age not to fall for his promises and excuses. He certainly wasn't falling for Mortland's dubious tale. Unfortunately, he feared Tessa would not see through the lieutenant.

Perhaps he wasn't giving her due credit. After all, she had refused more than once to take a turn with Mortland. But Tristan couldn't forget the imploring look she'd given him when his mother had urged him to give permission for her to leave. Had Tessa secretly wanted to take a turn with Mortland?

Tristan clenched his teeth. The devil, couldn't she see the man was unworthy of her? He'd called her by her Christian name, damn it all. No honorable man treated a lady with such disrespect.

He bowed his head, remembering the night he'd kissed and touched her. Who was he to point an accusing finger?

Hawk approached, standing silently for a while. "Did you eat something rotten? Your complexion is a nasty shade of green."

"The devil take you."

Hawk leaned his hip against the balcony rail. "Jealous?"

Tristan muttered a particularly foul curse.

Hawk's shoulders shook with laughter.

"Damn it, I'm worried about her."

"Did you know about Mortland?" Hawk asked.

He nodded. "Broughton told me he was investigating Mortland's disappearance. It was clear he thought the man dead. Who would not after two years without a word?"

"No doubt the French family consisted of a lonely war widow," Hawk said.

"Everyone else seemed taken in by his story." Tristan's jaw worked. "I'm worried Miss Mansfield fell for it, too."

"I doubt it. She seemed reluctant to walk out with him."

He wanted to believe Hawk, but he couldn't forget her beseeching look, one he couldn't interpret. "The way he persisted makes me think he has designs on her." Had she wanted to go, or had she made a silent plea for him to rescue her?

"He's probably sniffing after her fortune."

"I've got to protect her," Tristan muttered.

"You ought to protect him," Hawk said. "She rather looked as if she wanted to murder him when they left here."

"They've been gone too long. I must go to her," Tristan said.

Hawk made a sound of disgust. "Nine of the most eligible belles in the ton are vying for your attention, and you want to chase after the only one who isn't."

Tristan felt as if he'd fallen off a rearing horse and knocked his brains about. He'd not even given the bridal candidates more than a cursory thought. Even during his conversation with Georgette, his mind had wandered as she'd chattered nonstop. In shock, he realized he rarely thought about any of them unless they were present. But he thought about Tessa every single day. And night. Especially at night when images of her naked in his bed stole into his head.

Hawk peered at him. "You look as if a lightning bolt just struck you. What is between you and Miss Mansfield?"

Tristan stiffened. "I'm only concerned for her welfare. She has no male relative to see to her protection."

"Brotherly concern, is it?"

"Stubble it, I'm off to rescue her."

"And set all the tongues wagging? Not a good idea, old boy."

"I don't give a rat's arse." Then he strode past the guests, ignoring the invitations to stop and converse. Tessa was in trouble. He must protect her.

When he reached the stairs, Tristan found himself fighting the crowd returning to their seats. He continually muttered pardon as he squeezed past the other patrons.

Once he reached the foyer, he drew in a deep breath, scanning the dwindling crowd. Where was she?

He walked a few paces and then he spotted Tessa. She and Mortland stood before a painting. Tristan slowed his pace. Perhaps he'd worried needlessly. Nothing seemed untoward.

The lieutenant glanced over his shoulder at Tristan. A predatory gleam filled Mortland's eyes. Then he took Tessa's gloved hand and lifted it to his lips, startling her.

A red haze clouded Tristan's vision. He quickened his stride and halted a foot away. Tessa swerved her crimson face toward him. Then she snatched her hand back as if scalded.

Tristan braced his feet in a wide stance and stared daggers at Mortland.

An amused smile lit Mortland's pretty-boy face. "Miss Mansfield, I've obviously kept you from your duties too long."

Tristan offered his arm to Tessa. "May I escort you? The opera will resume shortly."

"Yes, please." Her face still red, she set her fingers on his sleeve.

Mortland bowed. "Thank you for the pleasure of your company, Miss Mansfield. I will relinquish you—for now."

Neither she nor Tristan spoke as they climbed the steps. She dared say nothing, for she was so overset she didn't trust herself to speak. How dare Richard kiss her hand? Oh, he would pass it off as a courtly gesture if she confronted him, but she knew he'd done it on purpose upon seeing Tristan. Richard's timing was no coincidence. She suspected he wanted Tristan and everyone else to think there was a romance blossoming between them. If he thought she would stand for his playing the part of a lovesick beau, he was in for a rude surprise.

After she and Tristan entered the box, the girls' mothers eyed her with suspicion. Tessa surmised they'd been gossiping about her reluctance to walk with the lieutenant. Her long absence and return with Tristan probably had inflamed their poor opinion of her. Doubtless they saw it as another character fault, along with her spinsterhood and her career.

Tristan halted and drew in his breath as if he were about to speak, but Anne appeared at her side, preventing him. He bowed, excused himself, and walked away.

Anne frowned. "Where is Richard?"

"Downstairs." Tessa fisted her gloved hands. He'd not changed at all. Richard had coerced her tonight, but she vowed he never would again.

Anne drew her aside. "Why did you frown when my brother asked you to walk with him?"

"He put me on the spot." Tessa's chest rose and fell with her agitation. "I am disappointed you did not discourage him."

Anne looked taken aback. "I saw no harm."

"In front of all the duke's guests?" Tessa said in a curt tone and winced at Anne's stunned expression.

"But we are all old friends," Anne said. "I never thought you would object or I would have deterred him. The duchess and Shelbourne approved."

"They could hardly refuse with a crowd watching."

"Their approval would not have been necessary had you accepted immediately," Anne said. "Truly, it was intermission, so I do not understand why you tried to beg off."

Tessa shook her head. "I am here for one purpose only—to assist with the duke's courtship. You know I take my matchmaking career seriously. Leaving the box sent a message that I am frivolous."

"I did not mean to make you uncomfortable." Anne worried her hands. "I was so elated over Richard's return I did not stop to think."

Tessa winced. "I understand." Richard had taken advantage of his sister's joy. Tessa knew he would continue to do so.

Anne swallowed visibly. "Geoffrey is angry at Richard for detaining you so long. He told me to reprimand Richard or he would. It is the first time Geoffrey has ever spoken in anger."

"Your husband is not angry with *you*."

"I imagined Richard's homecoming would be a happy occasion, but my thoughtlessness ruined everything." She regarded Tessa with misery. "Geoffrey did not approve of bringing Richard to Shelbourne's box, but I foolishly insisted. I let my impatience overtake my better judgment."

"I understand. It is over now, and we will forget it." But she never would. Despite Richard's claim that he only wanted friendship, his actions proved he'd not changed a bit. He was as calculating as ever.

Richard limped into the box, and Tessa could not suppress the shudder rolling along her spine.

He caught Anne's gaze and made his way over to them. "Anne, I might have known I would find you with Miss Mansfield."

"Richard, apologize to Tessa," Anne said. "You kept her from her duties much too long."

"I was so taken with her I quite forgot the time."

Tessa thought better of refuting him in the crowded box.

Lord Broughton joined them, his expression guarded. "Anne, Richard. We must return to our box," Lord Broughton said. "The performance will resume momentarily."

"Miss Mansfield, my sister and I will call on you soon," Richard said. "I look forward to reminiscing with you."

He knew she could not refuse if Anne accompanied him. If he thought to intimidate her, he was mistaken. "Uncanny, is it not?" she said. "I anticipated you would say those very words."

"Because we are old friends." He smiled.

She stared daggers at him. *No, we are enemies, and you will never corner me again.*

Chapter Eleven

*T*he next day, Tristan and Hawk entered the crimson drawing room for the appointed meeting to discuss the bridal candidates. Tessa sat with Julianne on the sofa across from his mother.

"You are late," the duchess said.

"My apologies." Tristan wished he'd not agreed to this meeting. If he'd given any thought to the courtship, he could tell them he'd already made his choices. Instead, he'd continued to worry about Tessa. He'd lain awake for hours, recollecting her reactions to the lieutenant. Afterward, he'd concluded she did not welcome Mortland's advances, but he could not be certain until he spoke to her. Regardless of how she felt about the lieutenant, Tristan meant to warn her. After what he'd witnessed and heard last night, he felt certain the man was a blackguard.

After they took seats, he glanced at Hawk. His friend's lazy grin hid the serious conversation they'd held before this meeting. At Tristan's request, Hawk planned to ask his cousin, Colonel Henry Bentham, to investigate Mortland's military career. Earlier today, Tristan had hired a Bow Street runner to follow Mortland in town and expose the lieutenant's every move.

Julianne turned to Tessa. "Everyone is agog over you and Lieutenant Mortland. You must tell us everything."

"There is nothing to tell. He is my friend's brother."

Julianne tipped her head. "I think the lieutenant is falling in love with you."

Tristan gripped the arms of his chair.

"Daughter, you are impertinent," the duchess said.

"It is of no significance, Your Grace," Tessa said. "I discourage all gentlemen because I've no intention of marrying."

Julianne's eyes popped wide open. "But why?"

"Because I do not wish to give up my independence or my matchmaking career," Tessa said with a saucy little shake of her head.

Tristan frowned. She'd indicated once before she didn't intend to marry. Every other woman he'd known thought of marriage as if it were the Holy Grail. But then, Tessa wasn't like any other woman he'd ever met.

The duchess fingered the ribbon holding her quizzing glass. "A lady of limited means may take up a respectable position as a companion, but you have no monetary need for a career, let alone a notorious one as a matchmaker."

"I perform a useful service for needy girls who wish to marry," Tessa said. "Last year, I made six successful matches. My career is unconventional, but it is a respectable one. With all due respect, I am performing a similar service for your son."

Hawk jabbed his elbow into Tristan's arm. Tristan jabbed him back.

The duchess glared at them. "Will the pair of you stop acting like schoolboys?"

"We should return to the subject of the courtship," Tristan said.

The duchess waved her hand in dismissal and turned narrowed eyes on Tessa. "Why are you so bent on remaining unwed? It is most unusual."

Tessa shrugged. "My uncle's wealth gave me the gift of freedom. I may do as I please. No man tells me where I may go, what I may purchase, or whom I may befriend."

Julianne clasped her hands and sighed. "Oh, it sounds wonderful."

Tristan glared at his sister. Naturally she ignored him.

Tessa turned toward Julianne. "Gentlemen assume they are superior in intelligence. They believe we are incapable of making sound decisions and insist upon ruling us as if we were little more than children."

Tristan scoffed. "No man of sense wants a senseless wife."

"Then why are girls taught to hide their intelligence in order to attract a husband? Hmmm? I think it is because men are so fragile they cannot bear to admit our sex is every bit as clever as theirs, if not more so," Tessa said.

Hawk pressed his hand to his forehead. "I feel faint. Where are my smelling salts?"

The duchess glared at him. "Will you behave?"

Hawk grinned. "Must I?"

"Enough," Tristan said. "Let us dispense with the courtship business."

Tessa nodded. "I know you are anxious to hear everyone's opinions."

He did not care what anyone thought, but he'd promised to listen.

Tessa turned her attention to Hawk. "Will you share your thoughts about the girls, my lord?"

He released an exaggerated sigh. "Despite my best efforts to charm the ladies, not a single one fell in love with me. I am heartbroken."

Tristan rolled his eyes.

Tessa smiled. "Perhaps Julianne has opinions to share."

"Oh, yes." She sat up straighter. "I like Georgette best. She takes interest in others and is kind to everyone."

"Can you cite an example?" Tessa asked.

Julie nodded. "Georgette wanted to help Amy Hardwick. She is so timid, others ignore her, but Georgette was determined and enlisted my aid. We helped Amy choose flattering gowns and encouraged her to cut her hair. Amy wishes to overcome her shyness."

"You have become bosom friends with Lady Georgette," Tristan said.

"And Miss Hardwick." Julianne's tone sounded defensive.

He tapped his thumb on the arm of his chair. "While you are helping Miss Hardwick, do you speak of me?"

"If you think they are taking advantage of me because of the courtship, you are wrong. They both worried you would think that, but I told them you are fair-minded."

"What I think," he said, "is that you cannot be objective because of your friendship."

"That is not true," Julianne said.

"Have you spent as much time with the other candidates as you have with them?" he asked.

"No, but I know Georgette and Amy are the nicest of all the girls."

"That is illogical. You admitted you do not know the others as well."

Julianne pouted. "I know they are jealous of Georgette because she is prettier than they are."

He lifted his brows. "Perhaps they are jealous of her friendship with you."

"Jealousy is to be expected," the duchess said. "The gels are competing against one another. Any hastily formed friendships among them won't last long."

Julianne shook her head. "Amy and Georgette will never turn on each other."

The duchess sniffed. "You are probably correct. No doubt Lady Georgette feels she has little competition from Miss Hardwick."

"Mama, that is unkind. Miss Hardwick suffers because others call her plain. I know her to be sweet and unselfish."

The duchess shook her fan. "Before you accuse me of being unkind you might look into your own heart. You chose Lady Georgette for your brother and completely disregarded Miss Hardwick, even though you think her sweet and unselfish. Can you deny it is because Miss Hardwick is plain?"

Julianne sniffed. "I meant to add I would be equally pleased if Tristan chose Amy."

"Your brother is a handsome man," the duchess said. "Naturally he will wish to wed a beauty."

Hawk snorted. Tristan shot him a warning glance.

"Duchess, what are your thoughts?" Tessa asked.

She lifted her nose. "The gels were all polite, and a bit frightened of me, as well they should be. Lady Georgette is a great beauty like her mother. But Miss Shepherd has inherited her mother's unfortunate tendency to punctuate every sentence with a twitter. As for Lady Elizabeth, I cannot recommend her."

"Why is that?" Tessa asked.

"I cannot abide her mother, Lady Durmont. She is a spiteful gossip."

Tristan made an exasperated sound. "I will not dismiss a young lady because you dislike her mother."

"Mark my words. Lady Durmont would make you a miserable mother-in-law," the duchess said.

"Duchess, is there something else about Lady Elizabeth you find objectionable?" Tessa asked.

"We hardly exchanged more than a few words. It was the same with the other gels. I need to spend more time with them in order to form better ideas of their characters."

"Thank you, Your Grace," Tessa said. "That was very helpful."

Tristan had heard enough. "Thank you all for your observations."

"But what have you decided?" the duchess asked.

Absolutely nothing, but he wasn't about to admit it. "Miss Mansfield, may I escort you?" When she nodded, they both rose. He meant to ask if he could call on her in an hour to discuss his decisions or the lack thereof. And then he would discreetly probe into what she knew about Mortland.

The duchess shook her fan. "Sit down, both of you, so that we may discuss which girls you should retain."

Tristan bowed. "Thank you, but I will make the decisions. You will excuse us, Mama."

"I will not."

He walked over to Tessa. When she took his arm, he started toward the door.

"Tristan, come back here at once," the duchess demanded.

And tell her he had no idea which girls he meant to keep? Before he knew it, his mother would have chosen his bride, and then they'd engage in a row. Better to ignore her.

"Mama," Julianne cried, "it is unfair. Make him tell us."

"I say, old boy," Hawk drawled. "It is rather unsporting of you."

"This is an outrage, Tristan," the duchess said. "After all we have done, you cannot deprive us of your decision."

He halted and turned toward her. "Have no fear. When I make my final decision, I will invite all of you to the wedding."

When they stepped outside the drawing room, Tristan drew Tessa away from the door and clasped her hands. She felt possessed, utterly engulfed by the warmth of his palms and the long fingers closed round her own. She inhaled and his male scent rushed into her head. Exhilarating sensations swept through her veins. His thick lashes lowered imperceptibly as he snared her with his intense blue gaze. Her brain turned to mush.

"May I call on you in one hour?" he murmured.

Breathe. Speak. Say something. "Yes," she finally whispered.

She did not hear the swish of skirts until it was too late. Tristan looked past her and released her hands. Tessa turned to find the duchess watching them with an arrested expression. Oh, dear God, had his mother seen them holding hands? The thought made Tessa's stomach churn.

The duchess frowned at her son. "I thought to find you in your study, but it seems you've not gotten far."

"I was on the point of escorting Miss Mansfield to her carriage," he said. "Afterward I have an appointment. I will speak to you when I return."

As Tessa took Tristan's arm, she darted a sideways glance at his mother, expecting to see her lips pinched with disapproval. Instead, an ironic half-smile curved her lips.

One hour later, Tristan entered Tessa's drawing room and claimed the chair across from her, noting the absence of her companion. "Did you decide to save Miss Powell the bother of attending only to be dismissed?"

"No, she went for a drive with Mr. Hodges. He is the young man who visited her at the opera last night. If you prefer, I will call for my maid."

"I'll try to recover my tender sensibilities." He saw no reason to belabor the issue of harming her reputation. Thus far, they'd encountered no problems, and he did not expect them now.

She regarded her clasped hands. "I hope your mother did not form the wrong impression earlier."

"She would have made it clear if she had." But he wondered how much she'd witnessed outside the drawing room. He'd better prepare a reasonable explanation just in case.

Tessa sighed. "I fear we set the wrong expectation with your family and Lord Hawkfield today. They obviously thought you would tell them your decision for the next round of the courtship."

"They made an incorrect assumption. I agreed to involve them, but as you saw, it proved useless."

"Not entirely. You did learn about your sister's friendships with Georgette and Amy."

"I knew about it. They called on my sister last week."

She stilled. "Did you speak to them?"

"Yes, briefly. I heard giggling in the hall and saw them scurrying toward the stairs."

"Did Georgette mention her friendship with your sister at the opera?"

"No." Why did Tessa's nose wrinkle whenever she mentioned Georgette's name? From the first, he'd sensed she disliked her, but Tessa had never actually said anything negative.

"Does their friendship trouble you?" Tessa asked.

"What am I to do about it? Prevent Julianne from seeing them again?"

"Do you think it is unfair to the other candidates?"

"My sister's friendships will not sway my decision," he said.

"It is causing strife among the other girls." Then she proceeded to relate the convoluted story involving the secret meeting at Lady Elizabeth's house. "Apparently Elizabeth and Henrietta instigated the meeting. I believe they are trying to malign Georgette."

"But you did not witness it."

"After I thought about it, I realized the two tattlers had no reason to fabricate the story. They clearly agreed with Elizabeth and Henrietta that someone should report to me."

"If you're so convinced, why did you not confront Elizabeth and Henrietta? You had ample opportunity to do so last night."

She leaned forward. "If I confront them directly, they will twist the incident to make themselves appear innocent."

"I have no wish to be embroiled in the girls' squabbles. Let them work it out for themselves."

Her green eyes flashed. "You won't be so cavalier if you marry someone who is constantly involved in intrigues."

His jaw hardened. "Do you think Elizabeth and Henrietta capable of betrayal?"

"You spoke to them last night. What do *you* think?"

He couldn't recall much about those conversations. In truth, he'd been far too preoccupied with Mortland, a subject he meant to broach with Tessa. "They seemed pleasant enough." He paused and added, "To my face."

She blinked.

"May I make use of paper, pen, and ink at your desk?"

"Yes, of course."

He crossed the room, sat, and located paper. Afterward, he dipped a quill into the inkwell. "What are the names of the two tattlers?"

She joined him, standing behind his shoulder. "They were only the messengers."

The light scent of roses curled through his senses, momentarily distracting him. "And childish, do you not agree?"

She sighed. "Charlotte Longham and Catherine Cresswell."

He frowned, unable to recall much about them, but it

did not signify. Best to go forward with those he meant to invite. He scrawled the names: Lady Georgette Danforth, Miss Sally Shepherd, and Miss Priscilla Prescott. He started writing Lady Suzanne, but his brain seized. The devil, she was the Earl of Lockstone's daughter, but he couldn't recall the family surname.

"Thurgood," Tessa supplied.

He dipped his pen. "I knew that." He wrote her last name and sat back.

"You're eliminating Elizabeth and Henrietta?" Her voice registered surprise.

"I trust your judgment." Perhaps if he placed his trust in her, she would speak frankly about Mortland.

Tessa rested her hand on the top of the chair, inadvertently brushing the back of his coat. His flesh tingled all over.

"There are only four left," she said.

He heard disappointment in her voice and added one more name, one he'd debated over week after week.

She moved to his side. "You decided to keep Amy Hardwick."

"For now."

Her brows lifted in a silent question.

"I had every intention of eliminating her, but I saw her with my sister and Georgette." He frowned. "She was laughing." The devil, he knew it was a stupid reason to keep her.

Tessa's smile could light the night. "You pretend to be gruff, but underneath, you are a very kind man."

He huffed. "I hope I'm not raising false hopes."

"She is one of five, and there are no certainties for any of them," Tessa said.

"I've got to release her after the next round," he said. "I

cannot deny she is a thoughtful young lady and improving under my sister's influence, but her timidity is a problem." He shook his head. "I've already kept her too long. Her chances of marrying are nonexistent this late in the season."

"That is true of all the girls," Tessa said, "but they all knew the risks from the outset."

"I need to make a decision soon. It's wrong to keep them dangling."

Tessa said nothing for a long moment. "Is there any one candidate you fancy?"

He set the quill aside, considering how best to respond. Of course, he'd have to be blind not to notice Georgette's beauty, but he wondered about the sincerity of her friendship with Julianne. Ultimately, there was something lacking, something intangible, that he couldn't quite put his finger on. "Now that their numbers have dwindled, it will be easier to choose." But even as he said the words, doubts plagued him.

Tessa's gaze skittered away. Then she squared her shoulders as if she were about to face a hangman. Tristan frowned. Something troubled her.

She cleared her throat. "Surely you have a favorite."

You. The second the thought popped into his head, he stood up so fast he bumped into her. He caught her upper arms to keep her from stumbling. "Sorry," he said.

He knew he should let her go, but they stood toe to toe, and her skin felt so soft. The very air between them crackled, like the stillness before a crack of thunder. His heart raced, and suddenly he felt robbed of breath.

The thud of approaching footsteps outside alerted him. Someone rapped on the door.

He released her, and they turned in unison. For several anxious seconds, Tessa stared, as if incapable of speech.

"Could it be anyone but Gravesend?" Tristan whispered.

"No, he would never show anyone up when you are here, not without asking me first." Then she called out, "Come in, please."

"I beg your pardon, my lady," Gravesend said. "I installed Lady Broughton and Lieutenant Mortland in the ante room. I thought it best to consult you first."

Tristan's heart stampeded. They had grown too complacent and were in very real danger of being discovered alone.

Tessa looked shaken. "Tell Lady Broughton I am indisposed."

"Don't. My carriage is out front," Tristan said. Damnation. Certain scandal loomed.

"Gravesend, send for my maid," she said. "When she arrives, you may show the guests upstairs."

After the elderly butler shuffled out, Tristan blew out his breath. "Thank God for Gravesend and your quick thinking."

"I'm sorry," Tessa said. "If it were anyone but Anne, I would ask my butler to turn them away."

"We must act nonchalant," he said.

"We will tell the truth. We met to discuss the courtship."

"There is something I must discuss with you after they leave," he said.

"Please do not keep me in suspense. I'll worry the entire time they are—"

Lady Broughton's muffled voice sounded from outside the door. "Richard, we should have waited."

Tessa whirled round and gasped. "He defied protocol," she whispered.

Tristan wasn't at all surprised. "Be calm," he murmured.

"Why should that butler keep us cooling our heels when we are her old friends?" Mortland said. "And why is she with Shelbourne behind closed doors?"

"I'm sure her companion is there," Lady Broughton said.

Tessa touched his sleeve. "Allow me to answer any questions. I have a plan."

His jaw worked. He damned well would defend her.

"Please, for my sake," she whispered. "I am counting on you."

Yet another rap sounded. "Why does she not answer?" Mortland said.

Tessa clasped her hands. "Come in, please."

Lady Broughton entered with her insufferable brother. Mortland held one arm behind his back. What the devil was the man hiding?

Tristan edged closer to Tessa, standing near her shoulder. While Tessa exchanged greetings with them, he stared daggers at the lieutenant. *I'll protect her from the likes of you.*

"I am sorry to keep you waiting," Tessa said. "I instructed Gravesend not to disturb me during meetings."

Lady Broughton's brows lifted. Her skeptical expression worried Tristan.

Mortland offered Tessa a bouquet of wildflowers. "I saw them at the park this morning and couldn't resist."

Bloody hell. It was exactly the sort of romantic gesture she adored. Not long ago, she'd tried, unsuccessfully, to reform Tristan himself.

Suppose you were competing with another man for a girl's affections. The other gentleman brings flowers and sends poems. What would you do to top him?

Shoot him.

Tristan longed for a dueling pistol.

"How thoughtful, Lieutenant." When Tessa reached for the flowers, Mortland had the gall to brush her hand with his fingers.

"My maid should arrive shortly. I will ask her to bring a tea tray and a vase," Tessa said.

Mortland bowed in Tristan's direction. "Shelbourne, what a fortunate circumstance to meet you again so soon."

"Mortland," he grumbled.

The lieutenant looked about the room. "Miss Mansfield, where is your companion?"

Tristan's hands itched to pummel the bastard.

Tessa ignored the question. "Shall we be seated?" Tessa led the way and perched on the settee. She held the bouquet in her hands and smiled at Lady Broughton, who sat across from her.

Tristan took up a stance in front of the fire and crossed his arms over his chest. He meant to intimidate Mortland by watching his every move.

When Mortland sat at the opposite end of the settee, Tristan gritted his teeth and turned his attention to the poker. He picked it up, brandishing it like a sword as he considered Mortland over his shoulder. Temptation gripped him.

The maid arrived. Upon setting eyes on the poker, she faltered. Well, hell, he wasn't in the habit of frightening servants. He reluctantly set the poker aside.

While Tessa instructed the maid, Tristan scowled at Mortland. The man only had eyes for Tessa. Eyes that ogled her lush body.

"Miss Mansfield," Mortland said, "I feared you had come to harm when you did not answer the knock immediately."

"One cannot be too careful of drawing rooms," Tristan drawled. "The danger boggles the mind. Carpets to trip on. Candles to overturn."

Tessa's lips twitched.

The tea tray arrived. Lady Broughton arranged the flowers while Tessa poured. Tristan accepted a cup, noting that Mortland refused.

The lieutenant rose and limped about, examining the pastoral paintings. "What an exquisite drawing room."

No doubt he was calculating the value of every item.

Suddenly the cad turned. "Do you still dabble in watercolors, Miss Mansfield?"

Tristan recalled that Mortland's family had called on Lord Wentworth often. Perhaps Wentworth had displayed Tessa's paintings proudly.

Lady Broughton returned to her chair and smiled at Tessa. "Richard told me he used to watch you from afar while you painted at your uncle's lake."

Tristan almost growled. He should have guessed Mortland had spied on her. Probably undressed her in his mind, too. Tristan entertained thoughts of beating the lustful images out of Pretty Boy's head.

Pretty Boy wandered over to the sideboard and lifted the brandy decanter, regarding Tessa with a lovesick smile. "May I?"

"Of course," she said.

Tristan returned his empty cup to the tray and glanced at Mortland. A yellow curl fell over the fop's forehead as he splashed brandy into a glass. The valet must have spent hours applying hot tongs to those girlish locks.

"Where *is* Jane?" Lady Broughton asked.

A look of discomfort flitted through Tessa's eyes. "She is otherwise occupied."

Tristan blamed himself. He'd broken his promise never to put Tessa in a compromising position again.

Mortland walked over to the escritoire behind the settee. He leaned over and set his fingers on the list. A muscle in Tristan's cheek jerked at the sight. "Lieutenant, are you in the habit of reading private correspondence?"

Tessa's cup rattled on the saucer.

Mortland pivoted, feigning innocence. "I simply noticed the paper on the desk."

Lady Broughton's lips thinned. "Richard, you will give the impression you are prying."

Mortland clapped his hand over his heart. "I would never."

You just did, you bloody bastard.

Mortland sipped his drink and limped over to Tristan. "I say, Shelbourne, you must have all the gents grumbling. You've taken all the prettiest gels off the market." He glanced over his shoulder at Tessa. "Well, nearly all."

Tristan clenched and unclenched his fists. Since he couldn't hit the man in front of the ladies, he decided to put Mortland on the defensive. "So, Mortland, you've only just returned to England. How did you know where to find your sister?"

"When I was well enough, I traveled to Paris, where I

found English newspapers. Imagine my shocked delight upon discovering she'd married the Earl of Broughton."

"Interesting," Tristan said. "I am surprised you did not write to your sister."

"I wished to rush home to England and surprise her."

Tristan narrowed his eyes at the man's bald-faced lie.

Lady Broughton's expression grew grim as she contemplated her cup. Tristan figured Broughton had raised the same question.

"Tessa, we have interrupted your matchmaking discussions long enough." Lady Broughton set her dish of tea aside. "I will call on you again soon."

"Anne, we've only just arrived," Mortland said.

"Richard," she chided. Then she glanced at Tessa. "You will excuse my brother. He has been away from England too long and has forgotten the proprieties."

"I'm sure it's all the fault of those pesky French peasants," Tristan drawled.

Tessa cleared her throat and warned him with her eyes. He arched his brows in answer.

She ignored him and rose along with Lady Broughton. "I am glad you called, Anne."

Lady Broughton bobbed a curtsey. "Richard?"

Mortland gulped down the rest of his brandy, confirming that the pretentious fop had the manners of a goat. He returned his glass to the sideboard and escorted Lady Broughton as far as the door. There, the cur stopped to confer with his sister. Tristan was tempted to toss his dandified arse down the stairs.

"What a splendid idea, brother." Lady Broughton faced Tessa with a bright smile. "Do say you will join us for dinner tonight."

"I regret I must decline."

Pretty Boy wagged his curly head. "We shan't take no for an answer. You must say yes."

Tessa, ever the lady, maintained her serenity, even at Mortland's insistence. "Another time, perhaps."

"Tomorrow night, then," Mortland said.

Tristan refused to allow the cur to beleaguer Tessa any longer. He strode across the carpet until he towered over the lieutenant. "Your insistence borders on abuse."

"I say, Shelbourne, you are touchy about such trifling matters."

Tristan itched to slam his fist into the man's face.

"Gentlemen, this is quite unnecessary," Tessa said. Her soft footsteps padded across the carpet until she came to stand before Lady Broughton. She squeezed her friend's hands. "Anne, I am unable to commit to social engagements this week until I have confirmed plans for the courtship."

Lady Broughton nodded. "Richard, please come now."

Mortland regarded Tristan with a smirk, and then at last he followed his sister out of the drawing room.

Tessa shut the door. She rested her hands there, without saying a word.

The devil. She was angry with him. "I'll not apologize for defending you," he said gruffly.

She faced him. "I know you meant well, but you only succeeded in goading Lieutenant Mortland."

"Did you expect me to ignore his disrespectful treatment of you?"

"He is like a child seeking attention," Tessa said. "If you ignore his bad behavior, he will see there is no reward in it."

"He is a man. You do not know the foul things men think."

Her brows lifted. "Does that include you?"

He wasn't about to answer her. "I didn't like the way he looked at you."

"If looks could kill, you would have committed murder today," she muttered.

"He spied on you while you painted," Tristan said. "I find that disturbing."

A guarded expression stole over her face. Then she seemed to collect herself. "I am more concerned with the present. He is bound to embarrass Anne again and again."

"I am concerned about you," Tristan said. "Stay away from him."

Anger sparked in her green eyes. "You will not give me orders."

"Do you welcome his addresses?" Tristan blurted out.

Her lips parted. "I thought it rather obvious last night I do not."

Relief filled him temporarily, but Mortland's determination worried him. "Don't admit him into your drawing room. You will only give him opportunity."

"I cannot refuse him when he accompanies Anne."

She did not understand the man had dishonorable intentions. "You saw the way he persisted when you refused the dinner invitation. He will try to coerce you into doing his bidding."

"Credit me with enough intelligence to thwart him," she said.

"The way you did at the opera?"

Her face flushed bright red.

He'd botched that one, but he had to make her understand. "Tessa, all I want is to see you safe."

"I will see to my own safety."

Frustration gnawed at his gut. He wanted to throw her over his shoulder, take her someplace safe, and lock her up if necessary. Since kidnapping was illegal, he needed a less forceful method of protecting her. He must think of a way to remove her from harm's way.

"We should discuss the activities for the next round of the courtship," she said. Then she walked over to the settee and sat.

Tristan decided to join her there and claim back the territory. He braced one hand on the cushion and angled his body toward her. She adjusted her position so that she faced him as well.

"You have a plan?" he asked.

"I think a poetry reading is in order. The girls would be ever so smitten and—"

"No poetry."

"Very well, I will play the pianoforte, and you may waltz with each of the girls." She gave him a challenging look. "That way you may judge if they are graceful or not."

"No dancing," he said.

"You disapprove of all my ideas." Tessa leaned toward him. Naturally his gaze dropped to the rounded tops of her breasts. A spark of heat shot to his groin. She kept talking as if blissfully unaware of the heart-stopping view she offered him. Determined to get his mind out of the gutter, he lifted his gaze.

He never made it past her ripe mouth. His brain seized on his favorite fantasy. Tessa on her knees between his thighs. Closing her plump lips over his cock. Naturally he got hard.

Tessa snapped her fingers, startling him out of his lusty contemplation. "Tristan, you are not listening. Do not try to deny it. I see the glazed look in your eyes."

"My mind was pleasurably occupied," he said in a voice better suited for the boudoir. He hoped she wouldn't notice he was aroused. His skintight trousers hid nothing.

"Well, I shan't repeat myself. We will discuss the court-ship tomorrow when you are not so preoccupied."

When she rose, he stood as well. He met her gaze and could not look away. Gradually her eyes softened with a languid expression. Her lips parted a little. The ragged sound of her breath mingled with his own.

The tension between them grew taut. He sensed her answering desire, and every muscle in his body urged him to close the scant distance between them. He wanted to pull her into his arms. He wanted to remove the pins from her curls and let down her hair. He wanted to press her soft curves against him, where he ached for her, but he knew even the slightest brush of her soft skin would send him up in flames.

"I had better go," he said in a hoarse voice.

She looked dazed.

With the last vestiges of his restraint, he bowed quickly and strode from the room.

Chapter Twelve

After arriving home, Tristan gave instructions to his secretary to travel to Hollincourt, Tessa's country seat. His secretary would pretend he was looking over properties in the county and stop in the village near Tessa's home. He would mingle with the populace and discreetly inquire about Mortland.

Tristan would leave no stone unturned in digging up Mortland's past. Having met the bastard, Tristan had concluded that Tessa's uncle had not purchased the commission out of generosity. It would have made more sense for Mortland to follow in his father's footsteps and take orders in the church. Instead, Tessa's uncle had bought him a possible death sentence with that commission. Tristan suspected the Earl of Wentworth had meant to get rid of Mortland.

After concluding the business with his secretary, Tristan leaned his head in his hands. He knew Mortland would use Lady Broughton again and again to gain entrance to Tessa's drawing room. Sooner or later, Mortland would trick Tessa. Tristan was sure the man would stop at nothing to get her alone. He couldn't even think beyond that point because it made him wild to beat the blackguard senseless.

Bloody hell, she was in as much danger from him as she was from Mortland. He'd lusted after more women than he cared to count, but never before had he experienced anything like his uncontrollable craving for Tessa.

He could not trust himself to be alone with her again. If he went too far, he'd have to marry her, and that would set off a scandal he'd never live down. He could not subject Tessa or his family to dishonor. Their meetings would have to take place at his home. He groaned, thinking of his mother's interference, but there was no other choice. He'd best make the request now.

Tristan found his mother reading a book in the red drawing room. She whipped off her spectacles and set them aside as if she didn't want him to see her using them. He made no comment. In the past year, he'd seen her holding newspapers at arm's length. She'd taken to grumbling about small print.

She inspected him. "Your cravat is rumpled."

He said nothing and sat beside her.

She arched her brows. "Well? Do you plan to keep me in the dark?"

Ordinarily he would have done so, but he needed her help. "I've a favor to ask. I wish to hold the next courtship session here."

She leaned across the sofa and felt his forehead.

Tristan swatted her hand away. "What are you about?"

"Checking for a fever."

"I thought you would be pleased."

"Of course I am." She found her fan and applied it. "I suppose your matchmaker will insist upon being present."

"Her name is Miss Mansfield, and yes, she will attend."

"How many girls remain?" she asked.

"Five."

"What sort of activity do you have in mind?" she asked.

"We are still in the planning stages." He didn't tell her he didn't have the foggiest idea.

"Hmmph. I shall send for Miss Mansfield tomorrow. If the event is to take place here, I must approve first."

"What? You don't endorse orgies?"

She snapped her fan closed and rapped his knuckles.

"Ouch!" He snatched his hand back, shaking it.

"There is something else I wish to discuss with you," she said. "What do you know about Lieutenant Mortland?"

He grew wary. "I never met the man before last night."

"You need not have met him to have heard about him."

"All I knew before last night was that he had been missing in action for two years."

Her eyes narrowed. "Shortly after Miss Mansfield took a turn with the lieutenant last night, you went in search of her. Why?"

Until he had evidence, he had no intention of discussing his suspicions or his investigation with anyone but Hawk. "The opera was about to resume."

"Poppycock. Now tell me the truth. Why did you feel compelled to rescue her?"

"Why did you encourage her to go with him?"

"Because her flimsy excuses were causing a scene. I feared she would bring censure upon herself. One can hardly blame her after the lieutenant called her by her Christian name. His manners are deplorable."

He said nothing.

She frowned. "He may be dangling after Miss Mansfield's fortune."

Tristan bounded off the sofa and paced before the hearth.

"You are agitated," his mother said.

"She has no one to protect her," he muttered.

"She wouldn't be in this predicament if she were not so attached to her independence. Someone needs to take Miss Mansfield in hand. All that money and freedom have swelled her head. She courts disaster flaunting her independence and bizarre matchmaking schemes. Society barely tolerates her, and that is only because of her late uncle."

Tristan said nothing. Tessa's career, coupled with her self-imposed spinsterhood, made her an easy target for gossip.

"I've concluded she wrapped Wentworth round her finger," Mama continued.

Tristan could well believe it. She'd cajoled and hoodwinked him any number of times.

"Of course she needs a husband. Honestly, Wentworth neglected his duty when he failed to arrange her marriage."

"He was dying."

A coal dropped and hissed. Tristan retrieved the poker, removed the screen, and stirred the fire.

"Do you plan to tell me what happened?" his mother asked quietly.

He set aside the poker and adjusted the screen. Then he returned to the sofa. "It is not my habit to reveal confidences, but I am making an exception because you have the wrong impression of her."

When he finished telling her what Tessa had sacrificed for her uncle and Lady Broughton, his mother considered the information with a faraway look in her eyes. "Her caring nature is a positive sign. From what you've told me she is not selfish. Perhaps she only needs guidance."

"She devoted so much time to caring for others that she neglected herself," he said.

His mother knit her brows. "Her uncle is dead. Lady Broughton is married. There is nothing to hinder Miss Mansfield now."

"She thinks she's on the shelf."

"Now that is ridiculous. Foolish gel to throw away happiness for the sake of pride. And I assure you it is pride standing in her way." She smiled. "I shall find her a husband."

"What?" Tristan stared at his mother as if she'd spoken in a foreign tongue.

"Her breeding is flawless. She is attractive. With her figure and fortune, she is as eligible as the younger gels, if not more so." She sighed. "Of course she will have to give up her ridiculous career."

"Mama, you are not to play matchmaker."

She ignored him. "Certainly I shall look well above that lieutenant. She can do much better. I'm thinking a marquess."

"You will stop thinking."

"Miss Mansfield could reach as high as a duke, but you're obligated to the bridal candidates. There are quite a few bachelor earls. She will likely have to settle for one of them."

"For the last time, you will not meddle in her life."

"Very well. *You* find her a husband."

"No," he growled.

A smug smile played on his mother's lips. "Either you do it or I will."

He'd be damned if he would stand aside and watch another man pay court to Tessa. Ogle her goddess body. Stare at her lush mouth. He fisted his hands.

"You are the one who said she has no one to protect her," Mama said. "Who better than a husband?"

He wanted to smash something. He would not find her a husband. He would not let his mother do it. He couldn't. Because he'd pound his fists into any man who dared to even look at Tessa.

"Never mind," his mother said. "I will find her a husband."

Fire seared his lungs. He couldn't breathe. Couldn't just sit there. He bounded off the sofa and paced the drawing room again. His fists clenched and unclenched.

He wanted her. He couldn't have her. He didn't want any other man to have her.

The devil. If he didn't do something, his mother would find her a husband. Probably some sweet-talking swain who would bring her flowers and read poetry. He couldn't let that happen.

"Why are you so restless?" his mother asked.

Tristan halted. With considerable effort, he brought the turmoil racing through his blood under control. Slowly he turned to face his mother. Then he realized she'd handed him the perfect means to stifle her interference. "You will leave the matter to me."

Tessa was passionate about her independence. When she learned about his mother's nefarious plans, she would balk. But he couldn't call on her again. Damnation. He'd have to find some way to warn her.

The next day, Tessa followed the butler across the checkered marble floor of the ducal mansion for a requested appointment with the duchess.

Just as she reached the stairs, Tristan walked out into the hall and strode toward her. Her heart fluttered when he smiled. Then he dismissed the butler and escorted her upstairs.

The solid muscles of his arm made her aware of his strength. Unable to help herself, she glanced at him from beneath her lashes. Although she had memorized his features, she still felt a jolt at the sight of his boyish grin. Memories of the way he'd kissed her at Ashdown House, as if he were starving, flooded her brain. Hot, demanding, thoroughly sinful kisses that had stolen her will to resist.

Yesterday something had passed between them just before he left her town house. His heated gaze had thrilled her. The wanton inside her had wanted him to kiss her again, but of course he had not. He'd promised never to touch her again, and he was a man who kept his word. Her honorable Tristan, she thought. But he wasn't her beau, and the thought weighed heavy on her heart. She told herself her secret feelings for him were only for a little while. All too soon she would have to give him up to another. For now, she would not ruin what little time they had left together.

He gazed at her as they climbed the steps. She let herself fall under the spell of his beautiful blue eyes, committing him to memory.

"I asked my mother to hold the next courtship session here for the sake of propriety," he said.

His words doused her like a bucket of ice water. "Oh."

"We cannot take any more chances. Mortland found us alone in your drawing room. We know he spied on you in the past and is likely to do so again. If he sees my carriage at your town house again, he may spread gossip, if he hasn't already. My mother's presence will lend respectability to our meetings."

She averted her face because she feared he would see her disappointment. "So we are to include your mother in future decisions?" she said in a small voice.

"There is a smaller room adjacent to the red drawing room. My mother will chaperone from there. We'll not have complete privacy, but I won't risk your reputation again."

"I understand," she said. They would never be alone again. The realization saddened her far more than it should.

They reached the landing. "There is something I need to speak to you about afterward," he said. Then he frowned as muted feminine voices sounded from the open drawing room door. Tristan slowed his pace. "Apparently my mother is entertaining."

As they neared the door, Tessa recognized Lady Durmont's voice. "Duchess, that spinster has taken over your role. It is an insult to you."

Tessa inhaled sharply.

"On the contrary," the duchess said. "Miss Mansfield

has done me a favor. You might consider retaining her to find wives for your sons. It is high time they gave up sowing wild oats."

Tessa silently cheered. *Well done, Duchess.*

Lady Durmont continued. "She has influenced the duke and turned him against my Elizabeth."

"She's got her claws into him," Mrs. Bancroft added. "My Henrietta thinks she means to have him for herself."

The words scorched Tessa's face. Oh, God, had she let her feelings for him show? She prayed Henrietta was shooting in the dark. But it mattered not. The two dragons were shredding her to pieces. Her legs trembled.

"Walk in there like a queen," Tristan said softly.

Tessa lifted her chin. She would not give those two cats the satisfaction of seeing her humiliation.

He led her inside. Lady Durmont and Mrs. Bancroft rose and curtseyed. "Your Grace," they murmured simultaneously.

Tessa noted they did not even recognize her presence. Tristan gave them a curt bow and then shot them a freezing look. The two dragons looked at each other with alarm as they sank into their chairs. Evidently they'd realized he'd overheard their nasty remarks.

The duchess inclined her head. "Miss Mansfield, it is a great pleasure to see you."

She used every ounce of her strength to make a graceful curtsey.

Tristan led Tessa over to sit on the sofa next to his mother. Then he took a chair near her and glared at the dragons.

Tessa took silent pleasure at their fearful expressions.

The duchess faced the two matrons. "Miss Mansfield

and I are making plans for the next courtship session."
The duchess smiled. "I will hold the event here."

Mrs. Bancroft winced. Lady Durmont looked as if
she'd eaten something rotten.

The duchess drew her quizzing glass up to her eye.
"Lady Durmont, you are very pale. Are you unwell?"

"I am beside myself with worry for my poor Elizabeth," she said. "When she received the letter of dismissal
this morning, she took to her bed."

Mrs. Bancroft dabbed a handkerchief under her moist
eyes. "Henrietta wept when she received her letter."

The duchess lowered her quizzing glass. "I am sure your
daughters will recover quickly. The young are resilient."

Lady Durmont turned to Tristan. "Your Grace, I
beseech you to reconsider. You cannot deny my Elizabeth
is the finest flower among all the belles."

Mrs. Bancroft sniffed. "My Henrietta is a lark among a
flock of wrens. No other girl can match her sweet soprano."

Apparently Mrs. Bancroft was as tone deaf as her
daughter.

"Well, Henrietta is a sweet girl, but of course my Elizabeth is a true incomparable," Lady Durmont said.

Tessa almost snorted.

The two women turned their appeals to Tristan, speaking over each other in their efforts to convince him of the
dubious merits of their daughters. Tristan regarded them
with icy boredom.

The duchess rapped her fan on the sofa arm. "Ladies,
please. Such conduct is unbecoming."

Lady Durmont bristled. "Duchess, if it were your
daughter, you would defend her."

"I teach my daughter by example. Ladies, you will

excuse us. I have kept Miss Mansfield and my son waiting too long."

When the duchess rose, the two dragons had no choice but to do likewise. Tessa and Tristan stood as well. Lady Durmont lifted her pointed nose as she marched out the door.

Mrs. Bancroft clutched her handkerchief and hesitantly approached Tristan. "Your Grace, I beg you to reinstate Henrietta."

He regarded her with hauteur. "Please convey my best wishes to your daughter for her future happiness."

Her lower lip trembled as if she were on the verge of weeping.

"Good day, Mrs. Bancroft." He bowed.

She scowled at Tessa and then quit the drawing room.

Afterward, Tristan regarded his mother. "Those two vicious cats are not to set foot inside our house again."

The duchess fingered the ribbon of her quizzing glass. "They are disagreeable in the extreme, but they are not the only ones blaming Miss Mansfield."

"What?" Tristan practically shouted.

"Lower your voice," the duchess said. "Do you want the servants to hear?"

"I will not stand for anyone mistreating her," he said.

Tessa turned to his mother. "Duchess, why would they blame me? From the beginning, your son made it clear he is making the decisions."

"Pride," she said. "It is far easier to blame you than to admit he rejected their daughters."

Tessa clasped her hands in her lap. "It is my fault. The courtship was my idea. I should have realized the eliminations would cause strife."

"Their mothers agreed to the conditions," Tristan said. "If you will recall, I gave the girls the option to bow out. All of them knew that eventually I could choose only one."

"Logically, you are correct, son. Emotions, however, are never rational."

"Something must be done," Tristan said. "I won't let the ton besmirch her when she's only done her duty by me."

Tessa would not have called her efforts duty. After all, she'd made the choice to help him, but she thought it best to pick her battles and let this one go for now.

The duchess nodded. "We will invite the remaining five girls and their mothers to my drawing room for the next courtship session. I will host the event next Friday and champion Miss Mansfield."

Tessa stilled, unable to believe her ears. The duchess meant to counter the gossip those two dragons would and probably already had spread. Why would she when she'd disapproved of Tessa's involvement in her son's courtship from the start?

The duchess toyed with her quizzing glass and gave Tessa a knowing smile. "You wonder why I offered to help you."

Tessa almost dissembled, but she knew the duchess would not respect anything but the truth. "I admit I am surprised."

The duchess nodded. "I know you overheard those two cats. And yet you walked into this room with your head held high. I would have done the same myself. So I decided to help you."

Tessa wondered how many times the duchess had held her head high in the face of her husband's philandering. "I am grateful, but I must think of the young ladies. I fear it may prove awkward if the mothers observe. The girls are likely to become nervous." And Tristan would be uncomfortable as well, she silently amended.

"We can hold the session in the adjoining drawing room while my mother entertains their mothers here," Tristan said.

"What exactly are you planning?" his mother asked.

"I wish to interview them," Tristan said.

The duchess released an exasperated sigh. "That brings to mind another matter. Several of the mothers have brought to my attention that this courtship is lacking all semblance of romance. No flowers, no poetry, not even a single dance. And they are also concerned because you are not spending equal time with each of the girls. Many feel you favored Georgette too much at the opera."

Tessa bit her lip. He hadn't completely ignored the other girls, but he'd made his partiality to Georgette clear.

Tristan folded his arms over his chest. "I am conducting *my* courtship the way I see fit."

"You're not courting the girls. You're interviewing them as if they were servants," the duchess retorted.

The tension between them seemed ready to erupt. Tessa decided to intervene. "Perhaps there is a compromise."

Tristan and the duchess swerved their gazes to her.

She drew in a breath. "Rather than a straightforward interview, we will play a question-and-answer game."

Tristan huffed. "I have serious decisions to make, and you want to play games?"

"There is a purpose. You will have the opportunity to ask any questions you wish, but since it will be a game, the girls will feel at ease and respond naturally."

He nodded. "If I interview them, they will say what they believe I wish to hear. Brilliant idea, Miss Mansfield," he said.

She smiled. "I'm glad you approve."

"I will send out the invitations posthaste," the duchess said.

"We should invite Julianne and Lord Hawkfield to participate as well," Tessa said. "Their observations will be useful."

Tristan scoffed.

The duchess's blue eyes lit up like the lanterns at Vauxhall. "A wonderful idea, Miss Mansfield. You can put the idea in Hawk's mind that he needs a wife. Lady Hawkfield would be ever so grateful if you found her son a bride."

"Mama, no matchmaking," Tristan said in a stern voice.

"Miss Mansfield will take care of the matter, dear. She is an expert."

Tessa shook her head. "Duchess, I already offered my services at the opera, but Lord Hawkfield declined."

"You what?" Tristan almost shouted again.

Tessa held her finger up to her lips.

"Hawk is a stubborn bachelor," the duchess said. "Miss Mansfield, you will use your matchmaking wiles on him. Perhaps he will fall in love with one of the gels Tristan doesn't want."

"Why not feed him the scraps from my plate, too?" Tristan grumbled.

The duchess ignored him. "Miss Mansfield, what is your opinion of Hawk?"

Tessa blinked. "Er, he seems a jolly sort of gentleman."

"He is a rogue and a charmer." The duchess fingered

her quizzing glass. "I believe he needs a strong-willed woman to reform him."

Tessa stilled. "Well, you can lead a horse to water, but you cannot make him drink."

A sly expression appeared in the duchess's eyes. "Unless you make him thirsty."

"Enough, Mama," Tristan said in a stern tone. "You will cease this matchmaking scheme."

"I have a suitable lady in mind for him," the duchess said. "He is an earl, and I'm certain his mother would approve."

Tristan bolted off the sofa. "Absolutely not."

The duchess regarded him with an odd, knowing smile. "I see no objection."

"I object," he gritted out.

"Duchess, who do you have in mind for Hawk?" Tessa asked.

Tristan glared at his mother. "Do not even consider answering that question. We have an agreement. You are not to interfere."

"See that you apply yourself," the duchess said with a sniff.

Tessa watched them with bewilderment. Their cryptic conversation gave her the impression she'd missed something, but she could not figure it out for the life of her.

Chapter Thirteen

Tristan tugged at his tight cravat as if it were a matrimonial noose.

He sat in a circle with his sister, Hawk, and the final five bridal candidates in preparation for the parlor game. In the adjoining red drawing room, his mother entertained the girls' mothers.

Their daughters whispered and cast surreptitious glances his way. Then they dissolved into giggles. Tristan met Hawk's amused gaze. The bridal candidates were the sort of young girls they had both avoided for years. They reminded him of his little sister. Sweet, innocent, immature girls.

The reality of the situation slammed into his head like a hammer. He was obliged to wed one of them. The day he'd told the girls he would choose only one, he'd made an explicit promise. Their parents and all of society expected him to choose one. To do otherwise meant dishonor to him and his family. He had no choice.

Well, he had five choices, and at the moment, not one of them appealed to him.

When Tessa took a chair beside him, she leaned over and whispered, "You seem a bit discomposed."

"I am not," he said through gritted teeth. He'd merely succumbed to a moment of panic. All men got cold feet when faced with the end of their bachelorhood. The best cure for irrational emotions was rational thinking. Forcing himself to consider the situation logically, he mentally reviewed his duchess qualifications.

1. Age twenty-one: Only Miss Hardwick qualified. Since he couldn't envision bashful Amy as a duchess, he amended his age requirement—downward.
2. Single, never married, and of noble birth: Check.
3. Training in planning social events and managing servants: Georgette and Amy, the least childish of the five, had helped plan that disastrous barge trip. A bad omen.
4. Intelligent conversation: Snort.
5. Sound judgment based on rationality rather than emotion: Debatable.
6. Gracefulness, dutifulness, modesty, and decorum: Check. Then he recalled the name calling and shoving at the speedy courting session. Uncheck.
7. Virtuous: Check. Well, as far as he knew.

And of course he wanted passion. He looked at Georgette, the prettiest of them all, and tried to envision her in his bed. He conjured up an image of her grasping a sheet to her chin with her eyes squeezed shut. Thinking of England, no doubt.

He reminded himself it was his duty to teach his virginal wife the pleasures of lovemaking. While he'd never bedded a virgin, he'd certainly kissed one. The memory of Tessa's abandoned response stirred his blood. Despite her innocence, she'd reacted passionately to his every touch. Surely it would be the same with his wife. After all, he had an arsenal of seduction techniques. But he could not deny his reaction to Tessa was different. From the first moment he'd seen her, he'd desired her. And that desire had only grown over time. Even now, he was much too aware of the rustle of her skirts, her soft breathing, and her rose perfume. Damnation, he had to stop thinking about her.

No more lusty visions of her naked in his bed. Naked in a bath. Naked in a field of leaves. Naked on his lap. No, no, no.

She leaned toward him. "Are you ready?" she murmured.

No. "Yes."

She clasped her hands and smiled at everyone. "This is a new sort of guessing game, one I invented especially for the courtship. Beginning with Lady Georgette, each of the bridal candidates will ask the duke a question."

While she continued to explain the convoluted rules, something to do with the girls' seeking the advice of Julianne and Hawk, Tristan's thoughts wandered. He couldn't ask what he really wanted to know. *Will you be an angel in the ballroom and a temptress in my bed?*

After a great deal of giggling among the girls, Tessa managed to get them to settle in for the game. "Lady Georgette, you may begin."

She smiled, revealing her twin dimples. "Your Grace, how many girls have you kissed?"

The other girls tittered.

"None," he said.

"That cannot be true." Priscilla Prescott straightened her back like a broomstick.

Tessa shook her head. "No one is allowed to help her, unless she appeals to Lord Hawkfield or Julianne."

Lady Georgette turned to Hawk. "My lord?"

"Let me think." He counted in French on his fingers. *"Un, deux, trois, quatre, cinq, six, sept, huit, neuf, dix."* He glanced up. "I've run out of fingers."

"Try not to strain your meager brain," Tristan muttered.

The girls burst out laughing.

"Shall we continue?" Tessa said. "Georgette, you must declare true or false."

Uncertainty flitted through her eyes. "Um, false?"

Tessa turned to him. "Is her answer correct?"

He'd missed this particular rule. "No."

Georgette twirled a blond curl. "You've never been kissed either?"

The other girls snickered behind their hands.

Tristan shrugged. "I have never kissed a girl, but I have kissed women."

Tessa smiled. "That was a trick. Now it's your turn to ask Lady Georgette a question."

He'd missed that rule, too. "I believe Lady Georgette already answered my question."

Georgette released her curl. She looked confused. "I did?"

Julianne made an exasperated sound. "Georgette, you goose. You admitted you've never been kissed."

Georgette blushed. "Of course I would never be alone

with a gentleman, much less kiss one. Mama says it gives gentlemen ideas." She frowned. "She would not tell me what ideas."

Hawk feigned a perplexed look. "I wonder what she meant."

"Ahem," Tessa said. "I believe it is Miss Shepherd's turn."

The round-faced brunette scrunched her forehead as if deep in thought. Suddenly she brightened. "I have it. Your Grace, do you prefer dogs, horses, or sheep?"

He wondered if his ears were clogged. "Miss Shepherd, did you say sheep?"

Sally twittered. "Oh, yes. My brother Charles adores our sheep. He gives all the ewes names. His favorite is Louisa. Isn't that sweet?"

Do not laugh. Whatever you do, do not laugh. He made the mistake of glancing at Hawk, who slid down in his chair, his shoulders shaking. Tristan covered his mouth with his fist.

Tessa narrowed her eyes, as if warning him. "Your answer?"

"Er, horses."

Sally pouted. "You don't like sheep?"

"True," he said.

"They are not abiding by the rules," Priscilla said.

Tristan glanced at Miss Prescott's broomstick posture and imagined her standing that way while he tried to get her nightgown off. She'd probably insist on keeping it on. He mentally crossed her off the list.

Sally blinked. "Did I do something wrong?"

Tessa gave her an indulgent smile. "You did well. Now, it is the duke's turn to ask Miss Shepherd a question."

He thought a minute. "Think about a time when you did something you knew was wrong. Tell me what happened." He hoped it had nothing to do with little lambs.

"Not long ago, I did something very bad," Sally said. "I stole my sister Sarah's love letter and read it."

Julianne's eyes lit with mischief. "What did it say?"

Sally wrinkled her nose. "It was all nonsense to me. The gentleman signed himself as Lord Randy. He said he wished to plunder the treasure in the bush and claimed he carried a candlestick in his, er, unmentionables."

Hawk bent over, wheezing and coughing. Julianne pounded his back. Georgette cried out, "He's choking."

Tristan looked up at the fat cherubs painted on the ceiling, seeking divine intervention from the gentleman upstairs.

When all the young ladies expressed their concern for Hawk's health, Tessa assured them he would survive. "Let us continue. Miss Prescott, I believe it is your turn."

She pushed back her shoulders, thrusting out her flat bosom. "What is your favorite dish?"

"Pickled eels," he said.

She turned to Julianne. "True or false?"

Julianne shrugged. "True."

"I disagree," Priscilla said.

"You are correct." Tristan glanced at the mantel clock. This game was proving a colossal waste of time.

Tessa nudged him with her elbow. "You may ask Miss Prescott a question."

He returned his attention to Miss Prescott. Even though he'd crossed her off his list, he must ask her something. He decided to test her insistence on following rules. "Miss Prescott, when you are confronted with a dilemma, where right and wrong are not necessarily clear, how do you make a decision? You may cite an example."

"Oh, it is always clear to me what is right and wrong," Priscilla said with confidence. "I abide by the proprieties in every situation."

She'd confirmed his opinion of her. "Thank you. That will be all."

"Lady Suzanne, it is your turn," Tessa said.

Suzanne considered him from beneath her lashes, a practiced, coquettish look. "Your Grace, why did you select me as one of the final five candidates?"

Actually he'd eliminated the ones he knew didn't suit. The others, with the exception of Amy, remained by default, but of course he wouldn't admit that. "I selected all of you because you were the nicest girls."

Suzanne pouted like a child. The chit had obviously been hoping for a compliment. When Tessa asked her to declare his answer true or false, she answered true in a miffed tone.

"Do you have a question for Lady Suzanne?" Tessa asked him.

"Yes. Lady Suzanne, what do you consider to be your greatest asset?"

She dipped her chin. "Oh, I should not say."

"Why?" he asked.

"Is he allowed to ask that?" Priscilla the rule keeper said in her snooty voice.

Julianne snorted. "He's a duke. He can do whatever he wants."

Hawk pouted. "I'm so jealous," he said in a falsetto voice.

Everyone laughed, with the exception of Priscilla, who pinched her lips.

Tessa calmed everyone. "Lady Suzanne, you may continue."

By now, Tristan had already forgotten what he'd asked her.

Suzanne dipped her chin again. "Mama says my best asset is my beauty, but of course, beauty must be more than skin deep."

Tristan gazed at her, expecting more, but she only batted her lashes.

"Now it is Miss Hardwick's turn," Tessa said.

The shy girl contemplated her folded hands. When her silence stretched out, the other girls fidgeted. Once again, Tristan wondered if he'd done Amy a disservice by keeping her in the courtship this long. She'd seemed to improve under his sister's influence, but when faced with a crowd, she shriveled.

Priscilla made an exasperated sound. "Amy, if you cannot think of a question, then pass."

Tristan gripped the arms of his chair. "There is no time limit."

"I am only trying to help her," Priscilla said. "It is obvious she does not have any ideas."

Amy lifted her chin, and this time, she didn't hesitate. "Miss Prescott, I realize my silence makes you uncomfortable. However, I am mindful that there is an important purpose underlying the game. Therefore, I wish to think carefully before I speak."

Julianne punched her fist in the air and grinned. Georgette squeezed Amy's hand. Hawk winked. "Well said, Miss Hardwick."

Tristan regarded Amy with newfound respect. "Take all the time you need, Miss Hardwick."

Though she blushed, Amy regarded him steadily. "I am ready, Your Grace." She drew in her breath as if mustering her courage. "What is the single most important quality you seek in a wife?"

Amy had stunned him. Of all the girls, she had asked a question of significance, one that cut straight to the heart of the courtship. He reviewed his qualifications again and decided he'd left out an important item. "Loyalty," he said.

"Miss Mansfield, may I ask the duke a clarifying question?" Amy asked.

Tessa looked at him. "Your Grace?"

"Of course," Tristan answered.

Amy exhaled, but her gaze never wavered from him. "Loyalty can mean many things. What does it mean to you?"

"A thoughtful question. For me, loyalty means my wife will act with honor and always be truthful with me."

Amy nodded. "Honesty is important in any close relationship. A marriage without trust would sour quickly."

"Once trust is broken, there will always be suspicion thereafter," Tristan said.

"True or false?" Tessa said gently.

Amy kept her gaze on him. "I know he is telling the truth."

When everyone else started chattering, Tristan tugged on his sleeves, unable to look at Amy any longer. Of the five, she alone had shown maturity and intelligence in her questions and responses. On paper, she fit most of his qualifications. Possibly all, for he'd wager she'd had nothing to do with the decision to take a barge to Ashdown House. He'd felt she understood him in ways the other girls did not. As much as he respected and liked her, he knew he was the wrong man for her. She would be much happier as the wife of a clergyman, a role where her husband and the parishioners would appreciate her quiet thoughtfulness.

The mothers entered and made a great to-do about all the laughter they'd heard. All complimented Tessa on her suggestion for a parlor game. Tristan glanced at his mother, who stood at the door with a secretive smile. Obviously she'd succeeded at championing Tessa.

This afternoon, his mother had agreed to let him speak to Tessa alone after the parlor game, provided he broached the subject of marriage. At last, he'd have the opportunity to warn Tessa.

Tristan made a point of speaking to each of the girls and their mothers as they departed. When at last he came to Mrs. Hardwick, her sweet smile reminded him of her daughter. "Amy has told us how much she admires you."

Amy blushed and lowered her lashes.

"I am honored by your regard, Miss Hardwick," he said. But he didn't feel worthy of Amy's admiration. He'd kept her in the courtship out of pity and judged her only for what he saw on the surface. Today, the girl he had judged least likely had exposed the shallow side of him.

The duchess shooed Hawk and Julianne from the yellow drawing room. Then she addressed her son. "I will leave you to discuss the eliminations with Miss Mansfield. You will also address that other matter."

After she left, Tessa glanced at him. "I am surprised your mother did not insist we include her."

"I convinced her we needed to discuss the courtship

in private." He started pacing in front of the marble fireplace.

"Tristan, what is troubling you?"

"I should have eliminated Amy Hardwick weeks ago."

"Amy has benefited from the experience," Tessa said.

He halted. "I gave her preferential treatment week after week. Today, I'd decided to eliminate her. But tell me how I'm to do it when she outshone all the others."

She had to reassure him. "Today she showed incredible courage. While your sister helped her, you are equally responsible for her transformation."

"I take no credit for her improvement."

"Not long ago, you told her if she didn't believe herself worthy, no one else would. Today she stood up for herself. She has learned her own worth."

"She would never be able to withstand the scrutiny of being my duchess. But if I eliminate her, I'll feel as if I've kicked a puppy."

"You have given Amy a gift she will take with her the rest of her life."

"She'll conclude I'm a cad who judged her by appearances only, just like all the others. And make no mistake. I did."

Tessa had encouraged him to make allowances for Amy. Now she must convince him that he'd done the right thing. "She will not forget your kindness."

"Miss Hardwick deserves much better than crumbs from me. Hell, I don't deserve her."

Tessa thought his concerns and admiration for Amy showed how much he'd progressed since that first day he'd asked her to make him a match. But they needed to discuss the other bridal candidates as well. "I believe you learned more than a little about the five girls," Tessa said. "Come, let us sit and review your opinions of all of them."

He pulled out a chair for her and sat in one directly across.

"Now, think carefully about each one," Tessa said. "How would you describe them?"

"The beautiful one, the witless one, the spiteful one, the vain one, and the bashful one."

His sarcasm shocked her. "Tristan, you are not taking this seriously."

"Seriously, I know you far better than I know them."

The blood drained from her face. "You mustn't say such a thing."

"It's the truth."

His words sent wave after wave of guilt crashing over her. She ought to have encouraged him to spend more time with the girls. Instead of suggesting he take them for a ride in the park, she'd kept him all to herself in her drawing room. She'd told herself he needed her guidance, but she'd wanted him to flirt with her. Foolishly, she'd seen no danger in pretending for a little while that he was her beau. And in doing so, she'd failed him.

Guilt would not help him now, so she forced herself to concentrate on the situation at hand. "You chose the five girls above nineteen others," she said. "What did you base your decisions on?"

He shrugged. "I eliminated those I knew were unsuitable. What else could I do? There were so many, it was impossible to spend sufficient time with them."

Tessa winced. She should not have invited twenty-four girls, but she'd wanted everyone to know she was making him a match. At the time, she'd thought they both would benefit, but she'd put her own ambition above his needs.

She still had a chance to salvage the situation. "This is my fault, but we will rectify it now. Since their numbers have dwindled, you can court each of them individually."

He scoffed. "Do you really believe if I spend more time with them it will change anything?"

His words shook her. "What are you saying?"

"They aren't likely to reveal new depths to me, with the exception of Amy, who did so tonight. The others are too immature."

"But you spoke at length with Georgette at the opera." *And the entire time I wanted to tear you away from her.*

"Do you know what we talked about? Or rather what Georgette talked about? Balls and dancing."

"I suppose you found it difficult to deter her from frivolous topics." The moment the spiteful words flew from her mouth, she wanted to kick herself.

"We were in a crowded opera box. Did you think we discussed serious topics there?" he said in an exasperated tone.

"Tristan, you have expressed doubts about all of them. I am concerned." An inner voice told her she'd ignored the warning signs. She'd even hesitated asking whom he favored because she'd feared he would admit it was Georgette. When he'd failed to name the blond beauty, she'd secretly rejoiced. The memory shamed her.

"Doubts or not, I must go forward." He drew in a breath. "Eliminate all but Amy and Georgette. My mother will invite both girls and their parents to Gatewick Park for a house party. I will make my final decision there."

Panic set in, clawing at her lungs. No, he couldn't end

it like this. "You have not formed an attachment to either of them. If you invite them to your home, you will signal you mean to marry one of them." *Not Georgette. Please not Georgette.*

He stood and stared hard at her. "Isn't that what this courtship is about? Everyone expects me to choose one of the candidates."

She rose on shaking legs. "You cannot marry out of obligation. It is not fair to you or the girls. You must tell them you have not developed tender feelings for them, and you do not wish to mislead them any longer. Tell them they are free to court other gentlemen."

"Do you think that will satisfy their fathers? You have not considered the consequences. No father would allow me to court his daughter for fear I would jilt her. All of society would condemn me and *my family* by association. I have no choice but to marry one of the bridal candidates. To do otherwise would be tantamount to dishonor."

Her temper ignited. She'd blamed herself, but he had a responsibility as well. "I did not agree to make you a match only to see you marry for duty."

He loomed over her. "Why else would I marry?"

"Mutual affection. Shared interests."

He huffed. "You mean love. I know you cling to romantic ideas about marriage, but I've no such illusions. I must have an heir in order to ensure the succession. If I fail, the property will default to the crown, and the ducal title will die with me. The future of my birthright is at stake. Cold, hard duty is the only reason I seek a wife."

"I know you must marry, but duty does not preclude love." She held her palms up. "You can have it all."

"Enough, Tessa. I know what you want. I understand

why you believe in love matches, but your parents' marriage was an anomaly. I've always understood what was expected of me, and every one of those twenty-four girls understood as well. When I gave twenty of them the opportunity to withdraw, only Miss Hardwick tried to leave. The others did not dare defy their parents. You are the only one who refuses to acknowledge this is a dynastic marriage, a marriage of necessity."

She could hardly breathe. "All the times we met, you pretended to listen, but you were merely placating me." Her voice had risen as she spoke, but she was frustrated and scared.

He shook his head. "I never misled you. From the beginning, I told you I could not promise to marry for love. The only promises I made were to treat my wife with respect and dignity, and to remain faithful."

She'd wanted him to open his heart to one of the girls, but the only heart she'd opened was her own. And God help her, she was relieved yet horrified that he did not love either Amy or Georgette.

Tristan folded his arms over his chest. "I cannot defy society. If I do, I will set off a scandal that will hurt my mother and sister. I will not bring dishonor upon them."

She saw implacable determination in his beautiful blue eyes and knew she'd lost the battle before she'd begun.

An hour later, Tristan sat in his study, staring morosely at the dregs of brandy in his glass. He still wanted to smash something, but Hawk would rib him mercilessly.

Tristan's gloomy thoughts returned to his mother's delighted surprise upon learning of the house party. She'd spoken of grandchildren. Julianne had danced a little jig because she would have a sister by summer.

He'd been in no mood to warn Tessa about his mother's ridiculous matchmaking scheme.

Hawk returned from the sideboard with the decanter and topped up their glasses. Then he lifted his glass. "A toast to your impending engagement."

"Piss on you." He'd done what he'd set out to do and made his family happy. By summer, he'd be a married man. Tristan muttered a vulgar and very old English word.

Hawk chuckled. "Cold feet?"

He didn't answer. Earlier when Tessa had taken her leave, he's started to follow her, though he'd not even known what he meant to say. Hawk had intercepted him. In an aside, his friend had said only one word. *Don't.*

Hawk knew. He'd said words to that effect at the opera. Tristan wanted the only woman he couldn't have.

He downed a mouthful of brandy, burned his throat, and grimaced. Better to burn from liquor than from wanting her. "The devil," he said. "I've a right to mourn my bachelorhood."

"Quite so," Hawk said, and took a swig.

Tristan gulped another mouthful. "You're the next victim," he said evilly. "My mother told the mischief-maker to find you a bride."

Hawk's arrested expression looked comical. "You'll tell Miss Mansfield I'm a scoundrel, the worst rake in London."

Tristan huffed. "Rakes are her specialty."

"She nabbed you. That's proof enough." Hawk frowned into his glass. "How did she manage?"

"Dropped her fan. Let me step on it. Smiled her siren's smile. Next thing I knew she'd reeled me in."

"I warned you," Hawk said. After a pause, he added, "How did she rope you into courting two dozen chits?"

"Tricked me." Tristan swigged brandy again and swiped his mouth.

"She's diabolical," Hawk said. "Let me top up your glass. You need to get stinking drunk."

They downed two more glasses without a word. Then Hawk belched. "Someone needs to stop her."

"It would be easier to stop a cannonball." Tessa was relentless, determined beyond all common sense. She was also impulsive, impetuous, and passionate. And so damned tempting with that goddess body, those lush lips, and her sharp wit.

"I've got a plan," Hawk said.

"This ought to be entertaining," Tristan muttered.

Hawk waggled his brows. "Revenge."

Tristan snorted and took another drink.

"What does she fear more than anything?" Hawk asked.

"Nothing. Trust me, the woman is fearless."

"Think," Hawk said.

"Can't. My brains are soaked."

"She's a happily-ever-after spinster. You heard her. She loves her independence. What is the worst thing you can do to her?" Hawk slapped his thigh. "Marry her!"

He scoffed.

Hawk set his empty glass aside. "Admit it. You've got a bad case of lust for her."

"The devil take you."

"He probably will." Hawk traced his finger round the

rim of his glass. "It's forever, old boy. Do yourself a favor and cut the other two chits loose."

Tristan pinched the bridge of his nose. "I'm committed." There was no turning back.

"You can't cry off. But the chits can."

Society decreed a gentleman could not end an engagement, but the lady could do so. He didn't know the reason for the rule, but it mattered not. "Their families are pressuring them. They'll do their duty." And so would he. He massaged his burning chest. Probably the brandy.

"Scare them off," Hawk said. "You're positively frightening when you scowl."

"I'll not bring dishonor upon the girls or my family."

Hawk's demeanor turned serious. "Hang society. They'll forget in time."

He shook his head. Tessa believed in love and fairy tales. He believed in reason and duty. Even if the two girls weren't standing between them, he knew a marriage between them would never work. He played by society's rules in order to preserve the honor of his family and the dukedom. Tessa acted on impulse, heedlessly leaping into one mad scheme after another. His mother had said it all. Society barely tolerated her. The very qualities he admired the most in her—her independent spirit and her fearlessness—would rip them apart if she did not conform. And conforming meant giving up her freedom and career, something she'd sworn never to do.

There were other insurmountable problems. Because she'd orchestrated the courtship, the jealous cats would shred her to pieces if he married her. Society would conclude the two of them had played the girls and their families false. They would condemn them. His mother, sister, and future children would suffer as well.

No matter how much he desired her, no matter how much sheer physical passion sizzled between them, he could not marry her.

"Old boy," Hawk said. "If you want her, move the mountains to make it happen."

Tristan shook his head. "It's impossible." After uttering the words, he added Tessa to the list of things he'd sacrificed for duty the past thirteen years. Cold, hard duty.

Chapter Fourteen

Tessa sat in her drawing room, trying to finish a letter to her steward. She had many duties to attend to before leaving for Gatewick Park on Monday morning, only two days away. For the past week, she'd spent hours helping the duchess make plans for the house party, but she'd seen Tristan only briefly. He'd bowed and greeted her in a distant fashion. Tessa had maintained her composure until she'd entered her carriage. And then she'd fought back tears all the way home. For a man who was bound to marry another. For a man she'd failed.

She could do nothing to stop him from marrying for duty. The duchess had sent the invitations for the house party. The scandal sheets had printed the news. In all the clubs, gentlemen made wagers. Most placed their bets on Georgette, but one of the papers declared Amy the dark duckling, a hateful reference to the ugly duckling label others had applied to her. Tessa had thought Amy safe from public notice among the crowd of girls, but she'd never expected Amy to progress to the very end. She was ashamed for doubting the sweet girl. Amy had made the final round with no special favors.

The house party was almost at hand, and Tessa realized Amy could not win. If Tristan chose her, she would spend a lifetime enduring the ton's scrutiny, and if he rejected her, she would suffer public defeat. Tessa almost wished he would reject Amy, because then the papers would forget her eventually. It would be far better to end the suffering quickly. But the thought of his choosing Georgette hurt so much Tessa wasn't sure if she ought to attend the house party.

She could not quit this late because that would raise suspicion and give the blasted papers more fodder. She had a duty to Tristan and to both of those girls.

Tristan's courtship was not the only reason for her vexation. She had received an unwanted parcel earlier today. Anger simmered inside her at Richard's audacity, but she refused to dwell on him. She had sent the gift back immediately without a message. Under no circumstances would she allow Richard to beleaguer her again.

Gravesend appeared and announced Anne. Tessa's shoulders stiffened. Her faithful butler knew she despised the lieutenant. Earlier in the week, she'd discovered two giant footmen in her home and learned Gravesend had hired them for her protection. So she wasn't surprised when he sought to reassure her. "Lady Broughton is alone," he said. "I know you have an appointment with the Duchess of Shelbourne today, so I thought it best to consult you first."

Tessa glanced at the clock. "Show her up, Gravesend, but please have my carriage ready in thirty minutes."

When Anne entered the drawing room, Tessa joined her on the settee. Gravesend promised to instruct a maid to bring a tea tray.

After he left, Tessa smiled at her friend, relieved that Richard had not accompanied her. "I am sorry I could not attend your dinner party last week."

"I'm surprised to find you at home," Anne said. "Richard and I called twice this week."

Gravesend had told her. She'd not bothered to hide her relief. "I have been very busy with the courtship, but your visit is a welcome respite."

Anne spoke about all the people who had called to pay their respects to Richard. Tessa smiled and managed not to show her revulsion. When the tea tray arrived a few minutes later, she poured and handed her friend a cup. "It seems you have been busy as well."

"I heard about the house party," Anne said. "Are you attending?"

"Yes, of course."

Anne toyed with her cup handle. "Were you planning to tell me?"

A dozen times, she'd thought of calling on Anne, but she'd not wanted to face Richard. "Between assisting the duchess with the plans and packing for the journey, I've scarcely had a moment to myself."

"Jane will feel ill at ease at the duke's estate. She may stay with me," Anne said.

"That is very kind of you, but Mr. Hodges's married sister has already invited her." Tessa believed he would propose to Jane soon.

Anne frowned. "Why should she stay with strangers? You know she would be easier if she were at my home."

Tessa would not. She could easily imagine Richard interrogating Jane and tricking her into revealing more than she should. "Jane already accepted the invitation."

"I see." Anne set her cup aside and took a deep breath. "There is a reason I called today."

Tessa knew what her friend meant to say.

"You wounded Richard when you returned his gift."

He'd sent the watercolors to remind her of the past. Richard had known doing so would discompose her. "I accepted his flowers, but you know other gifts are inappropriate."

"I know it wasn't precisely correct, but he only meant it as a sentimental gift from an old friend."

She could not tell Anne that her brother's intentions were not innocent.

Anne smoothed her skirts. "You did not even send a note."

She'd been so angry she'd not stopped to consider Anne's reaction. Then again, why should she justify her actions when Richard had ignored proper etiquette? "Under the circumstances, I felt no explanation was required."

Anne looked at her miserably. "I know you are angry with my brother and do not blame you. He wanted to apologize, but I felt it better if I came alone. I am sorry for his impertinence that day in your drawing room."

"I felt your embarrassment as if it were my own. Regardless of his conduct, it does not change my regard for you. I've always felt you are the sister of my heart."

"Yet you have stayed away. I know you've been busy with the courtship, but we've always made time for each other. I can only conclude it is because of my brother."

Tessa measured her words. "His persistence at the opera and again in my drawing room disconcerted me. Each time I thought of calling on you, I feared he would try to coerce me."

"I rebuked him for his unmannerly conduct. He felt bad because he'd allowed his enthusiasm to run away with him." Anne gave her a weak smile. "I believe he truly wishes to make amends."

Tessa doubted his sincerity, but kept her thoughts to herself. Richard had meant to manipulate her at the opera. The flowers and watercolors were his way of drawing her into his web. He'd lost the opportunity to gain her fortune long ago, but he'd not given up. Today, he'd learned she would not tolerate his insufferable pursuit.

"Will you join us for dinner, Tessa?"

She bit her lip at the hopeful look in her friend's eyes. Soon she must call on Anne or risk alienating her. But the memory of the watercolors repulsed her anew. Tessa knew she could not face him so soon because she doubted her ability to hide her disgust of Richard. "Please forgive me, but I must decline. The duchess is expecting me this afternoon, and afterward, I have much to do in preparation for my departure on Monday. When I return, I promise to call."

Anne looked down at her clasped hands, but said nothing.

"Is something else troubling you?" Tessa asked.

Anne looked at her. "Richard asked me to convey his concern about you. He was shocked to find you alone in your drawing room with Shelbourne. My brother believes Shelbourne is risking your reputation."

Her temper flared. "Give Richard a message. Tell him

he'd better not discredit Shelbourne's honor. Your brother is no match for a duke. And while you're at it, tell him I'm no damsel in distress."

"I share Richard's concern. If this becomes general knowledge, it will ruin you. Do not meet Shelbourne alone again. He never should have persuaded you in the first place."

"He asked, and I agreed. It is a business relationship."

Anne shook her head. "You told me you are friends, and you even agreed to address each other by your Christian names."

"We became friends in the course of our discussions about the girls."

Anne gave her a dubious look.

"If you knew him as I do, you would not worry. He is very devoted to his family and treats the bridal candidates with the utmost respect."

"You seem to have forgotten his reputation, but I have not. From the first night he met you at my ball, I sensed he'd marked you as a conquest. He looked at you in a most improper manner—as if he were undressing you with his eyes."

"Your fancies have taken flight," she said. But when they were alone that last time, he had regarded her with heated intent. He knew how to snare her with his blue eyes, and God help her, she could not resist him.

"He has used a slow siege to disarm you. Little by little, he's gotten one concession after another. You are blind to what he's done, but I am not."

Tessa fumed. "You have twisted events when you do not know all the circumstances."

"What worries me the most is the way you respond to

him," Anne said. "I saw the secret looks the two of you exchanged in your drawing room that day. You were communicating without words. There is an intimacy between you. I worry you have developed tender feelings for him."

Tessa averted her heated face. "I am his matchmaker. What you sense is merely friendship." As she spoke the words, her heart squeezed. He meant far more to her than he should, but she dared not admit it. Dared not show it.

"Can you honestly tell me he has done nothing improper?"

She laughed. "According to you he has carved one hundred notches in his bedpost. So the answer is no."

"I know you well. You employ sarcasm to evade questions you do not wish to answer, but I care too much about you to let this pass. Look me in the eyes and tell me the truth. Did he seduce you?"

She met her friend's gaze. "No." He had not seduced her. She'd welcomed his kisses and touches that night at Ashdown House. And though she ought to be ashamed, she knew she would never regret it.

Anne exhaled. "Thank God."

The clock chimed the half hour. "I'm sorry, Anne, but I must leave for my appointment with the duchess."

As they walked out together, Anne sighed. "I do feel more at ease after speaking to you, especially since the duke's courtship is almost over. Everyone will say you made the most prestigious match in the nation."

Yes, she would achieve her own ambition, and no one would ever know she'd failed him.

Two hours later, Tessa set her quill aside and rubbed her wrist. "Duchess, what else may I help you with?"

Julianne groaned. "Oh, do not ask. Mama is sure to torture us with another task."

"You needn't worry, daughter. We are done." The duchess removed her spectacles. "Dratted things are a nuisance."

Tessa smiled, remembering how Uncle George used to misplace his all the time. "I had no idea how much work it is to plan meals for a house party."

"Your uncle did not entertain?" Julianne asked.

"Only the neighbors. We lived quietly in the country." She shrugged. "I've never even attended one before."

The sound of footsteps drew Tessa's attention to the door. Tristan bowed. "Am I interrupting?"

"Not at all," his mother said. Then she regarded her daughter. "Julianne, you have ignored the pianoforte all week. You must practice."

"But, Mama, I'm tired from all the planning."

"You dawdled and gossiped most of the time. I'll not listen to any arguments."

"I promise to practice tomorrow," Julianne said in a wheedling tone.

Tessa's lips twitched. She doubted Julianne would sway her mother.

The duchess rose. "You will excuse me, Miss Mansfield. I mean to have a private word with my daughter."

After they left, Tessa regarded Tristan. He looked very handsome in his blue coat and buff trousers. She'd missed him terribly, but she mustn't show her feelings. "I should leave."

When she stood, he strode across the room and took her hands. Her breath hitched. Forbidden feelings flooded her heart.

"You are well?" he murmured.

She nodded.

Worry clouded his blue eyes. "Has Mortland used his sister to gain entrance to your drawing room?"

"They called twice while I was here assisting your mother." She paused. "Anne came alone today. I was very glad to see her."

Tristan furrowed his brows. "I'm surprised Mortland did not insist upon accompanying her."

"Anne told him to stay behind so that we could talk privately. She is like a sister to me." She debated how much to tell Tristan and decided to be honest about everything except Anne's concern about her relationship with him.

When she finished telling him about the gift she'd returned and her conversation with Anne, Tristan scowled. "Mortland will persuade his sister to call tomorrow or the next day. He cannot resist your fortune or your beauty."

Her heart turned over. She knew she was plain, but his words lifted her battered spirits all the same.

"I've heard rumors he's racked up ruinous debts," Tristan said.

Oh, dear God. Poor Anne had no idea.

"I do not know if Broughton is aware, but do not admit Mortland even if he calls with his sister," Tristan said. "I cannot rest easy otherwise."

"Anne will not call in the next two days. I refused her dinner invitation on account of all I must do before leaving for the house party," she said.

"You will be safe from him next week," Tristan said. "When we return, I will speak to Broughton on your behalf."

She inhaled sharply. "I cannot allow you to fight my battles for me."

"I will protect you," he said gruffly.

She forced herself to say what she must, though she wasn't ready to face losing him to another. "You will be engaged and soon will marry. I cannot become dependent upon you." The day her uncle died, she'd realized there was no one to rely upon, no one to advise her or help shoulder the burdens.

His blue eyes filled with determination, and though he said nothing, she knew he meant to intercede. "Mortland and Anne caught us alone in my drawing room. I'm sure Broughton knows. If you go to him, Broughton will question your involvement. You will make matters far worse for both of us."

He scowled.

"You know I am right." She released his hands. "I must go now."

He offered his arm. "I'll escort you."

Tristan walked with her to her carriage. Foolish woman. He didn't give a damn about her independence. He would confront Broughton next week.

As her driver let down the steps, Tristan faced her. "I feel in my bones Mortland will try something in the next two days. Promise me you will send for me if anything happens."

"Nothing will happen. Even if he tries to call, Gravesend won't let him in."

"He'll concoct some ruse," Tristan said. "Swear to me you'll be careful."

"You're as bad as Gravesend with your worries," she said. "He employed two brawny footmen to protect me. He did not even tell me."

Tristan nodded. "Good. I'm glad to hear Gravesend is looking out for you." She had no idea he'd secretly met her butler in a coffeehouse. The old man had gratefully accepted Tristan's offer to hire the two giant footmen. What Tessa didn't know wouldn't hurt her, but Mortland could. Tristan refused to let that happen.

On Sunday night, Tessa's carriage turned into Grosvenor Square and jounced toward her town house. She'd attended a dinner party at Mr. and Mrs. Brook's elegant home, where she'd left Jane for the following week. Tessa liked Mr. Hodges's married sister. In a whisper, Mrs. Brooks had confided her brother planned to propose to Jane next week. Tessa had silently rejoiced. With a sigh, she realized she would soon need a new companion. Perhaps one of Jane's younger sisters would be willing to fill the role.

Weariness made her a bit lightheaded. Tomorrow she must rise early to travel with Tristan and his family to Gatewick Park. The journey would take all day. She'd packed and made so many arrangements she could hardly recall how she'd managed. The moment she arrived home she planned to retire immediately.

When the carriage rolled to a stop, John, her driver, opened the door and let down the steps. She descended and saw John staring at a hackney two doors down. "Looks suspicious," he said.

The backs of her hands prickled. She recalled Tristan's worry that Richard would try something. Was he waiting for her inside that carriage? With those debts he'd incurred, he would be even more desperate to get his hands on her fortune.

Stop being foolish. Richard was unmannerly and relentless when he wanted something, but he wouldn't risk doing something that would bring Broughton's censure upon his head.

The hackney door opened. Richard stepped out. Anger spurted in her veins. How dare he try to call upon her at this late hour? "John, deter him until I'm safely in the house."

"Yes, my lady."

"Tessa," Richard called out in a hearty greeting.

She started up the walk at a brisk pace. A cold gust of wind blew her pelisse about and whipped through her gossamer skirts. Behind her, she heard John arguing with Richard.

"Tessa, wait," Richard shouted.

John's angry voice rang out. "Sir, leave her be."

She despised Richard more than ever for his effrontery.

The front door opened. Gravesend called out, "Hurry, Miss Mansfield."

She increased her pace, but the sound of rapid, uneven footsteps behind her made her furious. She looked over her shoulder. John was following Richard as fast as his bulk would allow.

"Go home, Richard," she called out. "John, attend to the carriage."

"Tessa, I must speak to you," Richard said, hurrying despite his limp.

He was gaining ground on her. She picked up her skirts and ran toward the house. Her reticule bumped her leg, jangling the coins inside. As she neared the door, Gravesend stepped back. Bells rang. Her butler was summoning the big footmen.

She stepped over the threshold and tried to shut the door, but Richard caught it. "Why are you running away from me?"

"It is after midnight. Go home and leave me in peace."

He shoved the door, and she stumbled back. Then he barged inside and slammed the door behind him.

"You are not welcome here ever again." She pointed at the door. "Leave this instant."

"I must speak to you," he said. "I cannot let you go with Shelbourne tomorrow. I'm worried about you. Anne is worried. Don't go with him, Tessa."

She whirled around. "Gravesend, tell the footmen to escort him out." She took two steps, but Richard caught her arm.

"My feelings for you have never changed, and when I saw him in your drawing room—"

"Let me go, you fool," she hissed.

Gravesend stepped in front of him. "Unhand the lady this instant."

Richard let her go. Then he pushed Gravesend so hard against the wall, the mirror above the hall table reverberated.

"You blackguard," she cried as she ran to Gravesend. "Oh, God, are you hurt?"

"Run," Gravesend croaked.

Richard grabbed her arm again and pulled her to his chest, hurting her with his tight grip. His eyes filled with contempt. "You made me a promise eight years ago, and then you betrayed me. I spent years in the filthy army because of you. You owe me."

The liquor on his breath made her stomach roil. "Let me go," she cried, trying to wriggle out of his grasp.

"Stop resisting," he gritted out. "I know what you've been doing with him behind closed doors. You think you've gotten away with it, but not this time. You're coming with me tonight."

Tessa kicked him and wrenched out of his grasp. She picked up a vase of daffodils on the hall table and threw it at him. It shattered on the floor. Richard laughed, took a step, and slipped. He fell on his bad knee and moaned. Then he rolled to his side and writhed on the floor.

"Serves you right, you bully," she cried.

Tom and Jack, her two brawny footmen, raced through the great hall. Seconds later, Tom yanked Richard's arms from behind and pulled him to his scuffling feet. Richard howled like a dog.

"Hold your tongue," she hissed.

A curly lock flopped over his scarred brow. He bared his teeth. "Bitch. How many times did Shelbourne have you?"

She marched up to him and slapped his face so hard, he jerked.

Richard's lip curled. "Tell them to turn me loose or I'll spill your dirty secrets to Shelbourne."

Jack planted him a facer. Richard cried out.

Tessa's nostrils flared. "Lower him to his knees, Tom." She regarded Jack. "My uncle once told me where to hurt a gentleman who becomes too fresh." She glanced at Jack's boots. "Will you do the honors?"

"Gladly, my lady."

On impact, a guttural sound came out of Richard's mouth. Then Jack slammed his fist into Richard's other cheek. His head went limp.

"He'll be quiet now," Tom said.

Upon her request, Gravesend produced a leather bag

of coins. With shaking hands, she rummaged in her reticule and added more money to the purse. Then she addressed both footmen. "Take the servants' entrance. Search him before you take him outside. Strip him of any weapons, money, valuables, his shoes, and his coat. Make sure he's vulnerable. There's a hackney two doors down. Be quick, and try not to attract attention. Pay the driver well for his silence. Escort our unwanted guest to a dangerous location and dump him. I presume you know the foulest place?"

Jack cracked his knuckles. "Aye, my lady."

After they hauled Richard off, Gravesend shuffled over to her. Her entire body starting shaking uncontrollably.

John hurried as fast as he could through the great hall. "My lady, are you hurt?"

"N-no. Th-thank you for trying t-to help."

"The dastard is gone," Gravesend said. "You may return to your post."

John pulled on his forelock and left.

Afterward, Gravesend looked at her sorrowfully. "My lady, I failed to protect you."

"Y-you have done so. Are you hurt, Gravesend?"

"Don't worry about me." Gravesend took her arm. "Let me help you upstairs."

She made it as far as the staircase, but her legs wobbled so badly she had to sit on the step. Tessa bent over and held her head in her trembling hands.

"My lady, I am sorry I failed you."

She glanced up at her faithful servant. "P-please, you must not blame yourself."

Gravesend's white brows furrowed. "I promised your uncle I would look after you."

"And you have done so." She must rouse herself, so he

would not worry. After she stood, she grasped the banister for support. "He is gone now and will never return."

"I fear he will," Gravesend said.

She realized she'd made a critical mistake. Eight years ago, her uncle had sent him off to war. She should have sent Richard to the docks where a press gang could take him away. Oh, why had she not thought of it? Because he'd surprised her, and she'd not thought, only reacted. He was like a rat. He'd scurry out of the filthy slums and make his way back.

"Let me send a message to Lord Broughton," Gravesend said.

"It's very late, and I must rest. I'll contact him after I return from Gatewick Park. I will be safe with the duke next week."

"The duke is a fine gentleman," Gravesend said. "Do you recollect that night he called very late?"

She hesitated, remembering their row about Caroline Fielding. "Yes, I recall the night."

"After the duke left, he returned only a few minutes later. He saw a suspicious hackney close by. He asked me to set up a guard that night."

Had Richard been spying on her then? Before he even contacted his sister? Probably so.

"The duke is protective of you, my lady," Gravesend said.

The news made her heart squeeze. Her knight in ducal armor. "We shall keep a footman posted at the door from now on."

"Tomorrow, be sure to tell the duke about that fiend breaking into your home," Gravesend said. "He'll take care of the villain."

Tessa dared not involve Tristan, not when Richard had threatened to spill his guts. If Richard acted on his threats, she could not bear for Tristan to partake in her scandal.

She bid Gravesend good night and walked up the stairs. Her heart still beat madly. Richard would surface again and crawl back to his sister. Tessa figured he probably thought *she* was too afraid to contact Broughton. Afraid of what Richard would reveal.

After she confronted Broughton next week, he would refuse to harbor Anne's brother. Richard would never manipulate Anne again. He would have no money. No place to stay. No one would receive him. His reputation would be in shreds. But he would have nothing left to lose, and she knew he would seek vengeance. She would take extra precautions from now on. The next time he came looking for her, and he would, she would make sure his next journey took him far, far away from England.

Chapter Fifteen

The sun painted gold streaks in the soot-filled sky as Tristan directed the two enormous footmen who carried Tessa's trunks as if they weighed no more than pillows.

A crisp breeze chilled his cheeks, an invigorating sensation. He felt easier knowing he could protect Tessa from Mortland at Gatewick Park. On Saturday, he'd received the first report from the Bow Street runner. As he had expected, Mortland frequented the lowest gaming hells and prostitution houses. No doubt the lout was disease-ridden. Tristan would ensure Mortland never came close to Tessa again.

He hoped he would receive the military reports on Mortland before he returned to London, and then he would show all the evidence to Broughton. He would demand Broughton hand the cur over to a press gang. Sending him away from England was the only way to ensure Tessa's safety. He didn't give a damn about her worries. When it was done, he'd tell her. She would be so relieved, she would forgive him.

Hawk climbed out of the second carriage and stretched his arms. "Might as well walk about while I can."

Julianne descended from the lead carriage, lifting her frothy skirt and petticoat. Tristan frowned as he caught Hawk ogling his sister's ankles. "Julianne, return to the carriage at once."

"I want to stretch my legs," she said.

His mother clambered out of the carriage his sister had vacated. "Where is Miss Mansfield?"

He fisted his hands on his hips. "Would everyone please return to the carriages?"

Naturally they ignored him.

Tristan consulted his watch. "I will see what is keeping Miss Mansfield." Then he turned, only to find her hurrying toward him with a netted reticule swinging from her wrist. He pocketed the watch and met her halfway up the walk. She looked a bit tired, but it was early. He offered his arm, and when she clasped his sleeve with her gloved hand, something inside his chest tumbled over. "You look very pretty," he murmured as he took in the short emerald cape that matched her bonnet ribbons.

She blushed and eyed the carriages. "Oh, my, we are to have outriders as well."

"I don't like to leave matters of safety to chance. Come along. We need to be on our way."

When he reached the carriages, he meant to send Tessa off in the same one as his mother and sister. But his mother complained that one of the ladies would have to ride with her back to the horses, which apparently was too *distressing* for females.

Tristan sighed. "Julianne, you may ride with Hawk and me."

"Oh, no," she said, shaking her head. "You will complain as soon as I take off my slippers, as you always do."

"You will do as you're told," Tristan said.

"Mama, I will not ride with him. He will lecture me all day."

"Probably," the duchess said.

Hawk winked at Julianne. "I'll ride with you and Miss Mansfield."

Julianne clasped her hands. "We will have a jolly journey. Tristan, you can ride with Mama."

"And leave me to suffer your brother's complaints for hours on end? No, thank you," the duchess said.

Hawk waggled his brows. "Old boy, no one wants to ride with you."

Tristan glanced at Tessa. The last time he'd seen her, in his mother's drawing room, he'd been too worried about Mortland to even consider telling Tessa about his mother's matchmaking scheme. But now his mother had unwittingly handed him the perfect opportunity to warn Tessa. "Miss Mansfield?" he said.

"No," his mother said. "It would be improper for you to ride alone in a closed carriage with her. We must think of Miss Mansfield's reputation."

"Mama, may I speak to you privately?" he said.

She followed him a few paces away. "The answer is no."

"We are falling behind schedule already," he said. "And this will give me an opportunity to speak to her about that subject nearest and dearest to your heart."

She hesitated. Then she frowned. "We cannot afford to risk any gossip about her."

"Mama, you have seen my protective instincts toward

her. It is brotherly concern." Any moment he expected a thunderbolt to strike him for that bouncer.

"Well, let me speak to Miss Mansfield."

He followed his mother, telling himself he was doing it for Tessa's sake.

"Miss Mansfield," she said. "My son has expressed a brotherly concern for your welfare."

Hawk snorted. Tristan glared at him.

The duchess frowned at both of them and then returned her attention to Tessa. "As I was saying, my son has requested that I allow the two of you to travel together. Naturally I am concerned for your reputation. However, he has promised to speak to you about an important subject. You are no milk-and-water miss, but if you object, say the word."

Tessa bit her lip.

Tristan lifted his brows. Then he cast a sideways glance at his mother and returned his gaze to Tessa. He hoped she would understand his silent message.

She inhaled and nodded. "I believe there can be no objection to my acquiring a pretend brother for the duration of the journey.

The duchess nodded. "When we stop at inns, you and my son will take on new identities as brother and sister as an extra precaution. He will be Mr. Gatewick and you shall be Miss Gatewick."

Hawk leaned against the second carriage. "Why not call them Mr. and Mrs. Gatewick?"

"Stubble it," Tristan said, retrieving his watch. "We are already twenty minutes behind schedule. Let us be off."

His mother cleared her throat. "Tristan, you will endeavor to make yourself agreeable to her."

"I'm sure he will be a most attentive husband to Mrs. Gatewick," Hawk drawled.

The duchess marched over to Hawk. "Help me into the carriage, you scamp. I mean to have a word or two with you."

Tristan turned to Tessa. "Are you sure?"

Her lips twitched. "I shall be happy to ride with you, dear brother."

"I am fortunate you are so agreeable, sweet wife."

She laughed as he handed her up the steps. Once inside, he sat across from her and removed his hat. Tessa squinted as sunlight glared through the windows, so he pulled down the shades on both sides. "Better?" he asked.

"Yes, thank you."

Within minutes, the carriage rolled away. He checked his watch again. "We will change horses periodically, but about one o'clock we should arrive at the Hat and Feathers Inn for luncheon. The food is plain but decent."

"I knew you would plan every detail."

"That reminds me," he said, reaching beneath the seat. "Here is a rug in case it gets chilly along the way."

"Thank you." She shook out the woolen lap robe and tucked it beneath the high waist of her gown. With an impish grin, she kicked off her slippers and wiggled her stockinged toes. "I shall be very snug."

"No fair," he said. "I can't remove my boots."

"I would offer to assist you, but I fear I'd land on my backside. You will simply have to suffer."

She grinned and removed her bonnet, revealing her upswept curls.

"If I take off my coat, will you promise not to swoon?"

he asked. "For comfort, you understand. We have a long journey."

She fanned her gloved fingers near her cheeks. "I shall try to recover from the sight of your shirtsleeves."

He moved over to her seat. "Actually it's so tight I will need your assistance. If you don't mind, that is?"

"Not at all." Using her teeth, she removed her gloves, a move he found oddly erotic. The devil, he'd definitely been too long without a woman.

"Turn your back," Tessa said, "so I can slide off your coat."

After she helped him wrestle out of the tight sleeves, she tugged the ties of her cape. When she removed it, he pitched it, along with both their gloves and his coat, to the other seat.

He winked at her. "I wager my mother would swoon if she knew we were undressing."

Tessa burst out laughing. "You are very naughty."

"Guilty as charged." He looked at the other bench. The carriage wheels rattled on the cobblestones. "I should move to the other seat, but I'd have to shout for you to hear me."

"Your mother indicated you have something to tell me. So you may stay."

He knew Tessa would launch into a tirade when he told her about his mother's plans and wanted to wait a bit. So he stretched out his legs. "You are my first lady friend."

She gave him a suspicious look. "You are thirty years old. There have been more than a few women in your life."

He knew better than to respond.

"How many were there?" Tessa asked.

He chuckled. "A gentleman never tells."

She peered up at him. "Did you not consider any of them friends?"

"We never spoke about anything of consequence."

"Was it not awkward considering the, er, closeness?"

"You mean physical intimacy?"

She blushed and nodded.

The devil, he couldn't believe he was having this conversation with her. "I do not think you will like the answer."

She lifted her pert nose and made a sound of disgust.

He'd best tell her about his mother now and then move to the other seat. "I have a confession to make. My mother ordered me to find you a husband."

She gasped. "What?"

"That was exactly my response." He paused and added, "I agreed."

"How dare you?"

"Perhaps I should clarify," he said. "I agreed to take care of the matter."

"You are not to reverse roles. I am the matchmaker. You are not a husband hunter."

His chest shook with mirth.

"What is so amusing?"

"I only agreed so I could ward off my mother."

Tessa pouted. "That was very bad of you to tease me."

"I had rather hoped you would thank me for protecting you from my mother's matchmaking scheme."

"You have my undying gratitude," she said.

"Does that involve anything more substantial?"

"If you continue to thwart your mother, I'll kiss your boots," she said.

"I'd rather you kiss my lips." The devil. He'd let that slip.

She stared straight ahead. "I'd rather kiss a toad."

"Well, then, I shall find you a husband, dear sister."

She let the blanket slip and leaned toward him. He held his breath at the seductive expression in her eyes. Then she pulled his head down and kissed him quickly on the cheek. "There," she said, still holding his face between her small palms. "Consider yourself rewarded."

He caught her hands. "You'll have to do better than that." The words rumbled out, the undertones unmistakably sensual. He knew he was flirting with disaster, but couldn't help himself. When a ragged breath escaped her, his blood heated in response.

Their gazes locked. He rubbed his thumbs over the backs of her soft hands. She closed her eyes momentarily and inhaled.

He leaned toward her without thinking. Her lashes lifted and her lush lips parted. "Oh, you're not a toad."

"Will a duke do?"

She shook her finger and sat back, once again Miss Prim.

He wondered if she'd ever had a beau. The words tumbled out of his mouth. "How many men have you kissed?" he all but growled.

"A lady never tells."

He wondered if he was the first. The idea made his chest swell. "I wager no man ever kissed you the way I did."

She looked at him and arched her brows. "Fishing for compliments, Your Grace?"

"Does that mean I deserve one?" He remembered

her abandoned response and wanted her to admit she'd liked it.

She sat back and turned her attention to the opposite seat. "I barely remember it."

"Liar."

After a few minutes, she turned and narrowed her eyes. "Have you kissed anyone since me?"

"No."

Mischief glinted in her eyes. "Out of practice, are you?"

"Is that an offer?"

She lifted her chin. "I already gave you one kiss today."

"You call that quick buss on the cheek a kiss? I think you need lessons."

"Oh, do you have a teacher in mind?"

His gaze lowered to her mouth. God, her lips tempted him. "I am at your service, milady."

She shook her head. "Thank you, but I shall wait for someone with recent experience."

"Now you've thrown down the gauntlet." He wiggled his brows. "I must avenge my honor," he said in an overly dramatic tone.

Her lips twitched. "On the kissing field?"

He'd missed matching wits with her. "Shall we duel with our lips?"

"You may find yourself eating grass for breakfast."

He leaned down. "Ah, but I may fell you with a kiss."

Laughing, she pushed on his chest. It was a clear signal to stop, but her lips were only inches away. He couldn't breathe.

"What conceit," she said, averting her face.

He exhaled, disappointed and relieved at the same time. Of course he would not have kissed her. He'd set the wheels in motion, signaling he would propose to either Amy or Georgette. And he'd sworn never to dishonor Tessa again.

Granted, he had been tempted, but there was a world of difference between wanting and acting. He had complete control of his baser urges. But he could hear her soft breathing. *Idiot. Of course, she is breathing.*

She sighed, drawing his gaze to her profile. Her full, creamy cheeks and button nose made her appear very innocent. But her mouth was all sin, a delicious pink pout made for...

He had to stop thinking about kissing her.

The carriage turned, hit a bump, and sent her careening into him. His hand closed round her shoulder to protect her. The carriage evened out, but he didn't remove his hand. Just in case they hit another bump.

Now they sat hip to hip. Her soft thigh against his leg heated his blood. He looked at her, willing her to turn to him. Slowly she returned his gaze. Her expression softened, became languorous. He angled his head, drawing closer until he could feel her breath on his mouth. Almost taste her sweet lips. His own breathing grew labored. He knew he should look away, but she bewitched him.

Neither of them moved an inch. He was afraid if he did, he would lose the struggle and kiss her. She was breathing harder now. His skin tingled all over. He thought he would die from wanting her, from resisting her. Heat spread to his groin, and he thought he'd go mad with the effort to do nothing when his whole body shouted at him to take her, devour her lips, and thrust his tongue inside her mouth.

The rug slipped to the floor. "Oh," she said.

Saved by the rug, he thought. While he retrieved it, a voice in his head told him to move over and put distance between them, but he couldn't make himself do it. He glanced at her, longing to pull her into his arms and kiss her senseless.

Tessa snuggled under the woolen rug. Then her hand slipped out to cover a yawn.

"Tired?" he murmured. Damn, he'd lost the opportunity. He ought to be glad, but he wasn't.

She nodded, and a shadow passed over her face. "I did not sleep well last night."

"Are you worried about something?"

She hesitated. "All will be well." Then she yawned again.

"Lay your head on my shoulder," he said. When she did, he wrapped his arm round her shoulders. Without a thought, he nuzzled her hair. She yawned again and nestled closer to him.

Tristan congratulated himself for his restraint. He'd almost become accustomed to the feel of her curled up next to him. Tessa's breathing slowed, indicating she'd fallen asleep. The rocking motion of the carriage lulled him as well. He closed his eyes.

An indeterminable amount of time had passed when she turned her cheek into his neck cloth. She snuggled closer to him until her soft breasts pressed against his chest. His heart thumped, remembering the way she'd moaned when he'd palmed her breast at Ashdown House.

The carriage rattled and started swaying. Her head slipped lower. He tried to right her. "Tess?"

"Hmmm?"

"Tess, draw your legs up, and I'll help you lie on the bench." Then he would move to the other seat.

Matters quickly spiraled out of his control. She drew her legs up and rubbed her cheek against his chest. He stifled a groan. Then he tried to lower her head while attempting to ease out from underneath her. In one fluid motion, she turned on her side, laying her head on his thighs. Then she put her hands beneath her cheek. "Mmmm," she mumbled.

Lord save him. When she sighed, he could feel her breath whispering along the fabric of his tight trousers. Her lush mouth was only inches away from the bad boy in his drawers. He laid his hand on her soft hair, and the gesture made him think exactly where he wanted her lips. His groin tightened again. Desperately, he tried to turn his thoughts elsewhere.

Parliament? Tessa's breathing slowed, making him think of sleep. More than a few of the older gents snored their way through the sessions. He'd caught himself nodding off a time or two during some old windbag's speech. Hell, he'd caught the old windbags napping during his speeches.

She made a funny little feminine sound. Then she stretched out her legs. The rug fell to the floor. Her skirt and petticoat were hiked up to her knees. He had a front-row view of her shapely, silk-clad calves. With a hiss, he tried to will away the inevitable erection. *Down, boy.*

He vowed not to look at her legs, but every so often she moved them. The whisper of her silk stockings on the leather drove him mad. Unbidden, a wicked fantasy appeared in his head. His fingers itched as he imagined unrolling her stockings and kissing the flesh he revealed.

Bad Boy was begging to salute her. His skintight

trousers felt like a tourniquet. Then he worried the buttons on his falls wouldn't hold up to the pressure. He imagined the sound of fireworks. Pop, pop, pop.

Tristan stared up at the ceiling, wondering if it was possible to die of a damned erection.

Deliver me from lust.

Early evening shadows covered a quarter of the Black Swan Inn's courtyard. Tristan inspected the new team of horses. Satisfied, he assisted Tessa up into their carriage. The rattle of passing carriages and jangling harnesses frayed his overwrought nerves. For eight long hours he'd wrestled with temptation. He took a deep breath and climbed into the carriage, telling himself he could resist her for a little longer. This time, he sat across from Tessa, hoping distance would cool his unruly desire.

She removed her bonnet. "How much longer until we arrive at your home?"

"We will be there before nightfall." He set his hat on the seat beside him.

The horses started and the carriage rocked into motion. Soon the clattering of hooves on the cobblestones changed to pounding thuds as the carriage turned onto the road.

Tessa attempted to smooth out the wrinkles of her diaphanous white skirt. As she pressed her hands over the fabric, he could discern the dimensions of her shapely thighs. Heat spread through his veins. He turned his attention to the window and lifted the shade, pretending interest in the passing scenery.

A few minutes later, they hit a bump. He turned to her. "Rough start," he said, pulling the shade down.

The carriage started rattling and swaying. Her tense

expression worried him. "The road will smooth out soon."

She clutched the edge of the seat. "Is it safe?"

The reason for her fear dawned on him. Her parents had perished in a carriage accident. Grabbing the strap for balance, he stood, bending his head. The carriage swayed again.

"No, you must sit. It's dangerous." She sounded terrified.

In one long stride, he made it over to her seat and put his arm round her shoulders. "I will keep you safe."

The minute he uttered the words, the carriage jolted. She gasped. He could feel her trembling, so he clasped her hand. "Just a bit longer. I promise."

She gripped his hand hard during the bumpy ride. A half hour later, the sickening swaying eased. She released his hand and sighed. "Thank goodness." Then she removed her cape. "Oh, that is much better." She glanced at him. "May I help you with your coat?"

"God, yes." He turned his back. As she assisted him, her fingers brushed the silk fabric of his waistcoat, making him long for her to touch his skin. She folded the coat lengthwise and set it aside, a domestic gesture that for some odd reason tugged at him.

He settled back, putting distance between their bodies. "My mother cornered me at the inn. She insisted I speak to you about marriage again."

Tessa made an exasperated sound. "Did you tell her it was hopeless?"

"She is threatening to find you a husband if I fail."

"Heaven forbid." She straightened the neckline of her gown. "We must think of some way to divert her."

"My mother is a formidable woman and will not forget the matter easily. She is convinced you need a husband."

Tessa's eyes glinted with mischief. "I have it. As soon as we arrive at your home, I will pen a description of my ideal husband. The requirements will be impossible. You will honestly be able to tell her there is not a man alive who will please me."

"It won't work. My mother thinks you are more than eligible and could have your choice of suitors."

She found the rug and shook it out over her lap. "Tell your mother to stop meddling in my affairs."

"Tess, she is right, you know."

"I have no desire to marry, and you are not to broach the subject again."

"You are all alone in the world. I worry about you."

She regarded him with a defiant expression. "I am no fool, Your Grace. I can spot a fortune hunter at fifty paces."

Tessa had referred to him by his formal address, a sure sign she found his questions unsettling. "Is it fortune hunters you fear?"

"I fear nothing."

"Except marriage," he said.

She kicked off her slippers with more than a little force. "Oh, you are ridiculous. I already told you I prefer my independence and my career."

"You believe in happily ever after for everyone but yourself," he said.

Anger flashed in her eyes. "The women I make matches for have no choice. Their livelihoods depend on marriage. I do my best to ensure they find loving husbands." Her bosom rose and fell. "Even you do not have my freedom. You must marry to secure an heir, but I am not duty-bound. My uncle's title is dead. I am free to will my fortune to whomever I please."

"Is that what your uncle would wish for you?" he murmured.

"I am one of the richest women in England. Do you have any idea how rare that sort of independence is?"

He smiled. "I do, but you have not answered my question."

"My answer is that I do not have the usual inducements to wed."

He caressed her cheek. "There are other advantages to marriage."

"Oh, yes, I could wed, and then my husband would have complete control of my fortune. What a happy prospect."

"You could put it in trust before you wed, and then you would have complete control of it."

She huffed. "No man would accept a wife without a penny."

Her cynicism stunned him. Until now, she had given every impression of being an incurable romantic. "You believe in love for everyone but yourself. Why is that, Tessa?"

A mirthless huff escaped her. "I am hardly an eligible young miss, despite what your mother thinks. Everyone else has labeled me a spinster."

For years, she had sacrificed her own needs for others. Now she was caught up in a vicious cycle. She didn't believe any man would see past her spinster status unless he was bent upon possessing her fortune. And the damnable truth was she would never allow anyone to get close enough to see the woman beneath the labels of spinster and heiress. But he knew she was much more.

He thought about the way she thumbed her nose at society's rules. Maybe it wasn't heedlessness, but rather defensiveness. "Tess, you give so much to others, to your own detriment."

"I deny myself nothing. I have wealth beyond my means to spend."

Her angry retort made him smile. "I am not speaking of material possessions."

She rolled her eyes.

"You deny yourself family and companionship."

"I have friends."

"I know," he said. "But you are forgetting one benefit to marriage."

"You are trying to divert me from your courtship," she said. "We do need to discuss it. I am concerned about your doubts."

"We already discussed the matter. I'll not let you change the subject," he said. "Think of what you are missing."

She averted her gaze. "I am a matchmaker and am fully aware of the benefits of marriage, but they do not apply to me."

He cupped her cheek and turned her to face him. "You think not?"

"I—I know so."

"You do not sound certain," he murmured, caressing her silky skin.

"Wh-what are you doing?"

He winked at her. "I am trying to convince you of what you are missing."

A ragged breath escaped her.

He lowered his head and breathed near her ear, telling himself he only meant to prove his point. "Would you miss naughty whispers?"

"You are unseemly."

"Not convinced, I see." He turned his head until her breath whispered over his lips. "Would you miss tender kisses?"

"You are wicked."

He could almost taste her. "Want more?"

"You are indecent t-to ask."

"But I will." He reached round her, supporting her back as he leaned forward. The rug slipped. She drew back and gasped. He glanced down at the rounded tops of her ivory breasts. Then he lowered his head and blew between the shadowy cleavage. She whimpered.

Heat flooded his groin. The game had gone too far. When he lifted his head, her eyes fluttered open. "Now do you have an inkling of what you are missing?" he said.

She pushed his chest. "You are a tease."

He let her go. "I proved my point."

She sat up and lifted her chin. "You proved nothing."

He tickled her waist.

She cried out and wiggled away. He chuckled and tickled her again. The rug fell to the floor as she leaped to her feet, swaying with the carriage. Tristan grabbed her arm to keep her from falling. She tried to wrench out of his grasp. He tugged her toward him, trapping her between his legs. When the carriage rocked, she lost her balance and grasped his shoulders. Grinning, he jiggled her with his thighs. A sweet laugh escaped her.

Their eyes met. He looked longingly at her mouth. She wet her lips.

Then he did a reckless thing. He leaned forward and captured her lips. *Tell me no. Stop me. Tell me I am all but promised to another.*

She returned his kiss, and all rational thought fled.

He hauled her up onto his lap. She reached up, tunneling her fingers through his hair. He molded his lips to his, but it wasn't enough. He plucked at her mouth and licked her lips. When she gasped, he thrust his tongue inside. The instinct to devour her pounded in his blood, but he checked his rough urges. He savored her, slowing the rhythm to intensify her pleasure. She tasted sweet and tart, like sugar and lemon.

He surfaced for air, swearing to stop, but she placed her palm over his heart. "I want to feel your heart beating for me," she whispered.

"Kiss me," he said.

She touched her lips to his. He opened for her, an invitation. She tasted him uncertainly, as if he were some new delicacy. The truth dawned on him that this was new to her, only her second kiss. And only with him, he was sure of it. He let her explore, and as she grew bolder, the delicious ache in his groin heated to rock-hard arousal. Unable to hold back, he drew her tongue into his mouth and sucked. A soft, feminine moan escaped her. So he did it again and again. Then she reciprocated, and he groaned.

When he lifted his lips, she planted butterfly kisses on his cheeks and his jaw. Unable to help himself, he suckled her slender neck. Her fingers tightened on his shoulders as if she were afraid of falling.

One more kiss. Just once more. Then he would stop.

When their lips met again, her mouth opened to welcome his tongue. His need for her grew to a fever pitch.

Somehow his hands were fumbling with the small hooks on the back of her gown. When he freed the last one, he pushed her sleeves and her bodice down and freed her arms. She reached for his shoulders, and he caressed the tops of her breasts displayed above her stays. Then his fingers traveled over the hard boning of her busk. He kissed her again. Then he removed the busk and tossed it aside on the seat.

She gasped. He pulled down the top of her soft stays, revealing her powdery white breasts. "You are beautiful," he whispered, cupping her.

Her eyes drifted closed. He teased her nipples with his thumbs. Then he gently squeezed the distended buds. "Oh," she whispered.

He lowered his mouth and touched the tip of his tongue to one pert nipple. She arched up to him, so he did it again and again, teasing her until she clutched his head.

"Please," she begged.

Yes. He took her fully in his mouth and suckled hard. Her ardent, feminine moans and restless movements emboldened him. He lifted her skirts, sliding his hand over her velvety soft thighs. She opened for him with only the slightest coaxing. When he found the springy curls, he cupped her with his hand. Her slick, hot folds drove him mad with desire. He almost dipped his finger inside, but feared taking her virginity. He caressed her, explored, and found the sweet spot. She made a mewing sound in the back of her throat. He rubbed her rhythmically. "Like this?"

She arched up to him in answer.

His cock throbbed, grew harder, made him think dangerous thoughts. He wanted to straddle her over his lap and thrust inside her. But he could not, would not, must not, take her virginity.

She arched her hips and she was no longer damp, but wet, soaking wet. Her whimpers were the most erotic sounds he'd ever heard.

"Come for me, darling Tessa." He lowered his head and suckled her other nipple.

Her back bowed as she cried out. Then she collapsed.

He kissed her cheek. "Sweet, sweet Tess."

"I am floating," she mumbled.

His cock throbbed, almost painfully. Without thinking, he arched against her, but her soft bottom made the ache worse. "Sorry," he mumbled.

Her eyes flew open. She sat up, wriggling on his lap.

He groaned.

"Oh, no. Did I hurt you?"

"Don't move." He panted. "No, you had better move. To the seat."

She slid off his lap. He leaned his head back against the seat, gritting his teeth.

"Tristan?"

He peered at her, a mistake. Her kiss-swollen lips made the beast inside him want to howl.

She placed her palm on his chest. He inhaled. Her fingers skimmed over his waistcoat. Shock cascaded over him as he realized she was unbuttoning it.

"Tess," he said, his voice hoarse.

"Shhhh." Then she tugged his voluminous shirt out of his trousers.

He made a halfhearted attempt to stop her, but when her hands slid underneath his shirt, skimming up his belly to his chest, he lost the will to resist.

"Your skin is so hot," she whispered.

He would stop her soon. He would. He must. But oh, Lord, her touch burned him. Made him want, want, want.

As her hands trailed downward, he clenched his teeth. His cock strained against the confines of his trousers. He fought against the overwhelming urge to free himself.

Then her fingers trailed to one of the buttons on his falls. Alarmed, he grabbed her hand. "No."

"You don't want me to touch you?"

The throaty sound of her voice nearly undid him. "You cannot."

"Why?"

A huff escaped him. She didn't understand. "Because it is like shaking up a bottle of champagne and popping the cork."

"Oh." She looked disappointed.

He wanted her to protest. He wanted her to touch him. He wanted too much. And he had no right.

She kissed his lips. "Don't move."

Then she grasped his coat, rummaged inside, and dangled his handkerchief before his eyes.

When he realized her intention, it took all of his self-control to refuse. "No, I cannot let you."

She closed his fingers over the scrap of fabric and waved his hand. "This is a white flag. Say you surrender."

"Oh, God."

"Close enough." She gave him a siren's smile, and with agonizing slowness, she released the buttons on his falls and untied his drawers. When his engorged cock sprang out, her eyes widened. She started to touch him, and then hesitated. When she looked up into his eyes, he lost the battle. "Yes."

She swirled her finger round the drop of moisture. Then she clasped him. "Impressive," she whispered.

He surged in her hand. She smiled, bent down, and kissed him quickly. He must have died and gone to heaven.

She glanced up at him through her long lashes. "Did I hurt you?"

"Quite the opposite," he muttered. Then he wrapped his hand round her own and showed her how to pleasure him. Bless her, she caught on quickly.

He watched her the whole time. The pressure built and built, until the erotic spasms started and a hoarse sound erupted from his throat. She caught his cry with her mouth and covered him with the handkerchief. He shuddered as the throbbing ecstasy overcame him. Then his head fell back against the seat.

Disoriented, he awoke to the tickle of something soft beneath his nose. The scent of roses and woman permeated the fog in his brain. Hair, soft hair. Tessa's hair.

Awareness crept into his deadened brain in stupid spurts. Her cheek on his shoulder. His hand on her naked breast.

Good Lord, what had he done?

He realized his trousers were unbuttoned. The devil! He ought to be horsewhipped for what he'd done and what he'd allowed her to do.

A feminine sigh drew his attention to her face. Her eyes opened, and then she smiled, a sultry, well-pleasured smile.

She kissed his cheek. He turned to her, meaning to speak, to apologize, to do the devil only knew what. But somehow he found himself kissing her again, and whatever noble intentions he had crumbled. As soon as he tasted her, he sprang to attention.

He cupped her breasts, filling his hands to overflowing. At her quick intake of breath, he gazed down as he circled her distended nipples with his thumbs. Her head fell back as he pressed her breasts together and lowered his head to flick his tongue rapidly back and forth between her nipples. His cock grew rock-hard.

Her throaty moans emboldened him. He raised her up and pressed her thighs apart until she straddled him. Then he pushed her skirts out of the way, pulling her closer, until they were skin to skin, as close as they could be without joining. The sensation made him wild, insane with lust. He needed her, craved her, wanted to make her his in every way. The urge to penetrate almost, almost overcame him. And then he looked into her eyes and saw fear. "I swear I won't go too far."

She closed her hands round his erection. They rocked together, the ecstasy taking him to a mindless place where there was only her and him and this moment. Then he took her nipple in his mouth, sucking hard. She cried out. He wasn't far behind. A hoarse sound erupted from his throat as the sweet rapture overtook him, the waves beating in time with his heart. Quickly, she pulled the hem of her petticoat forward, wrapping it round his throbbing sex as his seed spilled over.

He enfolded her in his arms, and she buried her face on his shoulder. Then she mumbled something he did not understand. His heart galloped as rapidly as the thudding hooves of the horses. He gulped in air, unable to focus. When his breathing started to slow, a drunken, satiated stupor claimed him. His brain shut down. He closed his eyes and gave in to the little death.

Chapter Sixteen

A clattering sound awoke him. His muddled brain refused to work at first. Then he became aware of the vehicle slowing. Curving in a wide turn. Shouts outside. The carriage lurched to a halt. He nudged the shade aside. Bloody hell!

Tristan grasped her shoulders. "Tessa, wake up."

Her eyes opened. She looked dazed.

"Hurry, I've got to dress you."

She gasped. "Where are we?"

"Gatewick Park."

"Oh, my God." She covered her mouth.

He lifted her in his arms and stood her before him. "We must be quick." He pulled up her chemise and stays.

"Where is the busk?" She sounded frantic.

He found it on the seat, and with trembling hands, he tried repeatedly to insert it. At last, he managed to push it into place. He helped her with her sleeves and bodice. Then he turned her. She shook so hard, he was having trouble with the hooks. He forced himself to concentrate and managed the last one.

Voices sounded outside. In a panic, he grasped her cape and threw it over her shoulders. While she dealt with her bonnet and shoes, he tied his drawers, stuffed his shirt back into place, and fastened the buttons on his falls and waistcoat as fast as he could. She helped him into his coat.

He caught her face in his hands. "Meet me in my study later tonight. We will talk."

An arrested expression crossed her face. "I do not think that is a good idea."

"Tess, we've no time to argue now."

She inhaled sharply. "I am deeply sorry for seducing you. It did not occur to me you would become so distraught."

"What?" Had she forgotten to pack her brains?

"You must not worry, for I will still respect you tomorrow." She paused. "But..."

Tristan gaped at her. He must have pleasured her senseless.

A knock sounded at the door. They both turned to stare at it. Then she glanced at him and said in a rush, "I hope you will forgive me, but I cannot make an honest man out of you."

While Julianne played the pianoforte in the drawing room, Tessa pretended to be engrossed in the music, but she could not concentrate. The haze of Tristan's lovemaking still held her in thrall. She remembered the words he'd spoken in his chocolate voice. *"Like this?"* She squeezed her thighs together, remembering the exquisite sensations.

Tessa must be careful not to reveal her overwhelming feelings, but her heart overflowed and his sensual spell still enveloped her like a thick fog. But she must not show it. The duchess sat on the opposite end of the sofa, and her observant eyes missed nothing. She'd certainly missed neither Tessa's rumpled gown nor Tristan's wrinkled cravat when they'd descended the carriage a mere three hours ago, though she'd said nothing. Tessa prayed she'd attributed it to a long day of travel.

Soon Tristan and Hawk would arrive after imbibing their after-dinner port. She must not look at Tristan, for she feared everything in her heart would show on her face. At dinner, she'd dared to peek at him, and he'd returned her gaze over his wineglass. His blue eyes had smoldered as he'd returned her gaze. And she'd remembered his erotic words. *Come for me, darling Tessa.*

She would not regret today. Not ever. She'd stolen one afternoon of lovemaking with Tristan, incomplete as it was. Even now, with his mother seated on the same sofa and his sister playing, she recalled his touches and kisses. The way he'd watched her beneath his sultry lashes as she'd pleasured him. And his hoarse cry as he'd throbbed in her hands. She'd wanted to weep when it was over, but he'd awakened and taken her lips in a fierce kiss, as if he were starving for her. He'd made her feel wanted, desired, and loved.

And if what she'd done was wrong, and she knew it was, no one but the two of them would ever know. He knew, as she knew, they could never be. Like the star-crossed Romeo and Juliet, they had only the one stolen time together. No matter how much she grieved for him afterward, she would not regret one single moment of their lovemaking.

But now they were in his home. The girls and their families would arrive day after tomorrow. She shoved the thought aside. Soon enough she would witness him court two others, but she would face that heartache only when she must. For right now, she would keep him in her heart as long as she could.

She ought to be ashamed, and part of her was, but another selfish part of her wasn't sorry at all. Because she would carry the beautiful memory with her for the rest of her life and know that she'd given her heart for one day to the man she loved.

"Did my son speak to you?"

The duchess's voice startled her. Oh, God, did she suspect? Had she simply waited for the right opportunity? But no, she could not know. Tessa prayed she did not know. "I beg your pardon?"

"Attend me, young lady. Did my son speak to you?"

"Your son spoke of many things," she said. Oh, this was bad, very bad. She could hardly think because she was drunk with all her feelings for Tristan.

The duchess pointed her quizzing glass at Tessa. "I have noted the clever way you misdirect the conversation. I will not tolerate it."

"I beg your pardon," Tessa said. "It is an ingrained habit." She wasn't quite sure what the duchess meant, but Tessa thought she'd better act contrite. Not an easy feat for her.

"You have a nervous disposition, no doubt." The duchess narrowed her eyes. "Do most people fall for your diversions?"

Tessa stilled, unsure what to say.

"Answer my question," the duchess said.

"Um, most people do not seem to realize I have changed the subject." She glanced at the drawing room door. Perhaps she could claim weariness and leave. But she wanted to see Tristan once more tonight. Longed to see his expression, perhaps even one more secret look from him, one that acknowledged he knew it was over, but would always remember her. A look that said you are special, nothing like all those other women before. Or the one he must marry.

"I suppose it proves useful in thorny situations," the duchess said. Then she frowned. "Young woman, I am speaking to you."

Tessa swerved her gaze to the duchess. "I beg your pardon?"

"You did not answer my question. Did my son speak to you about marriage?"

She swallowed. Did the duchess mean a marriage between Tristan and her? Excitement and fear for what could never be rose inside her. Oh, she'd thought of it today. Let herself pretend for a while. Imagined the two of them tangled in sheets. Imagined touching his hot skin while he devoured her mouth, her neck, her breasts.

The duchess peered at her. "Did he mention any particular gentlemen?"

Just like that, reality crashed into her. "No," she said.

"Hmmph," the duchess said, and returned her attention to her daughter.

Tessa gripped her hands. How could she even have allowed herself to imagine a future with him? She could never marry Tristan. Even if it weren't for the girls and his noble intention to avoid scandal, she could not have him, even if he wanted to marry her. But she loved him.

She loved him.

Tristan didn't love her. He'd told her over and over again he didn't believe in love. For him, it was nothing but lust. She was no different from all those other women he'd taken to bed. No, she was worse. Because those women didn't pretend to be respectable. Those women didn't pretend he loved them. Those women weren't masquerading as his matchmaker while dallying with him.

How would the duchess feel if she knew the woman she'd championed at the parlor game had lured her son into an illicit one-day liaison? Tessa tamped down the guilt rising in her because she wanted to cherish her feelings for him for this one night.

Footsteps clipped outside the drawing room door. Tessa's heart squeezed as Tristan and Hawk strolled inside. When Tristan looked at her, she glanced at him from beneath her lashes, unable to resist.

Julianne stopped playing. Tessa broke eye contact with Tristan. Heavens, she must take herself in hand.

"Julianne, pray continue," the duchess said. "You are in want of practice." Once Julianne resumed playing, the duchess turned to her son. "Be seated."

Hawk strolled over to the pianoforte. Tristan sat right beside Tessa on the sofa. Oh, no. He sat much too close. She inhaled his delicious scent, a scent like a magic vapor that made her crave him. He shifted just a little. She glanced at his long fingers on the sofa, now only inches away from her own, and remembered what he'd done to her with his hands.

A discordant note banged from the pianoforte. "Hawk, you rogue," Julianne cried out, laughing.

Tessa dared to cast a sidelong look at Tristan.

He watched her with a determined expression. She glanced away. A horrible suspicion gripped her. Surely he did not mean to propose to her. No, he would not. He knew it would cause a horrific scandal. His mother did not suspect. If she had, she would have sent Tessa packing back to London. No one knew what they had done. Tristan had said he would not bring disgrace upon his family. Tessa breathed a sigh of relief. She was safe. And miserably, hopelessly in love with a man she could never hope to deserve.

"Tristan," the duchess said.

Tessa nearly jumped out of her skin at the sound of the duchess's voice.

"What did you do to Miss Mansfield?" the duchess said. "Look at her. She is uncharacteristically meek. I can barely get a sensible word out of her. I told you to make yourself agreeable to her."

His voice rumbled. "Was I not agreeable enough for your taste, Miss Mansfield?"

Oh, she wanted to box his ears for that double entendre. "You were . . . tolerable."

"Perhaps it is your turn to be agreeable, Miss Mansfield," he said.

She returned his gaze. What did he mean? Oh, my, did he think to continue their liaison? She could not. They could not. But a very naughty part of her imagined running through the grounds late at night, hand in hand, until they were well-hidden—and then he would swoop in for a lush, wet, and hungry kiss.

"Tristan," the duchess said. "I understand you spoke to Miss Mansfield about marriage. Did you get her to agree?"

"Not yet."

The duchess rapped her fan on the sofa. "If you do not apply yourself to finding her a husband, I will take over the matter."

"I will speak to her again tomorrow after breakfast," he said.

Tessa swerved her surprised gaze to him. He'd said he only wanted to warn her, but later he'd tried to convince her to marry. Perhaps he only wanted to discuss ways to divert his mother.

"Tristan," the duchess said. "Make sure she says yes."

Tristan gazed at Tessa with an expression so intent she could not breathe. "I will."

The next morning, Tessa descended the stairs and walked toward the breakfast room with her head held high. After a great deal of thought, she'd concluded she'd misinterpreted Tristan's meaning last evening. He would not risk scandal, not when both girls and their parents were expected to arrive tomorrow.

As for his mother's misguided matchmaking attempts, Tessa planned to dispatch them at breakfast and be done with the matter forever.

When she entered the dining room, everyone else was already seated. Tristan held out a chair for her, and for one heady moment, she inhaled the scent of sandalwood soap. "I'll fill a plate for you," he said.

"Toast only." She'd decided to start a slimming regimen and improve her figure. Of course she'd concocted the idea after imagining stepping naked out of a steamy bath only to find Tristan watching.

He set a brimming plate of eggs, sausages, and toast

before her. She spread only a smear of strawberry preserves on the toast. After finishing half, she set it aside, sipped her tea, and smiled at the duchess, who sat at the end of the table.

The duchess set her cup down and regarded her son. "Here is evidence of a nervous disposition. She cannot eat."

"On the contrary, Duchess, I am not nervous at all. After a refreshing night's sleep, I am myself once again," Tessa said. In truth, she'd lain awake for a long time, reliving Tristan's lovemaking. "Now that I am no longer suffering from travel fatigue, I wish to thank you for your concern about my marital status."

"We will discuss the matter after breakfast," Tristan said.

"No, we will discuss it now," Tessa said. "There is no reason for this meeting. I have made my arguments in the past and have no wish to repeat them. My mind is made up. I will not marry, and now we may discuss your courtship, which is the reason we are gathered here."

Tristan set his cup down. "You have no one to protect you. You know Mortland is after your fortune."

"My brawny footmen are more than equal to the task." She thought better of mentioning Mortland's invasion of her home two nights ago. If Tristan knew, he might confront Richard. And then Richard would confess everything—everything but his own perfidy. She could not bear for Tristan to know the truth about her.

The duchess cleared her throat. "Miss Mansfield, we are straying from the subject. You need a husband."

"For what? I manage quite well on my own, and as I've said previously, I enjoy my independence."

The duchess narrowed her eyes. "What of the estate? You must marry and have children so that one of them may inherit. Your uncle would want a family member to take over and ensure its prosperity."

"Since there is no entailment, I may leave it to whomever I please. Meanwhile, I consult with my steward and employ hundreds of other servants to see to the operation of the estate."

"Why should you bother with men's work? And who takes care of managing the housekeeping affairs? Do you relegate those duties to a servant?" the duchess said.

Tessa smiled, knowing her next words would impress the duchess. "But, Your Grace, I manage both the estate affairs and the housekeeping duties at the same time. Name one man who can say as much."

Silence ensued. Certain Tristan would glower because she'd topped him in duties, she cast a surreptitious glance at him.

He set his napkin on the table. "Are you finished with your breakfast, Miss Mansfield?"

"Indeed I am, but I will be happy to wait for everyone else." She returned her attention to his mother and found the woman regarding her with amusement. "Duchess, how may I help you today?"

"Miss Mansfield, I am astonished by all of your accomplishments," the duchess said. "May I enumerate them?"

Oh, dear, the duchess meant to put her in her place. "Your Grace, I did not mean—"

The duchess held up her hand. "No, let me speak without interruption. You don't strike me as overly modest, but you are not conceited either. Indeed, you devote yourself unselfishly to the needs of others. You nursed your uncle for years, took in Lady Broughton when she had no one, and as if that weren't enough, you've made matches for a number of poor wallflowers. You even took on the task of matchmaking for my son, a Herculean feat I couldn't manage. To top it all off, you manage the estate responsibilities of a gentlemen *and* a lady. While you are not one of the common beauties, your voluptuous charms are far more alluring to gentlemen. In short, Miss Mansfield, you are perfect."

"Duchess, I know my faults, and I most certainly did not mean—"

"Hush," the duchess said. "Tristan, you should have no trouble at all finding her a husband. When the eligible gentlemen learn she is on the market, they will fall at her feet."

Tessa stared at the duchess in horror. Oh, dear God. How had everything gone so wrong?

Hawk waggled his brows. "I say, Miss Mansfield, you are quite a catch."

The duchess looked at her son. "I've changed my mind. Take your friend off the list of potential husbands."

"What?" Hawk and Tessa said at the same time. She gaped at him. He gaped at her.

"The pair of you would spend all your time trying to outdo each other in some mischievous pursuit or another." The duchess regarded her son again. "She'll want some weak ninny she can twist round her little finger. Find her a man who will keep a firm rein, but won't break her in the process." She rose. "Tristan, get her agreement."

They all stood.

Tessa gritted her teeth and rose slowly. "No. I will not stand for anyone telling me what to do. Out of necessity, I learned to manage my estate and all the other responsibilities. I am not like other women. My career is important to me. It brings me joy. I am independent, and I like it. I'm not some wilting flower waiting for a man to rescue me. I see those ladies who go from their fathers' arms to their husbands' arms. I understand that is what they know and need. But I am not like them, and I can't change it. And I don't need a husband to keep a firm rein over me. How insulting. I rein myself."

Hawk grinned. "Duchess, will you reinstate me on the husband list? I find her passion most exciting."

The duchess fingered her quizzing glass. "Yes, I begin to see the possibility. She could put a firm rein on you."

"Stubble it," Tristan said. Then he turned to Tessa.

His eyes held an odd expression, one she couldn't interpret. "I wish to show you something." He held out his arm.

She relented because they needed to speak privately. But as he led her away, a stinging sensation rippled over her hands. She'd seen the determined look in his eyes last night. No, she would not borrow trouble. He understood as she understood that yesterday was yesterday. And done.

Chapter Seventeen

Tessa's stomach churned as he led her up one side of the U-shaped staircase. Neither of them spoke, but his severe expression spoke volumes. He'd probably wrestled with his conscience last night, but she would do her best to persuade him not to dwell on what could not be changed. They must put yesterday behind them. When he accepted the inevitable, and he would because he had no other choice, their forbidden friendship would end. An aching sadness spread through her veins, but she must not show her feelings.

When they reached the landing, he walked over to a winged statue in one of the enormous arched niches. "Eros," he said. "The Greek god of lust and fertility."

"Oh." Heat flooded her face as she recalled their intimacies yesterday. She'd responded with abandon to his every touch, but she would not allow shame to mar her beautiful memory. Soon he would marry, and all his kisses and caresses would be for his wife. She could not bear to think of it, but an image of Georgette's dimpled smile and slender figure rose in her mind. All her feeble hopes that he would always remember their lovemaking shriveled as she recalled his words. *I want to want my wife.* Sorrow engulfed her, for she knew he'd soon forget her when he took the exquisite Georgette to his bed.

Tristan continued walking, and she could not help noticing the other wall niches stood empty.

"I sold artwork after my father died," he said.

Her throat clogged, knowing how much he'd sacrificed for his family. "You did what you had to do," she said. Like him, she would do what she had to do and end what never should have started in the first place.

Upon reaching the gallery, he paused for a moment and took a deep breath. Her lips trembled. *Forgive me. I never meant to cause you anguish.*

He exhaled audibly and escorted her inside the long, rectangular room. She gazed at the numerous portraits lining the dark-paneled walls. Two crystal chandeliers hung from the ornately carved ceiling. A fireplace with a pale marble mantel stood at the far end of the gallery.

Tristan took her over to a portrait of a gentleman with a pointed beard and a pearl eardrop. "James Gatewick, the first Earl of Shelbourne," he said. "He served Henry VIII."

As he strolled on, she gazed down the wall. "Oh, look, that is your mother, is it not?"

"Yes." They walked over to the portrait. The artist had deftly captured the duchess's ironic smile. "Your mother was a great beauty. She still is."

Tristan led her to the huge portrait next to it. "My father," he said.

Tristan bore the same square jaw and thick-lashed blue

eyes as his late father. "You bear a strong resemblance to him."

"Until yesterday, I would have said I do not resemble him in character."

Her quick inhalation brought his gaze down to her upturned face. "I have not stepped inside this gallery since my father died," he said.

"Why?" she whispered.

"Resentment."

Tessa turned her attention to the portrait and glowered at it. "Your mother loved him. How could he betray her?"

"He was ten years her senior, well on his way to dissipation and dun territory when she met him. My mother's family traded her along with a generous fortune for a ducal connection."

Tessa regarded him with parted lips. "That is the reason you refused to marry for money."

"That and pride," he said.

"How did he die?"

"Predictably." His gaze strayed to the portrait again. "A cuckolded husband called him out. My father was drunk and misfired. His opponent shot him in the shoulder. The surgeon brought him home and dug the ball out, but the wound festered. He lingered for three days. Just long enough in his feverish state to beg my mother's forgiveness."

"And yours?" she said.

"I refused to see him."

A terrible suspicion gripped her. "Why did you bring me here?"

"I will not follow in my father's footsteps. It is my responsibility to restore your honor and mine."

Her heart knocked against her chest. "What are you saying?"

"You know, Tessa."

She started shaking. "I—I knew you would take all the blame, but you cannot absolve me of responsibility. I—I didn't stop you."

"No, I will not allow you to make excuses for my conduct. I swore never to touch you again at Ashdown House, but I broke my promise. There is only one way for me to make this right."

Panic clawed her lungs. "No. The girls. The families will arrive tomorrow."

"Shhhh," he said, placing his finger briefly over her lips. "Do not worry. I will speak to their fathers privately. The courtship was supposed to allow me the opportunity to know their daughters, but it has not worked as I'd planned. It will be a tricky business. The girls will have to cry off, but I also plan to pay a handsome sum to their fathers as restitution."

"I know you have doubts, but you must not end the courtship because of what happened between us," she said quickly. "We are consenting adults and—"

"Listen," he said, his deep voice silencing her. "In June when the season ends, you will return with my family to Gatewick Park. And then we will formalize our engagement."

She gasped. "No. Say no more, I beg you."

He took her by the shoulders. "Have your attorney arrange to put all of your fortune in trust before we marry. It will remain in your sole control." He smiled a little. "You see, there is a man who will wed you without a penny."

Oh, God, no. "It is not about my fortune," she said,

hearing the desperation in her own voice. "This cannot happen. The consequences are too terrible to contemplate. It is impossible, and you know it."

"Tess, you're shaking. Come sit with me." He led her over to a velvet bench and took her cold hands in his. "You're overset, but I will take care of you."

She started babbling. "I thought you understood. Yesterday was the one and only time for us. I never expected anything else."

"I dishonored you more than once." His expression turned resolute. "Your honor and mine are at stake."

At all costs, she must dissuade him. "We are both worldly. As much as I appreciate your honorable intentions, we did not go so far as to make an irrevocable mistake. No one knows. We will forget it ever happened."

"Impossible. I have intimate knowledge of your body. As you have intimate knowledge of mine. I can't pretend it never happened."

"Tristan, how can you ignore the scandal? Already I am accused of trying to sink my claws into you. It will hurt your family and the girls," she said, her voice rising.

He smoothed an errant wisp of hair from her cheek. "Last night, I thought long and hard before making my decision. I did not dismiss my obligation to the girls and their families easily. But I had to weigh that against the wrong I had done to you."

"I consented knowing there could be nothing more between us," she said. "I absolve you of any obligation to me, and you must accept."

He squeezed her hands. "Let me finish. I thought about what I would do if your uncle still lived, and I knew I would ask him for your hand in marriage. He is not here, but that changes nothing. Honor must be preserved. It is my duty to wed you."

His words stabbed her heart. Even though she could never marry him, she loved him dearly. And he'd all but told her he would never have proposed if he'd not felt duty-bound. He didn't even know he'd crushed her pride and broken her heart.

"I know this is not the fairy tale marriage your parents had," he said. "But you know as well as I do your uncle would brook no argument if he were here."

Her uncle's words spoken so long ago came to her. *If a man ever proposes, you must tell him.* She could not do it—could not tell Tristan the sordid truth. "We have no choice but to accept we made a mistake and put it behind us."

"Your fear is understandable under the circumstances," he said. "I know this is not how you envisioned your life. I cannot promise our marriage will be easy, but we will work it out as we go along. We do it all the time, so you know it's possible. In return, I offer you my family, my protection and devotion, and children. And Tess, what is between us—the passion—is rare. I never meant to compromise you, but we can be happy together."

She released his hands. "Can we be happy when such a marriage would cause pain to so many? Have you thought about how Amy and Georgette would feel? They would be humiliated and scorned. And you said you would never bring scandal upon your family. We cannot do this to them."

He frowned. "You urged me to call off the courtship because I have doubts, but I've no doubt about my duty to you. We will wed."

"I cannot," she said miserably.

He reared back as if she'd slapped him. "You are refusing me?"

"I am refusing to bring scandal upon you and your family." Her eyes filled with tears. She'd told him the truth, but he would not understand.

Tristan rose from the bench and stared at Tessa. A numbing sensation crept over him. The moment seemed unreal, as if he were standing outside his own body observing.

She hung her head. "I am so sorry," she whispered.

Tristan remembered something Hawk had said the first night he'd met Tessa. He'd chosen the only woman in the kingdom who wouldn't wed him.

Damn her! His face heated, and he turned his back on her. Damn her! He was a bloody duke—the most eligible bachelor in England. And she had refused him. He'd offered her everything, and she'd said no.

Running footsteps sounded outside the gallery. "Tristan? Miss Mansfield? Come quickly," Julianne said, excitement in her voice.

He cleared his throat, unable to look at his sister. "Julianne, please grant us privacy."

"Mama said you must come downstairs now. A carriage just arrived." She laughed. "Someone came a day early."

"We will be down directly," he said.

After his sister's footsteps retreated, he clenched and unclenched his hands. Then, with a deep inhalation, he forced control over himself. "Shall we greet the guests, Miss Mansfield?"

• • •

Tessa stood at the bottom of the horseshoe-shaped steps with everyone else. She managed a weak smile and clutched her shawl so hard her fingers hurt. Only the knowledge that others were there kept her tears in check. Oh, God, how could she have done this to him?

The breeze ruffled Tristan's dark, tousled hair as the guests descended from the carriage. He glanced back at her and then turned away. She bit her lip because she wanted to cry out, but she must not.

She was very close to breaking down. So she made herself watch the others to remind herself that she could not embarrass him. She must be strong for Tristan.

A silver-haired man stood talking to Tristan and Hawk. The Marquess of Boswood, Georgette's father, shook hands with them. Lady Boswood greeted the duchess. Julianne hugged Georgette. Tessa felt like a servant and was glad everyone ignored her. She stood there unseen, watching, waiting for the moment when she could escape to her room.

The marquess's voice penetrated her depressed thoughts. "We started out a day early. I wished to allow an extra day for the journey. My daughter is prone to motion sickness."

"Oh, Papa, must you mention it?" Georgette cried. Not a single wrinkle marred her pristine white skirts.

"Do not fret, daughter." Lady Boswood smiled at the duchess. "Georgette did not succumb to illness once. I believe she has outgrown the tendency."

Julianne drew Georgette aside. The two girls chatted and giggled as the footmen carried the trunks away.

"We made excellent time yesterday and spent last night

at the Black Swan," Lord Boswood continued. "I decided to journey on early this morning. I had no wish to expose my ladies further to the rougher classes who patronize country inns. It would be insupportable."

Tessa thought him far too high in the instep and disliked him for it.

"I hope we have not inconvenienced your family," Boswood said.

"Not at all," Tristan said. "My mother and Miss Mansfield have matters well in hand."

Lord Boswood regarded Tessa briefly with a cold, blank stare. She felt as insignificant as she had at the opera, but this time she was glad of it.

The marquess turned to his daughter and lifted his brows. "Georgette, will you continue to ignore the duke?"

Her smile fled. "I apologize, Papa."

Tessa watched the girl dip her chin as she approached.

"The negligence is mine," Tristan said, striding forward to intercept her. With a blush, she offered her gloved hand. When he lifted it to his lips, Tessa looked away, her heart shattering like breaking glass.

She was his worst nightmare. Only he had no idea. Must never know.

After luncheon, Tessa escaped to her bedchamber and leaned against the door. She would give back every farthing of her fortune for the chance to change the past. But she'd known for eight years what she'd given up. Stupid girl that she'd been, she'd not even realized until Uncle George had told her.

There wasn't a single moment that she'd accepted her

fate, but rather a gradual acknowledgment that it was real and irrevocable. Mostly, she remembered trying to atone by nursing her uncle, giving of herself in a silent plea for forgiveness. When he was near death, he'd asked her to forgive him. She'd cried so hard she couldn't see for the tears.

After that, she'd taken one step, one day at a time.

Disgusted with her self-pity, she walked to the bed and sank onto the edge of the mattress. She'd done the right thing, the only thing she could do, by refusing Tristan's proposal. Of course, it would never have been necessary if she'd not wronged him yesterday. And all the days before. All the days she'd selfishly led Tristan on by making herself sparkly and witty so he would spend more time with her. So she could pretend he was her beau. Yesterday, she'd crossed a line. Today, she'd humiliated him.

For years, she'd avoided gentlemen who expressed even the slightest interest in her, knowing she could never marry. It had been easy until he'd walked into her life. She'd fooled herself, even though Anne had warned her repeatedly. And she'd fallen headlong in love with him. Utterly, hopelessly, in love with him. She loved him too much to ruin his life.

Her eyes misted. Drat it all, she could not afford reddened eyes and a stuffy nose. In a few minutes, she must walk downstairs to the drawing room.

She pushed to her feet, found her fan, and waved it near her hot face. Soon she must face everyone and pretend nothing was amiss. And she must do so again and again. All week.

Georgette's muffled voice sounded through the wall adjoining their rooms. The girl most likely. The most beautiful girl. The one he would marry. She had no right to be jealous. No right to begrudge Georgette. No right to love Tristan.

Tessa glanced at the bedside clock, knowing she must leave shortly. With a deep breath, she resolved to sit as quiet as a mouse and avoid bringing undue attention to herself. She had no wish to do anything except disappear while sitting with everyone else.

Georgette's door opened and closed. Tessa listened for retreating footsteps. Instead a knock sounded, startling her. When she answered, she found Georgette and Julianne standing there.

Georgette smiled. "If you are ready, we thought you might wish to walk with us to the drawing room."

"Thank you." After retrieving her fan, she joined them in the corridor. She would remain calm. Whenever she felt the slightest bit discomposed, she would apply her fan.

As they strolled toward the stairs, Georgette looked at Julianne. "I wish Amy were here."

"She will come tomorrow," Julianne said. "I am so happy you both will be here this week. We shall have such fun together."

"You both must come to my bedchamber at night," Georgette said. "We can gossip for hours, as we did at Amy's house last week."

Tessa wondered if she'd been wrong all along about their friendships. Was Georgette sincere? Only time would tell.

The blond beauty turned to Tessa. "You must join us."

"I would not dream of interrupting," she said.

Julianne's blue eyes glittered with mischief. "Now that my brother eliminated that nasty Elizabeth and her lapdog Henrietta, we can tell you all the horrid things they did during the courtship."

Evidently Amy and Georgette had confided to Julianne.

They had reached the landing when Georgette halted. "I fear Miss Mansfield will think us cruel gossips."

Julianne regarded Tessa. "Perhaps Elizabeth managed to win you over as she did the other girls."

Despite all her heartache, Tessa managed a weak smile. "To borrow a phrase from your mother, do I look like I just fell off the vegetable cart?"

The two girls snickered behind their hands.

"We'd better be on our way," she said.

As they walked downstairs, the two girls talked about all the jolly times they would have during the week. They made plans to try on each other's gowns, alter the trims on their bonnets, and tell ghost stories at night. At first, Tessa felt relieved that the friendship seemed true and honest, but as they approached the drawing room, she realized they'd completely ignored the courtship. They'd not mentioned Tristan once.

She told herself it was only natural for them to make plans for themselves, but she worried anyway. Perhaps they didn't want to discuss Tristan in her presence. Tessa would feel awkward if they did talk about him. And her wounds were too raw to listen to Georgette speak of him.

Tristan had asked her why she didn't like Georgette. Tessa had taken an instant dislike to the girl and judged her when she didn't even know her. But on that first day, she'd seen Tristan's interest in the beauty. And then Tessa had unwittingly set out to malign Georgette, just like Elizabeth. On some deep level, Tessa had known the girl most likely would win him. And every moment afterward, Tessa had done all in her power to draw him to herself.

She had seduced him, whether he believed her or not. She'd led him to betray the girls he was courting. And he, honorable man that he was, had offered to marry her because he did not want to be a scoundrel like his father.

Tristan stood at the sideboard in the drawing room, so numb his hands felt like ice.

"Old boy, do you need help pouring the brandy?"

Hawk's amused voice reminded Tristan to keep his wits about him. He flexed his hands twice and poured two brandies. He did not trust himself to imbibe in his troubled state.

Fixing a stoic expression on his face, he handed drinks to Hawk and Boswood. While the marquess pontificated about a speech he intended to make next week in Parliament, Tristan nodded occasionally, but he paid scant attention.

Tessa had let him kiss and touch her. Touched him, by God. Given him all but her virginity. And then she'd told him they must forget it ever happened. She had given him a way out. Prevented scandal. He ought to be relieved. He wasn't.

"There they are," his mother said.

His sister and Georgette followed an unsmiling Tessa into the drawing room. All three curtseyed. Tessa sat apart from the girls and accepted a cup of tea.

"Excuse me," Hawk said. Then he claimed a chair next to Tessa and engaged her in conversation.

Tristan turned away. He would not let her see what her refusal had done to him. By God, he'd offered her everything, and she'd refused him.

Boswood cleared his throat. "Perhaps you would take me on a tour of the spectacular gardens."

Tristan knew better than to let Boswood corner him. "Perhaps another time," Tristan said. "My mother will take it very ill if we leave."

Boswood sipped his brandy. "Shall we move out of ear range?"

Tristan followed Boswood over to the open French windows overlooking the mansion's front entrance. The breeze stirred the marquess's thinning gray hair.

Bloody hell. Tristan couldn't allow his inner turmoil to distract him. Boswood was a ruthless politician with numerous allies. His ambitions knew no bounds. Every word he spoke was calculated to manipulate his opponents. Tristan could not let down his guard.

He kept silent as he gazed down at the parterre where a riot of colorful blossoms sprang alongside the tall, clipped hedges and conical shrubs. Long before his father had bled the estates dry, a landscape artist had designed the formal gardens. Tristan had planned to show them to Tessa, but everything had changed yesterday.

He had only himself to blame.

Boswood sipped his drink. "I had misgivings about allowing my daughter to participate in this courtship."

His mild tone did not fool Tristan. "Yet you allowed it."

"My wife convinced me our daughter stood no chance with you otherwise." Boswood's eyes glittered dangerously as he regarded Tristan. "You have a sister, Shelbourne. I imagine you would kill any man who played fast and loose with her."

He found the coy threat ridiculous. "Defense is the best

offense. I protect my sister to prevent any harm coming to her."

Boswood arched his brows. "Would you allow her to enter into a similar courtship?"

"If you disapprove of your daughter's involvement, you may withdraw her. I will not take offense."

"Does my daughter mean so little to you, Shelbourne? You would let her go so easily?"

True to his character, Boswood had laid a smooth trap, one intended to force Tristan to declare his intentions or risk insulting Georgette. "I have the highest regard for your daughter and for Miss Hardwick as well."

The marquess inclined his head. "A diplomatic response. While we have not always agreed upon matters of state, I appreciate your caution and your astute opinions."

Another of Boswood's famous tactics: Bowl over your opponent with a compliment and then go in for the kill. Tristan let the statement pass without comment, but remained alert.

The marquess looked out the window and said nothing for several minutes. When he spoke, his voice sounded rough. "She's my only daughter."

Tristan's neck prickled at the unexpected words.

After a few minutes, Boswood spoke again. "Her brothers were easy. Throw them out into the world, knowing they'll grow tough and wild until they settle down to their responsibilities. But I still see Georgette in braids carrying around a kitten like a doll. I know I can't keep her at home forever." Boswood looked at him. "But I won't give her up unless I know the man she marries will adore her as I do."

Boswood might as well have punched him in the gut.

Tristan met the man's eyes, knowing what it had cost the powerful politician to make such an admission. He understood how Boswood felt, for he felt the same way about Julianne. But Tristan could not tell Boswood what he wanted to hear, would not lie to the man. "One of the reasons I decided to hold the final session here was so I could get to know both girls better. In London, there is too much scrutiny—the scandal sheets, the ton. I feel an obligation to both girls—to give them equal consideration. But they should also have a say in the matter. And so should you and Hardwick." *Your daughters are too good for me.*

Boswood cleared his throat. "It's hard on the girls."

"I imagine it is," Tristan said. "All the decisions have been mine, though I gave them the opportunity to bow out."

"That is not what causes my Georgette anguish."

Tristan waited for him to supply the answer.

"The damnable thing is, Shelbourne, you chose the two girls who are fast friends."

And forced them to compete against each other. For him.

All these weeks, he'd given only cursory thought to the way the girls and their families felt about the courtship. He'd made an unspoken promise to choose either Amy or Georgette for his wife. Guilt seared his gut. Yesterday, he'd betrayed them.

They would never know, but he would.

He'd proven himself to be his father's son after all.

Chapter Eighteen

The letter from Tristan's secretary arrived Wednesday morning.

After breakfast, he sat in his private study reading the lines. The vicar, the tenants, and the villagers all praised Tessa. She made frequent donations to the poor and visited the sick. Tessa often patronized the village shops and made multiple purchases. All the shopkeepers knew she could find much finer goods in London.

He scowled as he realized his secretary had filled an entire page with glowing commentary about her. The devil. Tristan had asked him for a report on Mortland, not a syrupy ode to Tessa's many virtues. With an impatient sigh, he turned the page.

The following paragraphs about Mortland were not conclusive. His secretary had made several visits to the local tavern. No one had definitive information, but all had thought him a shiftless young man with no career aspirations. The local men confessed they were surprised when Wentworth purchased a military commission for Mortland. A few suggested the late earl might have caught Mortland at some nefarious deed. More ominously, shortly after Mortland had reported for military duty, one of the village girls had left suddenly for a supposed position as an upstairs maid at a grand manor in Derbyshire. She'd never returned, and her family had refused to speak to Tristan's secretary about her.

Tristan locked the letter in his desk and leaned back in his chair. Mortland might have gotten the village girl with child. Upon learning of it, Tessa's uncle would have made secret arrangements to send the blackguard away before he harmed another. Of course he would not have told Tessa or anyone else in order to save the village girl's family from embarrassment.

A tap sounded at the door. Hawk poked his head inside. "I have news if you've a moment to spare."

"Come in," Tristan said. After Hawk slouched in a chair before the desk, Tristan told him about the letter from his secretary.

"Your theory about the village girl sounds plausible," Hawk said. "My cousin Henry sent a report about Mortland's military career. Of those who remembered Mortland, most believe he deserted at Toulouse. With the confusion of the bridge falling, there was no proof."

"What about the French family?" Tristan asked.

Hawk shifted in his chair. "He might or might not have spent time with French peasants. What I do know is that my cousin's spies tracked Mortland in London. He's been there for at least six months, possibly longer."

"What?" Tristan stared at Hawk. "The Bow Street runner didn't uncover this information."

"Because he was only looking for Mortland's current activities. Where else could Mortland hide so well? The gaming hells and prostitutes would have drawn him," Hawk said.

"Mortland told me he contacted his sister after reading about her marriage in English newspapers in Paris. I should have guessed he was in London." Tristan frowned. "I'm surprised Broughton did not discover more in his investigation of Mortland's military career."

"My cousin looked into that. Mortland's superior officer thought the lieutenant dead and didn't want to unsettle Broughton, since he'd written on behalf of his wife."

Tristan scrubbed his hand over his face. "Bloody hell."

Hawk brushed his sleeve. "The overwhelming evidence proves Mortland is a bad character."

Tristan jerked out of his chair and paced before the fire. "I'd planned to talk to Broughton when we return to London. Broughton is no fool. He's bound to know Mortland is accumulating debts."

"You've got the proof you sought. Present it to Broughton. He'll cut off Mortland without a penny."

Tristan met Hawk's gaze. "It's not enough. Mortland wants Tessa's fortune. I'll have to get Broughton to agree to hand him over to a press gang. I'm sure Broughton will be only too happy to be rid of him."

Hawk lifted his brows.

"What?" Tristan said irritably.

"If you care for her, and I know you do, don't let her Christian name slip again."

The next day, Amy and her parents arrived. Tristan liked the rotund Hardwick, more so when the man confessed his grandfather came from trade—a shopkeeper. Hardwick didn't want it to come as a surprise. Tristan assured him it did not affect his opinion of Amy. He'd told Hardwick he held the greatest esteem for Amy and then wanted to kick himself when he saw the man's eyes light up with hope.

He didn't deserve Hardwick's daughter.

After luncheon, his mother insisted on taking everyone for a house tour. She'd left the gallery for last. Tristan took first Amy and then Georgette about the room, telling stories about his ancestors. Both girls had made polite comments, but he could tell they weren't much interested in the ducal battles of yore. He ought to have known better. And then he watched them gather round his sister, saw their animated expressions, and suspected they preferred Julianne to him.

His gaze strayed to Tessa as the entire party trooped to the other wall. He stilled at the sight of her pale complexion. She'd barely eaten today. Bloody hell, he'd damn well make himself stop watching her. By God, he would not worry about her. She was just another of his former lovers. He'd left them with nary a thought. He would forget her as well.

His mother stopped before the enormous painting of his father. "This portrait of my husband was commissioned shortly after Julianne's birth," she said.

Georgette and Amy exclaimed over Tristan's resemblance to his father. Tessa stood near his mother. Two days had passed since he'd brought her here. It felt like weeks.

His mother started relating her fairy tale version of her courtship. As she droned on, Tristan turned his face away. Lady Boswood exchanged a speaking glance with her husband. And then she regarded Tristan's mother with pity.

He strode off to the fireplace and leaned his hands against the mantel. Where the hell was his mother's pride? But then she'd never had any when it came to his bloody father. The man was dead. Gone. Dust to dust. She ought to thank God. But no, after thirteen years, she still refused to let go of her illusions. If he'd ever had any, he'd lost them after burying his misbegotten sire.

At the swish of skirts, he stiffened. *Leave me alone.*

Tessa walked up beside him. "Tristan," she whispered. "She needs to hold on to her happy memories of him."

He kept his eyes on the marble mantel and gritted out, "You know nothing."

She was silent for a moment. "I know a little. And I feel a lot."

He whipped his furious gaze to her. "You do not *understand*. They *know*."

Her eyes widened. "Know what?"

Tristan lowered his face to hers and gave her a cold look. "He flaunted his mistresses in public. In front of my mother."

She winced. "That explains why she only speaks of the courtship and nothing else. She wants others to know he loved her once."

A bitter laugh escaped him. "No, he loved her fortune."

The next afternoon, the duchess instructed Tessa to take all the young people out for a walk among the grounds. The elderly people, she'd said, would play cards indoors.

A cool spring breeze fluttered Tessa's bonnet ribbons. The oak trees across the lake were monstrously large, perhaps as old and venerable as Tristan's lineage. She stood well back, the silent observer, watching Hawk teach Julianne and Amy how to skim pebbles on the lake. Their laughter rang out periodically. Hawk, the consummate charmer, was teasing them. Amy learned quickly and skimmed a pebble over the glassy blue-green water. Hawk mussed her hair, and Amy danced a little jig with Julianne. They looked carefree and happy.

A shriek drew Tessa's attention to the right, where Tristan was pushing Georgette higher and higher on a swing. He met Tessa's gaze and gave her a cynical smile. Then he caught Georgette from behind, lowered the swing, and leaned over her with his face upside down, making the girl giggle. When he straightened, he cast a swift, hard glance at Tessa. Then he walked round the swing. He grasped Georgette's waist and lifted her up in the air, making her shriek again.

Tessa's heart knocked against her chest as he lowered Georgette slowly to her feet and held on to her waist. He gazed into the girl's wide eyes.

Tessa stood frozen in the spring sunshine as his words came back to haunt her. *He flaunted his mistresses in public. In front of my mother.*

He'd made sure she would see him. He meant to pay her back for refusing his proposal. He meant to flaunt Georgette because he knew she was jealous of the girl.

It was the opera all over again, only this time, he knew she was watching. She'd wounded him, and he meant to hurt her. Only this time, it wasn't a thousand knives stabbing her heart. This time, he'd thrust a single broadsword into her heart, the same one she'd imagined him wielding that first day he'd called upon her. She stood there bleeding from the inside out while he exacted retribution.

A burning sensation shot up through her throat, stinging her nose and her eyes. She whipped around, because she would not let him see the furious tears threatening to spill. Her side ached as she marched off faster and faster. She wished she'd never come. Never met him.

Running footsteps thudded behind her, and then a hand shot out to grab her elbow. Stunned, she stared up into Hawk's laughing eyes. He let her go, made a ridiculous courtly leg, and offered his hand. "Dance with me, mademoiselle?"

She glanced past him to see Tristan and the girls watching. Two could play this game, she thought. She looked at Tristan once more to ensure he knew she was about to do a little flaunting herself. Then she curtseyed to Hawk, and suddenly he led her round the grass in a waltz, a dance she'd only observed because no one ever asked. Hawk counted the steps the whole time, and she laughed as if she'd not a care in the world. Then he stopped, grabbed her hand, and propelled her along in a run toward the lake.

She was out of breath by the time they reached the edge of the water. Julianne's pretty blue eyes filled with misery. Tessa despised herself for hurting the girl, when she knew Julianne adored Hawk. But she meant to rectify the situation immediately. So she pushed Hawk at Julianne. "He's your prisoner," she said.

Julianne's eyes lit up, and she called Amy to help her. The two girls started leading him away. Tristan bent his head, speaking to Georgette. Her eyes shone as she curtseyed, and then she ran off to join her friends.

Tristan watched until they disappeared, and then he strode toward Tessa. She turned and walked in the direction of the house, because she owed him nothing.

"I never marked you for a coward," he called out.

She spun around, her face hot with anger, and marched toward him. He met her halfway and grabbed her upper arm. "Miss Mansfield, you are *my* prisoner for the next few minutes."

He left her not a second to protest as he took off. Tristan strode diagonally through the forest, off the path, and she struggled to keep up. Her lungs constricted, as much from fear as the grueling pace he set, but she vowed she would never show it. Then he stopped and backed her up against a tree, holding her wrists at her sides.

"Let me go," she said.

He released her, but he didn't step back. A muscle ticked in his cheek. He was breathing hard, his blue eyes stormy.

She drew in her breath. "I played your childish game back there, but I'll not make that mistake again. And I won't watch you use that little girl as a pawn in your quest for vengeance."

"Jealous?" he said.

Her temper ignited. "This is not about Georgette, and you know it. You are angry because I refused you. You ought to be relieved, but your pride is in it now. Do not for one moment suppose that you seduced me. We have been playing with fire from almost the first moment we met. Both of us knew better, but still we flirted and danced a dangerous game. I will not blame what happened in that carriage on being swept away by passion. We took precautions to prevent consummation, and that alone is proof we both knew exactly what we were doing. We let it happen because we both wanted to step right up to the bonfire and let the heat scorch us."

"The reasons do not signify," he gritted out. "I compromised you and did what any honorable man would do. But you made sure I walked away dishonored, not because of the scandal, but because you are afraid. You make matches for everybody else, but you won't risk marriage because you're too scared to commit yourself. And you use bravado to hide it."

She trembled. His furious blue eyes frightened her because he was too close to the truth, and he knew just enough about her life to put the puzzle pieces together. She must divert him to protect her secrets.

"I never misled you about marriage," she said. "I've explained my reasons for remaining single until I've hardly any breath left. You do not even realize you insulted me."

"I never insulted you," he said, his voice rising.

"Oh, yes, you did. You insinuated you would not marry me if you'd not compromised me."

"Do not twist my words. You know very well I had an impossible choice, but I chose to do the honorable thing by you."

"Do you even know how hypocritical you sound with all your talk of honor? You are by your own admission an unrepentant rake."

He inhaled. "That's a foul hit, and you know it. I told you the first day I called on you that I'll not apologize for my past liaisons. I swore to you I would remain faithful to my wife, and that is all that matters."

"You swore never to dishonor me again, and you broke

that promise. How am I to know you won't break your marriage vows?"

He glared at her. "Another foul hit. You admitted you were a willing participant. And you know you're the only woman I've touched since the day I met you."

"So I don't count?" she said, lifting her brows.

"Damn you," he said. "I walked through hell the night after I compromised you. You know I worried about the girls and their families. But all I could think about was how your uncle would feel if he knew I'd dishonored you and walked away. I made you an honorable proposal, and you refused."

"You did not even ask me. You just assumed I would agree." She gave him a bitter smile. "I suppose you believed it was a good offer for a spinster like me."

He took her by the shoulders. "Look me in the eyes and say that again."

She clamped her mouth shut, refusing to obey his command.

He yanked the bow under her chin and threw her bonnet on the ground. Then he tipped her chin up. "Look me in the eyes and say it again."

She would not surrender to him.

"Look me in the eyes and tell me you don't want me."

She trembled because she could not.

"Look me in the eyes and tell me you don't care about me."

She loved him, loved him still, despite their impossible differences.

"Look me in the eyes and tell me that if every obstacle, every single one, was removed, you would refuse me again."

Scoff at him. Divert him. Lie to him. But she could not.

"You cannot," he said. He cupped her face with his warm palms and long fingers.

As he lowered his head, her body responded to him against her will. She arched into him, felt herself yielding as his scent mesmerized her. The warmth of his body and his strong arms lured her to give in. She almost did, but she knew what he'd done. And that was enough to check her, to give her the strength to push away from him. To make her voice sharp.

"Congratulations, Your Grace. In the game of pride, you have evened the score."

He swore as she retrieved her bonnet and walked away.

She was still shaken by their argument today.

After dinner that evening, Tessa sat in the drawing room near the duchess, pretending to attend to the conversation. She felt incensed and sorrowful at the same time. He'd hurt her because she'd hurt him, and she wanted to go back in time to when they could match wits and flirt with a little danger. But in the carriage, they had gone too far. The intimacies they'd shared had made it harder, made her vulnerable to wanting and yearning. And now she ached and ached because she'd let herself fall in love with him.

She wanted him back, wanted all the enchantment, the pretensions, the dancing all around what was between them. If given the chance, she would do it all over again. Because she yearned so badly to be in his arms, touch his hot skin, and shatter apart from the ecstasy he'd shown her. She wanted to hear his hoarse cry when she pleasured him. Wanted to be skin to skin with him, one with him, wanted all of him for her own. And she could never have him.

The courtship was hurtling to its grand conclusion. Tomorrow the entire party would picnic at the lake, and then, on Saturday, Tristan would speak to both fathers. He would make his final choice, and she was powerless to persuade him to wait for love.

Today, he'd asked her if all the obstacles were removed, would she still say no. She ought to have lied, but she could not. For years, she'd used half truths and omissions to keep her ugly secrets safe. Anything to keep from lying outright, because she was ashamed of the lies she'd told her poor, grieving uncle. Tristan had not given her the opportunity to evade him, but afterward, she'd wanted to kick herself. She could have left sooner, but she'd been so furious with him she'd walked right into his trap. And now he knew the truth about her feelings for him.

She wondered if somewhere deep inside she'd wanted him to know. How could she be so stupid? Why did her heart still race every time she caught a glimpse of him? What had happened to her pride? She'd ceded everything to him today.

Even though he'd infuriated her, even though there was no chance of reconciling her friendship with him, no chance she could ever be his wife, she still wanted his happiness with all her heart. But she was powerless to stop him from making a mistake that would haunt him for the rest of his life.

She knew more than a little about regret.

Tristan would never experience the love he deserved, the love she knew in her soul he was capable of giving and receiving. She'd silently given her heart to him, but her unrequited love could not breach his heart. He was determined to marry for duty, and perhaps she ought to have realized it was his decision, not hers. After all, she'd balked when he and his mother had tried to convince her to marry.

Mr. Hardwick's hearty laughter rang out. He sat at the card table with Amy, Julianne, and Hawk playing whist. Across the room, Tristan sat on the window seat with Georgette. The girl talked continuously and twirled her curl. Then she touched Tristan's sleeve. Pain flared in Tessa's heart, and she averted her gaze. She'd watched the girl the past two days, ready to pounce on the slightest evidence Georgette was playing Julianne false to gain advantage with Tristan. But thus far, Georgette had displayed affection for both Julianne and Amy. Last night, Tessa had heard the three of them giggling in the next room for hours.

Georgette's sweet laugh invaded Tessa's thoughts. Unable to help herself, she stole another glance at the girl. This time, she noticed Tristan's thumb tapping on his thigh. She knew that gesture meant he was either impatient or perturbed. He sat silent, but how could he manage a word when Georgette chattered like a magpie? Tessa silently rejoiced because he wasn't taken with the girl most likely.

Shame followed on the heels of her spiteful thoughts. She started to turn away, but Tristan gazed at her with that intent expression she knew so well. She caught her breath, unable to look away. Despite everything he mesmerized her.

Georgette tapped her fan on his forearm and laughed again. A momentary, irritated expression filled his eyes, and then it was as if the ducal mask fell over his face. He rose with Georgette and escorted the girl over to her parents. Then he took a stance in front of the hearth.

"Miss Mansfield," the duchess said. "You will entertain us by playing the pianoforte."

Tessa preferred not to call attention to herself. "Perhaps the young ladies should exhibit."

The duchess drew her quizzing glass to her eye. "You are young and a lady. Therefore, you qualify."

Lady Boswood regarded Tessa with a speaking look. "How generous of you to defer to one of the girls. But of course you wish to encourage them since they are courting the duke."

Tessa heard the unspoken words: *And you are a spinster who should know her place.*

"Do play, Miss Mansfield," Mrs. Hardwick said. "Lady Julianne says you are quite accomplished."

Tessa kept her gaze upon Lady Boswood. "But I have many empty hours in which to practice." She enjoyed the stunned look on the woman's face, a confirmation perhaps that Lady Boswood had thought exactly the same thing.

"Gel, you remind me to add your talent at the pianoforte as yet another of your many accomplishments," the duchess said. Then she proceeded to inform Lady Boswood of every achievement she'd enumerated at breakfast yesterday.

By now the entire party had gathered round to listen. Warmth crept into Tessa's cheeks. Of course she appreciated the duchess's regard, but truthfully, Amy and Georgette deserved the attention.

"Is it any wonder Miss Mansfield is so particular that she has yet to find a husband?" the duchess concluded.

Stars above. Tessa cast a sideways glance at Tristan.

He looked momentarily amused, and then, as if he was remembering what had transpired today, his smile faded.

"Goodness," Amy said. "Miss Mansfield, do you sleep?"

Everyone laughed, to Tessa's relief. Determined to turn the topic away from herself, she glanced at Georgette. "Will you play for us? We missed hearing you at Ashdown House."

The minute she uttered the words, Lady Boswood's nostrils flared. Clearly Lady Boswood was sensitive about Georgette's illness at that rainy courtship session. To be fair, no proud mother would wish to see her daughter humiliated.

"Oh, I could not play," Georgette said. "My limited talents would seem poor indeed compared to Miss Mansfield's."

"Miss Mansfield, everyone has prevailed upon you to play," the duchess said. "Tristan, you will turn the pages for her."

Tessa winced. How could she endure being near him after all the harsh words they'd spoken today? But she'd learned the hard way at the opera that refusing only raised suspicion. So she rose and took Tristan's arm. Awareness of his strength brought back the memory of his protective arm round her shoulders in the carriage.

She missed those times when they could be at ease with each other, but for every easy time, there had been plenty of difficult ones. If she'd kept a more professional demeanor, she could have avoided hurting herself and him. But she'd wanted to touch his shining star and use it to advance her career. She'd not known her vow to open his heart would only break her own.

Upon reaching the instrument, he pulled out the sheet music from the bench and riffled through it. Then he set the sheets on the stand. Tessa swallowed hard. It was Pachelbel's Canon, the same music she'd played at Ashdown House.

Did he mean to communicate a silent message? The idea twined round her heart, but she must resist. Because she could not forget he would marry another. So she sat upon the bench and poised her nerveless fingers over the smooth keys.

The duchess approached and bent her head near Tessa's ear. "You will forgive me for embarrassing you earlier," she said.

"I appreciate your esteem, Duchess, but I fear Lady Boswood does not," she said.

"I've known her since we made our come-outs the same year," the duchess said. "She is one of those vain, aging beauties who spend their entire lives competing with other women. She goaded you because she knows you have my son's ear and fears you."

Tessa scoffed. "I doubt it."

The duchess looked at her. "You've no idea of the power you've wielded in this courtship, do you? Why do you think all those jealous cats gossiped about you? Because you alone had influence over my son. They feared you could make or break their daughters' chances."

Tessa glanced at Tristan. He looked away, but she suspected he was listening. "They overestimate my powers of persuasion and most certainly underestimate your son."

She knew he'd heard when he lifted his chin, all haughty, proud duke.

The duchess laughed softly and looked at her son.

"Gel, a clever woman knows how to wrap a man round her little finger."

Tristan tapped his fingers on the top of the instrument. "Are we here to gossip or listen to Miss Mansfield play?"

"Tristan," his mother said. "May I have a private word with you? Miss Mansfield, practice your scales in the meantime."

Tessa obliged and bit back a smile. The duchess apparently ordered everyone around. Tristan must have learned the tendency from her.

After a few moments, she looked over her shoulder to find the duchess still speaking to Tristan. Good heavens. The duchess was probably picking out a husband for her. Tessa shrugged. It wasn't as if the woman could marry her off in two days.

When Tristan returned, he leaned over her shoulder and straightened the pages of the music. "My mother insisted I meet with you in my study tomorrow to discuss potential husbands," he said in a low, velvety voice.

She shivered as his breath stirred the curl by her ear.

"We will use the opportunity to discuss my courtship," he said.

She nodded, placed her fingers on the keys, and tried to focus on the music. He meant to tell her his choice in advance. *Georgette.* The thought tripped her, and she played a discordant note.

He turned the page. "Do I make you nervous?"

"No." *You make me burn.*

She depressed the keys again, determined to live up to the duchess's praise. The haunting melody reminded her of the rainy night at Ashdown House. Reminded her of the ugly gown she'd worn and Tristan's hungry kisses, kisses that had made her feel beautiful and wanted. Each time he turned the pages, she breathed in his faint, masculine scent. She imagined him sliding onto the bench, bending her backward, and kissing her. Running his tongue along her lips and tasting her. She wanted to touch his hot skin and hear him make that rough sound in the back of his throat again. Most of all, she yearned for the girlish dream, the one where he knelt and declared he loved her beyond all reason. But there would never be a fairy tale wedding for her.

When she played the last notes, applause followed. She exhaled in relief and then turned to him. "Have you made your decision?" she whispered.

"We will talk tomorrow."

Tomorrow she must listen to him speak another woman's name. A girl's name. The girl most likely would be his duchess.

And after Saturday, Tessa would never see him again.

Chapter Nineteen

essa awoke to a knock on her door late Thursday night. Disoriented, she sat up and rubbed her eyes. It took her a moment to realize she was not at home in her own bed.

The knock sounded again. Through the wall, she heard a hoarse sound. With only the dying coals in the fire to guide her, she struggled to find her wrapper. While slipping her arms into the garment, she padded across the cool carpet and cracked open the door.

Julianne stood there, the light of her candle showing she wore nightclothes. "Miss Mansfield, will you come to Georgette's room? She is ill."

Tessa frowned. "Is Amy there?"

Julianne nodded. "Georgette is feeling bilious."

"Why did you not alert her mother?"

"Georgette begged me not to send for her." Julianne looked shaken. "I will explain later, but please will you help her?"

"Yes, of course." She followed Julianne next door.

Once inside, she found Georgette on the bed's edge, heaving over an empty chamber pot. Amy sat beside her, rubbing her back.

"She has barely eaten today," Amy said.

"Julianne, light another candle, please," Tessa said. "Georgette, why have you not eaten?"

The girl heaved again.

"N-nerves," Amy said.

"You are nervous, too?" Tessa asked.

"Yes, but I am not ill."

Julianne used her taper to light another candle. "Do not worry, Georgette. Miss Mansfield also suffers from a nervous disposition."

Tessa glanced at Julianne. "Come help me find water and a cloth."

Julianne led her over to the washstand and found a cloth. Tessa poured water from the ewer into the bowl. After wringing out the cloth, Tessa managed to coax Georgette to lie down and put the cool cloth on her forehead.

"Miss Mansfield," Amy said. "May I stay with her tonight?"

"You do not need my permission, Amy. Stay if it makes both of you less anxious."

"Thank you," Georgette whispered. The two girls settled under the covers. "I'm glad you're here, Amy."

"Julianne, bring your candle," Tessa said. "I wish to speak to you privately."

Once outside in the dark corridor, Tessa closed the door and faced Julianne. "Can you tell me what troubles them?" She suspected it concerned the courtship, but she was not sure what exactly bothered them and did not want to make assumptions.

Julianne fingered her long, jet braid. "They tell me they are nervous about the courtship, but they say very little because he is my brother. I cannot be neutral where he is concerned. But they are my friends, and I worry about them."

"Can they not speak to their mothers?" Tessa asked.

"Their parents are so excited. They don't want to disappoint them."

Chill bumps erupted on Tessa's arms. Were their parents pressuring them? She'd heard many stories of parents who forced their daughters into marriages.

"Miss Mansfield," Julianne said. "You are the only one among us who can be impartial."

Tessa winced. Up to now, she had not been impartial. She'd favored one girl and made negative assumptions about the other. But she could help them now, and in doing so, she hoped to help Tristan indirectly. "I will speak to them."

Julianne let out a shaky sigh. "Thank you. I hoped you would make such an offer." She paused and added, "It is hard for me, too. I love my brother, but I love them as well." She wiped her finger under her eye. "One of them will be my sister, and the other will not. I do not envy Tristan this choice. They are both wonderful girls."

Tessa's heart turned over. "My uncle used to tell me things happen for a reason. It will all work out in time."

After Julianne had padded down the corridor, Tessa entered the bedchamber. The covers rustled. In the light of the candle, she saw the girls holding hands on top of the covers. Her heart turned over.

She sat on the edge of the bed. "Are you better, Georgette?"

"My stomach is better," she said. "But we are both anxious."

"Anyone would be in your situation." Tessa took a deep breath. "Julianne asked me to speak to both of you. She feels I can be objective."

"You are kind," Amy said.

"You do not have to share confidences with me," Tessa said. "But if you decide to do so, I want you to know I will never tell another soul."

"I'm frightened," Georgette said.

"So am I," Amy whispered.

"If you tell me what frightens you, I may be able to set your minds at ease," she said gently.

"We are true friends," Georgette said. "When we found out we were the final two girls, we were excited at first."

"But then we realized we were competing with each other," Amy said. "It is awful."

"I never could have borne the courtship without your help, Amy," Georgette said.

Amy regarded Tessa. "All the other girls fell in with Elizabeth's scheme to get rid of Georgette."

Tessa's breathing quickened. She'd not known Amy and Georgette were aware of Elizabeth's plot.

Georgette regarded Tessa. "You do not know what Amy did for me. She was the only girl who stood up to Elizabeth and Henrietta when they plotted against me."

Tessa looked at Amy inquiringly. "What happened?"

"The day before we went to Ashdown House, Elizabeth sent me a missive. She said there was a hitch in the plans and set up a meeting at her house. When I arrived, I knew something was wrong because Georgette wasn't there. Elizabeth and Henrietta tried to turn me against her.

I knew they were jealous of Georgette. So I told them I would not listen to their slander and left."

"I'm not surprised after seeing them laugh when Georgette grew ill on the barge," Tessa said.

Amy nodded. "I couldn't believe the other girls joined in with them like sheep, but I suppose they were afraid of those two vicious girls."

"Miss Mansfield, I tried to be nice to the other girls," Georgette said. "But every time I paid one of them a compliment, they sneered."

Amy regarded Georgette. "On that first day when I dropped my pen, I envied you. You were so poised and beautiful. I didn't know that being pretty could be as hard as being plain."

"You are not plain, Amy," Georgette said. "All you needed were the right gowns to show your tall figure to advantage. Look in the mirror, and you will see how much you've transformed."

Amy smiled. "I had a bit of help from you and Julie."

"That reminds me of another matter," Tessa said. "The other girls were unhappy about your friendship with Julianne. How did that come about?"

Amy fingered the blanket. "I am responsible."

Stunned, Tessa stared at her.

"The day after we left Richmond, I happened upon Julianne at the milliner's shop," Amy said. "Julie expressed her disgust with those girls who had laughed at Georgette. So I confided what I knew about Elizabeth and Henrietta. Julie insisted we call upon Georgette immediately to lend our support."

"I would have quit if not for you and Julie," Georgette said.

"Perhaps it was wrong to involve Julie," Amy said, "but I believed the duke would eliminate me, leaving Georgette to face those horrid girls all alone. I knew the duke had only kept me out of kindness."

Georgette turned to Amy. "Do not belittle yourself ever again. I won't allow it."

"I know I earned this last round," Amy said. "The day of the parlor game, I remembered Shelbourne had told me no one would respect me if I did not respect myself. And I realized I was giving others permission to treat me cruelly. Everything inside me broke free. Why should I not express my opinions? And I am proud of myself."

"I'm proud of you, too," Tessa said. How wonderful justice had prevailed, for it so seldom did.

"We worried others would think we were taking advantage of Julianne," Georgette said. "So we made a pact never to discuss Shelbourne in front of her."

Tessa had misjudged Amy and Georgette. Both had suffered because others judged them by their looks, and Amy, the girl least likely, had shown her spirit by mounting a counteroffensive against the spiteful girls.

"We wish Shelbourne would choose us both," Georgette said.

Tessa's lips twitched. "I believe that is illegal. But if you are worried how this will affect your friendship, I can tell you that your concern says volumes. You will remain fast friends no matter what happens on Saturday."

Georgette squeezed Amy's hand. "We will."

"Now there is a serious matter I should discuss with you," Tessa said. "Sometimes young ladies and even gentlemen feel the need to please their parents. But marriage is for life. You must be very sure before accepting any gentleman's proposal. And you must find the courage to say no if you have any doubts. Will you both promise me to search your hearts before the duke makes his final choice?"

"Yes," they said in unison.

"The duke is a good man," Tessa said. "He will treat his wife with respect and dignity. And he will always be true to her."

"Thank you for telling us," Amy said. "Julianne says he is the best brother."

"He was very kind to us," Georgette said. "Even when we giggled like silly schoolgirls."

Tessa rose. "Sleep well." After she closed the door, she blinked back tears. They were sweet girls, and she knew one of them would make him a good wife.

She would be happy for him. But when she climbed into bed again, she could not help wishing for the impossible.

Early the next morning, Tristan paced his study, waiting for Tessa to arrive. Ever since she'd refused his proposal, he'd spent sleepless nights trying to make sense of all she'd told him. He'd even made a list of her reasons for refusing to marry in *general* and another for her reasons she would not marry *him specifically*. There were too many contradictions in her answers to satisfy him.

He'd told himself repeatedly to forget her. She'd refused him, and the memory still scorched him. But when he'd forced her to answer his questions in the woods that day, she'd not been able to deny she wanted him, cared about him, and more important, would not refuse his proposal if every obstacle were removed. Then she'd fobbed him off with a barb about pride and walked off before he could question her further.

Tristan was convinced she was hiding something from him, but he'd not the foggiest idea what it was. He wanted to know, burned to know. But to what end? Tomorrow morning he would make his choice, leave Gatewick Park, and once they reached London, he would never see her again.

He halted and squeezed his eyes shut. *I will conquer this obsession.* He must forget her, because tomorrow he would become an engaged man. And that would be the end of the courtship and his friendship with Tessa.

A soft knock sounded. He opened the door and caught his breath. Tessa looked adorable in a gossamer buttercup gown. He mentally kicked himself for noticing her clothing. It was a gown. An obstacle to naked flesh.

He forced his thoughts out of the gutter. "Come in," he said.

She entered, and he indicated one of the cross-framed armchairs situated in front of his desk. Then he sat beside her and drank in her sweet face, her luminous green eyes, and her made-for-sin lips.

"I have news that should bring you cheer."

"Oh?" he said casually.

"I cannot reveal specifics to you because I promised confidentiality, but what I can tell you is I spoke to both Amy and Georgette last night. I know how many doubts you've had, but, Tristan, I wanted to tell you that you chose well." She smiled. "There were some bumps in the road, but I feel absolutely certain now that you kept the two best girls in the courtship."

He said nothing, but he noticed she clutched her hands so hard her knuckles turned white. Not long ago, she'd tried to convince him to stop the courtship and wait for love. Now, on the basis of one conversation with Amy and Georgette, she felt certain one of them would make him a perfect duchess.

He wondered if she was trying to convince him or herself.

Tristan took a deep breath and uttered the words he'd prepared. "This is overdue, but I wish to thank you for everything."

Her smile was tremulous. "Even the speedy courting?"

He chuckled. "Even that and the ridiculous parlor game."

Her green eyes twinkled. "I shall never forget Sally Shepherd and the sheep."

"And the candlestick in Lord Randy's unmentionables."

She shook her finger. "You are naughty."

He wanted to tell her he would never forget her, but he kept the incautious words between his teeth. "Tomorrow morning, I will meet with Hardwick and Boswood in my study. Then I will ask permission to speak to Amy and Georgette alone." He paused. "My mother suggested you stay with her and Julianne in her boudoir. I will come to tell you my decision afterward."

She averted her gaze. "You've made your choice?"

He thought so, but he had today to make sure. At some point last night, he'd remembered what Tessa had told him at Ashdown House. *All any of us can do is make the best decisions we can and learn from our mistakes.*

Some mistakes, however, were permanent, irreversible.

A tap sounded at the door. He frowned and rose when his mother barged in.

"Miss Mansfield, I see you are discussing your need for a husband with my son, just as you should," the duchess said.

Tessa groaned.

"No need to worry," Tristan said. "I don't have a potential husband stowed inside my desk."

When Tessa tried to stand, his mother waved her back. "I will leave you to your discussion." Then she considered him. "I expect she will raise *one or two* objections. Do not take no for an answer."

Was he imagining a cryptic message behind her words?

She raised her quizzing glass to her eye. "Gel, do not disappoint me. Do I make my meaning clear?"

Tessa blinked. "Er, I'm not sure."

"Wrong answer," the duchess said. Then she turned back to him. And winked.

His jaw dropped.

"Close your mouth, son, and open the door for me."

Still stunned, he stood rooted to the carpet. What the devil was his mother about?

Another knock sounded at the door. He should have told the footman to guard his privacy, but he'd not expected anyone else to stir at this early hour. Before he could answer the knock, Julianne rushed inside and kicked the door shut. "Oh, I've not slept a wink. I cannot stand the suspense."

"Young lady," the duchess said in shocked tones. "Your manners have gone begging. You are not to kick the door like a hoyden ever again."

Tristan let out a loud sigh. "Julianne, I already explained I will tell you my decision tomorrow."

She threw her arms around his waist. "Tristan, you are going to be an old married man."

He looked at his mother over Julianne's head. "Best make the funeral arrangements now."

Tessa glanced at him. "Perhaps I should give your family privacy."

"Oh, no," the duchess said. "You are going nowhere until you agree to marry."

Julianne released Tristan. "Poor Miss Mansfield. You shall have to give up all your freedom and your match-making career."

"I am giving up nothing," Tessa said.

The duchess glared at her. "Oh, yes, you will."

Tristan rolled his eyes. "Mama, enough."

She lifted her quizzing glass to her eye again. "Are you abdicating?"

The door flew open. Hawk strolled inside and kicked the door shut.

"You are a bad influence on my sister," Tristan muttered.

Hawk rubbed his hands together. "Am I late for the family meeting?"

"I'm not family," Tessa said.

"But I thought you were Mrs. Gatewick," Hawk quipped.

Julianne snorted. "I thought she was Tristan's long-lost sister."

"Pretend sister," Tessa said.

Tristan whipped out his handkerchief. "I surrender."

When Tessa gasped, he realized what he'd just inadvertently done. *Here is a white flag. Say you surrender.*

"Exactly what is this meeting about?" Hawk asked.

"We are here to discuss Miss Mansfield's husband," the duchess said.

Hawk clapped his hand to his chest. "I am heartbroken." Then he grinned. "Who is the lucky fellow, Miss Mansfield?"

"I believe that is yet to be determined," she mumbled.

Hawk walked over to her. "And how large did you say your fortune is?"

Tessa shook her finger at him.

"Wentworth was reported to have assets worth at least a half million pounds," the duchess said.

Tristan stared at Tessa. "Is it true?"

When she held out two fingers on her lap, Tristan grasped the desk behind him to keep from staggering.

Hawk dropped to his knee and clasped her hand. "Miss Mansfield, make me the happiest of men."

"If it's a temporary offer, I'll take it," she said.

Tristan grasped Hawk's arm and hauled him to his feet. "Stubble it," he gritted out.

"Forgive me, Miss Mansfield," Hawk said. "I was overcome by love."

"For my fortune, you greedy rogue."

Hawk pretended to wipe a tear from his eye. "Crossed in love again."

Tessa smiled slyly. "Julianne, will you console him?"

Julianne's eyes danced.

"No," Tristan growled. He shot Hawk a menacing, don't-you-dare-go-near-my-sister look. Hawk fingered his cravat, as well he should, the notorious rake. Granted, Tristan had an equally disreputable reputation, but there was an unspoken code among friends that sisters were forbidden.

Tristan cleared his throat. "Enough of this nonsense. Let us go to breakfast."

"We cannot leave until Miss Mansfield agrees to wed," Julianne said.

Tessa rose. "I accepted Hawk's temporary proposal, so I'm off the hook."

"You are not getting off that easily. Nothing but a real engagement for you, gel," the duchess said.

Tessa glanced at Hawk. "Make it real, and I'll cry off after breakfast."

Hawk grinned. "Miss Mansfield, will you do me the honor?"

"For one hour," she said.

"But Mama forbade the two of you to marry," Julianne said.

"I've no intention of marrying him." Tessa winked at Julianne. "I know the perfect bride for him."

The duchess smiled slyly. "Miss Mansfield, after you throw him over, I have the ideal husband in mind for you."

Tristan scowled. What the devil?

The clock chimed nine times. The duchess gasped. "We will be late for breakfast. The guests." She started shooing everyone. "Hurry along."

"Mama, I need to speak to you about this husband business," Tristan said.

"It will have to wait," she said, looking harried. "We must keep to the schedule. Now off to breakfast."

"I just lost my appetite," Tessa muttered.

"It is your nervous disposition," the duchess said. "Never fear, a husband will cure what ails you."

A comfortable breeze stirred the awning erected above the tables for the picnic. Tessa sat next to the duchess. The conversation swirled round her. She gazed at the blue-green lake, thinking of the one at her uncle's estate—or rather hers. Even after four years, she still thought of it as Uncle George's property. Soon she would close up the

London town house and travel to Hollincourt. It would be the first summer without Anne.

She took a deep breath, because her eyes had started to mist, and she must not feel sorry for herself. There were many women in far worse situations. She was lucky compared to them. When she returned to Hollincourt, she would focus on charitable works and all her other duties. She would keep busy until she was so exhausted she collapsed into bed at night. And that way, she would not have time to mope about loneliness or lost opportunities. Or a man who had dazzled her for a short while. Uncle George had said things happen for a reason, and she must trust in that higher purpose. She would make a difference in the lives of others, meet new friends, and perhaps even travel. Her wealth meant she had opportunities very few women or men could enjoy.

She would give up every penny if she could have a husband and children. Tristan's children.

The duchess turned to her. "You have a poor appetite."

"It must be my nervous disposition." Tessa glanced at the other table where Tristan, Amy, Georgette, Julianne, and Hawk sat. Georgette was twirling her curl, a sign of her nervousness.

The duchess leaned closer to Tessa and whispered, "Do not fret. All will be well."

"I know," she said. "He chose the best girls for the final round." She wished she could express her opinion with more enthusiasm, but even though her head said she should be happy for him, her heart would not let him go.

The duchess regarded her with an enigmatic expression and then turned her attention to Mr. Hardwick. Tessa liked Amy's parents. They obviously loved their daughter very much. With a wistful sigh, Tessa wished Tristan would choose Amy, but she knew his doubts about her. Tessa knew far less, almost nothing, about his feelings for Georgette, but she'd seen him with the beauty at the swing. *I want to want my wife.*

The knives stabbed her heart again. There would be no surprises tomorrow morning when he made his choice.

After everyone consumed the seed cakes and pastries, the duchess announced a sack race competition. Tessa declined to join and said she would much rather observe. She needed to distance herself from Tristan, his family, and his friends, because she knew the pain of losing those she loved, and she'd come to care for the duchess, Julianne, and Hawk. She would miss Amy and Georgette as well. But their lives would go on without her.

She could not even imagine how she would go on without Tristan. Somehow he'd become her whole world, and now she must find a way to survive the horrible pain of losing him forever. She had no choice. Because she'd given up her choices eight years ago.

Tristan and Hawk picked their team members, and to Tessa's surprise, the duchess agreed to join her son's team. Tessa's shoulders shook as she watched the very proper duchess hop along in grim determination. Tristan's mother raced (or rather hopped) against Lady Boswood. Apparently the duchess wasn't above a little competition herself because she didn't bother to hide her satisfied smile upon trouncing Lady Boswood.

Lord Boswood approached Tessa and stood beside her. He didn't say anything for several minutes. Tessa wondered what he wanted. She almost said something, but she remembered Uncle George's advice. *Do not feel compelled to fill the silence.*

At last, Boswood cleared his throat. "My daughter told me you spoke to her and Miss Hardwick recently."

The backs of her hands prickled. He probably did not appreciate her interference, especially her advice to the girls to listen to their hearts rather than aim to please their parents. Again she said nothing. She kept her gaze on Tristan and Hawk as they hopped and called out good-natured insults at each other.

"You put her mind at ease," Boswood said.

She swerved her surprised gaze to him.

He watched the races. She glanced at Tristan as he handed off his sack to Georgette and helped her inside. The girl took two hops and promptly fell on her backside, giggling. Tristan ran to help her, and Hawk called him a cheat. Then Hawk ran to a struggling Julianne, picked her up, and carried her to the finish line. Tessa laughed.

Boswood turned to her. "Why in the world did you invite twenty-four gels to court him?"

She smiled. "I could tell you I only wanted him to have as many choices as possible. Or that I felt all those girls deserved an opportunity to court him. And to some degree, those reasons were true." She met Boswood's gaze. "But I would be lying if I didn't admit I recognized a golden opportunity to advance my matchmaking career."

He smiled a little. "If you were a man, you would make a formidable political opponent."

She thought of that day in her drawing room when Tristan had told her she would make a formidable barrister. The thought of him brought her gaze to the field. Tristan offered his arm to Georgette and started strolling.

Another little piece of Tessa's heart crumbled. "No, I wouldn't have the stomach for politics," she said. "I'm a woman, and I've a soft spot."

Boswood watched his daughter. "We all do, Miss Mansfield."

Chapter Twenty

$\mathcal{O}$n Saturday morning, Tessa's nerves stretched tighter and tighter as she sat on the sofa with the duchess in the gold drawing room. Everyone else took seats. Tristan had changed the plans, and now everyone fidgeted, waiting for him to explain.

Tristan stood in front of the fire dressed in a blue coat and buff trousers. His expression was solemn as he clasped his hands behind his back. Tessa drank in his features, committing them to memory—his black tousled hair, thick brows, perfect nose, and square jaw, freshly shaven, leaving only a hint of his heavy beard. Most of all she wanted to remember his brilliant blue eyes and the many times he'd gazed so intently at her.

The courtship would end this morning.

Her throat constricted. She clasped her cold hands so hard her fingers hurt. *Be happy for him. If you really love him, you will sincerely wish him happy.*

"I will make this brief," he said. "After due consideration, I encountered a problem."

She gaped at him. That first day of the courtship, she'd uttered similar words. When he slid a sly glance at her, she knew he wanted her to respond. "And what problem was that?"

"Both of them qualified," he said.

"Qualified?" Mr. Hardwick said, frowning.

"Clearly both ladies have unique and special qualities," Tristan said. "But I could not choose one over the other. In short, gentlemen, your daughters are perfect."

Georgette hugged Amy. "He chose us both after all."

Amy laughed. "Miss Mansfield said that is illegal."

The duchess made a strangled sound. Oh, dear, Tessa thought. The duchess probably worried the girls had feathers for brains.

Tristan held up his hand. "I will make a decision after we return to London."

Stars above. He was keeping them all in suspense. Drat him. He enjoyed holding that power over people. But her heart rejoiced, her silly heart that thought he'd reconsidered marrying for duty, when she knew nothing had changed.

Julianne pouted. "Mama, that is unfair. Make him choose."

Hawk winked at Tessa and then regarded Tristan. "I say, old boy, it is rather unsporting of you to keep us waiting."

Tessa's lips twitched. Hawk had purposely repeated the words he'd said the day after the opera.

Tristan cleared his throat. "After we return to London, I will call on each of the girls individually at their respective homes. This is an important decision—a lifetime decision. It is not something I take lightly. I hold both girls in the highest esteem." He looked first at Amy and then at Georgette. "I once told you that you have a choice in the matter. You still do. You have a say, you always have. I depend upon your complete honesty, ladies. Will you both promise me that you will contemplate all I've said before I call on you?"

"Yes," Amy whispered.

"Of course," Georgette said.

"We all have a long journey ahead of us today. I wish you all safe travels."

And just like that, her matchmaking role was over. Without the fanfare she'd imagined that first day he'd asked her to find him a duchess. She walked out with everyone else while he stood talking to Hawk. It was better this way, she told herself as she climbed the stairs. He'd crushed her fan one fateful night, offered to pay for it, and sought her out again after she'd fled. Before this day ended, she would tell him good-bye forever. And hold him in her heart all the days of her life.

The shadows reached halfway to the gates of Tessa's town house as Tristan escorted her to her door after the long journey back to London. The two burly footmen he'd hired had already carried off her trunks. He'd sent his mother home in the carriage with Julianne and Hawk.

He needed to say good-bye to Tessa.

They had ridden in separate carriages this time. He'd only seen her at inns along the journey. Now he glanced at her pillow-plump lips, remembering how the sight of her made-for-sin mouth had struck him stone senseless that first night he'd seen her at the ball.

She returned his gaze, her smile a little sad. All too soon they reached the open door. Gravesend stood there, stalwart and ready to serve his mistress.

Tessa turned to Tristan. "Will you shake hands with me?"

Tristan took her gloved hand, lifted it to his lips, and let her go.

Her spring-green eyes glimmered with tears. "I'll never forget you," she said, her voice a bit tremulous. "Goodbye, Your Grace." And then she fled inside, the same way she'd fled when he'd tried to give her his card at the ball the first night he'd met her.

Tristan rummaged inside his coat and handed Gravesend a folded paper. "My addresses in town and in Oxfordshire are listed. If she is ever in need, please send a messenger immediately."

Gravesend pocketed the paper. "On behalf of the late Lord Wentworth, I thank you for your concern for the little missy."

Tristan regarded the old man's white brows and lined face. "You are to be commended for your excellent service to your mistress."

Gravesend's tired eyes grew a little watery. "Lord Wentworth asked me on his deathbed to protect her. There wasn't anybody else, you see."

Tristan frowned. "At one time, Wentworth meant to send her to friends in London for her come-out. Could he not prevail upon them?"

"Rysinger had accepted a foreign post," Gravesend said. "Wentworth grew weak, so he asked his niece to write letters to his other friends. She never sent them."

She'd not wanted to leave her uncle or her home,

Tristan thought. When he offered his hand, the old man shook it. "Take care of her," Tristan said hoarsely.

After church the next day, Tessa walked up the pavement to Anne's town house. Tom and Jack accompanied her because Gravesend had refused to let her go without protection. She'd thought it a bit silly when she'd learned both footmen had stowed knives in their boots.

When they reached the door, Jack lifted the knocker. Tessa's stomach lurched at the memory of Richard bursting into her home. "Wait," she said.

"My lady, let us quit this place," Tom said. "You don't want to chance meeting up with that blackguard."

She took a deep breath and exhaled. "No, I only needed a moment to prepare. I have you and Jack to protect me. And I must resolve this business once and for all." Otherwise, she would never sleep peacefully again.

Jack rapped the knocker. When the butler answered, his eyes popped open when she insisted Jack and Tom must accompany her. She removed her shawl and looked up in surprise as Broughton walked into the entrance hall. He eyed her enormous footmen and drew her aside. "What is wrong?" he said in low tones.

She trembled. "Is Mortland here?"

"No, I turned him out a week ago today." Broughton's mouth thinned. "He stole the emerald necklace I gave Anne on our wedding day."

"Oh, no." She covered her mouth. Poor Anne.

"Tell me quickly what happened," Broughton said.

She related the entire story of what had happened after Mortland invaded her town house. "Because it was so late and I was leaving for Gatewick Park the next morning,

I decided to contact you when I returned. I fear he will retaliate."

Broughton winced. "Come with me to the drawing room. Say nothing of him to Anne. I don't want to cause her additional vexation. Afterward, I'll speak to you in my study."

A few minutes later, Tessa sat beside Anne on the settee and listened to her friend relate the same story about the necklace.

"My husband suspected Richard had lied about his absence after the war," Anne said. "In my heart, I knew something was amiss, but I wanted to give him a chance. I'm so sorry for the ill way he treated you, Tessa."

"Anne, you must not blame yourself."

"I wanted so badly to believe in the miracle of his return, and he took advantage of me."

"He's gone now, Anne," Broughton said. "He can't make you unhappy again."

Anne gazed at her husband. "You told me to think of our blessings, and there is so much happiness ahead of us." She spread her hand over her belly. Broughton's eyes softened.

Tessa swallowed. Why had she not thought of it?

Broughton laughed softly. "I fear we have given away our little secret."

Anne turned to Tessa. "It is early days yet, but I am certain. All the signs—"

Tessa enfolded Anne in a hug. Her eyes welled with tears. "I am so happy for you." *But I am so unhappy because I will never know your joy.* And that hurt all the more because she'd said good-bye to Tristan yesterday.

They broke apart. "Oh, look at me, weeping with happiness for you," Tessa said, rummaging inside her reticule.

She and Anne both dried their tears.

"Will you be the babe's godmother, Tessa? I could think of no one I would want more than the sister of my heart."

Tessa sniffed. "I would be honored." She would love Anne's babe as if the child were her own.

"Will you visit us at Clarewood?" Broughton asked. "Anne cannot bear spending the summer without you."

Things happen for a reason. "I shall for as long as you are willing to put up with me. But first, we must plan Jane's wedding."

Anne exclaimed over the news of Jane's engagement. They spoke of shopping for wedding finery for several minutes.

Broughton cleared his throat. "Anne, you should rest. I'll escort Miss Mansfield downstairs."

As they descended the stairs, Tessa fought the heartache threatening to overwhelm her. As happy as she was for her friend, Tessa was still raw with grief for Tristan. She'd known she would suffer, but knowing was nothing compared to the reality. The pain was physical, blinding, and with her always. *One footstep at a time. One breath at a time. One minute at a time.*

When they reached the marble floor, the butler walked into the great hall. Tristan and Hawk followed him.

Tessa inhaled on a ragged breath.

As if from a great distance, she heard Broughton greet them. Hawk carried a leather case. "I've papers you need to read," he said to Broughton.

Tristan stopped before Tessa. She gazed into his beautiful blue eyes. Time stood still as she drank him in and let her empty heart fill.

Broughton's voice brought her to her senses. "Gentlemen, I was about to discuss a grave matter with Miss Mansfield."

Tristan turned his attention to Broughton. "Is Mortland on the premises?"

Broughton shook his head. "Join me in my study. I'll explain everything."

While Broughton and Hawk strode ahead, Tristan escorted her at a much slower pace. "I received disturbing news about Mortland."

"What is it?" she whispered.

"I know he went to your house the night before we left for Gatewick Park."

She gasped. "How did you find out?"

"I hired a Bow Street runner. He'd sent the report to my London town house while we were in the country." He narrowed his eyes. "Why did you keep this from me?"

She could not tell him Richard had threatened to reveal their past to him. "There was nothing you could do, and I told you I meant to speak to Broughton after we returned," she said under her breath. "I do not want you involved."

"I am involved, and I will stay involved until that scoundrel is caught," he gritted out. "You'd better tell me the whole of it quickly."

"He forced his way into my house. My footmen apprehended him and took him to a seedy locale."

His jaw worked. "Did he hurt you?"

"No, but he shoved Gravesend into a wall."

"Bloody bastard," he muttered. "Tessa, he is dangerous. Whether you like it or not, I mean to protect you. You will not keep secrets from me."

She looked away. *My love, you've no idea how much I've kept from you.*

When they reached Broughton's study, Tristan sat in a chair beside her. Hawk handed the leather case to Broughton. "You will find detailed reports of the investigations Shelbourne and I conducted."

She swerved her stunned gaze to Tristan. He arched his brows, but said nothing.

Broughton read the papers. When Tessa asked to see them, Tristan shook his head. "The reports are explicit, and I do not want you to see the revolting details."

Afterward, Broughton regarded her with a grim expression. "I believe you are in danger, Miss Mansfield."

"He'll seek vengeance, but I mean to stop him," Tristan said.

"But how?" Tessa said. "He could hide for months. I have footmen to protect me, but I shall look over my shoulder constantly. I cannot live that way."

"We'll find him, Miss Mansfield," Hawk said.

She wet her dry lips. "He'll wait for the right moment to strike out again. He swore to make me pay for what I did to him." She could not tell them he meant to make her pay for her betrayal all those years ago.

Broughton set the papers aside. "I feel the blame. I've known his obsession with Miss Mansfield since the day he crossed my threshold. He asked too many questions and spoke about her constantly."

"He admitted he used to watch her paint from afar," Tristan said. "The blackguard spied on her." He looked at her. "I sent my secretary to the village near Hollincourt to sniff out old news. God, to think how close you came to harm makes me ill."

Her stomach roiled. Why had he not told her about his investigation at Hollincourt? *You're safe. It's been eight years. Not a whisper. No suspicion.*

"You *were* in danger," Hawk said to her. "There was a village girl who was not so fortunate. Her family sent her away and refuses to speak of her. You can imagine the probable reason."

"We've no proof, but it happened shortly after Mortland reported for military duty," Tristan said. "I do not think it is a coincidence."

Tessa's stomach cramped. She'd thought Molly had left for a position as a maid at a grand estate. No one had told her the rumors, but the tenants would not have dared to share salacious gossip with her. Certainly no one would have said anything to Anne or her father.

"We believe the unfortunate girl was the real reason your uncle bought Mortland's commission," Tristan said. "He must have wanted to get rid of him."

She averted her gaze. Tristan was wrong about the commission, but she could not bring herself to enlighten him.

"I'm relieved you escaped harm, Miss Mansfield," Broughton said. "His fixation on you was unnatural."

"He's bound to be sniffing after her fortune," Hawk said.

"I plan to step up my search efforts," Tristan said. "The man poses a serious threat to Miss Mansfield."

"My God, what is to be done?" Broughton said.

"I've hired men to search for him," Tristan said. "When he's captured, I want him handed over to a press gang."

"With pleasure," Broughton said. "I'll invent a story to explain his sudden absence."

Tristan regarded her. "I mean to capture him quickly, but I worry because you are alone."

"Miss Mansfield," Broughton said. "You and Miss Powell may stay here until Shelbourne finds Mortland. Anne would enjoy your company, and you would be safe here."

"I appreciate your offer, but he could hide for months," Tessa said. "I will take precautions."

Tristan looked intently into her eyes. "He invaded your home a week ago and abused your elderly butler. I fear he may try to abduct you."

Her stomach cramped again, but she forced herself to remain outwardly calm. "Gravesend has posted one of my footmen near the front door during the day. At night, one of them stands guard at the gates."

"Do not go out unless it is absolutely necessary. It's not worth the risk," Tristan said.

Tessa nodded, knowing she would feel vulnerable in a public place. The night Richard had forced entry into her home she'd witnessed his brute strength. He'd hurt Gravesend, and he'd meant to hurt her. She shuddered.

"Try not to worry," Tristan said. "I'll hire extra men to protect you. There are plenty of former soldiers who need employment. They'll be stationed out of sight to avoid attracting attention. I'll instruct them not to admit anyone at the servants' entrance. Deliveries will be left outside the door. Admit no one into your home."

Broughton frowned. "But what about Hodges? He'll want to call on Miss Powell after their recent engagement."

Tessa shook her head. "I don't want either of them embroiled in this madness." And she didn't want her problems to overshadow the couple's happiness. "I had better send her to his sister's house."

"I'll speak to Hodges and impress upon him the need to keep the matter quiet," Broughton said. "Miss Mansfield, you must warn Miss Powell."

"I did so today," she said. "I feared Mortland would try to corner her when she went out."

Tristan gazed into Tessa's eyes again. "Once I capture him, you need never fear him again."

Bile rose up in her throat. Richard had threatened to spill his guts, the same way he'd done eight years ago. She imagined Tristan's shock. His disgust. His anger.

Panic clawed her lungs.

For a moment, she could hardly breathe. But an image of Richard's smirking face rose in her mind, and all her anxiety heated into fury. She'd suffered enough because of that rat. Eight years ago, he'd marked her as an easy target, and she'd walked into his trap. He'd humiliated her, but she was no longer a gullible girl.

She couldn't stop him from making his ugly claims, but this time, she would not curl up like a victim and weep. When Tristan confronted her, she would deny Richard's every word, scoff and lie outright if she must. She refused to let Richard ruin her life again.

Her bravado vanished, and a shard of fear lodged in her chest. Tristan knew too much about her. She'd told him part of the truth that day Anne had given her Richard's letter, and Tristan would remember every detail. When Richard spewed her secret, Tristan would put all the puzzle pieces together. And he would loathe her for deceiving him.

Oh, God. She should have told him the sordid truth the day he'd proposed, but she'd not wanted him to know because she couldn't bear the shame. Now she could say nothing, could not confess in front of Hawk and Broughton. She'd waited till it was too late.

"We'd better leave now," Tristan murmured.

His gentle voice stung her heart. He didn't know she'd lied to him when she'd refused his proposal. He didn't know she'd deceived him about her past. He didn't know she'd masqueraded as a respectable woman.

If she had told Tristan the truth the day he'd proposed, he would have understood she'd fallen for the lies of a scoundrel. But he would never forgive her for letting Richard blindside him.

An hour ago, she'd thought losing him to another woman was the worst pain she would ever experience. She'd been wrong.

Chapter Twenty-one

Two weeks later, Tristan slammed his fist on his desk after the Bow Street runner departed. He'd gotten his hopes up, but they'd soon fallen flat. The runner had found Lady Broughton's emerald necklace in a notorious pawn shop in Petticoat Lane where the proprietor received stolen goods. The Bow Street runner had promised to redouble his search for Mortland in the gaming hells and bawdy houses.

The devil. For the past week, Tristan had stalked the worst districts of the city, asking questions and offering money to anyone who could supply information. All he'd gotten for his trouble were false leads. Finding Mortland in the sprawling slums was akin to looking for the proverbial needle in the haystack.

A knock sounded at the door. "Enter," he said.

His mother walked in and sat in one of the chairs before his desk. "Frustration is written all over your face. I take it there has been no progress in the search for Mortland."

"All I know is he has money, thanks to his sister's jewels." He related the information about the fence, and then he scrubbed his hand over his face.

She sighed. "You may never find him."

"I will not give up. No matter how long it takes, I will hunt him." Thirteen years ago, he'd refused to let ruinous debt defeat him. Through sheer determination, he'd succeeded, and he would again.

"I know you are prowling the slums at night," she said. "You are putting your life in danger."

"Tessa's life is in danger," he growled. The minute he uttered the words, he realized his mistake. Every muscle in his body tensed as he waited for his mother to express her outrage over his use of Tessa's Christian name.

She did not even blink: "I agree she is in peril. I do wish she would reconsider taking up temporary residence with Lady Broughton. Some excuse could be made—repairs to her town house or some such. It's foolish of her to stay locked up all alone."

"I'll call on her and try to persuade her," he said.

His mother fingered the ribbon of her quizzing glass. "That would not be wise since you've neglected to call on Lady Georgette and Miss Hardwick."

He stood and walked over to the hearth. After moving the screen, he retrieved the poker and stirred the hot coals. He knew he must honor his promise to the girls and their families, but he could not concentrate on them now.

"Tristan, you delayed your decision at the house party, and you are delaying again."

He continued to stoke the fire until it blazed. "It is a lifetime decision. I will not rush."

"Your inability to make a decision tells me you have

doubts. Call on Hardwick and Boswood. Tell them after much contemplation, you have concluded you are not yet ready for marriage."

He whirled around, still holding the poker. "I will not humiliate the girls and their families. The scandal would bring disgrace upon our family, too."

"Do not sacrifice your happiness for the opinions of society."

He set the poker aside and replaced the screen. "It is no small matter. You of all people know the consequences of scandal."

"Since you brought up the subject, we might as well discuss your father. Sit with me," she said.

He shook his head. "There is no point in opening up old disagreements."

"I'll not defend his mistreatment of us," she said. "But there are things you do not know. Will you listen?"

He joined her and regarded her warily.

"I should have spoken to you years ago about your father, but you resisted every time I tried," she said. "You've let your resentment fester so deep, you refuse to acknowledge your father had any good qualities."

He almost ended the conversation, but he kept silent. Let her make excuses for his sire. He'd refute every single one.

She searched his eyes. "No one is all good or bad. Those who make poor choices believe they are justified. Even that blackguard Mortland has his reasons for what he's done to Miss Mansfield."

He scoffed. "Yes, her money."

"Mark me. There is more to that story."

"You are right." He told her about the village girl and

his suspicion Tessa's uncle had forced Mortland to take the commission. "Mortland transferred the blame to Miss Mansfield. He wanted recompense and thought to woo her, so he could get his hands on her fortune. When she snubbed him, he decided to force her."

"You are undoubtedly correct, but we stray from the original matter."

He leaned forward, resting his elbows on his thighs. His mother didn't understand. He didn't give a damn about his long-dead sire.

"I think you need to know how your father felt about you."

Tristan knew his dissipated father had cared only about himself.

"The day you were born your father was ecstatic. You were a big, healthy boy. I wish I could describe to you the look on his face when he first saw you. He lifted you up and exclaimed over his perfect son."

Tristan scowled at the carpet. Did she think that made up for his father's cruelty?

"Your father was so proud of you," she said. "James would take you up on his horse and ride along the grounds. You were barely out of leading strings, but he was determined. When he discovered you'd learned to read at age four, he bragged about it to all his acquaintances."

He'd not known, but it changed nothing.

"I believe he wanted to be a good husband and father, but he let his resentment toward his own father overrule him. James could not forgive his father for forcing him to marry. Your grandfather had accumulated horrendous debts."

Tristan had known, but his father had gambled away the

fortune his mother had brought to the marriage. "Frankly, I've no sympathy."

"As I said before, I am not excusing him. I only want you to understand. I truly believe he loved me, but he didn't want to marry yet. He was seven and twenty, not ready to give up sowing his wild oats. But his father gave him no choice."

"He humiliated you," Tristan muttered.

She sighed. "I didn't understand his sudden coldness after we married. I knew my fortune was a draw, and families made arranged marriages all the time. I was too young to understand why he blew hot and cold. In the intervening years, I've come to realize his inability to reconcile his resentment toward his father affected his feelings for me. He fell into dissipation with his rowdy friends, gambling and drinking to excess.

"Five years after we married, I grew increasingly unhappy with his neglect. My father interceded and made empty threats. James realized I'd complained to my family. So he punished me by taking one mistress after another. He did not even try to be discreet. I blamed myself."

Tristan sat up and stared at her. "You did nothing wrong. He was weak and spiteful."

"I knew you felt powerless as a young man when you saw him with those women in our home. I didn't know what to say to you. I didn't trust myself not to break apart."

"He mistreated you and ignored Julianne. He wouldn't even see her after her birth because she wasn't the spare heir he wanted. The man was a selfish bastard," Tristan bit out.

"But you came," she said. "You held her and cried."

"I was a lad," he said gruffly.

"Your father only realized on his deathbed what he'd given up. When you refused to hear his apology, he wept."

"He made his own bed." Tristan looked at his mother. "He did not deserve you."

Her eyes filled with tears. "I held on to the happy memories of our courtship because I could not bear to think I'd wasted my life and heart on him."

His chest hurt. When he handed his mother a handkerchief, he felt like a devil. All these years, he'd refused to listen. He'd bristled every time she'd claimed to love his father. But Tessa had understood his mother's complex feelings.

"I count myself fortunate because I have you and Julianne," she said, folding the handkerchief into a square. "Despite everything your father did, you both turned out well."

"Mama, it was your influence that formed our characters."

She looked at him. "I watched you set out with grim determination to restore our fortunes. And you defied impossible odds. I'm very proud of you, son."

"Thank you." He swallowed hard. "Forgive me."

"I always understood," she said. "I love you, son, and whatever you decide about the girls, I will support you. But if you have doubts, do not let a sense of obligation force your hand. After all you've sacrificed, you deserve happiness. There is always a way around what may seem impossible."

He didn't bother to refute her, but there was no honorable way to back out now. Too many people would suffer.

"You must call on the girls and their families soon," she said.

"I've not been able to think of anything but capturing that devil, Mortland. Lady Georgette and Miss Hardwick have devoted the entire season to me. They could not court other gentlemen. I owe it to them to give careful consideration to the matter. I will write to their fathers and tell them an urgent matter has kept me away. Next week, I will call on them."

After she left, Tristan sat at his desk and penned the letters. Twenty minutes later, he rang the bell and instructed a footman to deliver them. Then he closed the door and leaned his back against it. He knew what he should do, but everything inside him rebelled.

For the first time in more years than he could recall, he closed his eyes and prayed for guidance.

Tessa retrieved her novel and walked downstairs to her drawing room. She kicked off her slippers and curled her feet beside her. She'd read *Sense and Sensibility* twice before, but she never grew tired of the story. After removing the ribbon marking her place, she read one page three times and realized none if it had registered.

She set the book aside and looked at the empty chair where Tristan had sat tapping his thumb impatiently so many times. How long would it be before the memories of his distinctive voice and brilliant blue eyes faded?

She missed him so much already she ached all over.

Sixteen days had elapsed since she'd last seen him. That first week, she'd jittered with nerves, expecting Tristan to call and condemn her. But the hunt for Richard had proven fruitless thus far. She suspected Richard knew he was a hunted man. He might have left London until the pursuit grew cold. Richard would bide his time, perhaps for months.

Tristan could not continue this quest much longer.

It was unfair to let him continue. He needed to focus his attention on choosing a bride and get on with his life, without her. Every additional day he remained embroiled in her problems was another day he delayed his engagement. He'd insisted upon protecting her, but he didn't know he was too late. She'd looked after herself all these years, and she would again.

She would hire men to track Richard. With her fortune, she could finance a veritable army to hunt him. Lord Broughton would provide her with the contacts she needed. Tomorrow she would send Tristan a letter informing him of her decision.

She would break this final tie with Tristan. The thought of never seeing him again sent a pang to her heart, but she could no longer prolong the inevitable. For both their sakes, she must end all contact with him. Though she would miss Tristan, she would always cherish her memories of him. Long ago, she'd resigned herself to a life without a love of her own. He would never know that in her heart he would always be her love.

Sorrow threatened to overwhelm her, but she would not pity herself. Resolute, she padded over to her escritoire and penned a letter accepting Anne's invitation to stay with her. Tomorrow, Tessa would send the letter, pack her trunks, and instruct Gravesend to close up the town house.

The tension that had gripped her for more than a fortnight eased a bit. She'd felt powerless and victimized hiding in her own home, but she'd proven herself capable of managing her own life since her uncle's death. Having made her decision, she felt more in control. She was not friendless, and she most certainly had abundant resources at her disposal.

With a sigh, she returned to the settee and started reading. The light in the room had begun to fade when Gravesend shuffled into the drawing room, his shaggy white brows furrowed. She set the book down, replaced her slippers, and stood. "Gravesend, is something the matter?"

"I hesitated to bring this letter to you. A ragged street urchin ran up to the gate and insisted upon leaving it with Jack."

She took the letter. Her heart nearly stopped as she recognized the handwriting of the address. Slowly she sank onto the settee and broke the seal.

"My lady, your face is ashen."

"It is from Mortland," she whispered.

"I will send for the duke," Gravesend said. "I swore to send him a message if ever you were in need."

She held up a staying hand. "Please be seated. Let me read it first. It may not warrant disturbing Shelbourne." But as she unfolded the page, her fingers shook.

Her lungs constricted as she read. Richard told her to follow his instructions exactly or she would pay. He told her to take a hackney to Hyde Park Corner at three o'clock in the morning and leave behind her bullyboys. He instructed her to bring a valise and fifty pounds. He didn't care how she managed, but she would do it or he would send Shelbourne a letter that detailed all her secrets. She shuddered at the crude examples he'd provided. But he didn't stop there. Richard said he couldn't wait until he finally had control of Hollincourt.

He meant to spirit her off to Gretna Green. She recalled his brute strength as he'd shoved Gravesend. He would think nothing of beating her into agreeing to wed him. Her chest rose and fell with each breath she took. "Never," she muttered. "You will never have Hollincourt."

"My lady," Gravesend said. "Did he threaten you?"

She looked up. "He is blackmailing me."

"Let me send for the duke now," he said.

"I had better read the rest first. We cannot make a mistake." As she turned to the next page, her heart beat so hard she feared it would burst out of her chest. Richard had threatened to ruin Tristan if she refused to do his bidding. He meant to send news of the duke's many assignations with her to the scandal rags.

She stared in horror at the evidence he'd provided. He'd listed dates and times of Tristan's visits to her town house, including the night she and Tristan had argued about Miss Fielding's engagement. Richard had been spying on her for weeks before he'd made his grand entrance at the opera. And of course he'd found her alone behind closed doors with Tristan.

Think. They could deny the accusations, but it would not matter. A scandal would erupt whether the information was true or not. But would the scandal sheets dare print such damaging information about the Duke of Shelbourne? Of course they would. They had never hesitated to report royal scandals.

Could she bribe them? She didn't have enough time. Oh, God, she had to prevent him from sending that letter, but she refused to submit to his demands. She would never put herself in Richard's power. Her life, if he let her live, would be worth nothing.

But it was not only her life at stake. She must inform Tristan immediately.

For a moment, terror paralyzed her, but she must not let fear overtake her. She must keep her wits if she hoped to stop Richard.

Think. Richard had used a child to deliver the message. He probably had other street urchins watching her house. Richard must not suspect she'd contacted Tristan. She needed Richard to think she was too afraid to tell anyone. It was the best way to catch him. Otherwise, Richard would suspect they'd planned to entrap him. And then he would come up with another scenario and another. The man who had figuratively risen from the dead would rise again and again. He was desperate now and wanted her fortune more than ever.

Tessa folded the letter and took the foul thing with her to the escritoire. "Gravesend, I must pen a letter to Shelbourne."

Her hands shook as she wrote. After sanding the ink, she sealed it and stood. "Gravesend, there is no time to lose. We need to spirit a message to the duke without attracting notice."

He looked shaken.

"If I don't act quickly, bad things will happen. Is there a way to get the message to Shelbourne without attracting notice from anyone who might be watching the square?"

"Yes, I'll see it done," he said. "I will send one of the young grooms round the alley."

"If Shelbourne is not at home, the groom must return immediately. I will then send word to Broughton to find the duke. It is imperative that he receive this letter as fast as possible."

"Yes, my lady." He took the letter.

"After you send it, bring Jack and Tom to the drawing room," she said. "Send one of the new guards to the gate."

She returned to the settee and wrapped her arms round herself. If Richard released the information to the scandal sheets, Tristan would partake of her dishonor. The papers would print a story stating he'd been dallying with her while courting the girls. He would be disgraced. Others would remember his father's flagrant liaisons. Everyone would scorn his mother and sister. Everything Tristan had worked so hard for would go up in flames.

Oh, God. Amy, Georgette, and their parents would not escape unscathed. The news would humiliate all of them. Anne and Lord Broughton would suffer. They were among the most powerful aristocratic families in England. The scandal would rock the nation.

Fear clawed at her lungs, but she must not succumb. If she made a mistake, Richard would ruin all of them.

Tom and Jack rushed into the drawing room. Gravesend followed, huffing and puffing in his effort to keep up.

She stood. "I sent a message to the duke asking him to send me a missive with a location where we can meet in secret."

Gravesend shook his head. "No, you cannot. I'll not allow it."

"You must trust me," she said. "Jack, I need you and Tom to lead me on foot through back alleys. I believe Mortland has spies watching the house and the square. Notify the guards to make sure the way is clear. When we are well away from the square, you will hail a hackney. Can you do this?"

"Yes, my lady, we will escort and protect you," Jack said.

"Gravesend, please find an old cloak from one of the maids that I may use to disguise my identity."

After they left, she paced the drawing room, waiting for Tristan's message. She prayed he would do exactly as she asked.

Chill bumps erupted on her arms. Tristan would ask to see the blackmail letter. But first, she must tell him about her past. She could not let him read that filthy letter without an explanation. The thought was horrific, but she needed his help. They must catch Richard. If anything went awry, Richard would make everyone who mattered to her pay.

Chapter Twenty-two

Tristan sat in his study with Hawk. They sipped brandy while making plans. After so many false leads, Tristan had concluded they needed an operative with experience in gathering intelligence. Upon Hawk's urging, Tristan had written to Boswood asking him to meet them tomorrow about a sensitive matter. The marquess had connections inside the Foreign Office. Half an hour ago, Boswood had sent a reply confirming he would call first thing on the morrow.

"We'll get the blackguard," Hawk said.

"I hope we find him soon. It's killing me to think of that bastard running loose. And frankly, I'm uneasy about Tessa's isolation. She can't go on like this much longer."

Hawk lifted his brows. "Tessa?"

"Stubble it. You know we're friends."

"Friends, is it?" Hawk shook his head. "If you want my advice—"

"Don't," Tristan said.

A knock sounded. Tristan frowned. "Come in."

The butler opened the door. "Your Grace, a messenger is here. He says he must bring a missive directly to you and wait for your reply. Claims it's urgent."

Tristan stood. "Send him in right away."

A gawky youth, not much above eighteen, handed him the sealed note. Tristan opened it. Shock cascaded over him. "Good God."

"What?" Hawk said.

He passed it to Hawk. "We've got to act fast."

Hawk swore a blue streak.

Tristan grabbed the note. "Where can we meet?"

"The love nest," Hawk said.

Tristan scrawled the address of Hawk's assignation place along with a message to Tessa on her letter. *Take the two big footmen inside the hackney—make sure they're armed to the teeth.* He handed it to the youth. "Come back tomorrow—there's a reward for making sure it gets there fast. Go!"

The youth pulled his forelock and took off lightning fast.

Tristan looked at Hawk. "Blackmail. What could he possibly have on her?"

"Don't think about that now. We need weapons," Hawk said.

Ten minutes later, they sped off in Hawk's carriage with dueling pistols and knives. "We'll vanquish the blackguard," Hawk said.

Tristan didn't know what information Mortland was using to blackmail her, but Tessa had said it was bad. He tried telling himself Mortland had only threatened to reveal finding them alone in her drawing room. But that hardly warranted a clandestine meeting. Whatever she meant to tell him, she did not trust putting it in a letter.

Tessa clutched her reticule on her lap as the hackney bore her along the dark, cobbled streets. The blackmail letter was inside the reticule. Her stomach clenched, but she could not let herself fall apart. She must use her head and shove aside her fears. Her shame. None of that mattered. Not now. All that mattered was ensuring that the only person who fell tonight was Mortland.

Jack and Tom took up the entire seat across from her. "Don't you worry, my lady," Tom said.

Tessa silently rehearsed the words she would say to Tristan. She would not make excuses or beg his forgiveness. Nothing could lessen the impact of her confession.

A few minutes later, the hackney rolled to a halt in front of a small town house. Jack and Tom got out first. Her legs shook as Tom helped her down the steps. The front door opened. Tristan ran down the pavement, tossed a purse to the hackney driver, and took her arm. "Hurry."

He instructed the footmen to follow and stand guard at the door. When he led her inside, a butler took her cape. Hawk walked out from the staircase. Tessa glanced around at the simple house—wood floors, plain staircase, and no paintings whatsoever. Bachelors apparently didn't care much for decoration.

"Follow me," Hawk said.

As Tristan led her toward the stairs, Tessa's stomach roiled. Now that the moment was at hand, she feared she would retch. But she could not succumb. *Think of him. Think of his family and friends. You can do this.*

When they reached the stairs, Hawk kept walking past.

"There's a little parlor this way. Not much furniture, but it'll do."

Pin-prick sensations stung the backs of her hands. She halted. "Wait." Her voice had sounded unbelievably calm.

Hawk turned, his expression inscrutable.

Tristan frowned down at her. "What is it?"

"I must speak to you alone," she said.

"But Hawk needs—"

"Please," she whispered.

"Go on, old boy," Hawk said. "I'll wait outside."

Tristan led her to the door. When he opened it, she walked inside, feeling as if she were struggling to awake from a nightmare. But the green chaise with ugly black tassels and the two mismatched chairs were all too real. When the door clicked shut behind her, she drew closer to the fire, seeking warmth. A coal hissed in the grate as if condemning her.

His footsteps thudded across the carpet and her pulse raced. She tightened the blue silk drawstrings of her reticule, a mindless attempt to hide her wretched secrets.

He stopped inches from her back, dwarfing her with his tall presence. Even if she'd not known he'd entered the room, she would have recognized the unique scent of him, a heady combination of sandalwood and primitive male.

When he put his hands on her shoulders, she closed her eyes, remembering his heated caresses. He had bared her body, but he'd not uncovered the secrets that tormented her soul.

"Tess, you're trembling," he said. "Let me take you to a chair."

She made herself turn and meet his gaze. "No, I must face you standing."

"I'm certain I know what he's holding over you," he said.

She searched his eyes. He might have guessed part of the demands, but his mild reaction spoke volumes. He didn't know she'd deceived him.

"Mortland threatened to spread word we'd had an assignation, didn't he?"

"How did you know?" she whispered.

"The night we argued over Caroline Fielding, I saw a hackney rolling past in your square," he said. "I thought it suspicious. Since then, I've discovered Mortland has been in London longer than he claimed. I'm certain he was in that hackney, spying on you," he said.

She drew in a hitching breath. "That was one of many incidents he listed. He named dates and times of all our meetings. He threatened to sell it to the scandal sheets."

"I'll stop him first," he said.

"He may have already sent the information. He wants vengeance."

"He's a fool if he thinks he can get away with it unscathed. If Broughton finds out Mortland threatened us, he'll not hesitate to denounce the blackguard. No one will believe his lies." Tristan paused. "What did he demand?"

Her knees shook. "Me."

Tristan's eyes blazed. "The bloody fiend. I'll see him dead first."

"He wants Hollincourt," she said. "He means to take me to Gretna Green and force me to wed."

"He named a place and time to meet?"

She nodded. "Hyde Park Corner at three o'clock in the morning."

Tristan grinned. "Don't you see? He set his own trap." He held his fist up. "I've got him in the palm of my hand."

His jubilant expression pierced her heart. *God give me the strength to tell him.*

Tristan took her by the upper arms. "Don't worry. He's got nothing to hold over you."

"Yes, he does."

"I can't imagine it's as bad as you think. Let me see the blackmail letter."

She tightened her fingers on the strings of her reticule. "There is something I haven't told you—about the commission."

A wary look came into his eyes. "What does the commission have to do with the blackmail letter?"

She wondered how he'd missed the obvious clues. But out of necessity, she'd become a master at deception. Like a magician, she'd used illusion and misdirection to divert attention away from probing questions. Tristan had seen only what she'd allowed him to see.

He frowned. "Why are you hesitating?"

She winced, knowing her next words would shock him. "My uncle did not force him to take the commission because of the village girl."

Tristan dropped his hands as if she'd scalded him. "It was you?"

Her lips trembled. "Yes."

"He raped you?" His words came out in a harsh whisper.

"It wasn't rape." She tensed, waiting for the moment revulsion showed on his face.

He stared at her as if in disbelief. "You told me you

didn't go to your come-out because you didn't want to leave your grieving uncle. But you didn't go because that devil got you with child."

"No, I was spared that agony." She'd wept with relief the day her courses had started.

"You lied to me," he bit out.

Her stomach quaked. "You made an assumption. I did not confirm or deny it."

"You deceived me."

"Y-yes."

His expression turned thunderous. "Your uncle forced him to take that commission. He sent him away for a reason. I want the truth."

"I swear I'll tell you the whole of it later, but we've not the luxury of time," she said. "I fell into a trap of my own making and his long ago. The story involves a negligent governess, an elopement that never took place, and my own complicity in my fall." She almost faltered, but she made herself say the rest. "It h-happened one time. Mortland wanted to s-seal the deal—make sure I showed up at the appointed place and time."

"Give me the letter," he said in a stern tone.

She'd dreaded this moment even more than her confession. "Before I do, I must warn you. It is vulgar and explicit. Mortland threatened to send the examples in the blackmail letter to you if I did not comply. He is counting on my doing his bidding because he thinks I am too afraid to tell you."

She shivered at the cold look in his blue eyes, but she must say the rest. "He thinks I will submit to his demands, but I know he's planning to send you the letter anyway. Mortland wants you to be livid because he sees you as a rival. I've known it since the night he saw you in the foyer at the opera. Do not fall for his trap. He knows you mean the world to me, and he's using my feelings as a weapon."

His jaw worked. "Give me the letter—*now*."

She tried to open the strings of her reticule, but she fumbled and dropped it.

He retrieved it and steered her over to a chair. Then he handed her the reticule.

When she pulled out the letter, her hand shook as she offered it to him. He strode off to the sideboard without a word. Oh, God, what if he believed all those filthy lies?

She wanted to call him back, beg him not to read the foul letter, and tell him none of it was true. But she knew Tristan would never believe her again. He hated her.

She pressed her fist to her mouth to keep from crying out.

Tristan slapped the letter on the sideboard. Damn her. She'd kept her ruinous secret from him and exposed his family to the risk of scandal.

He clenched and unclenched his hands. The minute she'd clapped eyes on that bastard at the opera, she'd known she was in danger. That was the real reason she didn't want to take a stroll with him. She'd known that blackguard might spill her secret at any moment. But when he'd warned her the next day, she'd pretended the bastard was no threat to her. She ought to have resigned on the spot because of the potential for scandal, but she'd thought of no one but herself.

He'd fallen for every one of her deceptions and worried about her safety. He'd put every ounce of his energy into hunting that bastard, and she'd not said a word. He'd hired men to protect her. Gone into the slums looking for that fiend. Postponed calling on Amy and Georgette. He'd turned his life upside down for her, and she'd lied to him.

All the things that had puzzled him about her fell into place. Mortland's use of her Christian name, the watercolors, and her refusal to wed. He'd offered to marry her because he couldn't live with dishonoring her. And she'd lied about her reasons for refusing him.

Even after her confession tonight, she'd had the nerve to tell him he meant the world to her. He knew she'd only told him because Mortland had forced her hand. She'd put him, his family, the girls, and their families at risk.

Right now, he couldn't afford to let his fury distract him. With a deep breath, he took out his watch. Five hours—that's all the time he had left to put together a team of men to apprehend the fiend. If he didn't catch that bastard tonight, an unholy scandal would erupt.

He pocketed his watch and opened the letter. The instructions matched almost all of what she'd told him, save for the demand she bring fifty pounds. Mortland had sworn to make her pay for her betrayal eight years ago. Tristan had no idea what that was about, but it did not matter now.

He turned the page, and his rage turned deadly cold. The bastard crowed over how many times he'd sampled her. Promised to rough her up and make her beg for his cock. Wrote in filthy language how he would make her pay for all the services she'd performed on His Grace with her whore's mouth. Mortland regretted he could not tell the duke in person about all the lewd acts she'd so willingly engaged in by the lake.

When Tristan reached the last sentence in the paragraph, he inhaled sharply.

I'll make you spread your legs in the dirt again.

Denial rose up in him. Mortland had meant to terrify her so she would submit to his demands. He'd threatened to send the foul letter to *him*. She'd said *it* had happened once. Mortland had wanted to ensure she'd show for the elopement. Having seen the cur in action, Tristan could well believe it.

But she'd deceived him repeatedly. He no longer knew what to believe, couldn't trust his instincts any longer where she was concerned.

The devil, was it true? An image rose up in his mind of Mortland's smug look when he'd kissed her hand at the opera. Bile rose in his throat, imagining that blackguard's hands all over her.

And he'd thought he was the first man to kiss and touch her.

He squeezed his eyes shut. Memories of the two of them in the carriage flooded his brain. He recalled her hesitancy when she'd touched him. She'd not known what to do. He'd had to show her how to pleasure him.

He'd bedded more than his fair share of women who were experienced in the sensual arts, and he would have known if she'd been acting. None of that mattered, he told himself ruthlessly. She'd lied to him all along.

Tonight, she'd blindsided him.

He folded the letter and put it in his pocket. He turned and almost stumbled at the sight of her. Her back was bowed. She held her fist to her mouth.

She'd only been eighteen years old.

He stiffened, resisting the overwhelming urge to comfort her. If she'd told him the circumstances earlier, he would have sympathized with her, but he would never trust her again.

He strode over to her. She lowered her hand, straightened her spine, and met his gaze. Tears welled in her eyes, but she blinked them back. He retrieved his handkerchief and handed it to her. She took it, but the threatening tears never fell.

"I have to prepare," he said. "It will be a long night. I am taking you to my mother."

She started shaking her head. "No, I cannot. My footmen will—"

"I do not have time to argue with you. I've only got five hours left to prepare. If I don't catch that fiend tonight, he'll embroil all of us in your scandal."

"Tristan, I never meant—"

"Hold your tongue." She shuddered at his terse command, but he would not make this easy on her. "You will do exactly as I tell you. Tomorrow you can make your full confession. No excuses. No evasions. No lies."

The first rays of dawn filtered over Wimbledon Common as Tristan force-marched a gagged and tied Mortland to the field. They'd had to give chase at Hyde Park Corner. The bastard had almost evaded on foot the two dozen mounted men and the speeding carriages in pursuit. Tristan had ridden on horseback after him. When they'd finally surrounded him, Tristan had dismounted and forced the lieutenant to the ground. He'd kneed Mortland in the back and gagged him so he couldn't spew filth about Tessa. Then Tom had frisked him and found a wicked blade in the cur's boot.

When they reached the field, Jack yanked Mortland's head back by his greasy curls. Hawk, Broughton, Boswood, Hardwick, and Tom stood as witnesses.

Tristan shed his coat and handed it to Hawk. Then he rolled up his sleeves and grasped the bastard by the chin. "I'll give you a choice, Mortland. I'll let you stand and fight me, though I promise you won't win. If you utter one word against the lady you threatened, I'll have Jack hold you in place while I beat you senseless. You'll be as defenseless as a babe."

Mortland glared at him.

"Untie the gag," Tristan said, fisting his hands.

Mortland snarled. "She spread—"

Tristan slammed his fist into the devil's mouth. Blood spurted out. All the fury erupted as bloodlust in Tristan's veins. He broke Mortland's nose, blackened both eyes shut, and pummeled his belly. The coward screamed and pleaded for mercy, providing a little entertainment for the other men.

Afterward, Tristan invited Broughton to have a go at the bastard. Broughton took out a handkerchief and wiped off Mortland's bloody face. "Just so I don't get my hands dirty." Then he pounded the blackguard.

Tom walked over to Tristan and told him of an interesting detail about the night Mortland had invaded Tessa's town house. With a cocky grin, Tristan strode over to Mortland and told Jack to lower the fiend to his knees. "I have a special punishment for you, one I believe the lady you wronged would appreciate."

Mortland whimpered.

Tristan kicked him in the groin. The bastard's head lolled. Jack shoved him to the grass, where he passed out.

After flexing his bruised hands, Tristan looked at the others. "Gentlemen, to the docks."

Tristan's mother met him in the hall. She eyed his bruised knuckles. "Barely a scratch."

"Where is she?" Tristan asked.

"Sleeping in my bed," she said.

"When she wakes, tell her to come to my study."

His mother's brows shot up. "You did not ask after her welfare."

"I'm exhausted and filthy. We'll talk later."

Her eyes blazed. "You blame her?"

A maid hurried past. "In my study," he gritted out.

She marched beside him, visibly bristling. After he shut the door, his mother turned on him. "I know your capacity for resentment, but you go too far."

His nostrils flared. "She lied to me and exposed all of us to scandal."

"She didn't send that blackmail letter. That villain did. I cannot believe you are blaming a defenseless woman. I taught you better."

"She has known from the night he showed up at the opera that he was a threat, and she said nothing. You defend her, but you do not know all the circumstances."

"I know that man hurt her. Last night, I held that young woman in my arms for hours. I tried to comfort her, but she kept saying she was unworthy. And I knew he'd seduced her. How old was she?"

Guilt flared in his chest. "Eighteen," he muttered.

"She was little more than a child. Younger than your sister."

"She is a grown woman now, and she deceived me *repeatedly*."

"Have you asked yourself why? Do you know what society would do to her? They would cut her. She would be ostracized, completely isolated because she has no family. It wouldn't matter that a scoundrel had seduced her. It wouldn't matter that she'd been young and naïve. She had no choice but to keep her secret."

"If she had told me, I would have understood," he bit out.

His mother lifted her chin. "Have you ever done something you're ashamed of?"

"Haven't we all?" he said, not bothering to hide his sarcasm.

"Then tell me your shameful secret," she said.

He shook his head. "Mama, enough."

"It's not easy, is it? And I'm your mother. You're assured of my love and forgiveness."

"You know I worried about her. I tried to protect her, and she withheld information from me when she knew I was hunting that cur. She waited until the last possible minute to tell me," he said. "And you expect me to forget? I can't do it."

"Then don't talk to her," she said. "She's too fragile. You'll break her. And I won't let you do it."

He couldn't breathe for a moment. "What are you saying?"

"All through the night, I told her over and over again that it was natural to cry," the duchess said, her voice shaking. "But she held it in for hours. I've never seen the like in all my life. And I thought, my God, she's held this in for years.

"At dawn, I told her it wasn't her fault. And only then did she weep. I finally got her to lie down and left her with my maid. But I could not stay away. I kept thinking she has no family. She believes herself unworthy of a husband and children. Her bosom friend is the sister of that fiend. I thought she might believe she had nothing to live for." Her voice broke. "I hurried to her and found her asleep at last. She was holding a handkerchief to her mouth. It was yours."

Aw, hell. Tessa had suffered for years in silence. She'd said nothing because she was afraid and ashamed. He'd known all along that scoundrel meant her harm. If he'd not been so blind, he would have guessed the man had hurt her long ago. He'd sworn to protect her, but when she'd needed him most, he'd blamed her.

"I cannot imagine how she's endured all these years," his mother said. "She must have been terrified that night at the opera."

Tristan stared at his mother as one realization after another slammed into his brain. "She never showed it. He coerced her, but she walked out of the box with her head held high. He sent her watercolors, and she sent them back. When Mortland invaded her home and hurt her butler, she got her footmen to rough him up and dump him in the slums. And she did not succumb to his blackmail threat. She sought my help and admitted her past indiscretion because she would not let him ruin our lives." And the day he'd proposed, she'd told him she would not bring scandal upon him and his family. She *had* tried to protect him.

"Most women would fall apart," he said, "but she never cowered before him. She's the bravest person I've ever met."

"Son, I admire her as well, but she's reached the limits of her endurance. I can tell her it wasn't her fault until I'm blue in the face, but she needs to hear it from you."

He closed the distance between them and enfolded his mother in his arms. "Send her to me when she wakes," he said.

After a few minutes, his mother stepped back, wiped a stray tear from her face, and sniffed.

"I'm sorry. I don't have a handkerchief," he said.

"Never mind that." She wrinkled her nose. "You need to bathe. You stink."

"Bloody hell," he said, laughing.

His mother swatted his arm. "Watch your language."

He took her hand and squeezed it. "Thank you for taking care of her."

"That is what mothers are for."

He left the study door open for her. The rustle of cloth brought his head up from the letter on his desk. She hesitated at the entrance, looking like a lost waif.

Tristan rose and strode over to her, noting the dark smudges under her reddened eyes. She looked drawn and defeated.

He shut the door behind her. "He's gone forever, Tess."

"Thank you," she murmured.

He led her to a chair and sat beside her.

She glanced at his right hand. "Your knuckles are bruised. You fought him."

"I beat him within an inch of his life."

An awkward pause followed, and then he recollected his manners. "May I get you a glass of sherry?"

She shook her head. "Last night, I remembered something you said to Amy at the parlor game. Once trust is broken, there will always be suspicion thereafter."

He saw sorrow and resignation in her eyes.

"I never wanted to deceive you, but I was afraid," she said.

"I know."

"Last night, you were angry when you realized I had not told you the real reason I didn't attend my come-out. That day I was overcome with shame and remorse when Anne handed me that letter. Afterward, you were so kind to me. I'd never discussed my past with anyone, not even Anne. You were the first person I trusted enough to reveal a few essentials."

"I understand now," he said.

She searched his eyes. "I thought you would be angry."

"I was, but it was unreasonable of me. It's not your fault."

"Though I am too late, I owe you an explanation," she said.

"You do not have to tell me." He didn't want to hear her confession. Didn't want to think about that bastard touching her, mistreating her.

"I need to talk about it," she said. "For eight years, I've held these secrets inside me." She put her fist to her heart. "You do not know the burden of guilt I carried. I deceived Anne to protect my reputation and to keep from losing her friendship. I told myself he was dead, and a confession would only add to her wounds. Even now I question whether I should tell her, but while such a confession might prove temporarily cathartic for me, it would only hurt her and ruin our friendship."

She had no one else to tell.

"I should have told you the day you proposed," she said. "You deserved the truth, and I could not make myself say the words. I knew I was unworthy. But when I refused you, it cut me to my very soul."

"You are not unworthy," he said.

"I was so young and stupid. I did not know a youthful mistake would forever alter the course of my life."

"Before you begin, I want to tell you something," he said. "The past does not change who you are now. You are still the brave Tess who faced dragons with your chin held high. The same Tess who stood up to me time and again. The same Tess who does the work of a man and a woman. The same Tess who finds husbands for girls everyone else ignores. The same witty, intelligent Tess who surprises me and makes me look at the world in a whole new way. The same Tess I couldn't help teasing. The same Tess I always looked forward to seeing every time I stepped inside your drawing room. And though I know he hurt you, I also know you are the strong woman you are because of the adversity you faced."

"And you are the strong man you are because of what you faced," she said.

He nodded. "We both had to grow up too early."

"After Richard was sent away to war, Uncle George told me if a man ever offered for me, I must tell him what happened."

He inhaled after hearing her use Mortland's Christian name, but he would not call it to her attention. She was looking back and probably not even aware of what she'd done.

"I knew I could never reveal my shame," she said. "I

could see in my mind the man's disgust. So I made the decision never to marry."

She'd only been eighteen years old when she'd given up all hopes of a husband and children.

When she hung her head, he knew he must reassure her. "I know that bastard took advantage of you when you were most vulnerable. You had lost your parents and your aunt."

"I knew better," she whispered.

"How did he manage to meet you alone?"

She returned her gaze to him. "I was so naïve. I thought we met by accident at the oak tree near the lake on my uncle's estate. Now I know he watched me and figured out my habits. I used to walk there with my watercolors. It was my dream place. I painted white knights on chargers rescuing damsels in distress."

He frowned. "Where was your governess?"

"She complained about boredom and insects. I sent her away, just as she intended. She took advantage of my uncle's melancholy and idled."

"Why did you not tell your uncle about him?"

"I was afraid he would keep me from seeing him. My uncle tried to guide me, but he was horribly listless after my aunt died. I had no friends or cousins. I was lonely. Anne was only fourteen, and those four years are vast when you are eighteen. I knew it was wrong to meet Richard in secret, but he charmed me."

"He seduced you," Tristan growled.

"At first, it was harmless," she said, "or so I told myself. Richard was the pinnacle of my life. He would paint a big X over my medieval knights, saying he was jealous of my imaginary beaux. You can imagine how that turned my head. It wasn't until I found out that I had a sponsor and was going to London for my come-out that things took a serious turn."

"What do you mean?"

"I foolishly told him about my come-out. In all my girlish excitement, I thought he would be happy for me. Instead, he grew sullen and said I would forget him. And then he begged me not to go, and I said he was being selfish. Then he ran away. So of course I felt guilty and went back the next day to apologize. He wasn't there that day, or the next. I went there every day for a week, and he did not come back.

"I might have escaped my fate if I had found a new place to paint or if I had told him to go away when he came back after that first week. Oh, but I was thrilled to see him. He told me he loved me, and I was bowled over. I thought I was in love with him. It was all very innocent and sweet at first."

Every muscle in his body tightened involuntarily, knowing she was about to reveal the part he didn't want to hear. For her sake, he must not show his hatred of the bastard, because she might interpret it as disgust for her.

"The week before I was to leave for London, he begged me to marry him," she said. "I was so naïve I actually told him to ask my uncle for my hand. Richard understood what I was too ignorant to figure out. He knew my uncle would refuse. Richard had no career, and truthfully, he was beneath me in rank. Right or wrong, my uncle would not have permitted the match on that count alone. Richard pointed out all these things to me. I was quite fond of *Romeo and Juliet*, and naturally saw our own story as equally tragic. So I told my uncle I wished to wait another year to attend my come-out. Then Richard proposed we elope and present my uncle with a fait accompli."

Tristan stilled. "You said you didn't elope."

"The day before, I met him at the lake. My conscience bothered me. I knew an elopement would wound Uncle George and cause a scandal. But I didn't want to lose Richard. So I told him I wanted to wait a little longer until my uncle's spirits lifted. Richard sensed my cold feet and accused me of toying with his heart." She laughed without mirth. "Of course I pledged my undying love for him. And that is when he told me to prove it."

Tristan inhaled.

She took a shaky breath. "I refused. He threatened to leave me forever if I did not. I told him no again. And he walked off. I have relived that moment so many times. If I had not called him back, my life would have turned out so differently. But I did. And I have had to bear the knowledge that I said yes."

Tristan let out his pent-up breath. "Tessa, he used your feelings to manipulate you. I saw my father play similar emotional games with my mother. It is abuse even if it is not a physical threat."

"I was so scared," she whispered.

He reached for her hand and squeezed it.

"Afterward, he told me to bring money. He was low in the pocket, but he loved me and said all would work out after we were married."

"I hope he rots in hell," Tristan muttered.

"That night, I tried to write a letter to my uncle," she said. "I cried the whole time. I could not leave my poor, sad uncle. So I woke him up in the middle of the night. I thought if I told him about the elopement, he would be so happy I'd confessed that he would let us marry. Of course I did not tell him what had happened. My uncle stayed very calm. Then he asked me where to find Richard and told me to sit quietly in the library adjoining his study. Richard did not know I was there." She paused. "I heard all of it."

"Your uncle told him he must accept the commission?"

"He told Richard he was a worm, not fit to crawl along the ground I walked on. Uncle George said he'd see him hanged before he let him marry me. I put my fist to my mouth to keep from crying out. But Richard had an ace in his pocket. He thought he'd sealed the deal. And then he told my uncle I had lain with him. I cannot even begin to tell you how mortified and ashamed I was."

Tristan was glad he'd beat the hell out of the bastard.

The clock chimed eleven times, drawing his attention. Then he returned his gaze to her. She was staring at her lap. "What happened afterward?" he said softly.

"Later, my uncle told me he never intended to let Richard near me again, but that day, he wanted Richard to reveal his true motivation—that he was after my fortune. Uncle George gave him two choices: Marry me without a penny or take a commission in the army."

"He chose the army," Tristan said.

"He said he'd rather join the stinking army than marry a fat chit." She looked at him. "I have felt ugly ever since."

"Tess, you are beautiful to me. The first time I saw you, I was struck dumb by your lush mouth and the laughter in your eyes. But it was your quick wit that intrigued me the most. No woman has ever challenged me the way you do."

She took a deep breath. "I promised you honesty, and I will say the words once. Then you must forget them."

His skin tingled, though he'd no idea what she meant to say.

"Mortland underestimated my uncle, and he underestimated me. He did not know I love you. I love you so much I would sacrifice myself to complete and utter ruin if it meant I could save you from scandal."

His heart thumped. She loved him. *Loved him.* A hot sensation rushed into his cheekbones and stung his eyes. He gritted his teeth, fighting for control.

Tears welled in her eyes. "You do not have to say anything. I know you will act with honor. But in my heart, you will always be my knight in ducal armor."

He wanted to get down on his knees and beg her to be his wife. But he'd made a pledge to two others. He wanted to break it, wanted to say to hell with society, but Tessa would not let him. She would never hurt those girls, and he could not bring disgrace upon them or Tessa.

There was one thing he could do for her, something he'd planned while waiting for her to arrive. He stood and helped her rise. "Come with me."

He led her to the hearth and set the screen aside. Then he removed the blackmail letter from his coat pocket. "I want you to burn his letter, and I will witness. When it is finally consumed, you will never think of him again."

She fed both pages at once into the fire. He held her hand until the papers and her past disappeared in the flames.

One week later, Tristan stood at the open window in his study, staring at the soot-filled sky. The door opened. His mother walked in and stood beside him. "You spoke to the two girls and their fathers?"

"Yes."

She cleared her throat. "I suppose one of the calls you made proved difficult."

He struggled not to laugh at her obvious attempt to wrangle the information out of him. "All in all, matters went far better than I expected."

She tried again. "Should I send out the invitations for the ball?"

He smiled. "Yes."

She swatted his arm with her fan. "You are purposely torturing me. Who did you choose?"

"I thought of surprising you at the ball."

"Insolent puppy. Tell me now," she demanded, "or there will be no ball."

He did.

She dropped her fan.

When he bent to retrieve it, his very proper mother muttered, "I'll be damned."

Tessa and Jane were discussing the wedding plans when Gravesend appeared at the drawing room door. "The Duchess of Shelbourne."

They both rose. Tessa had read the papers every day, expecting to hear of Tristan's engagement. Perhaps the duchess meant to inform her. Tessa's heart squeezed. She must be happy for him, even though her heart ached every time she thought of him. Which was about every five minutes. Next week six, she promised herself.

The duchess sat next to Tessa on the settee and turned her attention to Jane. "Miss Powell, I understand you are to make an advantageous marriage. Congratulations."

"Thank you, Your Grace," Jane said.

"I have a personal matter to discuss with Miss Mansfield," she said. "Will you grant us privacy?"

Tessa's lips twitched. How like the duchess not to mince words.

Jane fled the room as if *all* the society dragons were breathing fire at her.

"May I offer you tea?" Tessa asked.

"No, thank you." She opened her reticule and handed Tessa an engraved invitation. Tessa opened it. Her heart pounded as she struggled to keep the smile on her face. "Oh, he will announce his engagement at a ball. On Friday." *One week away.*

"My son will propose there."

Tessa gasped. "In a crowded ballroom?"

"He has spoken to the girls and their families at length," she said. "My son assured me all went well."

She swallowed. *It hurt. It shouldn't. But it did.* "So they know." Her voice had quavered just a little.

"He plans to honor both girls and their families. In this manner, he will show his great esteem for them and ensure that all of society is witness."

"Oh." She looked at the duchess. "Who did he choose?"

The duchess lifted her quizzing glass to her eye. "My son told me you like surprises. I assured him I would not give away his secret."

Tessa's lips twitched. "He did that on purpose because I surprised him."

"I believe *hoodwinked* is a more accurate word," the duchess said. "You will attend, of course. He wishes to acknowledge your efforts on his behalf."

Oh, it would be hard, but she must be brave for him.

And happy for him—in a year or so. "In that case, I certainly shall attend. After all, everyone will say I have made the match of the century." She frowned. That did not sound quite right.

The duchess cleared her throat. "I believe that is a possibility."

Chapter Twenty-three

$\mathcal{O}$n the night of Tristan's betrothal ball, Tessa's nerves threatened to overwhelm her. "Do I look presentable, Jane?"

"You look beautiful. Blue suits you," she said.

She had chosen the color in honor of his unforgettable eyes. "I suppose we should be on our way."

Jane's eyes registered sadness. "If I were a fairy god-companion, I would wave my magic wand and make sure your prince chose you."

Georgette would live the fairy tale tonight. "Let us go before I lose what little courage I have," Tessa said. After Jane had noticed her moping, Tessa had confessed she'd fallen a tiny bit in love with the duke. Jane had suspected Tessa had developed tender feelings for him.

When they reached the door, panic squeezed the breath from her lungs, but she would not disappoint Tristan. "I can do this," she said. "I will hold my head up high and sniffle like all the ladies. Sentimental feelings at such an occasion are to be expected."

"Very true," Jane said.

A knock sounded at the door. When Tessa opened it, Gravesend's weathered eyes misted a little. "Might I be permitted to say how very lovely you look tonight, my lady?"

"Thank you, Gravesend. Come along, Jane. We must not tarry."

"Two gentlemen are downstairs waiting to escort both of you," Gravesend said.

Tessa blinked. "Who are they?"

"I am sworn to silence," he said, puffing out his chest.

Tessa and Jane exchanged puzzled looks. Then they followed Gravesend down the corridor to the stairs. At the landing, Tessa paused. Hawk stood gazing up at her with a merry grin on his face. Beside him, Mr. Hodges turned and smiled.

"Oh, my goodness," Jane whispered.

In a daze, Tessa followed Jane down the stairs.

Hawk offered his arm to Tessa. "Shall we go to the ball?"

Tessa smiled a little. "He sent you."

Hawk winked. "He doesn't like to leave things to chance."

Moments later, the carriage wound through the streets of the West End. Then it slowed to a crawl, stopping and starting, moving only a few feet at a time. A mile of carriages stood in front of their vehicle, each waiting to deposit passengers. It seemed like hours before Hawk's carriage arrived at the wrought-iron gates. Then they were walking through the door of the ducal mansion and the stairwell was before them.

Hawk grinned at Tessa. "Well, Princess, shall we claim

privilege on those stairs?" He looked over his shoulder. "Hodges, follow me."

Then, as if by magic, the guests squeezed aside while Hawk led them up the curving staircase. At the landing, four footmen cleared the path for them.

The crowd stared as Hawk led her inside the grand doors. Tessa's heartbeat thudded in her ears. Or was that the buzz of voices? Ahead she saw a red-carpeted dais erected at the back of the ballroom.

Hawk led her to the duchess, who waited near the front of the stage. Then he stood beside Tessa.

Tessa curtseyed. "Your Grace."

The duchess raised her quizzing glass to her eye. "Miss Mansfield, I approve of your gown. Blue is your color."

"It is my favorite." Tessa craned her neck and caught a glimpse of Jane walking with Mr. Hodges, but the crowd swallowed her.

Julianne skipped up to her mother and peered at Tessa. "Miss Mansfield, your gown is gorgeous. You will be the envy of every woman tonight."

"Thank you, but I think someone else will soon be the most envied lady at this ball." She looked past the dais. Near the stairs, she spotted Amy, Georgette, and their parents. Both girls looked stunning tonight. Amy was tall and regal in a netted gown with a jade underskirt. Georgette looked beautiful, of course, in her white gown with a rose sash. Both girls appeared poised. Tessa was glad they'd learned the outcome ahead of time.

She craned her head, looking for Anne and Lord Broughton, but she could not see them in this crush. With a sigh, Tessa tapped the toe of her slipper, anxious for Tristan to arrive.

A parade of ladies walked toward them. Hawk leaned closer to Tessa. "My family—all female, you will note. My brother Will is languishing in some Italian villa, or so my great-aunt Hester reports. Watch out for her, she's a live one. And the white-haired lady is my grandmamma. She enjoys her heart palpitations, or rather, the attention she gets when she conveniently succumbs to them. Ah, here they come. Do me a favor, Princess, and tell them you're done making matches for rakes."

In the next few moments, she discovered Hawk had a rather eccentric family: grandmamma of the famed heart palpitations, the countess and her three married daughters, who insisted they'd gone into a decline upon hearing of their brother's ill-fated one-hour engagement, and Great-aunt Hester, who inspected Tessa and boomed, "Hah! She bamboozled Shelbourne with her bosom."

After they moved on, the duchess leaned toward Tessa. "Dreadful woman. She buried five husbands and keeps a faux mummy in her drawing room."

The connecting door opened, and the crowd hushed. Tristan strode in and headed for the dais. Tessa caught her breath. He looked very handsome in his formal black tailcoat and breeches as he climbed the short steps. When he reached the center of the stage, he put his hands behind his back.

"Ladies and gentlemen," he said, projecting his distinctive voice so that all could hear. "Thank you for attending. It is an honor to share this occasion with so many friends."

After a pause, he drew in a breath. "Most especially, I wish to thank the twenty-four beautiful young women and their families who started out this journey with me.

Much as I would have liked to marry all of them, I am not man enough for twenty-four wives."

Laughter erupted.

Tristan held up his hand. When the crowd quieted, he continued. "I am also honored to have my good friend Hawk here. He willingly attended many of the courtship events and even suffered a night at the opera. It was courageous of him since he is mortally afraid of catching wife-itis."

Tessa smiled as laughter broke out again.

"Of course, I am also indebted to my sister, who was under the mistaken impression she could engage in mischief while I was preoccupied with my courtship. And I wish to honor my mother." He made a very formal bow to her. "She thought her lectures fell on deaf ears, but eventually I saw the error of my ways."

Then he turned to gaze at Amy, Georgette, and their parents. "Will you join me?"

The girls linked arms and walked up to the dais. Their beaming parents followed, standing behind them. Tessa was glad the girls had remained friends, and it seemed their parents had as well.

Tristan addressed the girls. "Miss Hardwick and Lady Georgette, I honor both of you. It is to your credit that you have remained steadfast friends throughout the courtship."

Murmurs of approval sounded within the crowd.

Tristan continued. "Miss Hardwick and Lady Georgette, you are here for a reason. From the very beginning until the end, both of you demonstrated rare strength of character. I am awed by your unwavering loyalty and friendship. I also wish to pay my respects to Lord and Lady Boswood and Mr. and Mrs. Hardwick. Thank you for allowing me to court your wonderful daughters."

Tessa's breath hitched in her throat. She had assumed he'd chosen Georgette, but she could not be sure. He might have chosen Amy. Tessa gripped her hands hard. The suspense was almost unbearable.

Tristan cleared his throat. "During the courtship, I recognized there was an imbalance. All the decisions were mine, and yet the young ladies could not court other gentlemen. I thought this unfair to them, so I told them they had a choice in the matter. They had the option to withdraw at any time, and I promised I would understand."

Only a few coughs pierced the silence.

Tristan continued. "At a house party, I came to know Miss Hardwick, Lady Georgette, and their parents better. There was and still is friendship among all of us. But I began to worry if we were all not feeling a bit of obligation because of the public nature of the courtship. We all enjoyed our time together, but I felt something missing. So I decided to call on Lady Georgette and Miss Hardwick after we returned to London.

"Earlier in the courtship, I'd asked all the ladies what they expected out of a marriage to me. This time I posed the question a bit differently to Lady Georgette and Miss Hardwick. I asked them what they most desired from a husband. Mind you, I spoke to them separately, so imagine my astonishment when they both gave the same answer."

Tristan paused again, keeping everyone on pins and needles. "And they said love," he finished. "So I found myself asking another question."

Numerous male chuckles followed.

"I asked Lady Georgette and Miss Hardwick if they

loved me." He grinned at both of them. "And they astonished me again. Both reassured me of their great esteem and even mentioned I wasn't a bad-looking fellow."

More laughter followed. Tessa's eyes misted. She'd not failed him after all.

"Naturally I lamented the lack of passion in their regard, but I understood if they wished to withdraw. Now here is the part I found somewhat peculiar. Both girls assured me their decision was a near thing, but Miss Mansfield told them the law did not permit me to marry both of them."

Mr. Hardwick shook his head, making the crowd laugh louder.

When Tristan turned to the girls again, the crowd hushed. "Miss Hardwick and Lady Georgette, I wish you happiness and most of all, I wish you love."

Thunderous applause erupted. Tristan took the opportunity to bow to their families. Tessa clasped her hands and regarded the duchess. "Oh, that was wonderful. Like watching a play." Then she frowned. "Oh, dear. I suppose I'll have to arrange another courtship for him next season."

The duchess fanned herself. Hawk made a choked sound. Julianne snickered behind her hand.

Some of the guests began to head for the refreshment tables, but they halted when Tristan held his hand up once more. "Ladies and gentlemen, may I have your attention again?" He paused for silence. "You may be thinking what now? But a certain lady once told me some of the most wonderful things in life are a surprise."

Tessa clasped her hands to her heart.

"One night at a ball, I was searching for a bride, and I stepped on a fan quite by accident. When I looked up, I saw a lady with laughing green eyes. I offered to pay for her damaged fan, but she reassured me its death was a kindness as it was quite ugly." He looked down at his sister. "Julianne, will you do the honors for me?"

Tessa accepted the ugly little fan and smiled. It was so wonderful of him to recognize her. He must know how much it meant to her.

"Miss Mansfield," he said, "Julianne and I were unable to find any fans with putrid green paint, but my sister assured me this one is hideous."

Tessa laughed with everyone else. She was so touched.

His smile faded, and he took a deep breath. "I wish to honor you, Miss Mansfield."

Hawk offered his arm. "Princess, may I escort you?"

Tessa's heart started racing as she took Hawk's arm. "I do not understand."

The duchess took the ugly fan and leaned closer. "Don't disappoint me, gel."

Tessa's nerves jangled as Hawk led her round the dais and up the steps. Then he winked at Tristan and retreated. She stood there, dazed. Tristan beckoned her with his fingers. She walked forward, feeling as if she'd done this once before. He gazed intently into her eyes when she stopped before him. Then he reached into his coat, drew out a sealed paper, and offered it to her. "A gift for you," he said.

A hush descended over the room.

She broke the seal with trembling fingers. The silence unnerved her as she unfolded the page. Her breath caught at the words.

You are my one and only, for all eternity.

The same words her father had written to her mother every day of their marriage.

The paper fluttered to the carpet as he took her hands. Then he kneeled before her. She gasped, along with two hundred other guests.

His beautiful blue eyes were shining as he gazed up at her. "Tessa, I love you with all my heart. If you will agree to be my duchess, I will honor, protect, and love you all the days of our lives."

Tears streamed down her cheeks. How could she turn down the proposal of the decade? The century! "Yes," she whispered, gazing into his beautiful blue eyes. Then she projected her voice. "Yes, I will marry you. I love you so very dearly. And I will honor, protect, and love you all the days of our lives."

He rose, snatched her up in his arms, and swung her round and round. The crowd roared.

Then he set her down. She smiled up at him, feeling like a fairy princess after all. In front of all society, he captured her lips in a very unseemly, naughty kiss.

The crowd at the ball had thinned by three o'clock in the morning. Tessa hugged Anne, who promised to call the next day. Afterward, Tessa squeezed Amy's and Georgette's hands. When she promised to find them husbands, the duchess groaned.

Tessa laughed. "I suppose I should consult my fiancé first."

The duchess sniffed. "By next spring, you will be too busy with my first grandchild for a matchmaking career."

Tristan smiled at Tessa. "My duchess can have a career and a baby if she likes. She's perfect, you know."

Hawk clapped Tristan on the shoulder. Then he kissed Tessa's hand. "I am heartbroken."

"Careful, I may let her arrange a courtship for you," Tristan said.

Hawk held up his hands as if to ward her off. "Have mercy on this bachelor."

A few minutes later, Tristan took her aside. "At last, we have a moment alone."

"How did you know I would say yes when you proposed?"

"You told me you loved me," he said. "And I knew then what I'd denied for weeks and weeks. I had fallen head-long in love with you, and I could not live without you."

Her heart squeezed. "I love you," she whispered.

The duchess approached. "I have a confession to make. Really, I thought the pair of you would catch on, but then you only seem to have eyes for each other."

"What?" Tristan said.

"Son, you were appallingly easy to manipulate. All I had to do was threaten to find her a husband. You were wild with jealousy. It was clear to me the two of you were mad for each other. All you needed was a little push. The carriage arrangements were a near thing, however."

Tristan scoffed. "Mama, you refused when I first asked to ride with her."

"From the moment you spoke your first words, you said no when I said yes. I knew if I refused, you would tell a bald-faced lie to get her alone." The duchess lifted her nose. "Never let it be said I didn't arrange your marriage."

Tessa laughed. "Duchess, I never suspected a thing."

"You must call me Mama now," she said. Then she whispered in her ear. "I could not have chosen a more per-fect bride for him."

Tessa's eyes misted a little. "Thank you, Mama."

Soon the ballroom emptied of all the guests. Mama claimed she couldn't find her spectacles. She couldn't see too well in dim corridors without them, especially near her son's bedchamber. Then she collected Julianne and quit the ballroom.

Tristan drew Tessa into his arms. "Today is my thirty-first birthday, but I didn't make it to the altar," he said.

"Close enough," she said.

His blue eyes heated. "Duchess, do you have a gift for me?"

Her lips twitched. "Did you lie about your birthday?"

"Yes." He wrapped his arms round her and captured her lips. He opened her mouth and did wicked, wicked things with his tongue. And his hands. She felt him harden against her belly. Desire inflamed her.

When he lifted his head, she felt breathless. He gazed at her with that intent, seductive expression she knew so well.

"I hope your bedchamber isn't far," she said.

"Let's make a run for it," he said in that velvety, chocolate voice that made her crumble like cake. Then he grabbed her hand, and they ran to the stairs, laughing like a pair of naughty children.

Once inside his bedchamber, he started working on her ball gown feverishly, but she knew a moment of self-doubt. "I wish you were the first," she whispered.

He turned her round and cupped her cheek. "If you had gone to London all those years ago, another man would have snatched you up. Back then, I had nothing but a hardened heart and debts, nothing to offer a wife."

"Uncle George told me things happen for a reason."

"I love you," he said. He sought her lips. The initial soft kiss heated quickly. He kept peeling off the layers of her clothing, stopping often to kiss her skin. She got his coat, cravat, waistcoat, and shirt off. They both laughed as he struggled with the laces to her stays. Finally he pitched it to the floor and lifted her shift over her head. When he cupped her breasts, she made an ardent sound. He growled. She ran her hands over his chest, kissed him there, and made short work of his trouser buttons. When she clasped him, he hissed in a breath, and then he shed the rest of his clothing.

He stripped back the covers and tumbled her to the bed like a starving man. "I dreamed of this so many times," he said, breathing heavily. The heat between them ignited. She cried out as he suckled her, caressed her, and then kissed his way down her belly. He spread her thighs and did the most amazing things with his tongue. She arched her back, crying out with the pleasure.

He rose over her. "I want you. I crave you. I will never get enough of you." He slid one finger, then two inside her, stretching her. "I'll go slowly. You're really tight."

"My big, strong man," she said.

He made a male sound of pleasure in the back of his throat. Then she clasped him, guiding him. He entered her inch by inch, and the whole time, he never took his eyes from hers. She loved him very much for it because she needed that reassurance this first night of their lives together.

It was beautiful to watch him, to feel him stroke her inside, to be one with him. To be his. She swept her hands down his back, smoothing over his hips, and a hoarse sound came out of his throat. She pressed against him, rocking her hips. He reached between them and caressed her in a place that made her wild. "Like this?" he said.

She panted, "Yes." He angled higher within her and withdrew. He did it again and again and again. Then she stilled and cried out. He growled near her ear, "I can feel you clenching all around me."

He thrust inside her faster and faster. She clung to him, wrapping her arms and legs round him, because she never wanted to let him go again. A deep, male sound came out of his throat, and when he collapsed atop her, she kissed his cheek, slightly scratchy with his heavy beard. She was so happy and stunned by the intensity of it all. "I love you," she whispered.

When Tristan awoke, she still clutched him tight with her arms and legs. He thought he must be crushing her, so he disentangled himself. She made a little mewing protest. With a chuckle, he pulled her back to his chest, nestling her bottom against him like an inverted spoon. Then he filled his hand with her breast. As he drifted between wakefulness and sleep, she laughed.

"What is so amusing?" he mumbled.

"When I decided to make you a love match, I never dreamed it would be me."

He nuzzled her neck. "Mmmm."

"Tristan? I'm too excited to sleep."

"Must be your nervous disposition." He closed his eyes.

She turned to face him. "Oh, you're sleepy."

He rolled onto his back, pulling her on top of him. "Wake me up, darling."

"I think I like this," she said, as he helped her figure out how to ride him. Bless her, she caught on quickly.

A few hours later, a ray of sunlight pierced through the crack in the drapes. Tristan eased out of bed and found paper and pen at the corner desk. After he had sanded the ink, he slipped into bed, tucked the folded note beneath her pillow, and watched her sleep. His heart filled with joy. "You are my one and only, for all eternity," he whispered.

Lady Julianne Gatwick has written
a single girl's guide to enticing
unrepentant rakes.
The only problem: No one
can know she wrote it.

Please turn this page
for a preview of

How to Seduce a Scoundrel

Available in mass market
in July 2011.

Chapter One

A Rake's Code of Conduct: Virgins are strictly forbidden,
especially if said virgin happens to be your friend's sister.

Richmond, England, 1817

He'd arrived late as usual.

Marc Darcett, Earl of Hawkfield, twirled his top hat as he sauntered along the pavement toward his mother's home. A chilly breeze ruffled his hair and stung his face. In the dwindling evening light, Ashdown House, with its crenellated top and turrets, stood stalwart near the banks of the Thames.

Ordinarily, Hawk dreaded the obligatory weekly visits. His mother and three married sisters had grown increasingly demanding about his lack of a bride since his oldest friend had wed last summer. They made no secret of their disappointment in him, but he was accustomed to being the family scapegrace.

Today, however, he looked forward to seeing that oldest friend, Tristan Gatewick, the Duke of Shelbourne.

After the butler admitted him, Hawk stripped off his gloves and greatcoat. "Are Shelbourne and his sister here yet?"

"The duke and Lady Julianne arrived two hours ago," Jones said.

"Excellent." Hawk couldn't wait to relate his latest bawdy escapade to his friend. Last evening, he'd met Nancy and Nell, two naughty dancers who had made him an indecent proposition. Not wishing to appear too anxious, he'd promised to think over the matter, but he intended to accept their two-for-the-price-of-one offer.

The fastidious Jones eyed Hawk's head critically. "Begging your pardon, my lord, but you might wish to attend to your hair."

"You don't say?" Hawk pretended to be oblivious and peered at his windblown locks in the mirror above the foyer table. "Perfect," he said. "Mussed hair is all the rage."

"If you say so, my lord."

Hawk spun around. "I take it everyone is waiting in the gold drawing room?"

"Yes, my lord. Your mother has inquired after you several times."

Hawk glanced out at the great hall and grinned at the giant statue next to the stairwell. "Ah, my mother has taken an interest in naked statuary, has she?"

The ordinarily stoic Jones made a suspicious, muffled sound. Then he cleared his throat. "Apollo was delivered yesterday."

"Complete with his lyre and snake, I see. Well, I shall welcome him to the family." Hawk's boots clipped on the checkered marble floor as he strolled toward the cantilevered stairwell, an architectural feat that made the underside of the stone steps appear suspended in midair. At the base of the stairs, he paused to inspect the reproduction and grimaced at Apollo's minuscule genitalia. "Poor bastard."

Footsteps sounded above. Hawk looked up to find Tristan striding down the carpeted steps.

"Sizing up the competition?" Tristan said.

Hawk grinned. "The devil. It's the old married man."

"I saw your curricle from the window." Tristan stepped onto the marble floor and clapped Hawk on the shoulder. "You look as if you just tumbled out of bed."

Hawk wagged his brows and let his friend imagine what he would. "How is your duchess?"

A brief careworn expression flitted through his friend's eyes. "The doctor says all is progressing well. She has two more months of confinement." He released a gusty sigh. "I wanted a son, but now I'm praying for a safe delivery."

Hawk nodded, but said nothing.

"One day it will be your turn, and I'll be the one consoling you."

That day would never come. "And give up my bachelorhood? Never," he said in a flippant tone.

Tristan grinned. "I'll remind you of that when I attend your wedding."

Hawk changed the subject. "I take it your sister is well?" His mother planned to sponsor Lady Julianne this season while the dowager duchess stayed in the country with her increasing daughter-in-law.

"Julianne is looking forward to the season, but there is a problem," Tristan said. "A letter arrived from Bath half an hour ago. Your grandmother is suffering from heart palpitations again."

Hawk groaned. Grandmamma was famous for her heart palpitations. She succumbed to them at the most inconvenient times and described them in minute, loving detail to anyone unfortunate enough to be in the general vicinity. Owing to Grandmamma's diminished hearing, this meant anyone within shouting range.

"Your mother and sisters are discussing who should travel to Bath as we speak," Tristan said.

"Don't worry, old boy. We'll sort it out." No doubt his sisters meant to flee to Bath, as they always did when his grandmother invoked her favorite ailment. Usually his mother went as well, but she'd made a commitment to sponsor Julianne.

A peevish voice sounded from the landing. "Marc, you have dawdled long enough. Mama is waiting."

Hawk glanced up to find his eldest sister, Patience, beckoning him with her fingers as if he were one of her unruly brats. Poor Patience had never proven equal to her name, something he'd exploited since childhood. He never could resist provoking her then, and he certainly couldn't now. "My dear sister, I'd no idea you were so anxious for my company. It warms the cockles of my heart."

Her nostrils flared. "Our grandmother is ill, and Mama is fretting. You will not add to her vexation by tarrying."

"Pour Mama a sherry for her nerves. I'll be along momentarily," he said.

Patience pinched her lips, whirled around, and all but stomped away.

Hawk's shoulders shook as he returned his attention to his friend. "After dinner, we'll put in a brief appearance in the drawing room and make our escape to the club."

"I'd better not. I'm planning to leave at dawn tomorrow," Tristan said.

Hawk shrugged to hide his disappointment. He ought to have known the old boy meant to return to his wife immediately. Nothing would ever be quite the same now that his friend had married. "Well, then. Shall we join the others?"

As they walked up the stairs, Tristan glanced at him with an enigmatic expression. "It's been too long since we last met."

"Yes, it has." The last time was Tristan's wedding nine months ago. He'd meant to visit the newlyweds after a decent interval. Then Tristan's letter arrived with the jubilant news of his impending fatherhood.

Hawk's feet had felt as if they were immersed in quicksand.

After they entered the drawing room, Hawk halted. He was only peripherally aware of his sisters' husbands scowling at him from the sideboard. All his attention centered on a slender lady seated on the sofa between his mother and his youngest sister, Hope. The candlelight gleamed over the lady's jet curls as she gazed down at a sketchbook on her lap. Transfixed, Hawk let his gaze roam over the filmy scarf tucked into the neckline of her bodice. The tantalizing glimpses of the tops of her pert breasts heated his blood.

Good Lord, could this delectable creature possibly be Julianne?

As if sensing his stare, she glanced at him. His heart

drummed in his ears as he took in her transformation. In the past nine months, the slight fullness of her cheeks had disappeared, emphasizing her sculpted cheekbones. Even her expression had changed. Instead of her usual impish grin, she regarded him with a poised smile.

The sweet little girl he'd known all his life had become a woman. A heart-stoppingly beautiful woman.

The sound of his mother's voice rattled him. "Tristan, please be seated. Marc, do not stand there gawking. Come and greet Julianne."

Patience and his other sister, Harmony, sat in a pair of chairs near the hearth, exchanging sly smiles. No doubt they were hatching a plot to snare him in the parson's mousetrap. And why wouldn't they? He'd reacted to Julianne like one of the numerous smitten cubs who vied for her attention every season. Determined to take himself in hand, he strode over to her, made a leg, and swept his arm in a ridiculous bow of a sort last seen in the sixteenth century.

When he rose, his mother grimaced. "Marc, your hair is standing up. You look thoroughly disreputable."

He grinned like a jackanapes. "Why thank you, Mama."

Julianne's melodic, low laugh reverberated along his spine. "Hawk," she said.

All the air squeezed from his lungs. The raspy quality of that one word captivated him. Helen of Troy's face had launched a thousand ships, but Julianne's voice could fell a thousand men.

The silence in the drawing room recalled him to his senses. He set his fist on his hip and waggled his brows. "No doubt you will break a dozen hearts this season, Julie-girl."

She regarded him from beneath her long lashes. "Perhaps one will capture my affections," she said in her sultry voice.

Christopher Marlowe's infamous words echoed in his head. *Sweet Helen, make me immortal with a kiss.* Where the devil had that foolish thought come from? He'd best watch out. The bewitching Julianne was strictly off-limits and not for the likes of him.

Especially not him.

Hope stood. "Marc, take my seat. You must see Julianne's sketches."

Uh-oh. The narrow space meant he'd be seated hip to hip with her, but he could hardly refuse without seeming churlish. The moment he sat beside Julianne, his temperature heated several notches at the feel of her thigh next to his. Her light floral perfume muddled his brain. Naturally his groin tightened. He'd best play the clown to divert his thoughts from leaping into the gutter where they were wont to land. So he tapped the sketch. "What have you got there, imp?"

She showed him a sketch of Stonehenge. "I drew these last summer when I traveled with Amy and her family."

"Stonehenge is awe-inspiring," the countess said.

He thought Julianne far more awe-inspiring, but he dutifully looked on as she turned the page. "Those are some big rocks."

Julianne laughed and swatted him. "You've not changed a bit."

He met her gaze. *But you have, Julie-girl.*

Heavy footsteps thudded outside the drawing room doors, drawing his attention. Everyone stood as Lady Rutledge, his great-aunt Hester, lumbered inside. Gray sausage curls peeked out from a green turban with tall feathers. She took one look at Hawk's mother and scowled. "Louisa, that statue is hideous. If you want a naked man, find yourself one who is breathing."

Hawk's mouth worked with the effort not to laugh out loud.

"Hester, please mind your words." The countess fanned her heated face.

"Bah." Hester winked at Hawk. "Come give your aunt a kiss, you rogue."

When he obliged, she muttered, "You're the only sensible one in the bunch."

Tristan bowed to her. "Lady Rutledge."

Hester eyed him appreciatively. "Shelbourne, you handsome devil. I heard you wasted no time getting your duchess with child."

His mother and younger sisters gasped. Patience cleared her throat. "Aunt Hester, we do not speak of such indelicate matters."

Hester snorted and kept her knowing gaze on Tristan. "I heard your duchess has gumption. She'll bring your child into the world without mishap, mark my words."

Hawk considered his wily old aunt with a fond smile. Eccentric she might be, but she'd sought to reassure his old friend. And for that alone, he adored her.

He led Hester over to a chair and stood beside her. Her wide rump barely fit between the arms. After adjusting her plumes, she held her quizzing glass up to her eye and inspected Julianne.

"Aunt Hester, you remember Lady Julianne," Patience said, as if speaking to a child. "She is Shelbourne's sister."

"I know who she is." Hester dropped her quizzing glass. "Why are you still unwed, gel?"

Julianne blushed. "I am waiting for the right gentleman."

"I heard you turned down a dozen proposals since your come-out. Is it true?"

"I've not kept count," Julianne murmured.

Hester snorted. "There were so many you cannot recall?"

Noting Julianne's disconcerted expression, Hawk intervened. "Mama, I understand we've a bit of a problem. Grandmamma is claiming illness again, is she?"

His mother and sisters protested they must assume Grandmamma was truly ill. Finally, Aunt Hester interrupted. "Oh, hush, Louisa. You know very well my sister is only seeking attention."

"Hester, how can you say such a thing?" the countess said.

"Because she makes a habit of it." Hester sniffed. "I suppose you and your girls are planning to hare off to Bath on a fool's errand again."

"We cannot take a risk," Patience said. "If Grandmamma took a bad turn, we would never forgive ourselves."

"She ought to come to town where she can be near the family. I offered to share my home with her, but she refuses to leave her cronies in Bath," Hester said.

"She is set in her ways." Hawk grinned down at his aunt. "Few ladies are as adventurous as you."

"True," Hester said, preening.

The countess gave him a beseeching look. "Will you write William to inform him?"

"I'm not sure of his address at present," Hawk said. His

younger brother had been traveling on the Continent for more than a year. "Do not worry, Mama. He'll tire of wandering and come home eventually."

Montague, Patience's husband, lowered his newspaper. "He would come home soon enough if you cut him off without a penny."

Hawk ignored his least favorite brother-in-law. "What of Julianne? Her brother brought her all this way. Mama, can you not stay behind?"

"Oh, I could not ask such a thing," Julianne said. "I can stay with either Amy or Georgette. My friends' mothers would welcome me, I'm sure."

Aunt Hester turned to Hawk. "Her friends' mothers will be too busy with their own girls. I will sponsor Julianne. She will be the toast of the season."

A long silence followed. Hawk's mother and sisters regarded one another with barely concealed dismay. They thought Hester a few cards shy of a full deck, but he knew his aunt was prodigiously clever, if a bit blunt in her manners.

The countess cleared her throat. "Hester, dear, that is too kind of you, but perhaps you have not thought of how exhausting all those entertainments will be."

"I'm never tired, Louisa," she said. "I shall enjoy sponsoring the gel. She's pretty enough and seems lively. I'll have her engaged in a matter of weeks."

Tristan eyed Hester. "We're in no hurry for Julianne to marry. She's young yet."

Hester looked at Julianne. "How old are you, gel?"

"One and twenty," she said.

"The perfect age for marriage," Hester said. "Now that the matter is settled, let us go to dinner. I'm starved."

• • •

After the ladies withdrew from the dining room, Hawk brought out the port. His sisters' husbands exchanged meaningful glances. Tristan kept silent, but watched them with a guarded expression.

Montague folded his small hands on the table and addressed Hawk. "Lady Julianne cannot stay with Hester. Your aunt's bold manners and rebellious ideas would be a bad influence on the girl."

Hawk met Tristan's gaze. "Join me in the study?"

Tristan nodded.

They both rose. When Hawk claimed a candle branch from the sideboard, Montague scrambled up from the table. "Patience will stay behind and look after Julianne."

"My sister is determined to go to Bath," Hawk said. "She will not rest easy unless she sees our grandmother is well." The last thing he wanted was to expose Julianne to his sister's acrimonious marriage.

"You know very well your grandmother feigns illness," Montague said. "If your mother and sisters refused to go, that would put a stop to this nonsense."

Hawk realized Montague had seized the opportunity to keep his wife at home. The man constantly queried Patience about her whereabouts and upbraided her if she even spoke to another man. "I'll discuss the matter with Shelbourne. Gentlemen, enjoy your port."

He had started to turn away when Montague's voice halted him.

"Damn you, Hawk. Someone needs to take responsibility for the girl."

Hawk strode round the table and loomed over his

brother-in-law. "You've no say in the matter." Then he lowered his voice. "You will remember my warning."

Montague glared, but held his tongue. Hawk gave him an evil smile. At Christmas, the man had made one too many disparaging remarks about Patience. Hawk had taken him aside and threatened to beat him to a bloody pulp if he ever treated her disrespectfully again.

As he and Tristan strode away, Hawk muttered, "Bastard."

"Montague resents your political influence, your fortune, and your superior height. He feels inferior and engages in pissing matches to prove he's manly."

Hawk wished Montague to the devil. The man had campaigned for his sister's hand and showered her with affection. He'd shown his true colors shortly after the wedding.

When they walked into the study, the scent of leather permeated the room. Hawk set the candle branch on the mantel and slumped into one of the cross-framed chairs before the huge mahogany desk. The grate was empty, making the room cold. He never made use of the study. Years ago, he'd taken rooms at the Albany. His family had disapproved, but he'd needed to escape his father's stranglehold.

Tristan surveyed the surroundings and sat next to Hawk. "The study is virtually unchanged since your father's death."

He'd died suddenly of a heart seizure eight years ago, closing off any chance of reconciliation between them. A foolish thought. There was nothing he could have done to change his father's opinion of him.

"Your father was a good man," Tristan said. "His advice was invaluable to me."

"He admired you," Hawk said. Tristan had singlehandedly restored his fortune after discovering his late wastrel father had left him in monstrous debt.

"I envied your freedom," Tristan said.

"I had an easy time compared to you." Hawk's father had never let him forget it, either. Unbidden, the words his father had spoken more than a dozen years ago echoed in his brain. *Do you even know how much it will cost to satisfy Westcott's honor?*

He mentally slammed the door on the memory. "Old boy, if you prefer, take your sister to one of her friends. I'll make excuses to my aunt."

Tristan shook his head. "Your aunt is right. Their mothers should concentrate on their own daughters."

"My aunt is a cheeky old bird, but she's harmless enough. Hester will enjoy squiring Julianne about town."

Tristan glanced sideways at Hawk. "I've a favor to ask."

A strange presentiment washed over Hawk. He'd known Tristan since they were in leading strings, because their mothers were bosom friends. At Eton, he and Tristan had banded together to evade the older boys who liked to torment the younger ones. Hawk knew his friend well, but he'd no idea what his friend intended to ask of him.

Tristan drew in a breath. "Will you act as my sister's unofficial guardian?"

Hawk laughed. "Me, a guardian? Surely you jest."

"As soon as the fortune hunters discover I'm out of the picture, they'll hover like vultures over Julianne."

"Your sister has been out in society for four years. She's too clever to fall for a fortune hunter's wiles."

"She's naïve. I won't feel easy unless a solid man is there to protect her from rakes."

"But I'm a rake," he sputtered.

Tristan regarded him with a stern expression. "But of course, you think of Julianne as practically a sister."

He understood the warning beneath Tristan's words. Among rakes, it was a point of honor to avoid virginal young ladies, especially friends' sisters. An image of Julianne's pert bosom rose in his mind. No, his regard for her was definitely not brotherly in nature. Knowing he couldn't trust himself with her, he sought to put Tristan off. "There's no need for a guardian. My aunt will look after her."

Tristan pinched the bridge of his nose. "I should stay in London to watch over Julianne, but I cannot bear to leave my wife. No matter what I do, I'll feel as if I've wronged one of them."

The devil. Tristan had never asked for a favor before. He was like a brother to him. Damn it all. He couldn't refuse. "Anything for you, old boy."

"Thank you."

Hawk swore he would resist Julianne. Each time he felt stirrings of desire, he would envision Tristan's reaction. That would douse any lusty urges.

"There's one more thing," Tristan said. "You're not going to like it."

He lifted his brows. "Oh?"

Tristan narrowed his eyes. "You will give up raking for the duration of the season."

He laughed. "What?"

"You heard me. There will be no ballerinas, actresses, or courtesans. Call them what you will, but you will not associate with whores while guarding my sister."

He scoffed. "It's not as if I'd flaunt a mistress in your sister's face."

"Your liaisons are famous." Tristan tapped his thumb on the arm of the chair. "I've often suspected you delight in your bad reputation."

He made jests about mistresses, jests that everyone including his friend believed. While he was no angel, Hawk couldn't possibly live up—or was that down?—to the exaggerated reports about his conquests.

Hawk shook his head. "I'll not agree to celibacy." He'd be in a bloody frenzy then, wouldn't he? A frenzy that would make resisting Julie-girl all the more difficult. Of course, he'd never admit *that* to his friend.

"You don't even try to be discreet. Julianne adores you like a brother. I don't want her disillusioned."

"I'll keep my liaisons quiet," Hawk grumbled. He'd better forget the ménage à trois with Nell and Nancy. It rather aggrieved him, since he'd never dallied with two women at once, but he couldn't possibly keep that sort of wicked business under the proverbial covers.

"Agreed," Tristan said. "Write periodically and let me know how my sister fares."

"I'll tell her to ignore Hester," Hawk said. "She'll grow accustomed to my aunt's blunt manners."

"When the babe is born, bring her home to me." He smiled. "Tessa already asked Julianne to be godmother. Will you be godfather?"

A knot formed in his chest, but he forced a laugh. "You would trust a rogue like me with your child?

"There is no one I trust more than you, my friend."

He cut his gaze away, knowing he didn't deserve his friend's regard.

THE DISH

Where authors give you the inside scoop!

♥ ♥ ♥ ♥ ♥ ♥ ♥ ♥ ♥ ♥ ♥ ♥ ♥ ♥ ♥

From the desk of Vicky Dreiling

Dear Reader,

The idea for HOW TO MARRY A DUKE came about purely by chance. One fateful evening while surfing 800+ channels on TV, I happened upon a reality show featuring a hunky bachelor and twenty-five beauties competing for his heart. As I watched the antics, a story idea popped into my head: the bachelor in Regency England (minus the hot tub and camera crew). The call to this writing adventure proved too irresistible to ignore.

During the planning stages of the book, I encountered numerous obstacles. Even the language presented challenges that meant creating substitutes such as *bridal candidates* for *bachelorettes*. Obviously, I needed to concoct alternatives to steamy smooching in the hot tub and overnight dates. But regardless of the century, some things never change. I figured catfights were fair game.

Before I could plunge into the writing, I had to figure out who the hero and heroine were. I picked up my imaginary remote control and surfed until I found Miss Tessa Mansfield, a wealthy, independent young woman with a penchant for matchmaking. In the short preview, she revealed that she only made love matches for all the ignored wallflowers. She, however, had no intention of ever marrying. By now I was on the edge of my seat. "Why?" I asked.

The preview ended, leaving me desperate to find out more. So I changed the metaphorical channel and nearly swooned at my first glimpse of Tristan Gatewick, the Duke of Shelbourne. England's Most Eligible Bachelor turned out to be the yummiest man I'd ever beheld. Evidently I wasn't alone in my ardent appreciation. Every eligible belle in the Beau Monde was vying to win his heart.

To my utter astonishment, Tristan slapped a newspaper on his desk and addressed me. "Madam, I am not amused with your ridiculous plot. Duty is the only reason I seek a wife, but you have made me the subject du jour in the scandal sheets. How the devil can I find a sensible bride when every witless female in Britain is chasing me?"

I smiled at him. "Actually, I know someone who can help you."

He scoffed.

I thought better of telling him he was about to meet his match.

Cheers!

Vicky Dreiling

www.vickydreiling.net

♥

From the desk of Carolyn Jewel

Dear Reader,

Revenge, as they say, is a dish best served cold. If you wait a bit before getting your payback, if you're calm and rational, you'll be in a better position to enjoy that sweet revenge. The downside, of course, is what can happen to you while you spend all this time plotting and planning. Some emotions shouldn't be left to fester in your soul.

Gray Spencer is a woman looking to serve up revenge while the embers are still glowing. She has reason. She does. Her normal, everyday life got derailed by a mage—a human who can do magic. Christophe dit Menart is a powerful mage with a few hundred years of living on her. Because of him, her life has been destroyed. Not just *her* life, but also the lives of her sister and parents.

After she gets her freedom at a terrible cost, the only thing Gray wants is Christophe dit Menart dead for what he did—before he does the same horrific thing to someone else that he did to her.

I know what you're thinking and you're right. A normal, nonmagical human like Gray can't hope to go up against someone like Christophe. But Gray's not normal—not anymore. She escaped because a demon gave his life for her and in the process transferred his magic to her. If she had any idea how to use that magic, she might have a chance against Christophe. Maybe.

The demon warlord Nikodemus has negotiated a

shaky peace agreement between the magekind and the demonkind. (Did I mention them? They are fiends, a kind of demon. And they don't take kindly to the mages who kill them in order to extend their miserable magic-using human lives by stealing a demon's life force.) Because of the peace, demons in Nikodemus's territory have agreed not to harm the magekind. In return, the magekind aren't supposed to kill any more demons.

Basically the problem is this: Gray intends to kill Christophe, and the demon warlord's most feared assassin has to make sure that doesn't happen.

Uh-oh.

After all that, I have what may seem like a strange confession to make about my assassin hero who is, after all, a wee bit scary at times. He's been alive for a long, long time, and for much of that time, women lived very restricted lives. Sometimes he is completely flummoxed by these modern women. It was a lot of fun writing a hero like that, and I hope you enjoy reading about how Christophe learns to deal with Gray as much as I enjoyed writing about it.

Yours Sincerely,

Carolyn Jewel

http://www.carolynjewel.com

♥   ♥

From the desk of Sophie Gunn

Dear Reader,

After years living in upstate New York, my husband got a new job and we moved back to my small hometown outside of Philadelphia. I was thrilled to be near my parents, brothers, aunts, uncles, and cousins. (Hi, Aunt Lillian!) But I didn't anticipate how close I would be to quite a few of my former high school classmates. Didn't anyone ever leave this town? My life had turned into a nonstop high school reunion.

And I was definitely still wearing the wrong dress.

One by one, I encountered my former "enemies" from high school. They were at the gym, the grocery store, and the elementary school bake sale. It didn't take long to realize two things. First, we had a blast rehashing the past. What had really happened at that eleventh-grade dance? What had become of Joey, the handsome captain of the football team? (Surprise, there he is now. Yes, he's the one walking that tiny toy poodle on a pink, blinged-up leash!) Second, we were still terrifically different people, *and it didn't matter*. We were grown-ups, and what someone wore or whom they dated didn't feel so crucial anymore.

Cups of coffee led to glasses of wine, which led to true friendship. But friendship that was different from any I'd ever known, because while we shared a past, our presents were still radically different. My husband started to jokingly call us the Enemy Club, and it stuck.

That was what we writers call an *aha moment*.

The Enemy Club would make a great book. Actually, a great series...

The rest, as they say, is history. Each book of the Enemy Club series is set in small-town Galton, New York. Four friends who had been the worst of enemies are now the best of friends, struggling to help one another juggle jobs, kids, love, heartbreak, and triumph as seen from their very (very!) different points of view.

HOW SWEET IT IS is the first book in the series. It focuses on Lizzie, the good girl gone bad. She made one mistake senior year of high school that changed her life forever. Now she and her teenage daughter get by just fine, thank you very much, with a little help from the Enemy Club. But then Lizzie's first love, the father who abandoned her daughter fourteen years before, decides to come back to town on Christmas Day. Lizzie imagines her life as seen through his eyes—and she doesn't like what she sees. She has the same job, same house, same everything as when he left fourteen years earlier. She vows to make a change. But how much is she willing to risk? And does the mysterious stranger, who shows up in town promising to grant her every wish, have the answers? Or is he just another of life's sweet, sweet mistakes?

I'm really excited about these books, because they're so close to my heart. Come visit me at www.sophiegunn.com to read an excerpt of HOW SWEET IT IS, to find out more about the Enemy Club, to see pictures of my cats, and to keep in touch. I'd love to hear from you!

Yours,

Sophie Gunn

♥   ♥   ♥ ♥   ♥

From the desk of Sue-Ellen Welfonder

Dear Reader,

Wild, heather-clad hills, empty glens, and the skirl of pipes stir the hearts of many. Female hearts beat fast at the flash of plaid. Yet I've seen grown men shed tears at the beauty of a Highland sunset. So many people love Scotland, and those of us who do know that our passion is a double-edged sword. We live with a constant ache to be there. It's a soul-deep yearning known as "the pull."

In SINS OF A HIGHLAND DEVIL, the first book in my new Highland Warriors trilogy, I wanted to explore the fierce attachment Highlanders feel for their home glen. Love that burns so hotly, they'll even lay down their lives to hold on to the hills so dear to them.

James Cameron and Catriona MacDonald, hero and heroine of SINS OF A HIGHLAND DEVIL, are bitter foes. Divided by centuries of clan feuds, strife, and rivalries, they share a fiery passion for the glen they each claim as their own. When a king's writ threatens banishment, long-held boundaries blur and forbidden desires are unleashed. James and Catriona soon discover there is much pleasure to be found in each other's embrace. But the price of their yearning must be paid in blood, and the battle facing them could shatter their world.

Fortunately, true love can prove a more powerful weapon than any warrior's sword.

There are a lot of swords in this story. And the fight

scenes are fierce. But passions flare when blood is spilled as James and Catriona showed me each day during the writing of their tale.

It was an exhilarating journey.

Catriona is a strong heroine who will brave any danger to protect her home and to win the heart of the man she never believed could be hers. James is a hardened warrior and proud clan leader, and he faces his greatest challenge when his beloved glen is threatened.

Because SINS OF A HIGHLAND DEVIL is a romance, James and Catriona are triumphant. Their ending is a happy one. Numberless Highlanders after them weren't as blessed. Later centuries saw the Clearances, while famine and other hardships did the rest. Clans were scattered, banished from their glens and hills as they were forced to sail to distant shores. Their hearts were irrevocably broken. But they kept their deep love of the land, their proud Celtic roots remaining true no matter where they settled.

Their forever yearning for home still beats in the heart of everyone with even a drop of Scottish blood. It's the reason we feel "the pull."

I hope you'll enjoy reading how James's and Catriona's passion for their glen rewards them with a love more wondrous than their wildest dreams.

With all good wishes,

Sue-Ellen Welfonder

www.welfonder.com